THE DEMON'S IN THE DETAILS

TOUCHED BY A DEMON BOOK 2

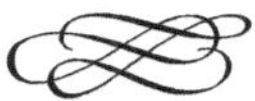

JEANNE OATES ESTRIDGE

The Demon's in the Details

Cover art: Paper and Sage, www.paperandsage.com

Editor: Karen Dale Harris, www.karendaleharris.com

Proofreader: Noël Kristan Higgins, the Queen of English.

ISBN: 978-1-949451-04-7

First edition: January, 2019

❀ Created with Vellum

"Not just no, but hell no." Georgia O'Keeffe Blackmon glared at her father and stepmother. "I'm not selling *John*."

The view from the floor-to-ceiling windows at the north end of her father's family room—the red sandstone cliffs and cloudless blue skies of Sedona, Arizona—was gorgeous, but Keeffe's gaze flashed right past it, to the opposite end of the room and a wooden pedestal topped by a Plexiglas case.

Inside the case, an eighteen-inch alabaster statue of an eagle soared upward, wings spread, its gaze fixed on the sky. The translucence of the stone gave the sculpture a transcendent quality. The sheer beauty filled Keeffe with bliss, and her anger moderated a little. Mom had been an incredible artist.

"I've been waiting since I was eighteen to take him home," she said. "After seven years, I'm down to my last thirty days. Why would I sell him?"

Dad responded to her question by burying his nose in his whisky glass, but Lilith, aka the stepmother-from-Hell, spread her hands.

"We're not asking you to sell it," she said. "We're just asking you to meet—"

"—someone who wants to buy him." Keeffe finished her sentence for her.

Lilith's lips tightened. Stepmom wore a black leather miniskirt that showed yards of what Keeffe had to admit were shapely and perfectly tanned legs. On her feet were strappy black sandals with five-inch heels. Her red silk top matched her toenails. Chunky red and black jewelry pulled it all together. Keeffe was aware of the contrast to her own outfit—a flannel shirt, faded jeans and down-at-the-heel Doc Martens.

Lilith didn't appear to have aged a day since she married Daniel Blackmon ten years ago. Probably because she was sucking the life force out of her husband.

"Be reasonable, Keeffe," she said. "I'm an art agent. Given your financial situation, I would be remiss if I didn't help you find—"

"My financial situation is fine." Keeffe cut her off with what was, mostly, a true statement. Lilith's face turned pink with annoyance, but before she could respond, the doorbell rang.

"That must be Seth." Lilith shot Dad a glance that looked like a warning. She left the room, her stiletto heels rat-a-tat-tatting on the hardwood floor like a machine gun firing.

The hair on the back of Keeffe's neck prickled. She wasn't much when it came to book-smarts, but she was good at reading people. This felt like more than just one of Lilith's intermittent attempts to convince her to sell her sculpture.

She turned to Dad. "Who is Seth?"

"Seth McCall, some Internet billionaire Lilith is helping select art for his new house." Above Dad's russet beard and mustache, his nose was a patchwork of broken veins. His drinking had taken a drastic uptick after he remarried.

"You don't really want me to sell *John*, do you?" Keeffe asked.

Dad's eyes flashed to the doorway where Lilith had disappeared, like he wasn't sure he was authorized to have his own opinion. *Come on, Dad. Grow a pair.*

He held up a hand. "That's between you and Lilith."

Nope. Not today, anyway.

A moment later, Lilith returned, accompanied by a blond guy who looked to be in his late twenties. He was tall, probably a foot taller than Keeffe's five-three. Above torn jeans hanging low on his hips, his T-shirt hugged six-pack abs. He must spend some serious gym-time to get abs like that. Sleeves of tattoos ran up both muscular arms and a tiny silver ring graced his left nostril.

He seemed oddly familiar. It took Keeffe a moment to realize why. He reminded her of the statue of Leonidas at Thermopylae that stood at Sparta. The statue was modern, but it had made Leonidas her personal choice for hottest historical figure of the ancient world.

Lilith introduced them and Keeffe's heart thumped a little until her gaze reached his eyes. They were a silvery-gray, with no hint of humanity, like a statue's sightless, soulless eyes. Instinctively, her fingers sought the little silver crucifix Mom had given her for her first communion. She instantly felt better. Safer.

Then McCall smiled, the killer smile Leonidas might have had if there had been modern dentistry in ancient Sparta. The sense of a soul gone missing disappeared.

"Hello, Keeffe." He extended his hand, his voice as smooth as acrylic flowing from a tube.

The handshake brought them close enough that she could smell his aftershave, an expensive mix of sandalwood and leather. She steeled herself to look at his eyes again, but they were now ordinary gray eyes.

Still, she had to resist the urge to take a step back. "What brings you to Sedona?"

McCall's gaze shifted to Lilith, focusing on her melon-like breasts. *Ew.* Lilith looked great, but she had to be twenty years older than Seth, minimum. After a long moment, he dragged his attention back to Keeffe.

"I heard it's great here in the winter. I can hike and mountain bike, even though it's January. I just built a house at the south end of town. Lil is helping me decorate." He looked across the room to the eagle, soaring inside its Plexiglas case.

"My sculpture isn't for sale," Keeffe said.

"Everything's for sale," he said easily. "It's just a matter of settling on a price. What would you take for it?"

"Nothing."

"Well, that's affordable." His smile was like a warm caress, but it left Keeffe cold. He headed toward the sculpture.

"No amount of money could convince me to sell," she told his back.

"I saw one of your mother's crucifixes at a church in Sicily." He threw the words over his shoulder. "And another in Majorca. Her work is magnificent. I want to own one of her pieces."

Keeffe followed him across the room, "Perhaps one of the churches would be interested in selling."

She stroked the Plexiglas case. A bronze plaque on the base read, *John*.

"Why is it named *John*?" McCall stood beside her, his thumbs hooked into the pockets of his jeans, unconsciously framing his genitals.

At least, she hoped it was unconscious.

"He's an allegorical representation of John from the Bible," Keeffe said. "My sister and brothers own the other three."

"Three what?"

"Evangelists."

"Huh?" His gorgeous face was completely blank. Clearly, he had never attended catechism class.

"Evangelists. You know—Matthew, Mark, Luke, and John. They wrote the gospels."

"Okay, sure," he said.

Why did he even want her statue? He clearly wasn't religious. She looked at *John* again, studying the clean lines of the wings, the sleek head, and fierce gaze. The eagle's soaring form was magnificent in its own right, but its meaning was the source of its real beauty.

"My mother was working on this piece when she died," Keeffe said. Inside the case, the bird's left talon wasn't quite freed from the stone. "She sculpted him specifically for me. You can't put a price on that."

"I'll give you a hundred and fifty thousand dollars for it."

Keeffe's jaw tensed. Even if she'd been interested, that was far less than *John* was worth. It was exactly what she would have expected, though. Just as she was finally about to win permanent possession of him, Lilith had brought in someone to rip her off.

"No, thanks," she said.

"Two hundred."

Keeffe glared at McCall. "He's not for sale."

McCall glanced at Lilith. She gave a tiny, almost imperceptible nod. Every follicle on the back of Keeffe's neck snapped to attention.

"Two fifty," he said.

Whatever the eagle was worth to him, he was worth more to her. When Lilith had moved in, barely a year after Mom's death, she had cleaned house, getting rid of not only Mom's clothes and personal items, but also her artist's tools. This statue and a small notebook were the only things Keeffe had left of Mom.

"Not just no, but hell no."

McCall glanced at Lilith's chest again and licked his lips. Gross. Then he turned to Keeffe and smiled his sexy, caressing smile. At least, it would have been sexy if he weren't such an asshat. He could barely take his eyes off Lilith's breasts, and right in front of Dad, too.

"Let me take you to dinner and we'll talk it over," he said.

Have dinner with someone she had no interest in, so that he could pressure her to sell something she had no wish to sell?

"No, thanks."

His mouth actually fell open. Evidently hot guys who also happened to be jillionaires didn't get turned down very often.

His eyes narrowed. "You're better off selling it to me than just losing it."

Keeffe stilled. "Why do you think I'm going to lose him?"

Lilith grasped McCall's upper arm. "Seth, perhaps we should—"

"Lil told me about your agreement," he said. "If you're not supporting yourself as an artist by the time you turn twenty-five, the statue becomes her property."

Keeffe's fists clenched at her sides.

"There are two problems with that statement." She spoke to

McCall, but her words were aimed at Lilith. "One, the statue doesn't become Lilith's, it becomes my dad's. And two, I *am* supporting myself. I make as much as a secretary does."

"Administrative assistant," Lilith said.

"Whatever you want to call it." Keeffe glared at her. When she was eighteen, she had been determined to get an art degree from Mom's alma mater in Pasadena. Lilith was equally determined Keeffe should take business classes at Coconino Community College in nearby Flagstaff. The resulting argument made Armageddon look like a tiff over which way the toilet paper roll goes.

After three weeks of shouting and slammed doors, Dad brokered a compromise: Cost wasn't the issue; it was about being practical. They'd pay for art school on the condition Keeffe signed a contract to repay them if, by her twenty-fifth birthday, she wasn't making as much from art as she would have from following Lilith's advice.

That would have seemed silly—how could an artist who wasn't even pulling in as much as a secretary ever hope to repay tens of thousands of dollars of tuition?—except they had *John* as security.

It was a gamble, but it had turned out okay. Over the past year, between Keeffe's canvases and the caricatures she drew outside Tlaquepaque Village during tourist season, she had made at least the average salary rate for an administrative assistant in this part of Arizona.

Another glance passed between McCall and Lilith. He had no real interest in her sculpture. Keeffe was willing to bet on it. No, Lilith had put him up to this. Her stepmom had wanted to take *John* away from her from day one. The only thing Lilith understood about art was its monetary value. Over at the bar, Dad poured himself another drink, shutting out the tension in the room. No help to be had there.

"I think it's time I took my sculpture home with me."

Lilith jerked. "I thought you decided it wouldn't be safe in your trailer." Her voice was sharp.

"Looks like it's not safe here either."

Lilith flushed, but it wasn't clear if that was from guilt or anger.

"Daniel, tell Keeffe how unwise it would be to try to keep the statue at her trailer." Her tone made *trailer* sound like *shack*.

Dad held up a hand. "Leave me out of this. I'm Switzerland. I'm neutral."

Lilith shot him a look that said he'd pay for that later. She turned back to Keeffe.

"If you're not concerned about it being stolen, think about the statue itself. We keep this house at a consistent seventy degrees and fifty percent humidity, summer and winter. Can you provide the same optimal conditions?"

Keeffe started to say, *It's made out of rock. It can handle a little dry air.* If you antagonized Lilith enough, you could sometimes make her pupils go rectangular, like a goat's.

Keeffe's brothers and sister claimed not to see that transformation, and in her anatomy-for-figure-drawing course in college, her professor had told her, flat out, that rectangular pupils didn't occur in humans. That trait was limited to goats, octopuses, and toads.

But Keeffe knew better. As a teenager, she had excelled at badgering her stepmother until her pupils reshaped into rectangles.

She'd spent a lot of her teenage years grounded.

She glanced at *John* again. His eyes were fixed on the heavens, away from trivial earthly concerns. She could almost hear her mother's voice saying, *Be the bigger person, Keeffe.*

She drew a breath. "I'm planning to loan *John* to museums."

She expected Lilith to relax once she learned the sculpture wasn't bound for the trailer park. Instead, to Keeffe's amazement, the circles of black at the center of Lilith's eyes lengthened and the corners squared off. Stepmom didn't like the idea of her predecessor's artwork going on tour. At all.

"I've talked to the Chicago Art Institute and the DIA in Detroit." Keeffe gave in to her baser instincts and pressed the barb deeper. "They both have churches nearby with Mom's crucifixes on display. They're very interested."

If she'd wanted to infuriate Lilith, she'd succeeded. Her stepmother's goat-like eyes blazed. If looks could kill, one of Lilith's stiletto heels would have hammered straight through Keeffe's skull right about now.

Then Lilith's charcoal-shaded eyelids swept down, hiding her weird pupils.

"Have you ever bothered to read that contract you signed?"

Keeffe caught her breath. Her cheeks burned as her eyes flashed over to McCall to gauge his reaction. Keeffe's dyslexia made reading a challenge, and Lilith knew it. Keeffe had tried to read the contract several times, but she'd never gotten all the way through it. Fortunately, McCall had wandered away to look at another statue, a she-demon with long black hair, horns, and an arrow-tipped tail.

Keeffe lifted her chin. "Clue me in."

"It really isn't in anyone's best interests for that statue to get stolen or damaged," Lilith said. "The contract specifies that it will remain here, in Daniel's custody, until you turn twenty-five and the terms of the contract have been fulfilled."

Keeffe waited for Dad to chime in, to confirm that of course he trusted her to take care of her mother's sculpture, and even to relinquish it, if necessary. Instead, he practiced his neutrality by adding another ice cube to his drink.

Keeffe's chest tightened until it felt like it might buckle. That statue was hers. She'd spent hours watching its delicate feathers revealed at the tip of her mother's chisels. She might not be able to breeze through a contract, but she could describe every hammer-stroke that went into that statue, and the other three as well.

Her sister and brothers had taken possession of theirs long ago. *John* was the only one still within Lilith's grasp. For the first time, it struck Keeffe that she might actually lose him.

Her palms grew sweaty. What other little tidbits were tucked inside that contract? She needed to read the thing, front to back, and make sure she understood every word, no matter how long it took her or how head-splittingly difficult it was. Lilith wasn't getting *John*.

Over by the bar, Dad watched them warily, while Seth tried to take the she-demon from her case.

Probably to feel her up.

Keeffe kissed her fingertips and pressed them against the Plexiglas protecting *John* before turning to face her stepmother.

"In thirty days, I'll be back to pick him up."

Lilith's pupils returned to a normal human shape. A tiny smile tugged at the corners of her lips. The hair on the back of Keeffe's neck stood up like porcupine quills. Evil stepmom was planning something, but what?

"When I do, he'd better be here." Keeffe took a shot in the dark. "If not, I'll be back with cops, lawyers, judges—whatever it takes."

Lilith smirked, as though to say Keeffe had no money to pay a lawyer. Hollowly, Keeffe realized she was right. She took a step forward until the rounded toes of her boots bumped up against the pointed tips of Lilith's stilettos.

"Understand one thing," she said, staring straight into Lilith's dark eyes. "It will be a cold day in Hell before I let you take my sculpture."

CHAPTER 2

*A*baddon, the Demon of Sloth, leaned his push broom against the hardened lava wall of Ring Nine and stooped to pick up the remote control that had just ricocheted off his skull. Across the ring, a trio of serpent demons, including Lamia, his former girlfriend, giggled and slithered out of sight.

Nearby, Satan beat his fists on the arms of his massive throne.

"Why is it that nothing in this fucking place works like it's supposed to?" His face was a deep burgundy. Oily black smoke streamed from his horns.

The question was clearly rhetorical, but Bad answered anyway. "Because DemSec hasn't been installing the patches on schedule."

During the five hundred years Bad had supervised DemSec, the satanic bureau in charge of outfitting demons for Aboveworld assignments, the department had expanded to assume responsibility for the technology throughout Hell. Under his guidance, demonic productivity had reached all-time depths.

Then one little mission went north and he was out of DemSec and into the maggot pit. He'd won his release a week ago, but Satan refused to put him back in the technology hub. Instead, he was assigned to Custodial Services.

Janitor duty was better than picking fly larvae out of his briefs, but it was no gig for a demon whose genius lay in figuring out ways to eliminate physical labor. He needed to get back where he belonged, and soon.

"If you'd put me back in charge of DemSec, I could get things straightened out." Bad tried not to think about what his replacement, Ornias, might have thrown away or destroyed since he'd taken over.

Satan pinched his skinny lower lip, considering. "You *have* been responsible for some of the greatest evils ever invented."

Bad's hopes rose, though what Satan said wasn't strictly true. Technology was morally neutral. It was how it was used that made it bad or good.

"So move me back," he said.

Satan shook his head. "You don't have the practical experience I need in that position. That last mission proved it. The director of DemSec needs more than technical expertise. He needs hands-on knowledge of Aboveworld. Ornias has worked more missions than any other demon down here."

Ornias was an action junkie with more muscles than brains. Bad controlled his impatience.

"I have field skills. Give me a field assignment and let me prove it. "

"You're a Hade." Satan looked him up and down, lingering on his horns and tail.

Bad drew himself up to his full height, which was still six inches shorter than Ornias.

"I'm aware of my heritage."

As a member of the tribe of miners and metalworkers that had peopled Hell before Satan arrived with his legions, Bad might not have the beauty of a fallen angel, but he had something better: brains.

"DemSec flourished under my leadership," he said.

Satan didn't argue the point. "I'll send you Aboveworld when the right kind of mission comes along."

"When will that be?" Bad actually had no desire to go Above. Human tech lagged so far behind Hell's it was a joke. Far too much up there still relied on manual labor. But if completing a field assignment was what he had to do to get DemSec back, then a field assignment it would be.

Satan shrugged. "It takes as long as it takes." He held out the remote. "Rewind this. I want to see what happened from the beginning."

Bad pushed a button on the remote. The giant screen facing Satan's throne lit up, displaying a wood-paneled room where three people argued. One of them was a burly, russet-bearded man Bad didn't recognize. The second was Lilith, Hell's leading she-demon. She had been involved in the failed mission that had doomed Bad to the maggot pit. Judging by the scene on the screen, she must have won her release a lot sooner than he had.

"She had other missions in play." Satan seemed to read his mind.

There was no point in expecting fairness in Hell. Bad turned his attention to the third person on the screen. She was small, a few inches shorter than he was, even. Beneath her flannel shirt and worn jeans, she was slender to the point of angular. Her ebony hair was swept back in a ponytail and her eyes—dark brown with an upward tilt at the corners—were fringed with lashes as dark as her hair. Her jaw was too strong for beauty, especially when it was thrust forward in anger, as it was right now.

It was her skin that held his attention, though. She had the golden skin tone of someone who lived where the sun shone a lot. Her glow seemed to light up the screen.

Satan snapped his talons. "Give me that thing."

Bad handed him the remote. Satan jabbed at the buttons. The screen went dark again.

"Bless it!" he snarled.

"If you put me back in charge of DemSec," Bad said, pushing his glasses higher on his nose, "I'll have everything humming again in no time."

Satan handed him the device. "I've told you what you have to do to get back to DemSec. Now make this work or you'll have maggots crawling up your ass again in no time."

Why was the boss so fixated on fieldwork? Earth was a cesspool of emotion. Humans made decisions based on feelings rather than solid data. It was no wonder things were such a mess up there.

Bad brought the screen back to life. Now the girl stared across the room, her face blissful. What had inspired such delight? He pushed a button to change the camera angle. An alabaster statue of an eagle came into view. Across the cavern of Ring Nine sat three other sculptures—an angel, a lion, and an ox—carved from the same translucent stone. One empty pedestal remained.

"I want that statue." Satan leaned forward, gripping the arms of his throne.

The statues were beautiful, if art was your thing. It wasn't Satan's thing, though. They must have some particular power. Bad touched the left temple of his glasses. Gehenna Glasses were his newest invention. He'd created them to pass the time in the maggot pit. They murmured into his ear, "Rachel Blackmon, American Sculptor," along with the dates of her birth and death.

On screen, Lilith left the room, returning a moment later with a fourth person, a human male so gorgeous Bad would have identified him as a fallen angel if not for his tattoos and nose ring.

"Have Lilith steal the statue for you," Bad suggested.

Satan shook his head. "The girl has to choose to give it up voluntarily."

Now why would that be?

Lilith's visitor attempted to buy the statue without success. Lilith sparred with the girl until she lost her temper and stomped out.

"Bless it all to heaven!" Satan's face darkened. More black smoke puffed from his horns.

This was not the outcome he'd hoped for.

"I don't understand the problem." Bad pushed his glasses back into place.

"Didn't you hear? The girl said she's made enough money to keep the statue."

"True," Bad said. "But Lilith appeared confident that she had things under control."

"Lilith would appear confident if armed guards were dragging her off to the Lake of Fire."

Also true.

"Describe the problem domain for me," Bad said. "I may be able to provide a solution you've overlooked."

Satan's face turned the color of a ripe plum. "Why aren't you sweeping?"

Bad stood his ground. "Because you need my expertise."

Satan scowled, but Bad stayed right where he was.

After a long moment, Satan said, "Ornias's first act in DemSec was to construct a population map to help us target our marketing efforts more effectively."

Bad's ears grew hot. Ornias couldn't build a population map to save his eternally damned soul. Bad had built that map. He'd identified all the selection criteria—poverty, violent crime, joblessness, educational attainment, drug overdoses, teen pregnancy, and a host of others. He'd run the resulting data through geographical software, creating a map with Earth's most vulnerable areas highlighted. He had been preparing to present his results to Satan the day the guards showed up to drag him off to the maggot pit.

He forced himself to take a deep, calming breath. There was no value in getting angry. Ornias had merely done what fallen angels always did, given the opportunity. He'd claimed credit for something he was neither smart enough, nor hard-working enough, to do on his own.

"Once we started looking at the map, we noticed some 'anomalies.'" Satan used air-quotes on the last word. The smoke coming from his horns grew thicker, blacker. "Areas that met the selection criteria but were trending in the wrong direction."

That was intriguing. "Were you able to identify any correlations?"

"It took a while," Satan said, "but we eventually realized eighty-seven percent of the affected areas contained churches with crosses or crucifixes sculpted by Rachel Blackmon."

Bad's jaw dropped. "Eighty-seven percent?" That went beyond statistically significant. It was all but a sure thing.

"It gets worse," Satan said. "The slopes of the trend-lines increased following her death."

Bad frowned. "They should have tapered off as people forgot about her."

Satan shot him a nasty look. "Well, they didn't. And they're continuing to grow."

Humans who could imbue things they touched with sanctity strong enough to affect other people were rare. The incidence of that sanctity extending beyond their lifespan was vanishingly small.

"How many affected areas did you identify?" Bad asked.

"Twenty-three."

Twenty-three? That was like having war break out at twenty-three separate locations.

Bad looked at the three statues on the far side of the chamber. "And now you're collecting up her sculptures, so they don't create more pockets of goodness."

Satan's horns chugged out smoke like a locomotive. His talons dug grooves into the arms of his throne.

"The crosses are in the worst possible places. The woman didn't care anything about money. She practically gave them away, to churches in densely populated areas of high poverty and crime."

Hell's prime battleground.

"Every one of those churches became a hub for redemption and restoration," Satan said. "Take Over-the-Rhine in Cincinnati—we owned that neighborhood for decades. Now it's a fucking tourist destination."

"Why don't you just buy up the crosses? If the churches are poor, they'll be glad to have the cash."

Satan's horns belched black smoke. "Just the kind of recommendation I'd expect from a demon with no field experience."

Bad reviewed his solution. It seemed sound. "What's wrong with it?"

Satan growled under his breath.

"We tried it. We offered to buy a crucifix from a church in New Jersey that was on the brink of closing. As soon as we made our offer, the people in the neighborhood banded together to raise money to keep the crucifix. In the process, they got to know each other, became a community. Since then, they've raised enough money to keep the church open, chased out a street gang, and instituted an after-school mentorship program."

No wonder Satan had that obsessive glint in his eye. They were losing ground hard won from the Enemy. Although Bad didn't view him as an enemy, exactly. More like an adversary, the way the CEO of one company might view the CEO of another.

"How many crosses have we collected since Lilith started her mission?" Bad asked.

For a moment he thought Satan would refuse to answer. Then he said, sulkily. "None."

Bad blinked. "So, Lilith's only achievement thus far is collecting the other three statues?"

"She's stopped the dad from painting," Satan said. "And prevented the boys from becoming artists."

"The father's works are sanctified, too?"

"Just the originals." Satan looked glum. "That woman was the fucking Mother Teresa of the art world."

Bad considered that.

"And you're concerned that if the girl loans her sculpture to museums near churches where her mother's crosses are on display, it will give them a booster shot?" If that happened, things would start to get better in a big way.

"Exactly," Satan said, but his eyes shifted away. There was more going on with those statues than he was telling.

Regardless, it still came down to getting the girl to voluntarily give up the statue. It was a challenging problem—Bad's favorite kind.

"So, the next deliverable is the girl's statue, correct?"

Bad interpreted Satan's grunt as an affirmative. "I assume the contract was written to our advantage?"

"Of course."

"But at this point, it's unclear where she stands as far as meeting the terms of the contract."

Another grunt.

"Why is that?" Bad asked. "DemSec should be able to pull digital records of all financial transactions involving the girl over the past year and compare the total against the parameters of the contract."

"They did that," Satan said. "Based on the numbers they pulled, she only took in about fifteen thousand dollars last year. But based on her lifestyle, it's clear she made more than that."

Bad frowned. Things were even worse in the technology division than he'd realized. On the other hand, DemSec's incompetence provided him with the perfect opportunity to demonstrate his own prowess. He murmured "Keeffe Blackmon" and tapped the right temple of his glasses. A second later, a profile scrolled up his lenses. He said, "Financial, last year," and a list of transactions appeared. The list was surprisingly short. Entire months passed without anything more than a cell-phone bill.

"Her electronic record appears to be incomplete," Bad said.

"That's what I just said," Satan said.

Bad's heart raced. This could be the assignment that put him back at the helm of DemSec.

"I could go up and figure out what's going on."

"You?" Satan looked him up and down dismissively, validating Bad's suspicion that, left to his own devices, Satan would never get around to sending him on a field assignment.

Bad stood taller. "Yes, me."

"And how do you propose to do that?"

"I wouldn't go in my own body, obviously. I was thinking in terms of a possession modality."

Satan's eyebrows lifted. "Possession." He tested the word out. "We haven't done a good possession in decades."

That was because under Bad's guidance, technological advances had made it possible for Satan's crew of fallen angels to go Aboveworld in their own forms, albeit somewhat genetically altered to make them appear more human.

"The girl was initially attracted to the man who tried to buy her statue. You could see it in her respiration and the dilation of her pupils," Bad said.

"It didn't turn into anything, though."

That attraction had terminated the moment she looked into his eyes, but Bad wasn't about to tell Satan that. It was better if the boss thought the girl found McCall's body alluring.

"The way he looked at Lilith offended her."

Satan raised one skinny eyebrow. "A Hade who can read face. Didn't see that coming."

Bad shrugged off the insult to his people, who were actually quite canny at reading body language. How else had they survived centuries of living side by side with the angel horde?

On-screen, McCall was trying to grab Lilith's ass without her husband seeing. She drifted out of range, but McCall followed her.

"That's another screw-up on Lil's part," Satan grumbled. "McCall was supposed to be her minion, but he does whatever he wants—which is mostly working out, playing video games, and banging Lilith whenever he gets a chance."

"Possession would be perfect, then," Bad said. "He's already in place. The girl found him physically attractive. I can take over his body and convince her to sell."

"Hold on," Satan said. "We just talked about you figuring out this technical glitch with the data."

"Why limit my scope?" Bad asked.

"Lilith doesn't play well with others."

That was an understatement.

"I won't interfere with her," Bad said. "I'll work on my own. Think of it as a backup plan."

Satan pursed his lips. "Can Hades even disapparate?"

"Of course," Bad said. "It's a skill, not a talent."

Satan worried his skinny lower lip. "I don't see the girl going for a nerd."

A lot of women were attracted by intellect and competence, but Bad didn't argue the point.

"You want the statue, right?"

Satan nodded. Bad's hopes rose.

"Well, I can get it for you."

For a moment, he thought he had it.

"Nah," said Satan. "I don't want to step on Ornias's toes."

Bad picked up the remote and tuned to a rerun of *The Jerry Springer Show*. A pair of women attempted to tear each other's blouses off while their baby daddy cheered them on.

Bad retrieved the broom he'd propped against the wall. This mission was custom-made for him, but Satan was too bigoted to perceive the full range of his abilities. And if he didn't get back to DemSec, the Hades would suffer. Inside Bad's pocket, his finger found a triangular button on his universal remote.

Fifteen minutes later, sweat beaded Satan's forehead. He stabbed at the thermostat in his chair arm. "Why is it so hot in here?"

"It's Hell." Bad pushed his broom in a long, smooth stroke.

The climate control system was another of his creations. Like any design worth its blueprint, it had a back door.

The chamber continued to warm. Inside his polyester coveralls, Bad sweated like a stonemason, but he kept right on sweeping. Once he was back in charge of DemSec, he'd be done with menial labor and back to using his strongest asset, his mind. After another five minutes, he heard the words he was waiting for.

"Come fix this thing," Satan roared.

Setting his broom aside, Bad went to Satan's throne and adjusted the climate control. The fans he'd installed in the rock walls picked up speed, but the air coming from the vents felt like a blast furnace.

He tapped the thermostat embedded in the chair arm with his fingertip.

"Hmm. The cooling system doesn't seem to be working."

"Then fix it." Satan's horns streamed smoke like a coal-fired power plant.

There was a balance to be weighed here. If Satan got any angrier, Bad could wind up in the maggot pit again. On the other hand, if he just let things ride, he might never get DemSec back. He rolled the dice.

"It's Ornias's system," he said. "I wouldn't want to tread on his toes."

Satan's face turned the color of a chili pepper. "You little piece of shit. I see what you're doing."

Bad locked eyes with him. "If you want to leverage my skills, put me in a position where they can do us both some good."

For a long moment, Bad's fate hung in the balance. He waited, arms folded, as sweat streamed down Satan's temples, sizzling as it rolled over the boss's hollow cheeks and dripped off the tip of his goatee.

"All right," Satan roared, "you can go. Now fix the air-conditioning."

But Bad made no move to adjust the temperature. Instead, he pulled out his phone and hit the record button.

"Agreement: If Abaddon delivers Keeffe Blackmon's eagle statue to Hell within nine weeks of the date-stamp on this message, Satan agrees to immediately place Abaddon back in charge of DemSec." He held out the phone to Satan. "Please say 'yes, I agree.'"

With the boss, you couldn't leave any wiggle room. Bad had learned that the hard way.

"Nine weeks?" asked Satan. "The girl's birthday is just a month away. Once she takes her mother's statue home, away from Lilith's influence, its power will grow exponentially. You'll never get it away from her."

Bad planned to have the statue well before the girl's birthday, but his motto had always been, "under-promise, over-deliver."

He spoke into the phone again.

"If Abaddon delivers Keeffe Blackmon's eagle statue to Hell within six weeks of the date-stamp on this message, Satan agrees to immediately place him back in charge of DemSec."

Satan fanned himself and glowered at Bad.

"Fine. Bring me that statue in the next six weeks and you can have DemSec back."

Bad held out the phone. "Please say 'yes, I agree'"

"Yes, I agree." Satan spat out the words. "But if you fail, your last stint in the maggot pit is going to seem like a picnic in Ring One."

Bad was already adjusting the temperature back to a comfortable level. He wasn't worried about what would happen if he failed.

He had no intention of failing.

CHAPTER 3

$\mathcal{B}$ad drove his Mini Cooper along a curving driveway of crushed rock, coming to a halt in front of a white stucco mansion. Behind McCall's huge house, red cliffs jutted beneath a cloudless sky. Tiny canyon wrens swooped from tree to nest and back again. Even though the air outside the car was a crisp forty-five degrees, the sun blazing overhead warmed the car to a comfortable temperature. Maybe coming Above wasn't so bad after all.

In the center of the house's red terracotta roof, a tinted-glass dome rose. Bad studied it with interest. Based on his research, the room beneath that dome was the perfect bait to lure Keeffe Blackmon to his side. With her in close proximity, he could study her and identify the best method of convincing her to give up her statue.

He leaned back in the car to pull a sturdy backpack from the passenger seat. Inside was all the tech he thought he might need while Above: his universal remote, a backup pair of glasses, an extra phone, a ring with keys that would open almost any door, and several other gadgets that might prove useful. He never went anywhere without his backpack. He rang the doorbell, grinning as the *Star Wars* theme sounded.

An old man with the rheumy eyes of an ancient tortoise opened the door. It was the demon Ronobe. Bad blinked. He hadn't known Ronnie was assigned to this mission. Satan hadn't mentioned him, and his name wasn't in the mission dossier.

"Well," said Ronnie, "if it isn't the baddest demon in all Hell."

Bad adjusted his glasses. "That's just a nickname."

"You're too modest."

"Not at all. I'm the smartest demon in Hell. I accept that title without equivocation. It's the assigning of moral judgments to inanimate objects that I object to." Bad lifted one eyebrow. "What are you doing here?"

Ronnie was a Hangel—half Hade, half angel. The identity of his parents was unknown. Centuries ago, the She-Wolf had found him beneath a wind-shattered bush in Ring Two and nursed him along with her own pups.

Rumor had it Ronnie had been a real Hell-raiser when he was young, but there was no sign of it today. He was the least ambitious demon in Hell, content to float along, making no effort to advance. His lack of drive made it unlikely he was here in competition with Lilith.

"Lil asked me to keep an eye on McCall," Ronnie said.

Apparently, Lilith's unwillingness to work with other demons was limited to demons who might try to claim credit.

"Is McCall here?" Bad asked.

Ronnie nodded. "Lil said you were coming, so I left some cocaine out for him."

Deep inside the house, a male voice chanted, "Cheez-*Its*. Cheez-*Its*. Cheez-*Its*." The chant grew louder with each iteration. "God damn it, Ronnie! Where are my Cheez-Its?"

Bad listened with dismay. "Cocaine's a stimulant. That is going to make this so much harder."

Ronnie's pendulous jowls swayed back and forth. "Lilith said you wanted him coked-up."

Bad should have seen that coming. Lilith was a babe, but she totally bought into the demon ethos that prevailed in Hell. She'd shiv someone with one of her dagger-heeled shoes before she'd share credit for a mission. It also provided a likely answer to his question about Ronnie's role. The old demon's lack of ambition made him the perfect wingman for a go-getter like Lilith.

"That's okay," Bad said. "I'll figure it out."

Before Bad could take possession of McCall's body, he would have to abandon his own. Ronnie led him to a large room with a pool table, a huge flat-screen TV, and a sectional sofa. A coffee table with a pair of game controllers, some comic books and a prescription bottle stood in front of the sofa. Prints from superhero comics and manga studded the walls. From a room down the hall, he could hear rhythmic grunts as McCall lifted weights.

According to the manual Bad found in the archives, *Human Possession for the Total Fucking Moron,* his essence would leave his body via his nose, appearing as coal-colored smoke just above his head. His body would be left in a state of suspended animation. He'd considered leaving it Below, but he didn't trust those jerk-offs from Ring Six not to steal his body and commit lewd acts on it.

He pressed the palms of his hands together and sucked a deep breath in through his nose.

"You'd better sit down," Ronnie said.

"Is it easier that way?"

"Not especially," the old demon said, "but it keeps your shell from falling over once you're gone."

Of course. Bad was a little embarrassed he hadn't thought of that. He sat down on the white leather sofa and started again, thinking demonic thoughts, just like the manual instructed. After twelve breaths, he opened his eyes. There wasn't so much as a wisp of smoke above his head.

Ronnie's ancient eyes surveyed him. "Think darker."

Bad pressed his palms together, took another deep breath and thought about the scene in *Harry Potter and the Goblet of Fire* where Voldemort kills Cedric Diggory. When he opened his eyes, a wispy cloud of pale gray smoke undulated above him. A second later, it streamed back up his nose.

"Darker," said Ronnie.

Bad nodded. He closed his eyes, pressed his palms together, and envisioned the part of *Dead Space 2* where the needle sticks you in the eye. This time, the cloud was twice as large, but it was still pale gray.

"Think about something bad you want to happen to someone else," Ronnie advised.

Bad's eyes widened. "Seriously?"

Ronnie shrugged his shoulders inside his too-large suit jacket. "I'm just telling you what works."

Bad closed his eyes again and thought about the scene in *Digital Devil Saga* where you eat your opponents. He gave one of them Satan's face. When he opened his eyes, his consciousness was no longer inside his body, but resided in a cloud of gray vapor hovering above his sideways-listing form. Sweet! Gravity Aboveworld was weaker than in Hell, but this was like weighing nothing at all.

"In there," Ronnie said, pointing to the workout room. "Quick, before you lose your ju-ju."

It turned out to be a lot harder to relocate when your being consisted of vapor molecules. Each molecule seemed to have its own agenda. Some went to scout McCall's home theater setup. Some went to check out the security system. A few wafted up to play in the ceiling fan. By the time Bad corralled them, part of his essence had streamed back up the nose of his body, which was showing signs of life again.

He dragged up an image of himself biting off Satan's ear and spitting it onto the floor. His entire consciousness coalesced into a dense, dark cloud. Before he could disperse, he zoomed down the hall and into the workout room, where McCall was now doing rapid pushups. Bad streamed up his nose.

There he encountered another setback. As soon as Bad attempted to take over McCall's neural circuitry, his host leapt to his feet and started screaming.

"Get outta me! Get the fuck outta me!"

An instant later, Bad found himself back in his own body, feeling like all the Hades in Hell were beating on his skull with their pickaxes. The manual had warned that headaches were a by-product of failed possession attempts. He squeezed his eyelids shut, waiting for the pain to subside enough to let him think. When he opened his eyes, McCall stood in front of Bad, fists clenched, glaring.

"Who the fuck are you?" He gave Bad the once-over. "Or do I mean, *what* the fuck are you?"

"I'm a demon," Bad said, wincing. "I've come Above to assist you in convincing Keeffe Blackmon to sell her statue."

"What are you talking about?" McCall bobbed from one foot to the other, like a boxer. He raised his shoulders and expanded his chest in a show of male dominance. With Bad's denser molecular structure, it was doubtful McCall could inflict any serious damage, but Bad preferred not to go down that path.

He repeated what he'd said, more slowly this time.

"I don't need any help." McCall displayed no resistance to accepting Bad's story. Either he was naturally gullible or someone— Ronnie or, more likely, Lilith—had told him about demons.

"Lilith sent me," Bad said, hoping McCall wouldn't text her to verify that.

McCall's shoulders dropped a few millimeters. "Lilith?"

"Lilith," Bad said firmly. "I'd like to offer you an arrangement."

McCall's posture returned to normal, though he continued to bounce on his toes. "What kind of arrangement?"

"Host me for six weeks and I will provide target-specific information, as well as demon skills, to increase your chances of success," Bad said.

"Huh?" McCall sniffed a long, juicy snort and rubbed his nose on his tattooed forearm.

Charming.

"Keeffe Blackmon." Bad dug deep for patience. "I have information about Keeffe Blackmon that will make it possible for you to convince her to sell you her sculpture."

He didn't actually. The dossier for the mission had been

pathetically incomplete, a perfect example of why he was badly needed back in DemSec.

"Sweet," said McCall. "Lil said if I can get the hippie chick to sell me the bird, she'll show me this trick she does with a mango and an ice cube."

"Excellent." Bad cut McCall off before he could share any further. "All you need to do is allow me to disapparate and take possession of your body."

"Disapparate?"

"Leave this body."

McCall's eyebrows flew up. "No way."

"I can guarantee your success."

McCall shook his head. "I'm not into cohabitation."

Bad touched his right temple and brought up McCall's Wickedpedia entry. According to his profile, he had never actually created anything. He had made his fortune by stealing other people's ideas and monetizing them.

"Perhaps we can work out an arrangement," Bad said. "I can give you brand-new technology, never before seen on Earth. In return, you allow me to share your body for the next six weeks."

McCall's eyes narrowed. "What kind of technology?"

Bad took off his Gehenna Glasses and offered them to McCall. "Touch the right temple and say 'Sedona, Arizona.'"

McCall put on the glasses and did as instructed. A sparkle came into his gray eyes.

"Now touch the left temple and look at that prescription bottle on the table."

McCall followed instructions again. The cocaine was evidently wearing off, because he'd stopped bouncing from foot to foot.

"Cool," he said, "but Google already made something like these."

"Not exactly like these," Bad said. "These are connected into Hell's databases. They also have the ability to record every interaction you make."

McCall fiddled with the earpieces. "How do they work?"

Bad removed the glasses from McCall's face and put them back on his own. "Possession first, specifications later."

McCall parked himself on the white leather couch and spread his arms along the back.

"Come on in."

Bad's first couple of tries were unsuccessful. Each time, before he could get firmly seated, McCall would expel him.

"I guess you're not really interested in making your next billion," Bad said when the splitting headache finally receded for the third time.

"I'm trying," McCall said, "but my survival instinct keeps kicking in."

They glared at each other in frustration. Then McCall's eyes fell on the prescription bottle on the coffee table. He opened the bottle, shook out three oval orange tablets and swallowed them.

"Give me fifteen minutes," he said.

Probably longer, given the presence of cocaine in his system.

To figure out the best way to get Keeffe Blackmon to give up the statue, Bad would need to spend time with her. He headed down the hall to check out the room beneath the dome he'd seen from outside.

He stopped in the doorway. The room was circular, with white, eight-foot walls. Tapping his glasses, he pulled up the Wickedpedia article about it. The glass vault was photochromic, keeping the light stable throughout the day. Full-spectrum lights, designed to mimic daylight, dotted the circumference of the room at regular intervals. He walked around the room, dictating notes as he walked. From an engineering perspective, the room was a marvel. From an artistic perspective, it was the perfect lure to draw in a painter.

When he returned to the family room forty-five minutes later, McCall was completely zoned out. Bad went through the process of disapparating again and surged up McCall's nose. This time he encountered no resistance. The pills had done their work.

Once he was in control, Bad looked down with serious awe at the body he was inhabiting. McCall's form was nine inches taller than his own Hade body, and every inch was ripped. He flexed his newly acquired arms and grinned as biceps like spinach cans strained against the sleeves of his T-shirt. He hooked a finger inside his waistband and dragged it out to check his junk. *Unholy shit.* If it was that big flaccid, what would it look like when he had a boner?

"Try moving around," Ronnie suggested.

Bad let the elastic waist of his jockeys snap back into place and got to his feet.

He took a step, awkwardly aware of the mechanics of lifting one foot while simultaneously swinging it forward and transferring his weight to the other foot and then back again once he settled the lead foot. He redirected some of his molecules away from McCall's prefrontal cortex to the more workaday parts of his brain. After a few more test steps, his movements became natural. He repeated the process with his hands until he could pluck a penny from the flat surface of the coffee table on the first try.

"Owned!" McCall's voice was deeper than Bad's. He liked the way it rumbled in his chest.

Looking up, he became aware of the rich colors of the world around him. The penny between his fingers was a shiny copper, the couch a creamy shade of ivory. The cliffs behind McCall's house, visible through the large windows on either side of the marble fireplace, shaded from pale orange to deep red to an eggplant tone in the shadows. The sky above the mountains was a shade of blue that made him understand why early humans had believed the sky to be the underside of Heaven. Humans had far more cones in their eyes than Hades. Hade eyes had evolved to work best in low light.

The riot of colors was astonishing.

"Don't forget that McCall is still in there," Ronnie said. "When he wakes up…."

Bad shrugged that off. He and McCall had a deal. For the next six weeks, he was driving.

He grabbed the shoulders of his empty Hade body while Ronnie grabbed its feet. Together they hauled it to a spare bedroom and put it on the bed. It lay there—short, dark, and a little hairy—sleeping peacefully.

He extracted the keys to McCall's Tesla from the pocket of his jeans and tossed them straight up, catching them in midair. His next task was to convince Keeffe to paint a mural in the dome room. While she painted, he would get to know her. From there, he would figure out how to get her to part with her statue voluntarily.

"Gotta go," he said. "I've got a date with an artist."

CHAPTER 4

Keeffe's trailer was old and decrepit, but her landlord had given her free rein to do whatever she wanted with the interior, so she was painting the living room and kitchen area to look like twenty-four hours in Sedona. The eastern wall featured a glowing sunrise in shades of yellow, pink, orange, and lavender. The ceiling cycled through a dozen shades of blue over to the western wall, which was the deep purple of night. The bottom half of the walls mimicked red sandstone cliffs under the different lighting conditions.

The mural was almost done. She would love to spend the evening working on it, but across the room, inside a dented metal footlocker that served as both filing cabinet and coffee table, lay the contract where eighteen-year-old Keeffe had scrawled her name in return for tuition money for art school. It would take coffee—at least four cups, enough to keep her up all night—to give her the mental energy needed to decipher the contract.

She groaned. What in the world had possessed her to risk losing the most important thing she owned?

Seven years ago, twenty-five had seemed far away. The mass production in China of Dad's paintings, which Lilith had arranged, had him rolling in money. It looked so easy, Keeffe figured she would be equally successful. And she supposed, at the back of her mind, she'd been certain Dad would never take away the statue Mom had made specifically for her.

Today she'd been forced to face the truth: she was wrong on both counts. She wasn't going to be an overnight success and Dad wasn't going to stand up to Lilith. As far as Keeffe knew, she was meeting the terms of their tuition agreement, but Lilith had written the contract, and today she had seemed far too smug. Keeffe needed to be sure there weren't any little gotchas waiting to trip her up at the last minute.

A search of her kitchen turned up no coffee. No surprise. Even small amounts of caffeine made her heart race and skip beats. Instead of a trip to the mini-mart, she decided in favor of dinner at her favorite dive. She wasn't procrastinating, she told herself. She was preparing.

Grabbing a pencil and her sketchpad, she headed out. After locking the flimsy aluminum door behind her, she threaded her way through the rows of broken-down trailers to the street.

The sun had already dropped behind the Black Hills, throwing deep shadows across the storefronts and turning the wispy cirrus clouds high in the sky into a palette of colors. She itched to go back and get her easel, to try once again to capture the incredible beauty that was Sedona at sunset, until a growl from her stomach reminded her she hadn't eaten since breakfast.

When a break came in traffic, she jaywalked across the street to Ernesto's Moonlight Grill. As she entered, an old-fashioned bell jangled overhead.

Inside, she took a moment to admire her handiwork. A couple of years ago, in return for a month of dinners, she'd designed the ceiling to create the illusion of a night sky. An inky black scrim covered a bank of LED lights, with pinpricks in the fabric to let tiny bits of radiance shine through. A titanium white moon, highlighted with touches of pale yellow, floated against the darkness.

It was reminiscent of Dad's work. He painted only cozy nighttime scenes. She would never box herself in like that.

At the sound of the bell, Ernesto's daughter, who was wiping down the massive wooden bar, looked up.

"*Hola*," Maria called.

"*Hola* yourself." Keeffe took a seat at the bar. "What are you doing here?"

The crowd was thin, typical for January. During tourist season, you couldn't get in the door at this time of night.

"The last girl quit unexpectedly," Maria said.

"That sucks."

"Tell me about it," Maria said. "So, what'll it be? Nachos and a Tecate?"

"Extra jalapenos," Keeffe said. "Instead of the beer—do you have free refills on coffee?"

Maria nodded.

"Make it coffee, then."

Maria looked surprised. "You never drink coffee."

"I've got a project to work on later. I need the jolt." Sometimes you did what you had to do.

Maria poured her a cup, then hollered the order for nachos through the opening in the wall to the kitchen.

Ernesto came through the swinging doors from the kitchen a moment later. A big man, his white apron stayed spotless, no matter how many hours he spent at the stove. His face lit up when he saw Keeffe.

"I thought I heard your voice," he said. "How's my favorite artist?"

"Craving your nachos." Keeffe grinned at him. "How's my favorite chef?"

He grinned right back. "*Bueno*."

What did it say about her that she was more welcome in a bar than at her own dad's house?

She dumped two packets of sugar into her cup and stirred. Behind her, the bell jangled again. Maria's eyes swept to the door, her face rearranging itself into a smile of welcome. Instead of calling *hola*, though, her mouth formed a silent *O* of amazement.

Ernesto's gaze followed hers. His eyes narrowed, and his shoulders hunched forward. What in the world had drawn such a mismatched pair of responses? Keeffe turned to see.

In the doorway stood Seth McCall.

Okay, that made sense. Their combined reactions summed up her own feelings about McCall. He was gorgeous, but something about him brought up her hackles.

"Hello, Keeffe." He slid onto the barstool next to hers.

"Hey." She moved her coffee cup a few inches down the bar.

"Nice place," he said, looking around.

He seemed different somehow. For one thing, he was wearing glasses, but it was more than that. She introduced him, trying to pinpoint the change.

"A pleasure to make your acquaintance." Maria's smile was more flirtatious than usual.

Ernesto's eyes traveled from Maria to McCall and back to Maria. "Who is taking care of my *nietos* tonight?"

Maria rolled her eyes. "Their father, because their grandfather made their mother come into work." She turned back to McCall, still smiling. "What can I get you to drink?"

"Whatever you have on tap."

Maria went away to draw him a beer. Ernesto disappeared back into the kitchen.

Meanwhile, Keeffe had figured out what was different about McCall. For one thing, he'd changed his aftershave. The leather and sandalwood smell had been replaced by—she took another sniff—the scent of chocolate. And not just any chocolate. Deep, dark, rich chocolate. The man smelled like a Ghirardelli factory. He literally made her mouth water. He smiled and she found herself smiling back.

That was when she noticed his eyes. Behind the heavy frames, they were brown—a brown as dark and rich as his chocolate scent.

"Were you wearing contact lenses this afternoon?" she asked.

For an instant, he froze. Then he touched his glasses. "Oh, right, I guess I was."

"You should stick with brown eyes. The gray is kind of creepy."

He blinked. "I'll keep that in mind."

Maria set his drink on the bar. "Your nachos should be out soon," she told Keeffe.

"Thanks." Keeffe gathered up her sketchbook and her coffee. "Can you bring them out to the booth, please?"

Maria's eyebrows rose, as though to say, *Seriously? You're walking away from that?* Keeffe ignored her and headed across the restaurant.

At a booth along the back wall, she set down her coffee and opened her sketchbook to the drawing she'd been working on before she went to Dad's. Drawn in charcoal, it was a series of concentric circles that narrowed to a vanishing point, like the top-down view of a cyclone.

"What's that?" McCall appeared beside the table.

She supposed she should have expected he'd follow her. "An energy vortex."

He studied the drawing. "Energy vortex?"

"It's a funnel shape in the earth that was formed by wind or water thousands of years ago."

"Interesting." His eyes were still on the paper. He actually seemed to be intrigued.

She thawed a little. "There are four of them in Sedona."

"Four?" His gaze sharpened. She got the sense of a penetrating intelligence she hadn't noticed that afternoon. "Why are they called energy vortexes?"

"Some people believe they create metaphysical energy."

His look of interest intensified, so she added, "Each one offers a different form of energy—masculine, feminine, or a masculine/feminine balance."

"That's just three," he said.

She nodded. "The last site, Bell Rock, has all three."

"What about you?" he asked. "Do you believe they really create energy?"

"They create something. The nearby trees look like a giant tried to wring them out like dishrags."

He pulled a phone out of his shirt pocket and tapped the screen, then frowned. After a second, his face cleared.

"Oops, wrong phone." Sticking it back in his pocket, he pulled another phone from his back jeans pocket. He spoke into it. "Check out the energy vortexes."

"Why do you carry two phones?" she asked.

"One's for business." He slipped it back into his jeans pocket.

She waited for him to plop down in the seat across from her, surprised to find herself almost disappointed when he didn't.

"Your dad said I might find you here," he said. "I have a business proposition I'd like to discuss."

Keeffe's jaw tightened. "I'm not selling my statue."

"Right," he said. "You made that clear this afternoon. May I join you?"

She stared up at him warily. He gazed at her with those soulful brown eyes while the mouth-watering smell of dark chocolate wrapped itself around her. Her pulse quickened. If Dad had told McCall where to find her, he must think this was a good opportunity. On the other hand—Lilith.

Deciding to give McCall the benefit of the doubt, she gestured to the far side of the booth. "Have a seat."

McCall sat.

"What's your business proposition?" She warmed her hands on her coffee mug.

"A commission, to paint a mural for me."

"A mural?" That was a surprise. At Dad's today, McCall's only interest appeared to be in Mom's work. He'd acted like he didn't even know Keeffe was also an artist.

"Indoor or outdoor?" she asked.

"Indoor. I have a room in my house that's round. Eight-foot walls, about twenty feet across, with a domed ceiling made of glass. I figured it would be a great spot for a mural."

"A domed room?" she said. What a cool-sounding space.

"The glass is photochromic, so the light stays even throughout the day." His eyes sparkled as he described it.

In spite of herself, she grinned. He was totally geeked out over this room. And he should be, because it sounded amazing. It would make a great canvas for a landscape. It couldn't hurt to find out a little more about it.

"What kind of subject matter were you thinking?" she asked.

"Uh...." He touched the right temple of his heavy glasses. His focus shortened, and his eyes swept back and forth, almost like he was reading something. His gaze returned to her.

"Scenes of superheroes."

She stared at him in dismay. "You mean—cartoons?"

"More like comic-book art or manga."

Keeffe sagged against the back of the booth, feeling like someone had just let all her air out. His eyes went wide.

"I mean, no." He faked a laugh. "Not cartoons." The way his voice squeaked, he might have been a cartoon character himself. "A cartoon mural would be ridiculous, right?"

"Not ridiculous. Just not my jam. I'm a landscape painter."

"Landscape?" he repeated. She could almost see him shifting gears. An enthusiastic smile stretched his lips. "A landscape would be great."

He was a terrible liar.

Keeffe stared at him through narrowed eyes. He was less annoying than he'd been this afternoon, but why had he changed his mind so fast? It made no sense.

"What made you choose me for this commission?"

"Lilith says that one day you'll be as famous as your father."

The mention of Lilith brought back his behavior that afternoon. Why would this uber-rich guy, who had the hots for her stepmom, want Keeffe to work for him? And why would Lilith recommend her? Her gut said that couldn't be good.

"I don't care for my dad's kind of fame."

"'Daniel Blackmon, Painter of Night.'" McCall sounded like he was reading from the advertising brochures. "He's sold thousands of paintings. What's not to like?"

"Nothing." Not if you didn't mind selling your soul for celebrity. Dad's paintings, replicated in China but hand-signed by him, were immensely popular, but he was scorned in the art world. That was probably why he drank so much.

"So, will you paint a landscape for me?" McCall asked.

She hesitated. It was tempting. The domed room sounded like a perfect canvas.

"You should get the kind of mural you really want. You won't be happy with it otherwise."

"I'm willing to pay fifteen thousand dollars."

Keeffe's fingers twitched. Fifteen thousand dollars was almost half what she'd made all last year.

Across the table, McCall was as still as a hunter. The memory of him following Lilith's cues, not to mention her boobs, returned. Given Lilith's long-running fixation with selling *John,* and McCall's interest in buying him, getting involved with the man was a bad idea.

She shook her head. "You wouldn't be satisfied with my work."

CHAPTER 5

ieldwork was both harder and more enjoyable than Bad had anticipated.

The misinformation on Keeffe's Wickedpedia page, stating that she was a cartoonist, had sent him down a blind alley. Had someone deliberately planted it to misdirect him? Maybe Lilith had gotten wind of his field assignment and made a preemptive strike. Or maybe Ornias wanted to reinforce his hold on DemSec.

Or it could be just another example of the poor quality of work being done in DemSec these days. Regardless, the Research Department would be one of the first areas Bad addressed when he was back in charge.

The enjoyable part was Keeffe herself. Her smile felt like sunlight warming him. Hell was such a dark place. He would miss the light up here when he went back.

The waitress arrived with nachos and a coffee pot. Keeffe drained her cup and set it down on the table with a thump.

"Girl, you're going to be up all night." Maria refilled her cup.

"Probably," Keeffe agreed, looking gloomy.

Maria left. Keeffe took two packets of sugar from the container on the table and tore them open.

"Do you always drink this much coffee in the evening?" Bad asked.

"No, but I need to—" She looked up to answer him and missed the cup. Sugar scattered across the table.

Swiftly, he counted the grains, moving his lips silently as he tallied. Two hundred and twelve spilled grains of sugar. Enumeration was a quirk displayed by anyone working for Satan, courtesy of the Adversary. It hadn't appeared in Bad until he went to work in DemSec.

Across from him, Keeffe stared. "Did you just count the sugar?"

He considered lying, but she was too observant. She'd never believe him. Instead, he shrugged sheepishly.

"I have some OCD issues."

"Lilith has the same compulsion." When she said *Lilith*, her lip curled.

She was not only observant but quick to see correlations.

She dug into the mess of chips and toppings. "Have some," she said around a mouthful of sour cream and salsa.

Avoiding the jalapeños, Bad selected a chip and tried it. It was delicious. Chalk one up for Earth. Everything in Hell was so spicy you couldn't really taste anything but the burn.

"Why don't you like Lilith?" he asked.

"Who says I don't?"

"Your expression when you mention her."

She shrugged. "Just normal stepmother-stepdaughter stuff."

It looked like more than that to Bad.

"Is she the reason you refused my commission?"

The twist of Keeffe's lips said he was right, but she shook her head and shoved another chip into her mouth.

After she swallowed, she said, "It's not what you really want."

"Yes, it is."

At that, she actually rolled her eyes. This girl was a tough sell.

"I heard you were a cartoonist," he said. "That's why I said cartoons."

"Who told you that?" She stuck her index finger in her mouth and sucked salsa off her fingertip.

Though she clearly didn't intend it as a come-on, the sight of her pink lips encircling her fingertip made his mouth go a little dry. Her lips looked as soft as she was tough.

He dragged his attention back to the mission. Tapping his glasses, he did a quick search of the dossier.

"I must have misunderstood. Lilith mentioned that your siblings are artists, too?"

"My sister Frida builds websites," Keeffe said, "and my twin brothers are designing a video game. I wouldn't call any of that art. Why would Lilith tell you that?"

Inside McCall's form-fitting T-shirt, Bad's armpits grew damp. He wasn't used to lying. "Let's compromise," he said with a smile. "Let's call them *art adjacent*."

"I don't believe in compromise." Keeffe crossed her arms. "Compromise is just another name for losing."

He blinked. "You're kind of take-no-prisoners, aren't you?"

Color rose in her cheeks. "So I've been told."

With Lilith as a stepmother, she'd probably had no choice. She'd had to either learn to stand her ground or get rolled over.

"That's okay." He selected another nacho. "There's nothing wrong with standing up for yourself."

Keeffe's arms relaxed and she actually almost smiled.

Finally, he'd said the right thing. "So, the cartoon thing," he dragged the conversation back on topic. "Your brothers do animation, right?"

"Yep," she said.

"I must have gotten my wires crossed. They're the cartoonists, you're the landscape painter."

"Correct," she said again, but she didn't offer to take the commission.

He pulled out his phone and typed "Keeffe Blackmon art" in the search box. A handful of images came back. He clicked on one of a twisted juniper against a backdrop of red rock and blue sky. It expanded to fill his screen. He drew in a startled breath.

"Is this yours?" He turned the phone so she could see the screen.

She nodded, almost shyly.

"It's incredible." Rapidly he clicked through the half dozen other paintings returned by his search. "You're an extraordinary artist," he said, with complete sincerity.

Her face turned pink with pleasure. She smiled, a full-on, stretched-lips, toothy smile that lit up the booth like a searchlight. Finally, he'd connected with her.

"I'll double the price for the mural," he said. "Thirty thousand dollars." After all, it was just money—and McCall's money at that.

Her smile faded. "No, thanks." The steeliness in her gaze warned him to drop it.

It was time to back off. To show her there were no hard feelings, he drew up the corners of McCall's mouth up in a broad smile.

"What's that about?" Keeffe asked. Her smile didn't have the wattage she'd displayed when he'd praised her work, but at least she was smiling again.

"Just having a good time," he said. Despite the mission setback, it was true. "It's good to get out. The problem with computer work is you spend too much time alone." He rearranged McCall's lips into a less expansive but still-broad smile. "I'm tired of thinking about SEO algorithms."

Keeffe cocked her head. "What's an SEO algorithm?"

"Search engine optimization. One of my products is software that determines the content of banner ads on web pages. I've been working on a new method to more closely align the displayed content to the interests of the viewer." When she didn't respond, he added, "You probably hate banner ads of any kind."

"Nope," Keeffe said.

He blinked. "You don't mind adware?"

"I don't have a computer, so it's not really an issue." She nibbled on a chip.

"You don't have a computer?" Bad was aghast. Then he realized what she meant. "Oh, you mean you have a tablet."

"Nope, no tablet."

He frowned. "You do everything on your phone?"

She reached into her pocket and pulled out an ancient flip phone. "On this? Hardly."

He held out his hand and she gave him the relic. Without conscious intention on his part, his fingers flashed over the numbered keys.

"What are you doing?" she asked, looking annoyed.

"Adding myself to your contacts." In fact, McCall had taken the initiative to do that, unasked. Before she could order him to stop, he said, "How do you deal with this? It doesn't even have a full keypad. And no Internet access."

He began to get a glimmering why her digital footprint was so small. He handed the phone back to her.

"Not a big fan of technology," she said.

That was just crazy. Technology ruled the world. Both worlds.

Bad tried to imagine simply choosing to ignore the wonders of the Internet, and failed.

"What do you do when you need to look things up?"

"I go to the library. They have a great collection of these things called books."

"I know a guy that still uses dial-up." He thought about Ornias. "Maybe I should introduce you."

"Maybe you should. He sounds like a great guy." Keeffe's tone was snippy, but a smile twitched the corners of her mouth.

She was a paradox. If she didn't like what he'd said, why was she smiling? If she didn't want to be awake, why did she imbibe caffeine so late? If she needed money, why didn't she take his commission? She was much more complex than his last girlfriend, and it wasn't just because she was warm-blooded.

The contradiction between her delicate prettiness and her utilitarian clothing, between her artistic sensibility and her complete lack of tact, between her incisive mind and her disinterest in technology, fascinated him.

Fieldwork was full of unexpected puzzles. He loved puzzles.

"Tell me about life as an artist," he said. "What does an artist do every day?"

She shrugged. "I paint. I teach art classes."

"That's it?" he asked.

"When it's tourist season, I draw caricatures."

"Do you ever use drawing programs?"

She wrinkled her nose. "You mean, like on computers?"

"Right."

"Uh, no." She looked at him like he'd lost his mind. "I get my inspiration from the real world."

What made this woman so technophobic? In order to get her to sell, he would need to understand her. In order to understand her, he would need to spend time in close proximity with her. To do that, he needed her to accept his commission.

"So be inspired." He lavished McCall's warmest, sexiest smile on her. In McCall's deepest, most persuasive voice, he said, "Come on, Keeffe. Paint the mural for me."

CHAPTER 6

"Nope. You need to find someone else." Keeffe gulped down the last of her coffee, then dug a ten out of her wallet and tossed it onto the table. "It was nice talking, but it's time for me to go."

"I've got it." McCall scooped up the ten and handed it back to her.

She didn't want him to pick up the tab, but she needed to get out of here. Away from his delicious chocolate scent. Away from his warm, fascinated brown eyes. It was getting harder and harder to fight the temptation to take his commission.

Anyway, she needed to go home and get to work on that contract. It was ten pages long. It would take her hours to decipher.

She wished she could take it to Frida or her brothers for help, but they didn't know about her reading issues and she planned to keep it that way. They knew she'd had trouble learning to read, of course. Mom had tutored her every night at their dining room table. But when Lilith came along, she put an end to the tutoring and advised Keeffe to keep her disability under wraps.

You don't want people to think you're a moron.

She really was the stepmother from Hell.

Keeffe called goodbye to Maria and headed for the door. Behind her, McCall stopped to pay the bill.

Outside, she waited at the curb for a chance to cross Sedona's busiest street.

"May I walk you home?" He appeared at her side before she could make good her escape.

"No need. I just live across the road." She steeled herself against his judgment of the run-down trailer park she called home, but he didn't give it a glance.

"Pretty town." He looked up and down the street. "It's great how sunny it is here."

"Right, because you like to hike and mountain bike."

He stared at her with something akin to horror. "What gave you that idea?"

"You did."

He blinked. "Right," he said. "Mountain biking and hiking, my two favorite pastimes."

His tone wasn't even remotely believable, but that afternoon, she would have sworn his enthusiasm was real. Another lie?

Then he smiled down at her, his brown eyes warm with laughter, and the aroma of chocolate swirled around her. Warmth blossomed low in her belly.

"This is just West Sedona." She attempted to break the spell he was weaving, but even in her own ears, her voice sounded husky. "You should see Uptown."

Light from an overhead streetlamp threw his cheekbones into high relief. "I'd like that."

"I wasn't offering you a tour."

"What were you offering me?" he asked, his eyes on her lips. The scent of chocolate grew stronger, inviting her to taste.

She licked her lips, knowing that could be interpreted as an invitation but unable to stop herself. "Nothing."

"Nothing?" He didn't take his gaze off her mouth.

"Nothing," she said, trying and failing to sound firm.

"Not even a kiss?"

Her back went rigid. "To pay for dinner?"

He stepped back, looking offended. "No. Because you want to kiss me."

She did want to kiss him. Over dinner he'd actually seemed like a pretty nice guy, appealing in a nerdy way. The way he reacted to her paintings—there had been no mistaking his sincerity. His jaw had dropped and, behind his glasses, his eyes had lit with admiration. She'd been in kind of a dry spell lately as far as sales, and it was balm to have someone truly admire her work.

Plus, he smelled delicious. Did he taste as good as he smelled? What the hell. There was only one way to find out.

She grabbed the front of his leather jacket and lifted her face. His mouth came down on hers, gentle but insistent. Under his persuasion, her lips opened.

He tasted like rich, dark chocolate, which she'd expected, but with a dash of cayenne thrown in, which she hadn't. His kiss warmed her lips like the peppers on Ernesto's nachos, making them tingle.

He cradled the back of her head and deepened their contact. Whatever his other issues, this guy knew how to kiss. He kissed like nothing existed in the universe but her, like a bomb could go off next to them and he wouldn't even notice. His single-minded focus was a little dizzying. She gave herself up to the intoxication of it, his tongue stroking hers. The peppery heat of it called up an answering warmth in her belly.

His lips moved on to place nibbling kisses along her jaw. The same zing warmed her skin as he worked his way to her ear. His breath lifted gooseflesh down the right side of her body clear to her toes. His concentration didn't waver. He was like a star, drawing her closer by sheer gravitational pull.

The muscles in her belly warmed, became liquid. She hooked her leg around his thighs and rubbed the inside of her thigh against his jeans. A passing car honked its horn, a long, jeering hoot. She ignored it, the friction making her sink more deeply into the heat of his mouth, carried away by the river of passion flowing through her veins.

The next thing she knew, the back of her head banged into the metal lamppost so hard her ears rang. His hips crushed her against the cast-iron base of the post, the ridge of his erection pulsing against her belly. The smell of chocolate disappeared beneath a gust of sandalwood and the peppery taste dissolved into the flavor of ordinary spit. *Bleah.*

She wedged her arm between them and shoved him away, gasping. It was hard to be sure in the dim glow of the streetlight, but behind his glasses, his eyes appeared to be gray. How could that be? It reminded her of Lilith, with her shape-changing pupils.

Keeffe was glad she'd resisted taking his commission for the mural. Something weird was going on here. Her suspicion that her stepmother had something to do with it returned. Her lust drained away like rainwater from an arroyo.

"My car is right there." He took her arm and tried to steer her toward a Tesla parked diagonally across two spaces.

She yanked her elbow out of his grasp. "Let's slow things down here, buckaroo."

He tried to pull her into his arms again. "Why? I want you. You want me. We're adults. What's the problem?"

She fended him off. "We barely know each other."

"What better way is there to get acquainted?"

"I'm gonna say, one that doesn't include our genitals."

She worried he'd persist, or even get mad. Well, she could get mad, too. Instead, he shuddered and his eyes seemed to darken. The scent of chocolate returned.

He nodded. "Fair enough. When can I see you again?"

This guy's train ran on two separate tracks. She had no business climbing on board either one of them. It was time to end her evening with Mr. Multiple Personality Disorder.

"I'll be in touch." This time, Keeffe was the one lying.

What did you do that for? Bad fired the question inside McCall's brain as Keeffe jogged across 89A and disappeared into a labyrinth of broken-down trailers. Things had been going great until McCall came roaring up and ruined everything.

"You were taking things too slow." McCall said as their body climbed behind the wheel of the Tesla.

This was actually the fastest pace that Bad had ever set for a first kiss. Connecting with someone was more about the mind than the body. It usually took him weeks, sometimes months, to reach the kissing stage.

"She's hot for my bod," McCall added. "We should try to get her together for a threesome with Lilith." He snickered. "Or do I mean a foursome?"

Ulck. Gross. If Bad was ever so fortunate as to get to make love to Keeffe, he'd have to figure out how to prevent McCall from being present.

We had a deal, Bad beamed the thought straight into McCall's cerebral cortex. *I get possession for six weeks. And at the end, you get the specifications for the glasses.*

"The deal didn't specify unilateral possession." McCall lifted their mutual shoulders in a shrug. "Just that I'd let you share my body for six weeks. Thanks to my hotness, you got a whole lot further with that hippie chick than you would have in your own scrawny hide."

True. Bad was a realist. *But your body made a lot more progress with me running the show than it ever would have with you in charge.*

"No way," said McCall. "If I'd been running things, we'd be in one of those tin cans right now, playing hide the salami."

What a pig.

"What's your deal, anyway?" McCall asked. "Lilith wants her broke. Why are you offering her money? And why are you offering her *my* money?"

She's not broke.

"Lilith said she's nowhere near making what a secretary makes." McCall's tone was smug.

Lilith only knows about Keeffe's digital transactions. Were you listening over dinner? She hates tech. She lives most of her life off the grid. I'll bet she's made at least as much in cash as she has in checks and credit-card payments.

"If her money went through the bank, Lil would know about it."

It didn't, Bad said.

"Then where is it?"

If Bad had to guess, he'd say that whatever Keeffe hadn't spent was probably under her mattress, or some other equally insecure spot in her trailer.

Lilith's arrangement is moot in any case. Keeffe is about to be offered a golden opportunity that will further her career. Something else DemSec's research department had missed. Bad had spotted it with a simple search of her siblings' data trails. *We need to get her to sign a contract to paint the mural before she learns about the other opportunity.*

"Wow." McCall's tone was admiring. "That's really evil."

It's not evil. Bad was offended. *I'm simply removing an obstacle to a goal.*

"Yeah," said McCall. "An obstacle that lets Keeffe Blackmon hang onto the thing she cares most about in the world. Dude, you are just like me. We see something we want and we take it."

Bad was nothing like McCall. He was a creator, an inventor, a dreamer of big ideas. McCall was a leech that sucked the blood of creatives like Bad.

Bad had no intention of wresting the statue from Keeffe's unwilling hands. His plan was to identify an object or opportunity for which Keeffe would happily trade the statue. To do that, he'd have to get to know her. That meant spending time together.

And that was why she had to paint the mural.

As Keeffe threaded her way through the trailer park, the coffee she'd chugged made its presence felt as a shivery sense of anxiety. Her stomach churned as she thought about McCall. What he did—you couldn't even call it bipolar. It wasn't like two extremes of the same person. It was more like there were two different guys living inside his body. One was a conceited asshat. The other was nerdy, sweet, shy —and a fabulous kisser. She needed to stay away from both of them.

By the time she got to her door, the coffee really hit her. Her hands were shaking so hard she could barely fit the key into the lock. Her heartbeat thudded in her ears. That was what happened when you mixed coffee, caffeine intolerance, and a handsy guy.

Time to forget about McCall and focus on the reason she'd drunk those four cups of coffee in the first place.

With quivering fingers, she cleared the art books off the footlocker and opened the hasps. After a couple of minutes of digging, she found the contract. She eyed it with loathing. Reading of any kind was challenging. Reading dense legalese was like climbing Chimney Rock without ropes.

She blamed Lilith for making her feel so embarrassed about her reading problems, but the truth was it had started before Lilith ever entered her life. It was a Blackmon tradition that when each child finished kindergarten, the graduate would select a favorite book and read it aloud to the family. Keeffe hadn't been around for Frida's reading, of course, but she remembered the boys double-teaming *The Polar Express*.

When Keeffe's turn came, she'd chosen *Make Way for Ducklings*. She'd been so proud. She'd started happily through the book, explaining what each picture meant, only to be stopped around page three when Claude yelled, "She's just making stuff up." He burst into laughter and Ed and Frida joined him. Mom had quickly shushed them, but the damage was done. Keeffe had hurled the book across the room. After that, whenever Claude wanted to annoy her, he called her "Duckling."

Now she carried the contract to the couch and sat down to decipher it.

Within five minutes, her head was whirling. The caffeine gave her energy, but the words were still a jumbled mess. Some letters, like *b*'s and *d*'s and *q*'s and *g*'s mimicked each other, so she had to stop to figure out what each one really was. It was tempting to toss the contract back in the trunk and give up. She took a deep breath and started again. This was too important to let her dyslexia get the better of her.

The first page described the loan. The amount was open-ended, but would be limited to tuition, room and board, books, and "reasonable living expenses." Keeffe had worked a part-time job all the way through college to pay for the tutors she needed to get through her classes.

On page two, there was a description of the salary goal she needed to meet. In the 365 days leading up to her birthday, she had to earn as much as the average administrative assistant, based on figures published by the Bureau of Labor Statistics. That she already knew, but for the first time she noticed a tiny number superscripted at the end of the sentence. She tracked the number to a note in the appendix. It stated that the salary figure would be based on the most recent listing in the BLS for job code 43-6011.

She frowned. She didn't know what job code 43-6011 was. When she'd researched the salary number a few years ago, she'd asked a librarian to look up the average salary for an administrative assistant in Flagstaff, the closest listing to Sedona. She didn't remember the librarian mentioning a BLS job code. She groaned. She'd have to go to the library tomorrow and double-check, just to be safe.

On page six, it said she would have to produce documentation for all money earned, in the form of dated bills of sale or bank statements. Since she kept most of her day-to-day money in a metal box at the bottom of the footlocker, bank statements weren't an option. Frida, who helped her with her taxes, insisted she track all of her sales on two-part sales slips, giving one to her customer and retaining the other for her records. For the first time, she was glad her sister was so fussy.

On page eight she ran across the clause stating that the collateral—her sculpture of *John*—would remain in her father's custody until her twenty-fifth birthday and the terms of the contract were met. How like Lilith to bury something so significant deep inside the contract.

After three hours of laborious decoding, Keeffe arrived at the tenth page. She'd never made it this far into the contract before. She closed her eyes and pressed the heels of her hands against her eyelids. *Hang in there.*

"The Borrower will demonstrate the ability to earn a living strictly through the application of artistic skills. The following activities reasonably will be deemed the product of her fine arts training:

a)Painting

b)Drawing

c)Sculpting

d)Teaching

e)Art-related consulting

"Failure to meet these terms will result in the Borrower being held liable for full repayment of all tuition, books, room and board, and miscellaneous fees incurred during her undergraduate education."

It didn't explicitly require she give up *John*, but where else would she get the money?

She searched her memory for any money she'd made in the past year for something other than art or teaching. When that yielded nothing, she felt a flush of pride. She might not be a superstar but she was supporting herself as an artist.

At the bottom left side of the final page was her signature. On the right was Dad's and, just beneath it, Lilith's. When Keeffe had questioned why her stepmother needed to sign it, Dad said his pre-nup with Lilith specified that she had final approval on any art-related financial decisions.

That was all there was to it, except for a dark smudge near the bottom of the page. As she'd handed her stepmother the papers after signing them, they'd slipped in her hands, giving Keeffe a paper cut. It bled, leaving a smear on the contract. Keeffe had offered to reprint the final page and sign it again, but Lilith had insisted on keeping the bloodstained copy, making a photocopy for Keeffe.

Keeffe wasn't done yet, though. She forced herself to comb through the appendices at the back, word by word. She was already juiced up on caffeine. Why waste it?

There, she ran across the note about job code 43-6011 again. Her unease returned, though she wasn't sure why. She had a safety buffer. She'd earned a couple of thousand dollars more than the contract required, but what if she'd been looking at the wrong number?

Maybe she should take McCall's commission after all.

She rejected the idea as soon as it occurred to her. Aside from Mr. Hyde's attraction to Lilith, it was probably not the best idea to enter into a business relationship when Dr. Jekyll's kisses make her want to climb him like a class three hiking trail.

She drummed her fingers on the lid of the footlocker. Without the commission, how could she generate extra income if she needed it? The bulk of the tourists that were her go-to source of quick money wouldn't be returning to Sedona till after her birthday.

Calm down, she told herself. This was the caffeine talking. In the morning, she'd go to the library. No point in panicking until she had the facts. She jotted down the job code on a piece of scrap paper and stuck it in the messenger bag that served as her purse.

As she placed the contract back in the footlocker, her fingers brushed against a dark brown, leather-bound book. Mom's final journal, where she had chronicled her work on *John*. Keeffe had swiped it from the long shelf of similar journals the day after Mom's funeral. Now she leafed through it, smiling at the sketches as Mom's concept for *John* took shape.

In the early drawings, this metaphor for the author of Revelation looked brooding, threatening. In one, his eyes were crazed, as though seeing the hallucinatory images that filled the final book of the Bible. Over the course of the drawings, his head lifted and his eyes cleared. Instead of apocalyptic visions, he seemed to see God.

Keeffe wished she could read the detailed pages of notes, but Mom's looping cursive was indecipherable. When Keeffe had realized she'd never be able to crack the code, she'd considered returning it to the shelf, but the pleasure of being able to look at Mom's sketches made her hang on to it. Later, when the other journals disappeared in Lilith's purge, she was glad she'd kept it.

First thing tomorrow, she'd go to the library. Come hell or high water, she was keeping her statue.

CHAPTER 7

The next morning, Keeffe was waiting outside the library when the doors opened, sipping a mocha latte from a to-go cup picked up at a convenience store. She needed the caffeine, not just to help her focus this morning, but to help her wake up. Last night's attempts at sleep were riddled with dreams of Seth McCall's mouth on hers. At one point, she woke up tasting dark chocolate laced with cayenne.

She took another sip and realized that she'd chosen the mocha this morning in response to a lingering craving for chocolate. *Get a grip, girl.*

While everyone else who'd been waiting for the library to open hurried toward the rows of public computers, Keeffe made her way to the information desk. Angela, the middle-aged librarian, greeted her with a smile.

"What are we looking up today, Keeffe?"

"I need to know the salary range for this job code." She handed Angela the note she'd written the night before.

Angela swung her screen around so Keeffe could see it and navigated to the Bureau of Labor Statistics site. As she worked, a couple of older people got in line behind Keeffe. She tried not to let their presence make her feel self-conscious. She had to get this right. She had no chance of retaining *John* if she didn't even know what the requirement was for keeping him.

"Here we go," said Angela. With the eraser on her pencil, she pointed to a row of figures.

Keeffe stared at the numbers, dumbfounded. She couldn't possibly be reading them right. The low-end number was sixteen thousand dollars a year more than the figures she'd been working from.

"Would you mind reading them to me?" she asked, low-voiced. "I, uh, I forgot my glasses."

Obligingly, Angela read the numbers aloud.

They didn't change. Panic swamped Keeffe.

"Are you sure?" she asked. "You helped me look up the salary for administrative assistants a few years ago and it wasn't anywhere near this much."

"I remember," Angela said, frowning. "Of course, these numbers change every year."

The old man behind Keeffe cleared his throat.

"Be patient, dear," said the old lady with him. "She'll be done soon."

"She's young," grumbled the old man. "Why can't she just look it up on her phone like the rest of them do?"

Keeffe's cheeks burned, but she refused to give up.

"Salaries don't change by sixteen thousand dollars. Not in just a few years," she told Angela.

"That does seem like a big jump." The librarian pressed a couple of keys. "I think I see what the problem is. Last time, we looked up 43-6014—a regular administrative assistant. The 43-6011 job code is for executive administrative assistants."

Keeffe had based her goal on a regular administrative assistant. Her ten-thousand-dollar buffer, which had seemed like it would be more than sufficient, wasn't enough. She was six thousand dollars shy of meeting the terms of the contract.

Angela printed out the pages in question, highlighting the job codes and salary figures, and gave them to her.

Numbly, Keeffe left the library. Of course, she could always take

McCall up on his offer. As soon as the thought crossed her mind, she dismissed it. Her reasons for refusing the commission were still just as valid as they'd been last night. She thought about his head-banging kiss. She tossed her empty mocha cup in the trash, remembering his chocolate and cayenne-flavored kiss. Maybe even more valid.

Inside her car, she stared out the windshield at the multicolored rectangles of sandstone that formed the walls of the library. She had just twenty-nine days to come up with six thousand dollars or lose *John* forever.

Why had she never looked at the contract in detail before?

Because you can't read, said a voice that sounded like Lilith's. *Because you're stupid.*

Even though she was sitting alone in her car, Keeffe's face burned. She blinked back humiliated tears.

There was no way that contract should have been based on the salary for an executive administrative assistant. The truth was, she could never have held down even a regular secretarial job, much less a job as assistant to an executive. Why hadn't she just admitted that to Dad at the time, instead of signing that contract?

Because she didn't want him to know that reading was a struggle for her.

It was a good thing Lilith wasn't here to see her now. Stepmom would totally get off on Keeffe crying because she'd stupidly walked into Lilith's trap.

At that thought, Keeffe's spine straightened. She might not win, but she would go down fighting. She was a good artist, damn it. Six thousand dollars represented only a couple of canvases. She just needed to put a little more effort into the sales end of things.

She returned to her trailer and loaded four paintings—done *en plein air* last fall before it grew too chilly to paint outdoors—into the hatch of her Honda. Then she drove down 179, circling through two roundabouts and swerving to miss a flattened armadillo. Ten minutes later, she arrived at Tlaquepaque Village, where the Red Rock Gallery operated. She'd had no sales in the past few months. Maybe fresh canvases would change her luck.

Her cellphone buzzed as she pulled into an empty parking space at the gallery. She pulled it out of her pocket and checked the screen. It was McCall. She pushed the "ignore" button.

She got out of the car and opened the hatch lid. With a whispered prayer beneath her breath, she retrieved the new paintings from the hatch.

Inside the gallery, Nancy, the owner, dusted a bronze sculpture of a cowboy astride a bucking pony. She looked up when the door opened, her face all set to break into a smile. When her eyes fell on the paintings in Keeffe's hands, the smile stopped mid-formation. Inside, Keeffe cringed, but she forced a smile of her own.

"My sales have been a little slow lately, so I thought it was time to freshen things up a bit." She positioned one of the new canvases on an eye-level shelf designed to give patrons an idea of what a painting would look like on their wall at home. The painting featured water rippling over the rocks of Oak Creek Canyon. The water glittered in the sunlight, so real you could touch it.

Nancy's face softened. "It's beautiful, Keeffe. You're a great painter."

The tension in Keeffe's gut unknotted a little, but before she could say thanks, Nancy added, "I just wish my customers saw your work the way I do."

A fresh wave of humiliation set Keeffe's cheeks ablaze. "Maybe these new canvases...?"

Nancy shook her head. "I wish I had a solution but it's happened too many times. A customer sees one of your paintings and they can't wait to buy it. But as soon as they pick it up, they change their minds. They can't put it down fast enough."

Keeffe stared at the canvas leaning against the wall, baffled. It made no sense. Her work was good. That wasn't just an artist's egotistical self-appraisal. She'd won award after award in college. Her senior show had sold out. She was a good painter.

"Is it the pricing?" With six thousand dollars to make up in just thirty—no, twenty-nine—days, she hated the idea of dropping her prices, but maybe she could make it up in volume.

"You're already priced lower than any of my other artists except the brand-new ones," Nancy said.

If Sedona loves you, she'll take care of you. That's what the artists in town always said. And having two famous artists for parents had given Keeffe a head start. When she returned to Sedona after college, the galleries in town had vied for her work. By the time she'd been home for three months, her paintings were showing in four different venues.

Everything had been good for the first two years. Then, a year ago, her sales had plummeted. Last March, one of her galleries had dropped her. A second followed suit in August, the third in September. The failures still smarted.

"No, price isn't the issue," Nancy said. "In fact, people often buy the next painting they pick up, even if it's more expensive. I've had a few people email me afterwards, though, sorry they didn't stick with you."

Keeffe tried to smile. "You could always ship them the painting."

"I tried that once," Nancy said. "They sent it right back." There was something odd in her expression.

"Did they say why?" Keeffe asked.

Nancy looked uncomfortable. "They said it had an unpleasant energy."

Keeffe wrinkled her nose. "What does that even mean?"

"I wish I knew." Nancy lifted her hands, palms up. "I'm sorry, Keeffe, but this is a small shop. I need to make every square foot count. I've got a new artist I'd like to give a chance."

Keeffe had gone to Sedona High with Nancy's daughter. She could play up that school tie, try to get a stay of execution, but pride sealed her lips. She bent to pick up the canvases she'd set on the floor.

"I'm sorry my work wasn't more popular," she said, her voice husky.

"I am, too." Nancy looked like she might cry. She went into the back room and brought out three more canvases.

She followed Keeffe out to the car. As soon as Keeffe opened the hatch, Nancy dumped the paintings she carried like she couldn't get rid of them fast enough. As she backed away from the car, she shivered a little and rubbed her arms. Keeffe had the sudden sense that, whatever Nancy might say to the contrary, she was relieved to have the paintings gone from her shop.

"Have you considered asking your stepmother for help?" Nancy asked. "With her connections, she might be able to hook you up with a private collector."

Keeffe shook her head but left it at that. There was no way she was going to air her family's dysfunctions in public.

"Maybe you should." Nancy's tone was encouraging. "She's been here half a dozen times in the last year. She really admires your paintings. Every time you bring in a new one, she's the first customer to check it out. She's really determined to find you an audience."

Maybe that was where the unpleasant energy was coming from. If anyone could infect a painting with unpleasantness, it was Lilith.

Keeffe returned to her trailer and unloaded the rejected canvases from her hatch. Disappointment sat on her shoulders like a five-gallon can of gesso. She had a few students lined up for art lessons, but it would take a lot of lessons to add up to six thousand dollars. She could set up with her sketchpad downtown and do caricatures, but the bulk of the tourists wouldn't arrive till after her birthday had come and gone. She had talked with a couple of local business owners about painting murals on the sides of their buildings. It wouldn't be consistently warm enough to paint outside until mid-February, but maybe she could get a deposit.

Because she had to do something.

To Bad's horror, McCall insisted on getting up at the first hint of daylight and riding his mountain bike up and down trails that were practically vertical, followed by lifting weights—and all before breakfast. Fortunately, after consuming a veggie and egg scramble, he'd agreed to let Bad command their body for a while.

Bad settled down in McCall's home office and combed both Hell's databases and Google for raw data about Keeffe and her family. He didn't want to be misled again by bad or missing information. Then he put together a list of places of interest and checked their feeds. He hit pay dirt on the library security cameras.

Once he was certain he had a better data net in place, he pulled up a contract template from Hell's legal repository. It was ten pages long and, in his opinion, weighted down with a lot of unnecessary clauses that would only make an already skittish Keeffe less likely to sign. He cut out most of the verbiage and added some specifics for the mural project.

He had just saved it—not to the repository, where Satan might see it, but to his phone— when Ronnie appeared in the doorway.

"Lilith's Miata just pulled into the driveway."

Lilith. Shit.

McCall roared to life inside their head. *It's Lil, bro. We are so getting some.*

Bad shuddered. *We are so not.*

Why not? McCall was outraged. *Lil's a babe. She's got this thing she does with a candle and a necktie—*

Bad did not want to hear about Lilith's sex techniques. *Do you know how old she is?*

She's insanely hot and....

As old as dirt.

I like older women.

Not this old. Lil was Adam's first wife.

Adam who?

The *Adam. The first man. Pre-Garden of Eden. I'm talking ancient.*

Lil was married before?

Seriously? That was the part McCall heard?

How in the world could McCall prefer Lilith to Keeffe, with her satin skin and sparkling eyes? Bad wasn't about to fornicate with Lilith. The mere idea squicked him out. He wouldn't be able to get it up for worrying about one of those stilettos stabbing between his shoulder blades.

Ronnie let her in.

"The boss wants to talk to us," she said.

Great.

When they reached the rec room, Ronnie had already tuned the TV to Hell's frequency. Opposite the couch, Satan's head filled the wall-sized screen. His face was the color of a pickled beet. Black smoke poured from his horns.

Woah, said McCall. *Who's that?*

It's our boss. Now shut up.

Maybe it was Lilith that Satan was mad at.

"You stupid fuck," Satan said as Bad entered the room in McCall's body.

Or maybe not.

Lilith's eyes glittered with triumph.

"I sent you up there to back up Lilith's plan," Satan said, "not to scuttle it. What are you up to with that new contract?"

DemSec must have picked up Bad's access of the legal repository. It was the first time he'd been on the downside of technological wizardry. He didn't much care for it.

"If you've been paying attention," he said, "then you know Lilith's plan was about to implode anyway. The girl is very close to reaching her goal."

"Bullshit," said Lilith. "She doesn't even know how much she needs to earn."

"Actually, she does," Bad said. "She went to the library this morning and looked it up."

Lilith's eyes narrowed. "How do you know that?"

"Last night over dinner, she mentioned that she uses the library for research, I set up facial recognition scans against feeds from the security cameras there. She visited there from nine a.m. this morning until nine-thirty."

"That doesn't mean she—"

"While she was there, a librarian accessed the BLS site. When Keeffe left the library, the security cameras showed her carrying a BLS printout.

Lilith's face flushed. "She still hasn't earned anywhere close to the amount she needs to."

"I disagree," said Bad. "Based on the data she provided over dinner last night, combined with social media searches for caricature sketches posted by buyers, I've done some extrapolations. I project that she's within five to seven thousand dollars of what she needs."

Lilith stilled. Clearly, he'd surprised her. She recovered quickly, though.

"She'll never make that up before her birthday." Lilith sat down on the couch and crossed her legs. McCall swiveled their head to watch her. "I've cursed every canvas she has for sale in this town."

"She doesn't need to sell paintings. On Monday, Saguaro National Park will publicly announce the recipient of their artist's residency, and it's Keeffe. It comes with a seventy-five-hundred-dollar award, payable at the start of the residency. It begins the day before her birthday."

Satan's gaze pinned Lilith. "You were supposed to be monitoring her activities. Why didn't you know about this?"

"I relied on DemSec," Lilith said. "They must have missed it."

"Keeffe didn't apply for the residency," Bad said. "Her sister filled out the application for her." And kept it a secret from Keeffe, as far as he could tell.

"How do you know about it when DemSec didn't?" Satan demanded.

"I cast a broader net."

"That place has fallen apart since Ornias took over." Lilith hitched her chin at Bad. "You need to put geek-boy back in charge."

Bad's jaw dropped. Lilith was actually on his side. Maybe hearing it from her would convince Satan.

Satan shook his head. "Ornias is adding structure and discipline that place has needed for a long time."

Bad frowned. It almost sounded like Satan had no intention of honoring his end of the bargain. He made a mental note to give that some thought once the current fire drill was over.

"What's in your contract, anyway?" asked Lilith.

"It says she'll paint a mural and I will pay her thirty thousand dollars—half up front, the other half on completion."

For a long moment neither Satan nor Lilith spoke.

"What the fuck?" Satan said finally, his horns puffing black smoke. "How does that get us the statue?"

Bad pushed his glasses up. "It will place me in close proximity with her for an extended period of time. During that time, I will get to know her and determine how best to convince her to give up the statue."

"In other words," Lilith said, "we give her thirty thousand dollars and get zip in return."

"McCall will pay for the mural, so it's not coming out of our coffers," Bad said.

At the back of his brain, McCall squeaked in indignation. Bad quickly set up barricades around Broca's region, the brain's speech center, so his host couldn't join the conversation. Satan and Lilith still didn't look convinced.

"When have I ever failed to resolve a problem I've worked on?" Bad asked.

Well, other than the failed mission that had lost him DemSec and landed him in the maggot pit. He didn't view that as his fault, though. His tech had performed exactly as designed. Satan had been looking for a scapegoat and settled on him.

"You're brainy," Lilith said. "No one is arguing that. But this isn't a technical problem. In fact, Keeffe Blackmon may be about the furthest thing from technology that exists in the world today."

"Be that as it may," said Bad, "she likes me."

"She likes McCall's ass."

And so does Lil. McCall tried to sidle over to her, but Bad halted him.

"But she likes talking to *me*," Bad said.

"You're going to have to get her to do more than talk if you want that statue."

Bad pushed his glasses up again.

"I'm confident I'll be able to persuade her. When her birthday rolls around and she collects that eagle sculpture from you, it will cement the bond between us."

Lilith's face turned scarlet. For a minute, he thought she might ignite right there on the spot. Her nostrils flared as she breathed in and out through her nose. After a moment, her color returned to normal. He had to admire her self-control.

"What if it doesn't?" she asked. "What if one of a million things goes wrong and before she ever collects the statue, she can't stand the sight of you. We need a fail-safe clause."

Satan stroked his goatee. "What are you thinking?"

Before Bad could object, Lilith jumped in. "I recommend adding verbiage saying that if she walks off the job, she has to return the deposit."

Bad frowned at her. "That's insulting. She'll never sign that."

Lilith smirked. "She's walked off jobs before."

"So if I add that clause, she'll think you were involved."

Lilith shrugged.

"I hate to break it to you," Bad said, "but she really doesn't like you."

"I like it," Satan said. "Put it in."

Reluctantly, Bad pulled up the contract and added another sentence. *In the event the artist abandons the work prior to completion, deposit will be refunded in full.*

By the time Keeffe arrived at the Sedona Community Center for the one o'clock Senior Watercolor class she co-taught with her sister, Frida, on Thursdays, her ego was flatter than the armadillo she'd seen on 179 that morning.

She arrived just as her sister-in-law, Jen, dropped Frida off. Jen's bee-stung lips and curvaceous figure made her every guy's fantasy, but she only had eyes for Frida. Today, Frida's tear-stained face looked even more miserable than Keeffe felt.

Oh, crap. It must be pee-on-a-stick day again.

Frida leaned across the console to kiss her wife and got out of the car. With the heel of one hand, she squeegeed tears from her cheeks.

Jen threw Keeffe a pleading look. Keeffe made a tiny gesture with her hand: *no worries, I've got this.* Jen's shoulders sagged with relief as she pulled away.

"No luck, huh?" Keeffe asked her older sister.

Frida shook her head, her lower lip trembling. Frida was tall and russet-haired, like Dad and the boys. Keeffe was the only one whose coloring displayed Mom's Asian heritage. Tears reddened Frida's eyelids, making her blue eyes look even bluer.

Keeffe hugged her. "I'm sorry, honey. Next month."

Frida's eyes filled again. "That's what we say every month."

"I know it feels like it's taking forever, but you have plenty of time to get pregnant. You're only thirty-three."

"And with every month that passes, my chances of getting pregnant decrease." Frida's shoulders were stiff with tension.

"You have years yet."

"It's not just the time. This is costing us a fortune. Our insurance doesn't cover intrauterine insemination. Every time we do IUI with donor sperm, it's like making a car payment on a BMW."

Ouch. Where were they getting the money for all this? Frida's website-design business was doing well, but not that well, and Jen was just a loan officer at the bank.

"I told Jen it's time to take it to the next level," Frida said.

Keeffe frowned. "What next level?"

"In vitro."

Keeffe stopped dead in the middle of the hallway. "You mean surgery?"

At the thought of Frida going under the knife, she broke out in a cold sweat.

"Oh, for heaven's sake, Keeffe. It's minor. Outpatient. I'll be fine."

"That's what they said about Mom's hysterectomy."

"IVF isn't surgery. It's a needle extraction."

Keeffe wasn't comforted. "But it's a general anesthetic, right? Or you could get one of those infections that's resistant to antibiotics. Why take that kind of risk?"

"We've already used up all the vials from our first-choice donor.

And there are only four vials available from our second choice. Jen wants to have a child, too, and we want the kids to have a biological relationship. That means sharing a donor. We can't do that if I'm going through vials of sperm like they're popcorn."

"So you're going to let them cut into you." Keeffe's fists balled at the terrifying thought.

"No knives, just a needle."

The risks of anesthesia and infection still loomed, but Keeffe bit her tongue. She had signaled Jen that she'd calm Frida down, not upset her more. "I'm just afraid of losing you."

Frida's face softened. "You're not going to lose me."

"And I hate the idea of IVF." Keeffe shuddered.

"Of course you do." Frida linked her arm through Keeffe's. "You hate every advance that's been made in the last fifty years."

"I do not."

"Then let me build you a website. You could advertise yourself and your paintings."

Frida would build the site, but she'd expect Keeffe to provide the content. The only thing Keeffe found harder than reading was spelling.

"Not interested."

Frida shrugged. "Have it your way."

They'd reached the end of the hall. Inside a large room with big windows and a colorful tile floor, two of their students were already waiting.

"What are we painting today?" Father Xavier had been their parish priest when they were children. Today he wore a polo shirt over a pair of loose-fitting jeans. A gold crucifix on a chain hung around his neck.

"Still life, Father X," Keeffe said.

Beside him, Sister Mary Grace had covered her white blouse and navy skirt with one of the smocks from the supply cupboard.

Frida extracted a wooden bowl and mesh bag of fruit from her bag. She placed the bowl on a high table in the center of the room and arranged the fruit for maximum contrast of colors, shapes, and textures.

The next half hour was chaotic as Keeffe and Frida helped their elderly students set up their easels and handed out watercolors and brushes to them all. Once the class settled down to paint, they had time to talk.

"Tell me about the guy at Ernesto's last night," Frida said as they strolled around the classroom.

"Geez," Keeffe said. "Word gets around fast."

"Especially if you dry hump someone right out on 89A."

Keeffe's face heated. "Was it you that honked?"

"Well, Jen, but yes."

"Things got a little out of hand."

"I'd say so. Who is he?"

Keeffe made a face. "Some Internet zillionaire who wants me to paint a mural for him." She stopped beside a student. "Nice work, Mrs. Dumbrowski. You really captured that banana."

The old lady smiled proudly.

Frida groaned. "Let's skip to the end. You turned down the commission, didn't you?"

Keeffe jammed her hands into her pockets. "He wanted me to paint cartoons."

Okay, so that wasn't strictly true. He'd claimed he would be happy with a landscape. Plus, he liked her work. A lot. At least, Dr. Jekyll did.

"Cartoons?" Frida seemed thrown for a minute, but she quickly rallied. "Okay, so that's not your style, but it's a commission."

"A commission to paint cartoons."

"Still...."

"Do you know how I met him? Lilith tried to get me to sell him *John*. Doesn't it strike you as just a tiny bit suspicious that now he wants to hire me?"

Frida rolled her eyes. "You think everything Lilith does is suspicious."

"Great pomegranate, Father X," Keeffe said. "Try adding a purple shadow at the bottom, to give it more dimension." She turned back to Frida. "Because it is."

"When are you going to get over hating Lilith?" Frida asked.

"I don't know. When is she going to get over being such a witch?"

"Lilith is not a witch." Father X dabbed purple paint around the bottom of his pomegranate. "She's a demon."

Both Keeffe and Frida turned to stare at him.

It was no surprise Father X didn't like their stepmother. As soon as Lilith married Dad, she had pulled Keeffe out of catechism class. Around the same time, Dad stopped taking Keeffe and the boys to Mass, opting to spend Sunday mornings in bed with his new wife. The boys were happy to sleep in, but Keeffe had missed the ritual of the holy Mass. As soon as she could drive, she started attending again.

"Sent by Satan," Father X added, his face thunderous, "to corrupt and destroy."

Keeffe blinked. Okay, that was a little strong, even where Lilith was concerned.

Sister Mary Grace cleared her throat, reminding them of Father Xavier's Alzheimer's diagnosis. He was still in the early stages, but the disease was already taking its toll.

"As long as you have purple on your brush, Father," Sister Mary Grace said, "it might be a good time to paint the grapes."

Father Xavier's face cleared like a quick-moving storm passing over the mountains. "Of course," he said. "The grapes." And he happily returned to his watercolor.

Keeffe moved on, a little shaken. It was one thing for her to believe her stepmother was evil. It was another to hear her childhood spiritual guide confirm that thought.

"You're really not going to take that commission?" Frida asked, after stopping to loosen a student's death-grip on her brush.

Keeffe dug her fists into her jeans pockets. "I haven't decided."

"Do you have something else lined up?"

"No." Judging from this morning's discussions at the Red Rocks Gallery, the opposite was true.

"Are you sure?" Frida's gaze was weirdly penetrating.

"Of course I'm sure."

Frida looked disappointed. Before Keeffe could ask why, she said,

"If you don't have anything else going on, why wouldn't you take this commission? Your birthday is coming up fast."

Keeffe fought down a spurt of annoyance. "I know when my birthday is."

"How close are you, anyway?"

"If you'd asked me yesterday, I'd have told you I had it locked." Keeffe explained what she'd learned from reviewing the contract the night before and her trip to the library that morning.

"Then why aren't you jumping all over this commission?" Frida asked.

"It's complicated." It was hard to say which would be worse—working for a guy she was attracted to, or working for an asshat.

"Don't get involved with the guy, just paint the mural. That room sounds great."

It did sound insanely cool. As though on cue, Keeffe's phone buzzed again. She checked the screen. "It's him."

"At least check it out," Frida urged.

After this morning's rejections, Keeffe really didn't have any other viable options. She stepped out into the hallway and tapped the answer button.

"Okay," she said. "I'll come check out the space."

"When?" McCall asked.

"I'll be there in an hour."

CHAPTER 8

Keeffe stared through the windshield of her Honda at McCall's mansion. Like many houses in Sedona, it was stucco. If she were painting it, she'd use titanium white, with blue and gray in the shadows. Maybe even some dioxazine purple, depending on the time of day.

In the center of the terracotta roof, a dome of tinted glass arched above the tiles. In spite of her misgivings, she was intrigued. The room McCall had described was an artist's dream.

Wrapping a woolen scarf around her neck, her only nod to the January chill, she got out of the car and marched up to the door. When she rang the bell, the *Star Wars* theme sounded.

Seriously?

After a few moments, the heavy door swung open, revealing an old man in an ill-fitting suit. His eyebrows, shaggy white tufts above smallish eyes, lifted in inquiry.

"I'm Keeffe Blackmon." This must be McCall's...butler?

The butler led her down a marble-floored hallway, past what appeared to be a fully equipped video arcade on the left and a mirrored workout gym on the right, to a gigantic rec room. At one end stood a black leather wet bar. Framed comic book covers dotted

"

three of the walls. McCall lounged on a cream-colored sofa, playing a video game on a flat-screen TV that took up the entire fourth wall.

On the screen, two long-legged women lunged at each other with broadswords. If they'd been real, rather than cartoons, their huge breasts would have made it impossible for them to stand upright, let alone wield heavy swords. In their comic-inspired world, even the five-inch heels on their boots didn't seem to affect their balance.

When McCall saw her, he tossed the controller onto the sofa and got to his feet. He smiled, not the arrogant I'm-God's-gift-to-women smile from after he kissed her, but a sweet, shy smile. And he was wearing his glasses.

She breathed a sigh of relief. Dr. Jekyll she could deal with. It was Mr. Hyde she was eager to avoid.

"Let me show you the room," he said.

She tossed her scarf on the back of the couch and followed him down the hall. He moved with the grace of a jaguar. The scent of cacao wafted to her nose. She swallowed. *Star Wars*, she reminded herself. *Video games. Cartoons.*

They arrived at their destination and her lust for her host fled, replaced by lust for the blank canvas in front of her.

The room was nothing short of spectacular. Keeffe turned slowly, assessing the possibilities. The diameter looked to be around twenty feet, yielding something in the range of five hundred square feet of wall space. The lighting was flawless. At her sides, her fingers twitched.

How gorgeous would this room be, painted as a landscape of Sedona? The majesty of Courthouse Butte, the shadowed mystery of Oak Creek Canyon, the soaring inspiration of the Chapel of the Holy Cross, the quaint streets of Sedona itself—all would make great subjects for a mural. If she layered on ultra-thin coats of glaze in the *sfumato* style, it could be breathtaking. This commission had the potential to make her name in the art world.

"Are you planning to cover the entire wall?" she asked, trying to sound casual.

He nodded. "The whole thing."

Crossing her fingers behind her back for luck, she said, "Did you decide what you wanted? Cartoons or a landscape?"

He opened his mouth, but no words came out. His jaw worked for a second. He took off his glasses and his eyes flickered and lightened to gray. She frowned. How the heck did he even do that? There were glasses that changed color depending on the light, but contacts? And why wear both?

He gestured with his left hand. "I figured on this side, we'd do Marvel." Then he waved his right hand. "And this side could be DC."

Disappointment hollowed out her chest. He must not have liked her landscapes that much after all. She took a deep breath. Maybe she could still salvage this.

"Would you be open to my interpretation of those worlds?" Artists had done some very cool work based on the comic book universe by not limiting themselves to the simplistic styles of the original artwork.

"I want it to look just like the comic books," he said.

Representing the beauty of Sedona would have allowed for almost endless permutations of color, gradients of reds and blues and golds and umbers. Reproducing comic book characters would limit her palette to the basics. It was drone work.

Instead of canyons and rocks and water and sky, she'd be reduced to depicting body suits and utility belts and winged boots. She wouldn't be able to paint in her own perspectives and dreams and hopes, bringing depth and meaning to the work. Instead, she would be restricted to silly, two-dimensional cartoon characters with *POW!* and *BAM!* in balloons over their heads.

She longed to tell him, not just no, but hell no, but with her birthday less than a month away, and after getting kicked out of another gallery this morning, she was in no position to turn down paid work of any kind. And, as Frida would be quick to point out, this wasn't just paid work; it was exceptionally well-paid work.

Keeffe had no choice. "I can do that," she said, without an ounce of enthusiasm.

Beside her, McCall seemed to wrestle with himself. Not just metaphorically—his shoulders heaved like he was actually engaged in a wrestling match. After a moment, he expelled a sharp breath. His eyes flickered back to brown.

"I want a landscape," he gasped. He put his glasses back on.

Oh, boy. Here we go again.

"I'm happy to paint whatever you want." Happy might be an overstatement, but even if she wasn't happy, he was the one paying. The choice of subject wasn't up to her.

"Definitely a landscape," McCall said. He picked up a sheaf of papers from a curved library table that hugged the wall. "I've got the contract right here."

Another contract. Keeffe took it from him like it was a snake.

"It's boilerplate." He pulled a pen from his pocket. "I'll give you fifty percent down. Just sign your name and I'll transfer the deposit into your account."

"Can't we just make a verbal agreement?" She wanted to ball up the papers and throw them at him. "You tell me how much you're going to pay me, I tell you what I'm going to paint, and we shake on it?"

"For thirty thousand dollars? I don't think so." He held out the pen. "Just sign at the bottom of the last page."

His voice was persuasive. All she had to do was scrawl her name on the bottom line and Lilith would have to concede. Keeffe could even start scheduling museum exhibits for *John.*

She looked at the contract. It was short—just two pages—but the print was much smaller than the one she'd signed with Dad and Lilith.

"I'll need to take it home and review it." She grimaced. More caffeine, when she was still jumpy from this morning's mocha.

"All it says is that you'll complete a mural for me within sixty days of signing. I'll pay you thirty thousand dollars, half up front, half on completion."

"Why the time limit?" she asked, more to demonstrate she was paying attention than because she really cared. She planned to dash off his cartoons as quickly as possible. Best case, a few weeks. A month at most. Sixty days gave her time to spare.

"It's a good idea to have a deadline in mind when you start a project." McCall looked businesslike. "Work expands to fill the amount of time you have to do it."

It was kind of a non-answer but, under the circumstances, it didn't matter.

"I'll need to read it before I sign," she said.

"Of course. Why don't you just do that now?"

Did he suspect she couldn't read? Fear made her snappish.

"I have to be somewhere."

He stilled. "When can I expect to hear from you?"

She felt like a steer being herded into a cattle chute with no clear view of what was at the other end. She wished she'd had a little more of this wariness when she'd signed that first contract with Lilith.

"What's your hurry?" she asked.

"I have another artist coming out later to discuss his vision for the space. Unless you're definitely going to paint for me?" He pulled out his phone. "In that case, I'll cancel the appointment."

She did not enjoy being pressured. "I'll contact you by early next week at the latest."

McCall smiled, but near the back of his jaw, a muscle ticked.

She might not be able to breeze through a contract, but she could read faces. He wasn't happy. And this was Mr. Nice Guy. Which reminded her…

"Why do your eyes change color all the time?"

His brown eyes went wide, like she'd caught him completely off-guard.

"I told you I wear contact lenses sometimes."

"No," she said. "I've seen them change right in front of me, even when you're wearing your glasses."

He swallowed, and she had a quick impression of a mouse that had run into an unexpected cage.

"Certain emotions can affect color dispersion in the iris." He tapped something into his phone and held it out to her. "You can read about it here."

She glared at him. "I'll pass."

Maybe she should just go ahead and sign. Without this gig, her chances of hanging onto *John* were practically nil. McCall had said the contract was just standard party-of-the-first-part legalese.

"Here you go." He pushed the pen toward her.

More pressure. Plus, she still couldn't shake the feeling that he had a motive other than love of art, just as he'd clearly been trying to buy *John* as a front for her stepmother.

"Come on," he said. "What do you have to lose?"

Her artistic integrity, for one thing. Dad was a perfect example of what happened to artists that sold out. And if there was something wrong with this contract, she could lose *John* forever. On the other hand, if she didn't sign this, *John* was as good as gone anyway.

As though he was reading her mind, McCall said, "This commission will safeguard your mother's legacy."

Her jaw set like iron. There were other galleries in town, and she could always get Frida to set up that website and sell her canvases there.

"My mom would never want me to sign up for something I don't want to do just to hang onto *John*. Anyway, it's not like her legacy would be lost, even if I did. My sister and brothers still have the statues she gave them."

His mouth opened like he was going to say something, but after a second he closed it without speaking.

Her grip on the contract tightened. "I'll take this home and look it over. If I decide I'm interested, you can compare my idea with the other artist's and see what works best for you."

McCall started to argue, but she tucked the contract into her messenger bag.

"I'll be in touch," she said, and walked out the door.

CHAPTER 9

*B*ack at her trailer, Keeffe settled down with another unwanted cup of takeout coffee and deciphered McCall's contract. Fortunately, it was much shorter than the one Lilith had written.

It said she would paint a mural of an agreed-upon subject to cover the walls of the designated room, floor to domed ceiling. She would finish within sixty days. He would pay her thirty thousand dollars, half when she signed the contract, the other half on completion. She would provide all paint and supplies. Everything looked fine until she got to the very end.

In the event the artist abandons the work prior to completion, deposit will be refunded in full.

Alone in her trailer, her temples pounded with anger. She knew exactly where the idea for that clause had come from—Lilith. Two years ago, her stepmother had set her up to paint a mural for another client, a rich old man with predatory eyes and grasping hands. Keeffe had been leery of accepting the commission but it was a lot of money, and she'd thought she could handle herself.

Her very first day on the job, he came into the room in a bathrobe that just happened to fall open. His behavior escalated every day. In the end, she'd had to walk away. She'd tried to keep his deposit, but he'd threatened to sue, and she didn't have the resources to fight him in court.

She thought about McCall's behavior at the lamppost. She would not be a victim this time. She could use some of his deposit to buy a stun gun. She'd keep it at her side and she wouldn't hesitate to use it if Mr. Hyde showed up.

She continued reading to the end of the second page. There were no other gotchas, and the contract had no appendices. All she had to do was decide if she was willing to trade her artistic integrity to keep *John*.

Her stomach growled. She hadn't realized how long she'd been studying the contact. Outside her trailer window, the sun was setting, with all the vibrant, nuanced colors she wouldn't be using in McCall's mural. She would take a walk to clear her head, then decide over nachos.

Grabbing her purse, she stuffed the folded contract inside so she could double-check the details.

She wasn't going to be anyone's patsy this time.

When "The Mephisto Waltz" issued from Bad's phone, he was expecting it. In fact, he was surprised he hadn't gotten the call sooner. He'd been preparing his arguments since Keeffe left.

"Conference call," Satan said. "Now." He disconnected.

By the time Bad got to the rec room, Ronnie already had the boss on screen.

"You didn't get her to sign," Satan said. His face was dark red, but Bad had seen it much darker. He wasn't mad, just micro-managing.

"She'll sign," said Bad. "She just needs time to review the contract."

Satan grunted. "When did you say that residency will be announced?"

"Monday."

"You're not really going to allow this dweeb to take over my mission, are you?" Lilith appeared beside Satan. She must be feeling really threatened to leave Sedona and make the long trip down the rings. Unless, of course, she'd installed a portal in Daniel's house. Bad made a mental note to check into that.

"I got the rest of the statues," she said. "I can get this one, too."

Man, did she ever hate sharing credit.

"You'll never get her to give it up without coercion," Bad said.

"It has to be voluntary." Satan's voice was tense. "Her choice."

What was the deal with Keeffe giving up the statue freely? That wouldn't affect its capacity to reinforce her mother's crosses. There was something else going on.

Let's get Lilith back here. McCall made a run at Broca's region, but Bad fended him off. *I'm horny.*

Bad was well aware of McCall's state. It made his skin crawl.

"That's the purpose of the mural," Bad reminded Satan. "It will let me spend time with her so I can get to know her well enough to convince her to sell me the statue."

"I've known her for ten years," Lilith said. "What makes you think you'll figure her out in a month?"

Because I'll be paying attention. Bad hid that thought from McCall.

"It's a bad plan. The money he's paying her makes her far less vulnerable. There's no advantage." Lilith directed her argument at Satan. "Who do you trust, me or geek-boy?"

"Neither of you." Satan tapped his talons on the arms of his throne.

"I'll get her signature tonight." Bad shoved his arms into his jacket, using the action to mask his struggle with McCall.

"You don't even know where she'll be," Lilith said.

"I'll find her." He already had a pretty good idea where. "We have plenty of cameras in place."

"She won't like you stalking her," Lilith said.

From the back of the couch, he picked up the scarf Keeffe had left behind.

"It's not stalking if I have a reason to see her."

Satan cut through all that. "How will you get her to sign?"

"She doesn't know her siblings have already sold their statues," Bad said. "I'm going to make sure she finds out."

Even after her walk, Keeffe still felt torn about her decision. The caffeine rushing through her veins wasn't helping. Maybe food would make things clearer.

That plan encountered a setback as soon as she walked into Ernesto's. Her brothers and their wives sat in the large corner booth.

"Hey, Keeffe," Claude hollered.

"Come join us," called Ed.

There wasn't really much left to think about anyway. What choice did she have? Setting up a website wouldn't happen overnight, and getting enough money in deposits for outdoor murals was a long shot. She headed toward her family.

Ed—Edouard Manet Blackmon—and his twin—Claude Monet Blackmon—were so alike most strangers couldn't tell them apart. Russet-haired and ruddy-skinned like Frida, they looked like Dad. The only nod to Mom's Asian heritage was their brown eyes.

Beside Claude, his wife, Suzanne, wore pale blue hospital scrubs. Her blonde hair was styled in a no-nonsense, easy-care bob. She looked exhausted.

"Boy or girl?" Keeffe asked.

Suzanne smiled tiredly. "Boy. Young couple. Their first baby."

Keeffe offered her a high five. Then she reached across the table to squeeze the hand of Ed's wife, Camille. Camille returned the squeeze. Her sister-in-law's face was an elegant system of planes that cried out to be captured on canvas. If Keeffe were a portraitist, Camille would have been one of her prime subjects. Her dark hair was swept back in a simple twist reminiscent of one of those ancient busts of Nefertiti.

Before Keeffe could slide into the booth, the bell jangled behind her. Automatically, everyone's gaze traveled beyond her, to the door. Her sisters-in-laws' faces molded into identical expressions of open-mouthed appreciation. If that weren't enough to tell Keeffe who'd just come in, her brothers' instant wariness would have done the job.

She turned to face McCall. "You're being a little stalker-y, dude."

He held up her scarf. "I thought you might need this."

She snatched it from his hands. "Thanks."

Then, because Suzanne and Camille clearly expected it, she made introductions.

"Is this the guy you were dry-humping against the lamppost last night?" Ed asked.

Keeffe's cheeks burned. If a story was embarrassing, you could count on the family grapevine to spread it. You could also count on her brothers to kick it up a notch, given an opportunity.

Predictably, Camille tried to smooth things over. "Would you like to join us?"

McCall smiled at her. "If it's all right with Keeffe."

She shrugged. When he moved toward her, though, she pointed to the other side of the table.

"You sit over there." She ignored the smirks from her brothers.

Maria came and took their orders.

After she left, McCall said, "I hear you guys have a video game company."

Ed nodded and a gleam came into Claude's eye. He was seeing McCall as a potential investor. Keeffe considered how she felt about that. Not good. She didn't really want McCall any more deeply embedded in her life than he already was.

That felt selfish, which in turn made her feel guilty. Getting an investor like McCall would be a tremendous windfall for them. Although, given McCall's dual personality, maybe it wasn't so selfish after all. He wasn't the safest choice of backer.

"Our first game releases in May," Ed said. "We've been developing it for four years, but we just quit our jobs and moved here to start working on it full-time last fall."

"What kind of game?" McCall asked. "Action? RPG? MMO?"

Her brothers looked at him with new-found respect. Maria brought their drinks and set them down.

"Role play, single-player." Ed's face lit with enthusiasm. "The story line is an art hunter searching for stolen artworks. We're going for the nine- to twelve-year-old market."

"Their graphics are gorgeous," Suzanne said. "And the story line is great. Camille's a writer, so she developed that for them. The beta release is getting great reviews."

"I'm impressed," McCall said. "Game development is crazy expensive."

Claude grinned. "We're looking for venture capital, if you're interested."

"Could be." McCall smiled the shy smile Keeffe associated with Dr. Jekyll, and she relaxed a little. "Tell me more about it."

"We're sourcing some of the animation from Poland, but we're doing most of it ourselves," Ed said. "We worked for Pixar as animators."

"Good deal. Sounds like you've got it figured out."

"Some of it, anyway," Claude said. "Since this is our debut game, we haven't been able to attract a lot of interest from investors yet. Everyone says it's too risky."

"Most game startups go belly up," McCall said. "How did you manage to get this far without external funding?"

Ed started to speak, but Claude interrupted him. "We've got over a million dollars of our own money tied up in it."

"A million dollars?" Keeffe leaned forward, stunned. "Where did you get that kind of money? Did Dad fund you?" It was a blow to think Dad would fund their game startup to the tune of a million bucks but insist she pay back her college tuition.

"Are you kidding?" said Claude. "With Lilith holding the purse strings?"

She relaxed a little. "Then where did it come from?"

Her brothers exchanged a look.

"We cashed in our 401(k)'s," Ed said. "Plus, we had some money from the graphic novels we wrote with Camille."

"And that was a million dollars?" Keeffe asked. "Wow. I had no idea Pixar had such a generous retirement package."

An awkward silence fell.

Keeffe's gaze moved from Ed to Claude and back again. Neither of them would meet her eyes. Suzanne was suddenly fascinated by her placemat. Only Camille was willing to look at Keeffe. Her expression was apologetic.

Realization struck Keeffe like a slap across the face. "You sold your statues."

Claude had inherited *Mark*, represented as a lion. Ed had gotten *Luke*, an ox. Their sculptures weren't as beautiful as *John*, at least not in Keeffe's opinion, but they were Rachel Blackmon originals. If *John* was worth a quarter of a million dollars, theirs paired together could have sold for at least twice that.

Their silence confirmed her suspicions. A fist seemed to clench around her heart. "How could you do that?"

"The game is taking longer to put out than we expected." Ed's voice was regretful. "We needed the money."

Keeffe's eyes burned with unshed tears. "I was planning to send *John* on a museum tour. I was going to ask if you'd lend your statues, too, to make a complete exhibit."

Ed reached a hand toward her. "Mom wanted us to pursue our dreams. She'd be happy *Mark* and *Luke* brought enough to fund our start-up."

Two of her mother's statues were gone, and for what? A stupid video game. Keeffe's stomach roiled. She pinned Ed with her gaze. "Who bought them?"

Another uncomfortable silence. Finally, Ed said, "A private collector who preferred to remain anonymous."

Which meant those statues were unlikely to see the light of day again during Keeffe's lifetime. Anger clogged her brain and loosened her tongue.

"I guess Frida and I are the only ones who value art above money."

Claude's face flushed. He clenched his fists. "Get real, Duckling."

Keeffe jerked like she'd received an electric shock. No one in the world could push her buttons like Claude. Across the table, she saw

McCall register her reaction, his gray eyes sparking with curiosity. Her cheeks blazed.

"Claude…" Suzanne put her hand on Claude's arm.

He shook it off. "How do you suppose Frida has been paying for her fertility treatments?" he asked Keeffe. "Jen is a loan officer, not a bank president."

His words were a gut punch. Just today she'd talked with Frida about her fertility treatments. Frida hadn't said a single word about selling off her inheritance to pay for them.

John was the only sculpture left. If she lost him, it would be like Mom's very existence in the family had been erased. How could her siblings place their own puny concerns above Mom's memory?

Then a new horror struck her. If she couldn't earn six thousand dollars in the next twenty-nine days, Lilith would insist she sell *John* to the highest bidder, too, and Dad wouldn't do a thing to stop her. All four of Mom's statues would be gone. For a moment, it felt like the air had been crushed from Keeffe's lungs.

She dragged in a breath. There was only one way to prevent it. She dug into her purse and pulled out McCall's contract.

Across the table, he stilled. His eyes were dark again, but unreadable. Was this a good idea?

She remembered her mother, her head tilted, a smile on her face as Keeffe shared the details of her school day… gaze fierce and intent as she chiseled *John* from the translucent chunk of alabaster…cool hand gentle on Keeffe's forehead when she was sick.

All Keeffe had of her mother were *John* and Mom's final journal. She'd do what she had to do to hang onto them. "I'll do your mural."

McCall shuddered and his eyes turned gray. They blazed with triumph.

Both sides of him needed to be knocked down a peg. "Just so you know, I don't sleep with clients."

Claude's jaw dropped. "Damn, girl."

McCall leaned back, draping his arm across the top of the booth. "That's okay. I don't sleep with employees."

Ed blinked. "Damn, dude."

Her sisters-in-law watched silently, eyes wide. McCall pulled a pen from his jacket. She took it.

"Do you want me to take a look at that before you sign?" Claude asked.

On the surface, the question was innocent enough, but Keeffe heard the insinuation underneath: *You know how you are about reading.* Her jaw set.

"I read it this afternoon."

Claude frowned at the papers in her hands. "Seriously, maybe you should let one of us look it over."

Because you're not smart enough to read it without our help. Keeffe heard the unspoken thought behind his words.

"The devil's in the details." Ed tried to soften the message, but it was still the same implication.

Keeffe's cheeks burned. She might not be a reader, but she wasn't an idiot. And, honestly, what did she have to lose? If she didn't sign, *John* was as good as gone. She scrawled her signature at the bottom of the page.

She gathered up the sheets and offered them to McCall. As he reached to take them, the edge of the bottom sheet sliced a paper cut in the joint of her index finger.

"Ouch." She yanked her hand away. A slim trail of blood edged the paper.

"Are you okay?" he asked, his brown eyes concerned.

She nodded, sucking on her finger. The coppery tang of blood filled her mouth.

"Okay, good." As he spoke, he bobbled the papers and somehow managed to slice his own thumb. Blood welled, leaving a smudged thumbprint on the page.

Ed's jaw dropped. "What are the chances of that happening?"

"Do we need to get fresh copies and start over?" Keeffe asked.

"No, that's okay." McCall scrawled his name on the blank line above his thumbprint. "These will be fine. Okay if I mail you your copy?"

"Sure."

With careful precision, he took pictures of the contract with his phone. Then he pumped his fist to the sky. "Yes!"

Keeffe blinked.

He cleared his throat. More quietly, he asked, "When can you start?"

To her surprise, euphoria filled her. It was the biggest commission she'd ever received.

"I'll be out tomorrow."

CHAPTER 10

*I*nside the mural room at McCall's house the next morning, Keeffe set down her sketch pad and pencils. "Can I borrow a tape measure?"

McCall hooked his thumbs into the pockets of his jeans. His long fingers framed his genitals. She didn't even have to look at his eyes to know they'd be gray.

"Didn't you bring one?" he asked.

"I don't own one." She fought down a feeling of defensiveness. "I usually just eyeball things, but this project requires a little more precision."

He shuddered like he was shaking off his cranky mood and his eyes darkened to brown.

"Sure," he said. "No problem." He disappeared.

As soon as he was gone, Keeffe wished she could leave, too. The elation she'd felt when she signed the contract the night before was gone, replaced by a sucking depression. It was such a gorgeous space. The thought of defacing it with a bunch of cartoons made her feel physically sick.

Get over yourself, girl. Those cartoons may not be your dream project, but they'll let you keep John.

Her phone rang. The area code was 520—Tucson. She didn't know anyone with that area code, so she let it go to voicemail. They didn't leave a message.

McCall returned. She was relieved to see his glasses were back in place. He handed her a yellow plastic device with a screen at one end.

Keeffe stared at it, repulsed. "What's this?"

"It's a digital tape measure."

"Don't you have a normal one?"

He looked puzzled. "A normal one?"

"You know, the kind where you pull out the tape and then push the button and zip, it retracts again."

"You mean a mechanical device." One of his eyebrows quirked in an expression that would have been cute if he weren't being such a jerk. "In this millennium, people use digital tape measures."

Keeffe folded her arms across her chest. "Lots of people still use manual tape measures."

He stared down his beautiful nose at her. "Lots of people over the age of eighty."

"Just because something's digital doesn't mean it works better," she said in an equally lofty tone. "Why do people insist on fixing things that aren't broken?"

Before he could respond, Ronnie appeared in the doorway. "I believe I have what the young lady needs." He held out a metal tape measure.

Keeffe plucked it from his hands. "Thank you, Ronnie." She awarded him a sunny smile, which made McCall narrow his eyes at the old man.

A look passed between them. She wasn't sure what it meant, but Ronnie raised his humped shoulders and disappeared.

She spent the next twenty minutes measuring and calculating. It would have gone faster, but just being in the same room with McCall was a distraction. He was measuring too, with his digital device. Wherever she went, he seemed to be there first, smelling like a freshly opened box of expensive chocolates. She made it a point not to brush against him because every touch was like a tiny firework. Their bickering should have been a turn-off, but for some reason, it had the opposite effect.

When she jotted down her last number, McCall pushed a button on his digital device and peered at the screen. He looked at her challengingly.

"What did you come up with?"

She checked her notes. "I make it five hundred and two square feet."

His face fell.

"Why, what did you get?" Keeffe asked.

"Same thing."

She grinned.

"But I could have had the answer fifteen minutes ago," he said.

She couldn't resist peeping up at him through her eyelashes. "Faster isn't always better, you know."

His eyes sparked, and he drew in an audible breath.

Before he could follow up, Ronnie reappeared. Grinning, Keeffe handed him the tape measure. The old man smiled at her, a twinkle in his eyes. He was kind of cute, in an ugly old man sort of way.

"Now that I have measurements," she said, "I'm going to head up to Flagstaff to buy supplies."

"Why don't you order them online and have them delivered?" McCall asked.

"I like going to the art supply store." She slipped her pencil and notebook into her messenger bag. "I like being able to browse the merchandise and talk to the people who work there and find out what works for other artists."

"You can get that in an online review," McCall said.

"Colors aren't always true online. Neither are people."

"People aren't always truthful anywhere."

She nodded. "That's why I like to be able to look them in the eye when I'm talking to them."

McCall, she was pleased to see, didn't have an answer for that.

Ronnie cleared his throat. "I made lunch—spinach salad, grilled salmon, and roasted pears—if the young lady would like to stay."

Gourmet food? Hand-prepared by someone else's hands?

"Of course I'll stay," she said. "Where can I wash up?"

Ronnie led her past a series of closed doors to an ornate bathroom. "We'll be lunching in the dining room," he said.

"And the dining room is where?" This house was so big it was insane.

"Fourth door on your left."

After she washed her hands, she wandered back in the direction she'd come from. Had he said left or right? She opened the door on the right. It was a bedroom. On the bed, a man lay sleeping. She stared in frozen fascination. At least, she thought he was a man.

He looked like he'd be maybe five foot six if he were standing, with leathery skin and curly black hair. Dark, silky hair covered his arms, almost like fur. Even more startling, he had a pair of little pink horns. An arrow-tipped tail hung over the side of the bed. His chest rose and fell in deep, even breaths.

McCall appeared at the end of the hallway. When he saw her, his brown eyes went wide. He hurried toward her.

"Who is that?" she asked. Or did she mean *what is that?*

Beads of sweat appeared on his beautiful forehead. He pulled her out of the room and closed the door.

"It's a robot."

"He was breathing."

"You just imagined that," McCall said.

Keeffe was still staring at the door. "He had horns and a tail. Why does a robot have horns and a tail?"

McCall swallowed. "He's Abaddon, a character in a video game one of my companies is developing."

"He looked so real. Can I see what he does?"

McCall maneuvered her toward the dining room. "There's nothing to see. He's not functional yet."

"I'd swear I saw him breathing."

"Don't be ridiculous," said McCall. "Robots don't breathe."

Keeffe looked back over her shoulder one final time.

It really had looked like the robot was breathing.

Bad chewed on his lower lip as he escorted Keeffe to the dining room.

You are lucky you have my bod to ride around in, dude. She was not impressed with yours.

That had been painfully clear. *Do you think she thought I was lying?*

You were *lying.*

But did she believe me?

I wouldn't.

Which was no help at all.

Ronnie brought the food, along with tall glasses of iced tea. Bad loved iced tea. In Hell, there was no iced anything.

To distract Keeffe from the horned body in the spare room, he asked, "What's your next step on the mural?"

"I make sketches. Then you approve them. Then I outline. Then I paint."

"Sounds good." From beside his plate, he picked up an iPhone in a pink case, pushed it across the table. In addition to allowing him to keep track of her movements, it would retire the antique she carried now.

Keeffe frowned, her fork suspended mid-air. "What's this?"

"A smartphone. I thought you could carry it while you're working on this project."

Her face set into the stubborn lines he was starting to associate with her. "No, thanks."

"It will let me get in touch with you if I need to."

She pulled her ancient flip phone out of her pocket and held it up. "I have a phone."

He eyed it with disfavor. "I remember. What do you use it for—to call Alexander Graham Bell?"

"Ha-ha."

"I want to be able to text you and be sure of it reaching you."

At that, her face shut down like a door slamming. "I don't text."

"Not on that thing. It would take half an hour to key in five words."

"I don't text," she repeated. She set her phone down on the tablecloth and picked up her fork again.

"Why not?" There had to be something deeper at work here.

"I just don't."

"Texting is perfect for asynchronous communication."

"A-what?"

"Asynchronous. Conversations where you don't necessarily need an answer right away. It's also good when you need to transmit reference information, like an address or a list."

She rolled her eyes. "You are the biggest geek I've ever met, and that includes both of my brothers."

He grinned. "Thank you."

"It wasn't a compliment," she said. "I prefer to talk to people."

"Come on. This is a huge project. There are going to be times when you'll need to let me know you're running late."

Her eyes narrowed. "Why would I want to do that? It's not like I'm going to punch a clock."

"What if I'm in town and you need me to bring back something for you—a paintbrush, maybe?"

"I don't expect you to run errands for me."

Bad took a deep breath and tried again. "I can load it with your favorite music."

"You don't even know what my favorite music is." She took a bite of salmon.

He arranged his face in McCall's most winning grin. "You could text me a list."

Instead of melting at his charm, she looked annoyed. "Read my lips. I. Don't. Text."

"It has a voice-to-text feature—you wouldn't have to type. You could just dictate messages."

She paused. He'd gotten her attention.

"And text-to-voice," he said. "It can read my texts to you when you're too busy to look at them."

She was wavering. He could see it.

"You can use it for research. It's easy. You won't even have to type anything. Here, let me show you. What's your favorite painting?"

She considered for a minute. "Probably *The Sleeping Gypsy,* by Henri Rousseau."

Not one of her dad's paintings. Interesting.

"I would have expected it to be a landscape," he said.

"Rousseau created the idea of a portrait landscape," she said. "I'm considering a similar idea for your mural."

He repeated the painting's name into the microphone, then showed her how to press a single button to send the resulting text to a search engine.

An instant later, an image popped up on the screen. It showed a painting of a dark-skinned woman clad in a rainbow-colored robe, sleeping in the desert beside some sort of stringed instrument and a clay water jar. A bright-eyed lion sniffed the woman's head but showed no interest in harming her. In the upper right corner of the painting, a full moon floated. The colors in the painting were muted, as they would be under the limited light of a nighttime sky. The overall effect was deeply peaceful.

Bad held up the phone so she could see the image, and for an instant her face softened.

"The backdrop reminds me of Sedona," he said.

She nodded. "Maybe that's why I like it so much."

He picked up her flip phone. "You can't do that with this relic."

She's not going to cave, dude. Lil tried to give her one back at Christmas and she wouldn't have anything to do with it.

That meant if Bad got her to carry the phone, he'd be one up on Lilith. That would get the boss's attention and demonstrate Bad's capacity for fieldwork.

Keeffe tossed her napkin on the table. It looked like McCall was right. She wasn't going to accept the phone.

There was only one thing to do. Bad stretched across the table to hand her back her phone. As she reached out to take it, he shot a wave of static electricity through McCall's fingertips. Before her fingers even touched his, a spark leapt across the gap. She yelped and yanked her hand away. Instead of dropping into her outstretched palm, the phone sank like a rock to the bottom of her untouched glass of iced tea.

"Crap." Swiftly, she inserted two fingers into the glass, but it was so tall and narrow she couldn't reach the phone. She pulled her fingers back out. A pair of bubbles floated to the top. She groaned.

"That was clumsy of me," Bad said. "Let me give you this smartphone to replace it."

She shot him a look rife with suspicion, but he met it with McCall's most guileless expression.

"You just paid me fifteen thousand dollars," she said. "If I wanted a smartphone, I'd buy one for myself,"

Ronnie appeared in the doorway with a small pitcher and a glass bowl filled with rice. He dumped Keeffe's iced tea into the pitcher, then fished out the cellphone and removed the back cover and battery.

"I understand that if you allow them to dry in a bowl of rice for a few days, they can often be restored to working condition," he said.

Keeffe smiled at him. "Still my hero."

"Thank you." He beamed at her. Then he cleared his throat. "Might I suggest that you consider transferring your service to Mr. McCall's device until yours is functional again? I'd be happy to take care of the necessary arrangements."

Keeffe's face said she wanted to refuse but, in the face of such graciousness, knew it would be churlish.

"Thank you, Ronnie." She sounded like the words choked her.

"Not at all, miss."

Once Ronnie returned from the kitchen, where he'd transferred the service with surprising quickness, McCall insisted on setting it up to receive email.

"I don't use email," she said.

"Ever?" He looked baffled. "Last night you said I could mail you the contract."

"I meant with a stamp. If someone insists on emailing me, Frida lets me know. She has my email address set up to deliver to her computer."

"That's just wrong. What's your email address?"

Reluctantly, Keeffe recited the address. She had no problem memorizing things like that. In fact, her memory was better than most people's because she used it more. It was reading that gave her fits.

His fingers flew over the keyboard. The phone dinged. He checked the screen.

"What was that?" she asked.

"I re-sent the contract as a test."

She held out her hand, but he didn't give her the phone.

"You'll get a lot more enjoyment out of it if you know how to use it." Then he insisted on giving her a half-hour lesson on its features. It truly was as simple as he'd claimed. She might even use that text-to-voice feature.

After a quick run up to Flagstaff to order supplies from the art store there, she called Ed to ask about his comic-book collection.

"Sure," he said. "Borrow as many as you want. Camille should be home."

A few minutes later, she rapped on the door of the vinyl-sided ranch Claude and Ed's families shared. From inside came the sound of Bob Marley singing "Three Little Birds" and children shrieking with laughter. The corners of her mouth lifted. That would be her nephews, the cutest three-year-olds in Arizona. *No hanging out*, she warned herself, *you've got work to do.*

Frida had razzed their brothers about sharing a home. "Just because you're twins doesn't mean you have to do everything together."

Ed said they were just being practical. Camille provided daycare for Noah, Claude and Suzanne's son. Sharing a home meant they didn't have to wake him and get him dressed before leaving for work.

After last night's conversation at Ernesto's, Keeffe suspected the sharing had as much to do with saving money as it did convenience.

When no one answered her knock, she balled up her fist and pounded. A moment later, Camille opened the door.

"Have you been out here long?" She smoothed her hair. "I was spelunking with the boys and I didn't hear you."

"Spelunking?" Keeffe followed her into the family room, where Camille and the boys had constructed makeshift caves from chairs and blankets. Noah and Andy were nowhere to be seen, but muffled giggles and twitching under the covers hinted at their whereabouts.

With a finger to her lips, Keeffe tiptoed over to a lump that looked big enough to accommodate two small boys and threw her arms around it. "Gotcha!"

The lump exploded into squeals of laughter.

"Aunt Keeffe!" Noah's blonde head, so like Suzanne's, emerged first, followed by Andy's dark curls.

"How are my favorite boys?"

"Did you come to play with us?"

Keeffe thought about the sketches she needed to get started on. "I did."

For the next half hour, she crept from cave to cave on her hands and knees, sat cross-legged under tables, and hid behind the sofa while the boys crawled all over her. When Camille called naptime, Keeffe struggled out from under the blankets and settled them in the twin beds in their room. They fell asleep almost immediately.

Sounds coming from the kitchen suggested Camille was making dinner.

"Thanks for the break." With a wooden spoon, Camille stirred something in a cast iron skillet. The smell of tomatoes and garlic drifted to Keeffe's nose. "Dinner may be on time for the first time this week."

"What are you making?" Keeffe smoothed the static from her hair and took a seat at one of the high stools that lined the counter.

"Sloppy Joes. I can usually slip spinach into it if I chop it up small enough."

Keeffe grinned. "Is that for Andy's benefit—or Ed's?"

Camille grinned back. "Both. Ed said you wanted to look at his comic books?"

Keeffe nodded. "For that mural for McCall. I need research material."

"Nice-looking guy," Camille said.

"He's a work of art." And a piece of work, but that was a different topic entirely.

Camille wiped her hands on a dishtowel and adjusted the flame beneath the skillet to simmer. "The comic books are in the garage, along with everything else we couldn't find space for. Prepare yourself for some real spelunking."

Keeffe followed her through the connecting door to the two-car garage that separated the halves of the duplex. It was stacked with boxes, tools, discarded toys, sporting equipment, and, above all, comic books. Boxes and boxes of comic books.

Keeffe whistled. "Wow. I can't believe Lilith let them leave these at Dad's for all those years."

"Claude told her they were worth a lot of money." Camille grinned. "We almost didn't get them back."

"Are they really?" If that were the case, why hadn't they sold the comics instead of their statues?

"No," said Camille. "They're not in good enough condition."

Keeffe picked a dog-eared Batman comic from the nearest carton and leafed through it. What she needed were images to bring some depth to the planned mural. She expected Camille to head back into the kitchen, leaving her to her task. Instead, her sister-in-law opened another carton.

"What are you looking for, exactly?" Camille asked.

Keeffe shook her head. "I don't know. I was never a comic book reader." Or any other kind of reader.

Camille lifted a Wonder Woman issue from the box. "I didn't expect to see her in here."

Keeffe laughed. "My brothers were always equal opportunity

obsessives." She reached for the book. "I'll have to see if McCall feels the same."

Camille handed her the comic book. Then, a little too casually, she asked, "How well do you know him?"

"Not very," Keeffe said. "I just met him two days ago."

"Really? I guess I thought..." Camille trailed off.

"That I'd have to know someone pretty well to practically have sex with them against a lamppost in downtown Sedona?"

Camille grinned. "Something like that."

"Usually, I'd say that's true. There's something about this guy, though."

"Makes you all tingly, does he?"

Keeffe thought about his two different personas. "Off and on."

"After you left last night, he talked with the guys about investing in Blackmon Media. He seemed pretty interested."

Dr. Jekyll might be okay as a business partner. Mr. Hyde would be a nightmare.

"Why are they interested in having an outside investor? I thought that was why they sold the statues."

"Even after selling, we're still short the half-million dollars we need to distribute and market the game effectively."

Keeffe gave a silent whistle. "That's a lot of money. What does he want in return?"

Camille caught her lower lip between her incisors. If Keeffe were painting her sister-in-law, she'd use quinacridone magenta for her lips, with just a touch of phthalocyanine blue.

"I majored in English, not business," Camille said. "I didn't really understand much of the conversation. There was something about McCall becoming an angel investor and a limited partner."

Keeffe might not know McCall very well, but she knew he was no angel.

"What does being a limited partner entitle him to?"

Camille shook her head, frowning. She was really worried. That was surprising, because she was usually unflappable.

"First-born male children?" Keeffe asked.

From inside the house, a voice yelled, "Aunt Cammy, Andy just peed his pants."

Camille groaned. "If that was all, I might take him up on it." She got to her feet. "It sounded more like a cut of the profits. If there ever are any." Inside the house Andy began to wail. "I better go. Do you want to stick around for dinner? I made plenty."

The discussion of McCall as a potential investor reminded Keeffe of her own contract with him. The sixty-day deadline should be ample, but she knew all too well that things didn't always go as planned. What she should do was go home and get started on those sketches.

Camille opened the door to the kitchen and the aroma of tomatoes and onions wafted out to the garage.

"Love to," she said.

Over dinner, Camille suggested dividing the mural into components with related themes for each area, to create a sense of cohesion.

"You can go with the four seasons of the year," she said, "or with morning, afternoon, evening and night."

It was a good idea. Keeffe just wished the mural interested her more. It seemed like such a waste to get a lucrative commission for a project that didn't capture her imagination. Then she told herself to stop being ungrateful. The commission would not only allow her to keep *John*, it would let her upgrade her lifestyle, maybe even buy a better car.

After dinner, Ed helped her sort through the comic books.

"After you left last night," he said, "McCall offered to bankroll us."

"That's what Camille was saying."

"He wants a thirty-four percent interest in the business in exchange for half a million."

"He wants a third?"

Ed nodded glumly.

"Half a million is less than you and Claude have invested, isn't it?"

She didn't bring up the statues. What was the point? What was done was done.

Ed set the top carton in the stack on the floor and opened the next one.

"And that's if you don't count our time. Without money for distribution and marketing, though, our game might as well not exist."

She could see that.

"The problem is if he has thirty-four percent, he can band with either one of us to overrule the other," Ed said.

"So stick together."

Ed gave her a wry look, and she nodded. Claude could be difficult sometimes.

"What do you think of him?" Ed asked. "You're usually a pretty good judge of character."

Keeffe was flattered. "Really?"

"I think so," said Ed.

"What color were his eyes when he made the offer?" she asked.

Ed scratched his cheek. "I don't know. Why?"

"Never mind." She chewed on her lower lip, thinking, then shook her head. "I wouldn't do it. Not unless you don't have any other options. The fact that he asked for thirty-four percent says he's planning to play you against each other."

"That's what I thought."

"But Claude wants to accept?"

Ed nodded unhappily.

"There you go," she said. "It's starting already."

For the next half hour, Ed helped her, selecting the comic books containing the most iconic images. Keeffe had to smile at his enthusiasm.

"Let yourself have fun with this," he said as he loaded her final selections into a box to carry out to the car.

"Sure," she said. "The money's good, at least."

He took her by the shoulders and looked down at her face. He wasn't as tall as McCall, but she had to tilt her head back to meet his eyes.

"I mean it," he said. "You can treat this as a punishment and let it make you miserable, or you can treat it as an opportunity to move out of your comfort zone and challenge your assumptions about yourself as a painter. One of the things that made Mom such a great artist was she was never afraid to try new things, move into new territories."

That was true. Mom had created crosses from barbed wire, Legos, matchsticks, even beer bottles. Every cross she did was totally unique. She built the first one from twisted branches found at each of Sedona's vortexes.

One of the things that had made their father so susceptible to Lilith's flattery was that he was afraid to change. Ed didn't say it, but Keeffe knew it was true. Determined to stay within the cozy circle of his homey little night scenes, Dad had begun to run low on ideas even before Mom died. His well of inspiration seemed to dry up completely when Lilith came along.

Keeffe leaned her head into Ed's shoulder. "Thanks."

He kissed the top of her head.

"Any time."

He was right. This was an opportunity to really dazzle McCall. She would make the most of it.

CHAPTER 11

*A*fter Keeffe left, McCall challenged Bad to a *Grand Theft Auto* tournament that kept them up till three a.m. Bad won, but not by much. McCall had great reflexes for a human, and it was clear he'd spent a lot of hours playing video games.

The next morning when Bad woke up, the body they shared was already seated at the counter in the big, sunny kitchen at the rear of the house. Ronnie, dressed in a long-sleeved shirt and gray suit pants covered by a white chef's apron, was frying eggs. Bad came to, feeling a little groggy. Possessing someone required a level of energy he wouldn't have predicted.

"So, like, I'm thinking about applying to become a demon," McCall was saying, around a piece of toast.

"A demon, eh?" Ronnie's hound-dog face was even longer than usual.

This was what happened to old demons. Even if they didn't screw up and piss off the boss, they eventually lost their edge. And then they wound up wet-nursing some jerk-hole like McCall.

"Yeah," said McCall. "I'd be a killer demon."

Bad waited for Ronnie to explain that humans couldn't become demons. If they came to Hell, they came as clients. But the old fiend just turned the eggs without responding.

"Everything your boss liked came from me. The asshole that's hitching a ride inside me didn't do diddly."

"That is not true." Bad took control of their mouth.

Ronnie turned to look at them. Was that disapproval on the old demon's face? He turned back to the stove before Bad could be sure, but it resurrected his question—why was Ronnie here?

Satan wouldn't have placed him here—McCall wasn't central to the mission. Bad suspected Lilith had placed Ronnie here. She was probably planning to gift McCall to Satan as a bonus.

McCall cocked their head. The kitchen swam woozily for a second.

"So you finally decided to join us, did you?" he said. "You really ought to work on that. The early demon gets the worm, bro."

"Bad is the Demon of Sloth," Ronnie said. "He's always loved a good nap."

Bad glared at him. One man's lazy was another man's efficient. In any event, the less McCall knew, the less ammunition he'd have in their ongoing war for supremacy.

"You're not a demon," Bad told McCall.

"I could be. I'd be a hella better demon than you. People would love me down there."

That was unlikely.

"Who came up with the idea of offering the Blackmons venture capital?" McCall said. "For that matter, who dry-humped Keeffe up against that light pole the other night?"

The recollection of McCall's hips pressing Keeffe against the light post sent a gust of anger through Bad. McCall needed to keep his crotch—and his hands and his lips—off her. Bad's reaction surprised him. It felt less like disgust at McCall's raunchiness than protectiveness toward Keeffe.

"If I was a demon, she'd have been under the table on her knees before we ever left the bar." McCall filled the shared part of their brain with a lurid video of Keeffe with her face buried in his crotch, followed by one of Lilith performing similar activities.

Their penis stirred. *Ulck.* The guy was like a stray dog, humping anything that moved. Bad called up an image of maggots and their erection wilted.

Maybe he should drug McCall again. Having the drugs in their shared system slowed down their physical actions and reactions, but at least he wouldn't have to put up with McCall's swinishness.

"Anyway, if you made such a great connection," McCall said, "why isn't she returning our texts?"

The last remnants of sleep fled Bad's mind. "You texted her?"

At the stove, Ronnie nodded lugubriously.

"Twice," said McCall. "She didn't respond."

"Of course she didn't respond. She told us she doesn't text." Bad hoped to change that, but it would require time and delicate handling, concepts McCall seemed to be unfamiliar with. Bad grabbed his phone. There were no texts to Keeffe showing in his messaging app.

Ronnie pointed to an iPhone lying on the counter. "He used that one."

Great. He pulled up McCall's texts. *RU up?* read the first. And then, a half-hour later, *How's it going?*

What an idiot. Bad took comfort from the fact that at least the texts weren't crude.

Bad picked up his own phone and selected Keeffe's number from the contact list. He pressed the call button. An instant later, she picked up the phone. He raised his eyebrows to drive home his point and then felt like an idiot. McCall couldn't see his own facial expressions.

"Good morning," he said into the phone.

"What do you want?" Keeffe all but snarled.

He blinked. "I was hoping I could take you to lunch."

"I'm working," she said. "Did you text me earlier, from a different number?"

He thought about disavowing those texts, but she already knew he carried two phones.

"Maybe," he said.

"Don't," she said, and hung up.

McCall shook their head. "Real smooth, bro. At the rate you're going, we're never going to boink her."

No, they weren't. Under no circumstances would Bad allow McCall to become intimate with Keeffe. Fortunately, seduction wasn't a necessity. Bad's intention was to become emotionally intimate with Keeffe, which opened the door to physical intimacy as well, but sex was neither a foregone conclusion nor a requirement for success. The requirement was trust.

Should their relationship blossom into something that included sex, he would never allow McCall to be present. Unfortunately, given his less than complete control over his host, he wasn't sure how he'd prevent it.

Worst case, he could drive her to quit without finishing the mural, but that was strictly a fail-safe. Bad preferred his original approach— getting to know her and then convincing her to sell him the statue voluntarily.

McCall turned back to Ronnie. "So, where do I apply to be a demon? Is there, like, an online form?"

Bad started to tell him that Hell didn't recruit demons from the mortal population but stopped himself. Let McCall have his dream. Maybe it would keep him busy so Bad could get some work done.

Keeffe spent the rest of the weekend in her trailer, building a model of the mural room. To get a sense of the scale of the work, she trimmed seven sheets of graph paper to eight by eleven inches and taped them together, overlapping each sheet with the next. She had no problems working with numbers. For the millionth time, she wondered why reading was such an issue.

When she set the model on the floor, it was a perfect, tiny replica of McCall's room. At the idea of filling so much wall space with comic book characters, she groaned. *Let it go. It is what it is.* Ed was right. It was time to break out of her comfort zone. She didn't much care what gray-eyed McCall thought about the mural, but she kind of wanted to impress the brown-eyed guy.

In line with Camille's suggestion, she divided the wall into eight panels. Each panel would feature one superhero in his characteristic pose. Then, she'd fill in the background with the setting and characters most associated with each—Gotham City, the Joker and Catwoman for Batman; Metropolis, Lex Luthor and Lois Lane for Superman.

At noon she took a break and wolfed down some peanut butter and crackers, finishing up with an apple. She thought about McCall's lunch invitation. Depending on which McCall she got, it might have been fun, but even with Dr. Jekyll, it wasn't a good idea to get involved with a client.

Other than the hour she spent at Mass on Sunday, she worked all day, scouring her brothers' collection and making notes about color palettes for each hero. That evening, she started sketching.

Monday morning at ten a.m., the phone buzzed with an incoming text. She glared at the device. The worst thing about phones was their ability to break your concentration.

A moment later, it buzzed again. With a growl she threw down her pen. She carried the phone over to the couch and shoved it under a cushion. She'd just sat back down when a muffled buzz sounded from the couch. What was so almighty important?

She tried to refocus on her work but found herself listening for the next buzz. From what she knew of McCall, he wouldn't give up until she responded.

As though to verify her perception, the phone sounded the Superman ringtone he had set up when he gave it to her. Growling, she retrieved the phone. She started to press Answer but stopped herself. McCall had said texting was good for asynchronous communication. Fine. Asynchronous it would be.

She brought up the first text and pressed the buttons he had demonstrated would make the phone read aloud.

"Some stuff showed up here," the mechanical voice said.

"What should I do with it?" said the second text.

"I can't just leave it in the hallway," said the third.

Pushing the Talk button, she said, "Put it in the mural room, period." Words magically appeared on the screen. She squinted at the letters, slowly confirming that they were the correct ones. She hit Send.

Almost instantly, she got a text back. She glanced at the screen and listened. "Will do."

"I'll be out tomorrow to prep the room," she told the phone and pressed Send.

"See you then," McCall responded a second later.

She had just held her first text conversation. With a sense of accomplishment, she got back to work. An hour later, the ringtone for an unknown caller chimed. The number was the same 520 area code that had shown up on her old phone on Friday. She pressed the Reject button. A moment later, the icon for voicemail appeared.

Curious, she tapped the voicemail symbol, then the speaker button, the way McCall had shown her.

"This is Annalisa Flora from Saguaro National Park," the recording said. "I'm calling in reference to your application to be our artist-in-residence. Please contact me at your earliest convenience."

Keeffe pulled the phone away from her ear and stared at it blankly. She hadn't applied to be an artist-in-residence at Saguaro—or anyplace else. The phone offered to let her listen to the message again. She pressed the 1 button.

The woman repeated what she'd said before.

A few months ago, Frida had told Keeffe about the residency and urged her to apply. Unwilling to admit she couldn't navigate the online application, Keeffe had insisted she wasn't interested.

She hit the callback button.

After exchanging greetings, Annalisa said, "Congratulations. You've been chosen to be our next artist-in-residence."

Keeffe listened in amazement. She clutched the phone like the offer might disappear if she didn't hang onto it. A grin split her face. "That's great."

Then she frowned. "How was I selected?"

"Based on your online application and the electronic portfolio you submitted," Annalisa said.

Frida had to be behind this. She must have built the portfolio from the digital copies she'd made of Keeffe's work, back when she was trying to coax Keeffe into building a website.

"We're very excited about having you," Annalisa said.

Last week, this opportunity would have saved Keeffe's life, or at least her statue. If she'd known she'd won it, she never would have signed on to do McCall's comic book mural.

"I'm very excited about the residency." And she was. From what she remembered, it was a chance to live at the park, down near Tucson, painting and working with visitors for a month. It would be a blast—and it came with a nice stipend. "When does it start?"

"You requested February tenth on your application."

The day before her birthday. Frida had been looking out for her.

The tenth was just over three weeks away. Keeffe looked at the model on the floor, now decorated with miniature comic-book scenes. If she painted like a madwoman, she would be able to complete it in time.

"That's perfect," she said. "I look forward to working with you."

Frida's house was an olive-green stucco in the Santa Fe style. Originally built in the 1970s, the updates she and Jen had done made it look much newer. The landscaping consisted of rocks and native southwestern plants, giving it a pleasantly harmonious feel. With four bedrooms, it had always seemed ridiculously large for two people. After McCall's place, though, it looked tiny.

Keeffe opened the front door and stepped into the living room. "Frida?"

Her sister appeared in the kitchen doorway, wiping her hands on a towel. Her face was grim. It didn't lighten when she saw Keeffe. She shook out the towel with a snap.

"What do you want?" she asked.

Wow. Hormone treatments always made her a little moody, but this was over the top.

"Are you okay?" Keeffe asked.

Frida's face didn't relax. "Claude called."

Uh-oh. So much had happened since Keeffe's argument with her brothers Thursday night, she'd forgotten all about it. She held out her hands, palms up.

"Peace. It was your statue and you had every right to sell it if you wanted to."

"You're right. I did." A muscle in Frida's jaw ticked.

"I just...it feels like every trace of Mom's legacy is being wiped away."

"Did it ever occur to you that my having a child is another way to ensure Mom's legacy lives on?"

It hadn't. "I guess that's true."

"Of course it's true. One-fourth of my child's genes will come from Mom. Those genes will be passed on to their children and their children's children. That's a lot more lasting legacy than any artwork."

There were cave paintings still around from tens of thousands of years ago. No one could trace their ancestry back that far. Keeffe didn't want to argue about it, though.

"Agreed," she said.

But Frida wasn't ready to let it go.

"Mom would have been over-the-moon at the thought of another grandchild. She loved babies. Remember how excited she was when she found out she was pregnant with Pablo?"

"Of course I remember." All of Keeffe's fears for Frida came rushing back. Pablo had died in Mom's womb, triggering the need for the hysterectomy that killed her.

The thought must have shown on her face because Frida said, "I'm not going to die, Keeffe."

Mom would have said the same thing.

"I know," Keeffe said. "I'm just...I know."

Her sister surveyed her with a combination of affection and frustration. "I know you're upset about the statues being gone, so here's some news that might cheer you up. Lilith has arranged to publish Mom's journals."

"Her journals?" Keeffe's first guilty thought was of the journal resting in her footlocker. No one knew about it except her. "I thought those were long gone."

"Me, too," Frida said. "It turns out they were just in storage."

"That's going to be one thick book," Keeffe said.

"Too thick. They're doing excerpts. Lilith has been working with an editor who's helping her choose the most interesting parts. They're titling it *The Artist's Soul.*"

"Is that a good idea?" Keeffe asked. A project to raise Mom's profile and make her better known contradicted every action Lilith had ever taken connected to Rachel Blackmon. There had to be some kind of catch.

"Why wouldn't it be?" Frida said. "I guess the publisher really loved them—said they were a window into the soul of a brilliant artist. Lilith says they'll make Mom's work even more valuable."

Which, in turn, would make Lilith even more determined to get her hands on *John.* Well, too bad, so sad. Now that Keeffe had this commission and the residency, keeping him was a lock.

"When does the book come out?" she asked.

"Sometime this spring," Frida said. "She just finished the final round of edits."

It was too late to add the final journal into the mix. Keeffe didn't know whether to be disappointed or relieved. "The final round? She really kept it to herself, didn't she?"

Frida shrugged. "Lilith's always kept things close to the vest. It's just who she is."

"Did you ever read the journals?" Keeffe asked.

"Some," Frida said. "They helped me cope after she died. The one where she talks about meeting Dad is really sweet, and I loved the one where she talked about sculpting *Matthew* and how she came up with the idea of representing him as an angel."

Matthew was Frida's statue. The one she'd sold to fund her fertility treatments.

"Do you know what happened to him?" Keeffe asked.

Frida shook her head. "Just that it was bought by an anonymous collector. They must have really wanted it, because they paid way above market."

Another anonymous buyer. Another of Mom's sculptures that likely wouldn't see the light of day again. Thank God Keeffe had managed to hang onto *John*. She wondered if Frida was sorry she hadn't waited until the journals were released, when the statue would be worth more, but she knew better than to ask. The boys certainly would be. It sounded like they needed all the money they could get.

"Is that why you came by?" Frida asked. "To ask about the buyer?"

"No, I actually came to thank you. Someone from Saguaro National Park called to say I was chosen for their artist-in-residence program."

Frida's face lit up. "That's great."

"It is, but I didn't apply for it."

Frida blushed. "I kind of filled out the application for you. Are you going to take it?"

Keeffe grinned. "Of course. I start the day before my birthday, so thanks for that, too."

"I've been on pins and needles, hoping you'd get it." Then Frida frowned. "Are you going to be finished with McCall's mural by then? I didn't know about the mural when I picked the date. Maybe you can change it?"

"It shouldn't be a problem. He just wants cartoons."

Frida gave her a sly look. "I guess the real question is, are you going to be finished with McCall by then?"

Keeffe lifted her chin. "It's a business relationship."

Frida laughed. "Just keep telling yourself that."

CHAPTER 12

"Good morning, Miss Keeffe. You're looking lovely today."

It wasn't just the roguish twinkle in Ronnie's eye that made Keeffe grin back at him. After she completed this mural, she'd be going to Tucson for a month-long dream residency. Her luck was finally starting to turn.

"Good morning, Ronnie. You're looking pretty handsome yourself."

"No fraternization between the employees, please." McCall's tone was jocular, but something about the look he shot Ronnie said he wasn't kidding. Keeffe had hoped for Dr. Jekyll, but it looked like she'd gotten Mr. Hyde instead.

She batted her eyes at Ronnie. "I'm afraid our date will have to wait until I get the mural finished."

Ronnie smiled even more broadly. "I'll be waiting."

McCall looked pissed, which made Keeffe chuckle louder than the joke deserved.

He reached for her portfolio. "What have you got for me?"

His tone was brusque, but before his hand could close on the portfolio, his elbow jerked. It looked like he was yanking his arm out of someone's grip, but no one was there.

She'd planned to show him the sketches first thing, but she decided to wait. She'd worked hard on those drawings, and she wasn't going to let Mr. Hyde dump all over them just because he was in a crappy mood.

She stepped back, removing the portfolio from his reach. "I'd like to prime the room first." If he didn't like that, too bad. Now that she had the residency, she didn't need his commission.

His eyes darkened to brown and his hand dropped to his side. "No, sure. I mean, whatever works for you."

He followed her to the mural room. In the middle of the floor sat a five-gallon bucket of Aqua Lock wall-prepping solution and two cardboard boxes. Pulling a Swiss Army knife from her pocket, Keeffe opened the first carton. Inside were rolls of plastic sheeting. The second contained metal pans, rollers, and packs of roller covers.

She turned to McCall. "Do you have a ladder I can use?"

"Sure, it's in the...." He didn't finish his sentence. Sweat broke out on his forehead and his forearms flexed like he was doing isometrics. Then he blurted out, "The contract says you'll provide your own supplies."

This was exactly why she hated contracts.

"I'd call a ladder equipment, rather than supplies," she said, "but if you don't have one, I'll go buy one." It would take a couple of hours, time she didn't really have to spare.

He shrugged. "Works for me."

Would killing him breach the contract?

"I've taken the liberty of bringing a ladder for Miss Keeffe." In the doorway, Ronnie held an aluminum stepladder.

Keeffe crossed the room. She batted her eyes at him. "And that's why you're my hero."

He beamed down at her, but quickly retreated under McCall's glare.

"So are you going to show me the sketches or not?" McCall asked. His eyes were gray as storm clouds.

Keeffe set her jaw. "Not while you're in this lousy mood."

His jaw moved back and forth, but it didn't open. They stood there glaring at each other for a long moment.

Finally McCall said, through gritted teeth, "If you need anything, I'll be in the workout room." He hurled himself out the door.

Good riddance.

What is your problem? Bad asked as McCall stormed into the weight room. Bad hated working out. The only thing worse than the endless, tedious repetition was having to watch McCall strut and pose in front of the mirrors that lined the room. *I thought you liked Keeffe.*

"We're supposed to make her miserable, so she'll quit."

That was Lilith's plan, but it wasn't Bad's. He still intended to use persuasion.

Not yet.

McCall loaded up a barbell with weights. "If we're going to keep her around, let's bang her."

There was zero chance of Bad letting that happen. He thought about drugging his host again. If he couldn't get McCall to settle down any other way, he'd have to try that, despite the potential impacts to his own performance.

"You saw her at that lamppost." McCall started his repetitions. "She couldn't get enough of me."

That wasn't how Bad remembered it. Apparently McCall had run that incident through some kind of mental filter that let him figure as a hero.

If we make her mad too soon, she'll take that residency. If that happens, she'll never sell us the sculpture. And who knew when he'd ever see the inside of DemSec again.

"Nah." McCall was definite. "Once I boink her, she'll hang around like a dog panting for scraps."

Bad couldn't remotely imagine Keeffe hanging around and panting for anything.

Your opinion is duly noted.

McCall glared at him in the mirror, outraged. "Don't I get any say around here? I mean, it's my house. It's my body."

That's not how demon possession works.

"We'll just see about that."

McCall launched an attack, hustling Bad's neurons out of his pre-frontal cortex. Bad considered initiating a counter-assault, then decided on a more subtle strategy. He vacated the pre-frontal cortex without argument.

When McCall realized he had his forebrain to himself, he grunted with satisfaction. "Take that, asshole." He started his workout.

Bad waited until he loaded up a barbell with weights and laid back on the bench. As McCall lowered the weights toward his chest, Bad took control of his arm muscles. The bar came to rest on McCall's windpipe, cutting off his air supply.

Let's get something straight. Bad swarmed back into the front brain. *You need this body to survive. I don't.* McCall struggled for dominance, but lack of oxygen gave Bad the upper hand.

Mortals are fragile. I could leave this bar on your throat until you die. Then I'd just waft out of your corpse and go right back to my own body.

He expected McCall to panic, but the big lout wasn't easily cowed.

Your boss won't like that very much.

True, Bad said, *but I've recovered from worse.*

In the mirror tiles on the ceiling, McCall's face turned from red to blue. *Get this thing off my neck.*

Stop interfering with my relationship with Keeffe.

She was attracted to McCall's body, but thanks to his personality, her trust had stalled out on the bottom rung. If Bad was to make any progress toward his objective, she needed to perceive him as a nice guy, someone who could be depended upon to keep his word. This bi-polar act they kept putting on wasn't helping.

You can't make me. The thought was strangled.

Actually, I can. Bad relaxed McCall's arms a little more. The bar pressed harder on his windpipe.

McCall tried to breathe, but couldn't drag any air into his lungs. *This is bullshit.*

Above them, the mirrored ceiling swam with black dots. If McCall didn't give in soon, Bad would have to let up the pressure. Killing him would totally hose the mission and Satan would be livid.

After another few seconds, McCall's instinct for survival overcame his desire to reclaim his body. He thumped a palm on their leg, tapping out like an MMA fighter.

Bad lifted the barbell off his throat.

McCall sucked in a greedy breath. "You're an asshole."

Like a trained rat, he picked up the bar and started through the boring sequence of lifts that kept his body in magnificent shape.

How did he stand it? The repetition was mind-numbing. Bad had assumed, since his host had made millions via the Internet, he'd spend his days creating algorithms and doing market research, but McCall did neither of these. He'd made his fortune by stealing an idea from a classmate. There was little doubt he planned to repeat the maneuver with the Blackmon twins.

Maybe he really should become a demon.

Keeffe ripped open the package of tarps and unrolled the plastic, positioning it at the base of the walls. Unfolded, it extended out four feet, protecting the hardwood floor.

Setting her iPod to shuffle, she stuck her earbuds in her ears and got to work to the sound of Lana Del Ray's "Big Eyes." She pulled a screwdriver out of her bag and pried the top off the Aqua Lock. From her portfolio, she retrieved a long, narrow paddle she'd brought from home. She stirred the primer, scraping the sides and bottom of the bucket. When her arms burned too much to continue, she gave the bucket one final stir. That should do it.

The bucket was too heavy to tip and pour. This was a spot where she could have used McCall's help, but since he was in Mr. Hyde mode, she'd figure it out on her own.

She rummaged inside her bag till she located a travel mug. That would work. She dipped out some Aqua Lock and poured it into one of the metal roller trays. Then she pulled out a one-inch synthetic brush. She preferred natural bristle brushes, but when working with latex, they absorbed too much paint.

For the next two hours, she crawled along the floor, trimming the wall a couple of inches up. The hardwood was a lot tougher on her knees than Ed and Camille's padded carpet. She made a mental note to buy a set of knee pads.

The work gave her plenty of time to think. Too much time. Memory of McCall's first exploratory kiss by the lamppost infiltrated her brain. He had explained his changing eye color, but she'd never asked him why his scent changed, too.

She breathed in, imagining the smell of rich, dark chocolate. If she licked his skin, would he taste like cocoa? She straightened, sitting back on her ankles, and realized she'd gotten turned on thinking about him. That was a waste of time. At any given moment, there was only a fifty-fifty chance he would be brown-eyed and chocolate-scented.

Thank goodness this commission had a finite end date. If McCall ever stopped ping-ponging between nice guy and asshat, she could be in real trouble.

Two hours later, her knees felt like she'd been crawling over broken glass and her shoulders burned like the fires of Hell. When Ronnie appeared in the doorway to tell her lunch was ready, she was so stiff she could barely move.

By the time Bad got to the dining room, Keeffe was already at the table. He smiled at her, but she turned her head away and shook out her napkin with a snap. Was she still annoyed over the ladder conversation?

Man, that chick just does not know how to let things go. Before McCall could reengage, Bad presented him with a snapshot of himself as he'd looked in the mirrored ceiling tiles that morning, his face blue from oxygen starvation. Their lips closed.

For lunch, Ronnie served avocado, lettuce, and tomato sandwiches with an Asian slaw on the side. There was a tall glass of iced tea for Bad and lemonade garnished with mint for Keeffe.

Keeffe took a bite of her sandwich and smiled at Ronnie. "I could get used to having you cook for me."

Ronnie beamed. "It's enjoyable to cook for someone so appreciative."

Keeffe stared across the table at McCall, her chin high, as though daring him to comment.

"I hope you'll join me for meals while you're working here," Bad said. "I enjoy the company and Ronnie gets bored, cooking for just one person."

God, you are such a suck-ass. Despite McCall's disgust, Bad's words replaced the fire in Keeffe's eyes with wary pleasure.

"Thanks," she said. "I might do that."

Bad took a bite of the slaw. It was mouthwatering. Ronnie hadn't learned to cook like this in Hell. DemSec must have given him a chef's identity for this mission. At least some of the work Bad had done there was being carried forward.

"So, did you make good progress this morning?" he asked Keeffe.

"Not bad. How was your workout?"

"Good," he said. "I think I figured out how to solve the cryptography issue with my security algorithm." That, at least, was something he could do while McCall performed his endless repetitions.

She said, "That's good," and withdrew back into herself.

He still wasn't forgiven. Or maybe she'd just gotten tired of dealing with his revolving personalities. Time for McCall's next lesson.

You need to apologize to her.

Yeah, like that's going to happen. If you're so anxious to kiss her ass, why don't you apologize?

Bad had lost the ability to apologize the day he started working in DemSec, but he didn't want to tell McCall that.

You're the one who pissed her off. You apologize. He poked McCall's thalamus, the brain's pain center.

McCall yelped. Keeffe jumped, startled. Bad pretended like he'd stabbed himself in the lip with his fork.

After a few more jabs, McCall caved. "Sorry about the ladder thing this morning. I was just in a shitty mood."

As an apology, it was pretty pathetic, but Keeffe seemed to accept it, or maybe she had McCall pegged as such a jerk she didn't expect much.

"How's your robot coming along?" she asked.

Bad stared at her blankly.

She's talking about your body, dumbass.

"Right," he said. "My robot. I haven't had much time to spend on it."

"I'd really like to see it, once you get it working," she said.

Maybe you should climb back into your own skin and show her how it works, McCall jeered.

Bad repressed a shudder at the idea of Keeffe seeing him in his own form.

"Sure," he said. "That would be great."

Back in the mural room, the instant Keeffe picked up the roller, her shoulders howled in protest.

"Would you like some help?" McCall had followed her from the dining room. "I'm not an artist, but I have primed walls before."

She wanted to refuse, but she didn't have that luxury. She was on a tight timeline.

"If you like." She didn't bother to hide her wariness. It would be just like him to offer help one minute and then gripe about it the next.

"How about if I do the rolling while you finish trimming?" he said.

As long as he was willing, she might as well make the most of it. "Okay, thanks."

After setting the ladder next to the wall, she picked up a plastic bucket and ladled a travel mug full of Aqua Lock into it.

"Here, let me help you with that." He picked up the five-gallon container and poured Aqua Lock into her bucket. His arms flexed with the effort.

"Thank you," she said, and meant it this time.

He pulled a remote from his pocket and pressed a couple of buttons. The air filled with some kind of techno mix. She shoved one of her earbuds in place.

"You have an iPod?" he said. "I thought you didn't like technology."

If you were willing to let them shuffle, iPods required almost no reading but she wasn't about to tell him that. "I'm willing to make an exception once in a while."

But he still wasn't satisfied.

"You don't like techno music?" he asked.

She shrugged. "Not a lot."

"What do you like? I have a huge music library."

A huge library of equally geeky music, no doubt. "I'm good."

"Or I can hook your player into my system." His brown eyes were warm. His tone said he was eager to make up. He was sweating a little from the effort of hoisting that five-gallon bucket, and the odor of dark chocolate rolled off him.

Against her will, some of her annoyance dissipated.

She handed him the device and he inserted it into a dock. A moment later, "Kandi" by One Eskimo filled the room.

"Music over speakers is so much better than what you hear through these." Keeffe touched the earbuds still hanging around her neck.

McCall dipped his roller into the pan and rolled away the excess. "Most recorded music is engineered to be heard over speakers. To sound right through headphones, it needs to be recorded binaurally, with mikes placed where human ears would be. They don't bother to do that, so you lose the spatial cues when you listen through headphones."

"Good to know," Keeffe said. "I've been losing sleep over that one." The tips of his ears turned pink. She giggled. "Has anyone ever told you you're a nerd?"

"My last girlfriend," he said, "when she dumped me."

She'd probably gotten tired of dealing with his Jekyll-and-Hyde act. Keeffe leaned forward to feather Aqua Lock along the top of the wall.

"Why did she break up with you?" she asked.

"She said I was too needy."

Keeffe thought about his phone calls and texts. "I can see that."

"Ouch." He grinned when he said it, though.

Keeffe leaned out to paint the farthest area she could reach. "What was she like?"

McCall smiled, as though at some inner joke. "She was a snake."

Keeffe climbed down the steps and moved the ladder a couple of feet further along the wall. "I hate when guys do that."

He blinked. "Do what?"

He was so clueless.

"Trash the girl after a breakup."

"Believe me, if you met her, you'd agree." His dark eyes twinkled.

"Maybe she just felt like where you were going with your life wasn't where she wanted to go."

This time, his smile was rueful. "Well, that was definitely true."

Keeffe was done trimming long before McCall finished the roller work, so she grabbed the second roller and started on the far side of the room.

He rolled a long swath of primer onto the wall. "Why don't you like Lilith?"

He'd asked her the same question that first night at Ernesto's.

"When she married my dad, she cleaned house and got rid of my mom's stuff." Keeffe couldn't keep the bitterness out of her voice. "Like, everything."

"That sucks." He offered the clichéd sympathy she expected, but then he said, "If you could have one thing of your mother's back, what would it be?"

"Why? Are you going to get it for me?"

"I don't think that would be possible," he said seriously. "I asked because it will give me a clearer sense of who you are."

It was Keeffe's turn to blink. Something in her responded to his complete lack of gamesmanship.

"I don't know." She thought about it for a moment. "Her chisels, I guess." She heard the longing in her own voice and tried to reel herself back in. "Why am I even telling you this?"

"Because I asked. You mean sculpting chisels?"

She nodded. "What about you? Are your parents still around?"

"Yes," he said.

"Do you have a good relationship with them?"

He nodded. "Pretty good."

"So, unlike your girlfriend, they approve of your life choices?"

"I wouldn't go that far, but they're pretty live-and-let-live."

When her paint tray was empty, his was running dry, too. As he hefted the Aqua Lock container, she changed out the roller pans. They were so close his bare arm rubbed down the length of hers. The sense of connection she'd felt with him at Ernesto's that first night, just before he kissed her, was back. Then she remembered the way he'd slammed her against the lamppost. She snatched her arm away, nearly spilling Aqua Lock.

"Careful." His face was calm. If he had any idea what was going through her head, she couldn't tell it.

When they finally finished the room, Keeffe set her roller down with a groan.

"I hear you," he said. "I work out a lot, but this uses different muscles. My shoulders feel like they're on fire."

This frank admission of weakness was not what she would have expected from such a hard-body. She walked up behind him and rubbed his shoulders.

"Ahhh." He rolled his shoulders. "That feels good."

He was perspiring, and his sweat smelled like cacao. His spine moved sinuously, making his delectable ass wiggle. It was an unselfconscious wriggle, like a child might make, and not the preening display of his other side. He turned to face her. Behind his glasses, his eyes were the rich brown she was coming to associate with the guy she really liked.

"How are you doing?" he asked.

"My shoulders are pretty stiff, too." She tried to roll them, as he had done, but they were so tight they would barely move.

He prodded her deltoids. "Can I give you a shoulder rub?"

Was that wise? Probably not. She nodded anyway.

He turned her around and moved his hands expertly over her back. The flannel shirt she wore over her tank top should have dampened the sensual pleasure of his touch, but it didn't.

"Your shoulders are like rocks. Would you like a massage?" His offer was so matter-of-fact that it didn't sound like a come-on.

Still, better safe than sorry. "No, thanks."

"You'll feel a lot better tomorrow if you let me work on you."

She put her hands over his fingers, which were kneading her shoulders into mush, and stilled them. "I don't sleep with clients."

"Yes, you told me that." His voice was serene.

"No, seriously," she said. "I think it just confuses things."

"I can see where that might be true." He placed a thumb on each of her rhomboids and pressed. Her muscles melted like caramel into a latte. "The massage offer still stands."

She whimpered a little. "Really?"

"Really." He stroked a delicious pattern on her aching back.

Keeffe moved her head and winced. "Okay, I'm sold."

In the workout room, Bad set up the massage table. Despite the fact that the past two hours had been menial labor, which he ordinarily loathed, he'd enjoyed himself. Hanging out with Keeffe and chatting as they worked had been surprisingly pleasurable.

Get her to take her clothes off, ordered McCall.

Bad could feel their penis hardening. Gross. McCall was like a lot of fallen angels he'd dealt with over the years, who lived strictly for physical sensation.

Ignoring McCall, he flicked a switch to warm the massage table. Then he picked up a remote and pressed a couple of buttons.

Overhead, Enya warbled "May It Be" from the *Lord of the Rings* soundtrack.

"You have a massage table." Keeffe stood in the doorway to the workout room. Her wariness couldn't have been any more apparent.

He nodded. "I don't like the portable ones masseurs bring with them."

She stayed where she was. "Do you really know anything about massage?"

"I'll let you be the judge of that." He dimmed the lights and folded back the top sheet.

She took a step into the room.

"Make yourself comfortable," he said. "I'll be back in a minute."

Where are we going? McCall was outraged. *We were about to get our hands on that.*

Bad walked into the rec room. He opened the drawer in the end table where McCall kept the orange pills. After removing the child-proof lid, he shook a couple out into his hand.

What are those for? asked McCall.

To calm you down.

I don't need to be calmed down!

Yes, you do. Bad tossed the pills into their mouth. *We'll be standing very close to her. She's going to notice if I have an erection.*

McCall spit the pills across the room. *No way.*

Bad shook two more pills into his hand. *I can force you to take these. If necessary, I can get Ronnie to help me.*

McCall swallowed the pills. *I'll still be there, you know. Watching everything. Feeling everything.*

That was all right. There wasn't going to be anything to watch. Bad planned to restrict his touch to the strictly therapeutic.

Keeffe lay on her back, staring at the ceiling. She was still a little leery of McCall's intentions, but he started out by folding up the bottom of the sheet to uncover her right foot, leaving the rest of her snuggled in warm cotton. Maybe he was on the up and up. Maybe he really was offering a massage and nothing more.

He poured jasmine-scented oil on his hands and lifted her left foot. For a moment, he just held it, warming it between his palms. Then he began to rub the ball of her foot, smoothing it in the direction of her toes. After being on the ladder for so long, it felt wonderful. She found herself relaxing under his touch.

He circled her big toe with an oiled hand and began to milk it like he was milking a cow. At first it just felt good, but on the third or fourth tug, she noticed an answering tug in her core.

"How's my pressure?" he asked, giving her second toe an expert pull.

"Fine." The word came out a little choked. She lifted her head to look at him.

"Are you okay?" He tilted his head solicitously. "Warm enough?"

"I am." And getting warmer every minute.

He finished with her foot. "How does that feel?"

Like she wanted to get naked with him. Keeffe tried to focus on her foot. "Feels lighter." She flexed it. "Like it weighs less than the other one."

"That's because I released the lactic acid from your muscles." He covered her right foot with the sheet and moved on to the left one.

"Does anyone ever fall asleep while you're doing this?" she asked, although sleep was the furthest thing from her mind.

"Sometimes." He finished with her left foot and set it back on the table, refolding the sheet to expose her calves.

She smothered a sigh of relief that he was done with her toes, only to realize she had celebrated too early. His oiled hands kneading her calves made her want to give him access to other body parts. She'd worn yoga shorts to paint in, and when he stroked the sensitive flesh behind her knees, she stifled a groan. What would he do if she wrapped her legs around his waist and pulled him down on top of her?

Professional artists don't sleep with their clients, she reminded herself.

Not true, she answered. *Georgia O'Keeffe married her first big client.*

Even more frustrating was the fact that McCall didn't even seem to notice how turned on she was. Occasionally he would ask if she was comfortable or how his pressure was, but otherwise, he seemed content to let her enjoy her massage without interrupting her thoughts.

That would have been fine if she were just innocently enjoying a massage, but under the circumstances, a little interruption would have been welcome. As it was, she had nothing to think about but how much she'd like to turn this rubdown into a carnal act.

It was all she could do not to whimper when he finished kneading her thighs and moved his hands away. A man who could make her legs feel that good—what kind of magic could he do with the rest of her?

When her arms were like limp strands of spaghetti, he rolled her over onto her stomach and had her put her face in the cradle built into the table for that purpose. Through the opening, she could see his feet and legs. When he went up on his toes, his calves strained against the denim of his jeans. She barely managed not to moan out loud.

"Are you okay?" He leaned over to murmur in her ear. The smell of chocolate enveloped her.

"I'm fine." Her voice sounded like a parrot squawking, but at least she'd managed to get the words out.

He stroked the sides of her rib cage. Against the sports bra built into her tank top, her nipples hardened into chips of granite. With expert strokes, he worked the tension out of her upper back—or maybe he just displaced it. Her vagina felt like a clenched fist. In a few minutes, he would move on to her glutes. If his hands slipped between her thighs, she couldn't be responsible for what happened.

But he made no move to access the territory between her legs. She couldn't decide if she was relieved or disappointed. A few minutes later, she made up her mind: definitely disappointed. When he finished, he pulled the sheet back over her and layered a heated blanket on top of it. It would have felt like heaven if she were able to feel anything but lust.

"Feel free to lie here as long as you like," he said and left her alone in the darkened, scented room.

Arrggh.

After Keeffe got dressed and left, McCall mumbled, "Why didn't we screw her?"

We weren't going to screw anybody. Bad kept that thought to himself.

McCall had an enormous tolerance for the orange pills. He'd managed to stay awake but, fortunately, not awake enough to be a problem.

"She wanted to boink, you know." He sounded groggy, but also frustrated.

Yes, I got that.

"Then why didn't we?"

Bad ignored him. Taking advantage of Keeffe wouldn't be conducive to Bad's long-term plan—gaining her trust. He'd scored an important bit of information while they were priming the walls today. He now knew at least one thing that would help make up for losing the statue. If he could determine what Lilith had done with Rachel's chisels, and if they hadn't been destroyed, and if he could retrieve them, they could help incentivize Keeffe to give up the statue. That was a lot of *ifs.*

"We could have gotten laid." Anger seemed to be rousing McCall from his torpor.

Not my goal.

Which wasn't strictly true. Before the massage, Bad had given up considering a physical relationship with Keeffe. She wasn't necessarily out of his league, but she was out of his species. But forty-five minutes of stroking nearly every inch of her body had left him wanting her as much as she'd seemed to want him. Molding his hands over her firm muscles had brought home what a beautiful body she had. He'd longed to touch more of her satiny skin. He'd had to call up some of his worst memories from Hell to remain flaccid.

"It may not be your goal," McCall said, "but it is mine. I haven't gotten any since you've been here."

Bad empathized with McCall's disappointment, but it didn't alter his determination to treat Keeffe as off limits.

The mission has to come first.

McCall continued to complain until Bad challenged him to a *Call of Duty* playoff. They played for a few hours but at eleven o'clock, to Bad's surprise, McCall announced he was tired.

Thank badness. Tonight would be a good night to turn in early. While McCall had been missing sex, Bad had been missing sleep. He hadn't had a full night's rest since he'd been Above.

He awoke in the depths of the night to discover himself engaged in coitus. His first clue was that their hips were pistoning like a pile driver. The second was the animal smell that permeated the room. The sheets were tangled around his ankles and a sheen of sweat covered his skin.

For one horrified moment he thought Keeffe had returned and McCall had jumped her. Then the aroma of black licorice reached his nostrils. That wasn't Keeffe—that was Lilith. He wasn't sure whether to be relieved or squicked out.

For a moment he considered aborting this sexual engagement. It would take very little to plant an image in McCall's visual cortex that would wither his erection. But McCall had been so resentful at not pursuing coitus with Keeffe, maybe it was better to let him complete this sex act with Lilith. Bad regrouped in McCall's pre-frontal cortex and solved quadratic equations until they finished.

Once they were done, Lilith sat up and swung her legs over the edge of the bed. Bad tried not to notice, but Lilith naked was hard to ignore. Her sizeable breasts seemed immune to gravity, but Bad liked Keeffe's slim figure much better. McCall reached for Lilith's ass, but she batted his hand away.

"I need to get back before Daniel notices I'm gone." After pulling her low-cut sweater over her head, she stepped into a pair of insanely high heels.

She leaned over and gave McCall a kiss that made Bad want to gag. Then she sashayed out the door.

McCall drifted off to sleep, but Bad was wide-awake. His control over McCall was diminishing. If he didn't do something to change the trajectory, McCall would soon figure out how to take command whenever he wanted. And, deal or no deal, Bad was pretty sure he'd do just that.

CHAPTER 13

*B*ad was still dead to the world when "The Mephisto Waltz" issued from the phone lying on the nightstand. He groaned. A morning that started with a Facetime with Satan was not destined to be a good day. He picked up the phone.

"I need your ass down here," Satan said. On the little screen his face was burgundy.

Bad struggled to a sitting position. "What for?"

"Now."

Bad was still bleary, but even half asleep he knew if he vacated McCall's body, he might never regain possession. "What about my mission?"

"You can return later. Right now, I need you in Hell. Pronto."

"What do you need?" Bad asked. "I can prepare better if I know what tasks you want me to handle when I get there."

"It's colder than a snake's snatch down here." Satan's tone was a snarl. "We're freezing our asses off."

Oh, for the love of... "Did you call Ornias?"

"Fuck Ornias. It's your system. Get down here and fix it."

Bad tried to come up with an alternative that didn't involve yielding his tenuous grasp on McCall's body. Inside his head, McCall woke from the profound sleep of a man who had done a grueling workout, primed hundreds of square feet of wall space, and then engaged in intercourse for half the night.

Is that Satan on the phone? he asked.

Bad muscled McCall out of Broca's region before he could say something that would tip off the boss that Bad's command of his host was incomplete.

"If it's just the climate control system," he told Satan, "I can remote in from here and take a look."

"I don't want you to look at it from there," Satan said. "I want you to come fix it."

"I can probably get it working quicker from here." He'd brought all his remotes with him, just in case he needed them. Where had Ronnie put his backpack? He looked around the bedroom for the leather bag.

That moment of inattention was enough to give McCall an opening.

"Your demon sucks," McCall announced. "If you want a real demon, you should hire me."

Satan's gaze sharpened. "What the fuck was that?"

Bad scrambled to shut McCall up, without success.

"You're supposed to be all-powerful and this loser is the best you can do?" McCall said. "Recruit me. I'd be ten times the demon he is."

Satan's gaze sharpened into two laser-red points. "You don't have control of the subject."

"I do," said Bad.

"He so fucking doesn't," McCall said.

"I do." With an extreme effort, Bad shoved McCall back out of Broca's region.

Satan gave Bad a look that should have melted his phone. "I'll see you down here inside the hour." The screen went dark.

Shit. Shit. Shit. Shit.

Take me along. McCall was back already, verifying Bad's belief that his control over his host was waning. *Maybe I can smooth things over with your boss.* McCall pictured himself chatting with Satan like an applicant at a job interview.

He really didn't have a clue.

"That's not going to happen." It was hard to say which would infuriate Satan more—McCall's daring to trespass into the confines of Hell or Bad's allowing it.

Because you know I'd show you up for the loser you are. McCall's sneer echoed inside his skull.

The possession manual hadn't mentioned how claustrophobic it would be, living inside someone else's body.

Not to mention that as long as McCall was in residence, Bad couldn't pursue any kind of physical relationship with Keeffe. Aside from the squick factor of a two-on-one—the mere idea made Bad's metaphorical skin crawl—he didn't trust McCall not to take things somewhere pervy.

Maybe McCall really did need a come-to-Satan moment, a lesson in how the demon world really worked. Maybe he needed to see the kind of punishments the boss meted out, and to realize those punishments weren't temporary, like a human jail term, but eternal. Maybe he needed to experience the full extent, reach, and misery of the Hellish domain. Maybe Bad should take McCall to Hell and just leave him there.

Maybe he should.

He could allow McCall to tag along to Hell. It wasn't as if McCall would be the first tourist to visit the netherworld. That Italian had written a whole travelogue about his adventure. Once there, Bad would take McCall on a little visit to DemSec. Since McCall was more into monetizing inventions than creating them, he would be interested in the next wave of innovation that would be appearing Above. Knowing what was coming would position him to profit from it.

When they got to DemSec, Bad would draw McCall to one of the dark caverns beneath the technology hub. There, he'd extract McCall's soul from his body and seal it in a secure vessel designed for just that purpose. Then he could finish up this mission without his annoying twin interfering. Once the mission was complete, he'd reunite McCall's soul with his body and send him home.

"You know what?" he said. "You're right. Let's go to Hell."

With Ronnie's assistance, Bad exited McCall's body and reanimated his own. Compared to McCall's, it felt odd and undersized. On the other hand, it was much better suited to Hell's climate.

McCall stretched. "Oh, yeah. Much better without you hanging around, clogging up my brain."

Bad ignored that. Whether McCall liked it or not, once he had McCall's essence stowed Below, he would repossess McCall's body.

"Are you ready to go?" he asked.

"Not yet. A couple of years ago, I bought some boots to hike the volcano fields in Hawaii. I'll need them for Hell," McCall said.

One of Bad's first projects when he joined DemSec had been to put chiller coils under the floors in the areas frequented by Satan's staff. He didn't say anything, though. He didn't want to lessen McCall's enthusiasm in any way.

After McCall left the room to find his shoes, Bad turned to Ronnie. "I plan to leave McCall down there."

"Good," Ronnie said. "You've been letting him run roughshod over you."

What exactly was Bad supposed to do? He'd nearly suffocated McCall in the weight room, but his resulting mastery had lasted barely an hour. And he couldn't drug him all the time. Humans were very subject to addiction.

"I need to visit Ring Seven while I'm down there," Bad said.

Ronnie's shaggy brows pulled together. "Why Seven?"

"Reasons," said Bad. If things went north, he didn't want Ronnie implicated.

What Keeffe wanted, more than anything, were her mother's

chisels. Lilith's status reports indicated she had sent everything she'd cleared from the Blackmon house Below. Bad had hopped onto the inventory database and searched for the items Lil had turned in. Most of them had burned to ashes long ago, but the chisels were a high-grade tungsten-steel alloy, with a melting point of 6000 degrees Fahrenheit. There had been a couple of failed attempts to destroy them, then a transfer record indicating they'd gone to the high-temp furnace at the center of Ring Seven. According to the records, they were still there, awaiting the next big blaze.

"You'll need waders to cross the Phlegethon," Ronnie said.

Bad had his own scheme for fording the river of boiling blood that ran through Hell, but waders were a good backup plan.

"McCall has a pair in the garage, in the storage cabinet," Ronnie said.

"Does he have any other protective gear?" On Bad's way to the Burning Sands where the incinerator was located, he would have to pass through the Horrid Wood.

"For the Harpies?" asked Ronnie.

Bad nodded. The Horrid Wood was infested with vicious creatures with the heads of women, the bodies of giant birds, and the worst qualities of both.

"No," said Ronnie, "but he does have hunting camo."

If Bad couldn't protect himself, maybe he could pass undetected. "That could work."

"It's in the same cabinet."

Bad located the gear. His Mini Cooper was fine for him, but too small to accommodate McCall's height, so Bad stowed the equipment behind the driver's seat of McCall's four-wheel drive pickup truck. He could have requisitioned the equipment once he got to Hell, but if Lilith found out he was planning to return the chisels to Keeffe, she would throw a hissy fit, and there was no telling where Satan would land on that. He wanted the statue, but he had a bias favor of human misery.

Ronnie went back into the house, returning a few moments later with a key ring. He removed an old-fashioned skeleton key from the ring.

"The Ring Seven furnace is off-limits to most demons," he said. "Here's the key."

Bad had a master key, but he appreciated the gesture, so he accepted Ronnie's offer. Bad examined the key. The bow was not a simple oval, or even an elaborate scrollwork design like many old keys. Instead, it contained an engraving of an eye.

"Interesting," he said.

"It's sometimes useful," Ronnie said.

Before Bad could follow up, McCall joined them. Bad stuck the brass key in his pocket and held out his hand for the car keys.

"I'll drive," McCall said. Using his superior height, he held the keys out of Bad's reach.

He still thought this trip was going to be fun and games. Bad couldn't wait to correct that assumption.

"If Bad drives," Ronnie said from the doorway, "it will give you more opportunity to look around."

McCall thought about that. "Okay, you can chauffeur me."

He tossed Bad the keys.

Out on the road, Bad pressed the gas pedal almost to the floor. To get to Ring One, the truck would have to exceed 130 miles per hour, the speed at which the portal to Hell opened. Reaching that speed would be a challenge on the curving highways around Sedona.

Ideally, Bad would have driven to the interstate and entered the portal from there, but I-17 was at least twenty minutes away. Satan had once sentenced a demon to a year in the feces storms of Ring Three for keeping him waiting five minutes. Under Bad's foot, the truck accelerated until the needle quivered at 125.

McCall grabbed onto the strap. "Dude, if you wanted speed, we should have taken the Lotus."

Bad pushed harder on the pedal. Off a curve in the road ahead, the portal to Hell opened. Against a background of red rocks and blue sky, only the flickering flames lit the blackness inside the squat doorway.

"Woah! What's that?" asked McCall.

"That, my friend, is Hell." Bad jerked the wheel to the right.

The truck hit the berm and went airborne. McCall screeched. When the tires touched back down, they were in Hell. The truck careened onto two wheels as Bad swerved to avoid a stalagmite. Beside him, McCall hung on for dear life. Maybe now he would realize how fragile he was.

McCall threw back his head. "Yee-haw!"

Or maybe he was too stupid.

They rolled over a surface so rough even the heavy-duty tires and custom-made shocks on the 4x4 couldn't absorb the jolting. McCall bounced up and down, restrained only by his seatbelt. Bad gripped the steering wheel as the road threw them from side to side.

Occasionally a rock flew up and banged against the undercarriage. Bad expected McCall to complain, or at least to worry that the terrain would damage his precious vehicle.

Instead, McCall leaned forward to scan the Hellish landscape with eager eyes. "This place is seriously bad. I mean, like, bad."

"No kidding."

Alongside the truck, the river Phlegethon roiled, filling the air with the coppery smell of blood. Beneath the 4x4's tires, the surface grew worse. They rolled over a pothole so deep McCall's head banged against the truck roof. He laughed like a maniac, but Bad slowed the truck to a crawl. If they lost the oil pan, they'd have to walk the rest of the way down the Rings.

When they reached Ring Three, Bad turned on the windshield wipers. The wiper fluid was all but useless against the mix of snow, rain and excrement that fell constantly.

McCall wrinkled his nose. "Eww. That's gross, dude."

Finally, he was starting to get the picture.

They passed a garbage dump guarded by Cerberus, the three-headed hound. Naked, obese people picked through the garbage in search of something, anything, to satisfy their hunger. As the truck rolled past, one pudgy fellow tried to climb on board. One of the mongrel's heads swung around and, with a snap of its massive jaw, clamped onto the man's ankle. The man screamed as Cerberus dragged him back. The dog's sharp teeth raked puffy flesh, tearing through muscle and tendon. Gouts of blood squirted, dripping from the dog's jowls. He shook his victim like a rag doll as the man wept and pleaded.

Bad expected McCall to freak out, but he watched the scene with glee.

"Too bad we don't have those on Earth," he said. "It would be pretty hard to get past a guard dog like that."

"Don't you feel bad for the guy?"

"That fatty? No way. If fat camps on Earth worked like that, maybe some of those porkers would actually lose some weight."

This guy had less compassion than some demons Bad knew.

They rolled into Ring Four, the one dedicated to misers and wastrels. Surely McCall would empathize with these sinners. Opposing mobs, loaded down with boulder-like weights, stood behind glowing yellow lines. The individual members were dressed in fine clothes—silks and brocades, velvets and leathers, Gore-Tex and microfibers—the most expensive fashions of their respective eras.

"These guys look okay," McCall said. "What's their deal?"

"These were the souls who dedicated their lives to accumulating wealth and possessions."

"Oh, yeah?" McCall leaned forward, fascinated.

At the clang of a bell, the mobs raced toward each other, dragging their weights. They clashed together as they reached top speed. Some fell to the ground and were trampled by the opposition or even their own teammates. The sound of bones cracking and howls of agony rent the air. One brawny fellow swung his weight around him in an ever-increasing arc, taking out everyone who got in range.

When only a few bloody souls remained standing, another bell rang and the melee stopped. Each side pushed their weights back across their respective starting lines. Blood stopped dripping, wounds closed, and the crippled slowly straightened, in the recurring cycle of healing and harm that was the trademark of Hell.

Once they were in place, they turned to face each other, waiting for the signal to start again.

"Woah." McCall's eyes were saucerlike.

Ha. He had realized the eternal cost of his lifestyle.

"There's another reason why it's important to stay buff," he said, nodding sagely.

Or not.

When they reached Ring Nine, Bad parked the truck outside Satan's rec room and made his way through the enormous ebony doors. The air in the room was chilly. The boss sat on his throne, directly opposite the big screen, huddled inside black lynx fur. Braziers blazed on either side of him. At the sight of McCall, his face darkened and flames danced in his square pupils.

"What is he doing here?"

Bad shrugged. "He wanted to see Hell."

McCall bowed deeply. "Good morning, Your Highness. I'm a great admirer of your work."

Above the silky black fur, Satan's skinny eyebrows rose. McCall wasn't what Bad considered intelligent, but he was good at flattery.

"Great place you have here." McCall bowed low again. "The design is brilliant."

Inside his lynx-skin coat, Satan practically purred with pleasure.

"I was especially impressed by how each ring is custom-tailored to the offender," McCall added.

Oh, brother. "Let's go fix the heat," Bad said. With a little side trip to DemSec.

"I'd rather stay here and talk with His Highness," McCall said.

Leaving McCall behind to share his opinions of Bad's screw-ups was the last thing Bad wanted to do.

"He's busy. Come on. I'll show you our state-of-the-art climate control system."

"Dude, it's an HVAC system." McCall shivered. "And it doesn't even work very well."

"That's an operator error," Bad said automatically. "Anyway, I thought you wanted to see Hell's technology."

"I can learn more from talking to His Worship." He gave Satan a look of adoration.

Satan preened. "Leave him here."

In the face of a direct order, there wasn't much Bad could do.

"Is he the best you've got?" McCall asked as Bad walked away.

"By no means," Satan said. "But he has particular skills that are sometimes useful."

Great.

CHAPTER 14

It took Bad only a few minutes to figure out what was wrong with the climate control system. Someone—probably Satan—had been futzing with the thermostat again. He set it to start warming the rings in two hours. That should give him enough time to retrieve the chisels.

The incinerator sat in the center of the innermost circle of Ring Seven, the circle dedicated to clients who had been usurers in life. To get to it, he would have to make his way through the two outer circles, preferably without being caught. The chisels were the most effective gift he could give Keeffe. They would win her gratitude and from there, he hoped, her trust. Going through channels would be a huge hassle that could take weeks and might still end in failure. Bad didn't have weeks and he refused to risk failure.

Near the entrance to Ring Seven, he parked McCall's truck behind a bank of stalagmites, away from the eyes of the patrolling centaurs, and checked the time. It was 9:55 a.m. The centaurs took their morning break at 10:00. The minotaurs were supposed to relieve them, but it had been centuries since the last break-out, and they'd gotten lazy.

With his universal remote, Bad shut off the Ring Seven cameras.

As long as he wasn't captured, it would be impossible to prove he'd ever been here.

He pulled his backpack from behind the seat and put the remote into the bag, where it joined the molecular accelerator/decelerator he'd been working on before being hauled away to the maggot pit. He'd gotten through beta testing when his work was cut short. Today would be its first live use.

McCall's hunting camo fit easily over Bad's clothes. He stepped into McCall's chest-high waders and slid his arms through the suspenders. Once he had them adjusted to his satisfaction, he strapped on his backpack.

The outermost circle of Ring Seven was for people who had committed violence against others. They spent eternity submerged in the boiling blood of the Phlegethon. The more violent the offender, the deeper their assigned location. If they tried to move to a shallower spot, the centaurs chivvied them back with a hail of arrows.

Keeping concealed behind the stalagmites, Bad made his way around the edge of the ring to the best spot to cross the river. It wasn't the shallowest, being nearly waist-deep, but only five clients were assigned there. Unfortunately, they were the biggest, meanest clients. In their previous lives, they'd led prison riots and they looked like they'd gladly do it again. He considered turning back, but then he imagined Keeffe's face, shining with joy when he gave her the chisels.

He blinked. What was he thinking? He was doing this for DemSec, not Keeffe. Giving her the chisels was just a way to soften her up.

A moment later a bell rang. From beyond the stalagmites came the clip-clop of centaurs' hooves, heading for the break room. When the sound died away, Bad rounded the jutting column of limestone and waded into the river. Even through the insulated waders, the water was hot enough to poach an egg. His leathery hide felt like it was being parboiled.

He'd hoped to cross the river undetected, but the biggest, ugliest client spotted him almost immediately.

"Hey, boys," he called to the other four as he waded in Bad's direction. "Looky here."

The other four turned. When they saw how small he was, they made their way toward him, grinning. Bad swallowed. Evidently their years in Hell had done nothing to lessen their violent tendencies.

He pulled his molecular accelerator-decelerator from his backpack and set it to Decelerate. Then he touched it to the bloody surface of the Phlegethon and pressed the button.

Instantly, a layer of red ice formed across the top of the river, extending in their direction. Within a few seconds, all five men were frozen in place. Ice continued to spread as far as Bad could see. Snaps and pops in the distance suggested the freeze continued well beyond his sightline.

He frowned. The device's range was greater than his projections had indicated. What if the chain reaction didn't stop? News of the Phlegethon freezing over would certainly get Satan's attention. He shook off his concern. He could always reverse the process by setting the device to Accelerate. He waded across the still-fluid part of the river and scrambled onto the bank.

The other side of the river held an open plain. Beyond the plain stood some trees. The cumbersome waders slowed him down, but he didn't want to chance leaving them on the bank. He'd need them again for the return trip. At the edge of the forest, he removed the waders and hid them behind a rock.

The Horrid Wood was his least favorite location in all of Hell. All of the vegetation—trees, shrubs, even weeds—contained human souls. If you snapped off so much as a twig, the plant would bleed and the tortured soul within would cry out. Those cries, in turn, called down the Harpies, who used their claws to further wound the trees, prompting further shrieks.

Bad took a deep breath and slipped into the forest, picking his way through with agonizing slowness to avoid brushing against anything herbaceous. After what seemed like hours, he reached the burning sands of the innermost circle without bumping anything or anyone.

The burning sands were packed with people. In recent years, with the advent of hedge fund managers, the sands had become so densely populated that simply being there was a misery, even without the flaming cinders that blew in the eyes and scorched the skin.

Fortunately, there was a back route to the incinerator. Bad edged around the crowd until he found the locked gate. He tried opening it with his master key, but the lock didn't yield. He stared at it, frustrated. After all the effort it had taken to get here, surely he wasn't to be stopped by a simple mechanical lock? Then he remembered the key Ronnie had given him. It turned easily in the lock.

Inside the barrier, he combed through a pile of trash destined for the incinerator, finding the chisels right where the inventory database had indicated. Blackened from previous trips through less-intense Hellish fires, they had the initials "RMB" engraved on their handles.

He put them in his backpack and made his way back around the circle of burning sands before creeping into the Horrid Wood. He was deep into the wood when he stumbled over a tiny sapling in the heavy gloom. A shoot broke off and blood flowed from the break. The sapling shrieked. Bad cringed.

"Shush, shush." He tried to comfort the sapling, but its wails only grew louder, attracting the Harpies. They swooped down from the sky, tearing off branches as they came. Each torn branch added its screams to the cacophony. Within seconds, the entire forest ran with blood and echoed with heart-rending cries. Bad stared around him in horror. He hadn't meant for this to happen.

He dropped to his belly, sheltering beneath some low bushes, trying not to snag any twigs or foliage, but it was impossible not to brush against something. Within seconds, his camo was soaked with blood. He sniper-crawled across the forest floor, wincing as each tiny plant he touched let out a scream.

He had never missed the ability to apologize more than he did today. He took a deep breath. His contrition wouldn't reduce their pain. The best thing he could do for them was to hurry up and get out of there.

The edge of the forest was in sight when one of the Harpies spotted him. Calling to her sisters, she dived toward him, claws bared.

He flinched, anticipating the rake of talons across his flesh, but her claws met only backpack.

She flew away, screaming in frustration. Bad let out a chortle that was mostly relief. At the sound, she circled back and emptied her bowels on his head. Her sisters quickly joined her. By the time he exited the forest, guano crusted him from head to foot. The reek of ammonia made his eyes water.

He peeled off McCall's camo, wiping his hands and face as best he could. Grabbing the waders, he headed for the river. When he got there, it was frozen solid as far as he could see in either direction. His mouth fell open. The decelerator function was far more powerful than he'd anticipated.

On the far bank, the centaurs waved their arms and shouted at each other and the clients. Despite Bad's stealth, the clients, waist-deep in the ice, spotted him.

"That's the guy!" they bawled. "He did this."

The centaurs glared at him across the river of red ice. If he told them who he was, they would let him pass, but he didn't want word of his presence in Ring Seven to get out. If Satan found out about this little side mission, he might confiscate the chisels and Keeffe would never see them again. On the other hand, if he didn't identify himself, the centaurs would be waiting for him when he reached the other bank.

Centaurs were famous for their bad tempers.

There were three of them and only one of him. They were much bigger and far faster than he. They were armed with bows and arrows, while he had only his molecular accelerator-decelerator, which didn't work on living things. The only advantage he had over them was his brain. He tapped the temple of his glasses and skimmed their Wickedpedia bios.

The smallest of the centaurs was Pholus. When he saw that Bad wasn't coming any closer, he reached for his bow and fired an arrow across the frozen river. It arced halfway across before clattering onto the ice. The centaurs moved restively on the far shore. Nessus, the second centaur, shot another arrow. It went farther but still fell short.

"Come over here," shouted the third, pawing the turf, "and let us trample you to a bloody pulp."

The thought of being trampled was not appealing. Bad's body would heal, but the process would be extremely painful. On the other hand, if Satan found out what he was doing… The thought of Keeffe's face, lit with joy at the sight of the long-lost chisels, stiffened his spine.

What else did he have in his favor? In addition to their inferior brains, the centaurs had surly tempers and bodies that would not fare well on ice. Tossing the waders aside, Bad stepped onto the ice. From beneath his feet came a sound like a gunshot. The frozen blood was starting to thaw.

"That's it, little Hade." Chiron, the eldest of the centaurs, beckoned him. "Come. Let us mangle you beneath our hooves."

Bad trained his gaze on Pholus. "What are you?"

The smallest centaur lifted his head proudly. "We are centaurs—a cross between a human and an equine."

"You're kind of puny. You look more like a cross between a monkey and a burro."

The centaur's face darkened. Swearing, he dashed out onto the frozen river, only to fall, legs splayed, and skid across the ice. Bad pulled out the AC-DC and set it to minimum acceleration. Inching closer to Pholus, but still well out of reach, he touched it to the ice. A ring around the centaur instantly melted. Pholus fell through, up to his haunches. Switching the gadget back to Decelerate, Bad refroze the ice around him.

"Help me," Pholus shouted to the others on the bank. Nessus and Chiron sidled anxiously but made no move toward him.

"They won't help you." Bad pitched his voice loud enough to be heard on the far bank. "They're cowards." He looked at Nessus. "Everybody knows that. That's why they call him Nessus the Wussus."

"Don't listen," ordered Chiron, but Nessus was already leaping onto the ice.

Bad quickly trapped him, too.

Nessus reached his arms toward Chiron. "Pull me from this ice. Together, we'll flatten the Hade."

Chiron crept to the edge of the bank, but he shook his head. He was smarter than the other two, and he had better control of his temper. If Bad couldn't get to him through anger, it would have to be through fear.

Reaching behind his back, he tugged a shiny disk containing backup software from his backpack. Without giving Chiron a chance to see what was in his hands, he slung the disk as if he were throwing a Frisbee. It flew toward the centaur's legs. With a shout of fear, Chiron jumped straight up in the air. When he came back down, the bank gave way beneath him. Bad raced across the ice and trapped Chiron, and then pulled himself onto the bank. He headed for the truck, but the wails of the centaurs made him turn around.

"You can't leave us here, trapped in the ice to starve," Chiron said.

"It will melt before you starve," Bad said. That was certainly true. It was already starting to thaw.

"But if the clients get free before we do, they will harm us."

Bad looked at the villainous faces of the five clients. That was also true. With a groan, he returned to the river. Trying not to slip, he set the gadget for acceleration and touched it against the red ice, once near Chiron, a second time beside Nessus, and a third time near Pholus. Fissures appeared in the ice around each centaur.

"You'll be free soon," he promised.

He ran for the truck. Now he just needed to dump McCall and he'd be set.

$\mathcal{B}$ack at Ring Nine, Bad found McCall literally seated at Satan's knee, snapping a selfie with Satan beaming over his shoulder. Bad eyed the pair with misgiving. What had McCall told the boss to make him grin like that?

Now that the heat was back on, McCall's handsome face dripped with sweat. His human body was ill suited to the normal temperature of Hell. Satan had shed his lynx-fur coat. As soon as McCall snapped the picture, Satan's cheesy smile disappeared, but he lolled back against his throne, clearly at ease and enjoying the warmth.

They were an unlikely duo. What in the world had they found to discuss that had put Satan into such a rare good mood?

"Our biggest single expense is monitoring," Satan said as Bad came into hearing range. "I spend a fortune on stoolie demons."

The tightness in Bad's solar plexus relaxed a little. It sounded like the boss had spent the last couple of hours bemoaning Hell's cost structure, a favorite topic.

"With the right technology, you could eliminate that cost," McCall said.

Exactly what Bad had been trying to tell Satan for centuries.

"Tried that," Satan grunted. "When Lilith made Daniel Blackmon build her a house to replace the hovel he lived in with his first wife, we spent a fortune wiring up cameras and mics, but whenever there's something she doesn't want me to see, they mysteriously go on the fritz."

"I've got just the thing to solve that problem," McCall said.

Satan's skinny eyebrows rose. "What's that?"

That was more interest than Bad had gotten him to display in technology in the last century.

"I've created a wearable monitoring device—a camera, mic and display built into a pair of glasses. They have two-way communication, allowing demons to request and receive information real-time. I call them Gehenna Glasses."

That credit-grabbing jerk.

Satan looked tempted. Then he shook his head. "I'd never convince the troops to use it."

"Make it a requirement," Bad said, stepping around a stalagmite.

Satan shook his head "The loss and breakage rates would be astronomical."

"Of course they would," McCall said. "No one likes to be coerced. The way to create acceptance is to pick out a few key thought-leaders and convince them the tech is to their advantage—maybe early adopters get some kind of perk, like extra vacation or a better office. That creates buzz, which, in turn, generates demand."

"That might work," Bad admitted grudgingly.

"It will work," McCall said. "This is how I became a billionaire—getting people on board new technology."

Satan clapped him on the back. "We could use more go-getters like you down here."

Seriously?

"It's been such a pleasure talking with you, Your Majesty," McCall said, staring up at Satan soulfully.

"Ditto," said Satan. "I look forward to seeing you again." For once, his smile lacked its usual meanness.

Time to break up this bromance.

"Before we head back, I'll take you by DemSec," Bad told McCall. And he'd leave McCall's technology-pirating ass there.

"What's DemSec?" asked McCall.

"Hell's technology hub," Bad said. "In addition to providing identities and equipment for demons on Aboveworld missions, DemSec is our center for research and development."

To Bad's surprise, McCall looked less than excited. He didn't get what a cool place DemSec was.

"A lot of the tech you see on Earth gets invented here," Bad said. "We release our discoveries to Earth's scientists and entrepreneurs as opportunities arise. You'll see stuff down here that won't appear up there for years, maybe even decades." It used to be decades and centuries, but timelines had contracted as the Apocalypse drew nearer.

McCall still didn't look impressed. "Why would we want to give them our technology?"

So that was it. McCall had already flipped his badge. He considered himself part of Hell. Bad waited for Satan to correct that assumption, but the old devil just smiled fondly at the human.

"I need to get back Aboveworld." McCall got to his feet, looking so eager it made Bad's teeth hurt. "Back to the mission."

Satan beamed at him. "We need to be sure the girl turns down that residency, or at least postpones starting until after her birthday."

The phone Bad had given her had relayed her conversation with the woman at Saguaro back to him and to Hell. Bad fought down a feeling of guilt. He hadn't betrayed Keeffe. He had just used the facilities available to gather the info needed to achieve his goal.

Once Keeffe postponed her start date, Bad would convince her that her siblings' approach—trading the sculptures for what they truly desired out of life—was what her mother would have wanted.

"Once she does that," Satan said, "we'll have her where we want her. She can either sell us the statue, or we'll invoke the fail-safe clause."

Bad kept his face impassive, though he had no intention of invoking Lilith's fail-safe.

"Exactly," McCall said. "Now that I understand what's going on, you can count on me, Your Majesty. I'm a team player."

There was no such thing as a team player in Hell. If there ever had been, that demon had been duped and betrayed and backstabbed until he learned his lesson. There was no sense in trying to explain that to McCall, though. His eyes glowed with the light of a freshly minted convert, ready to throw himself on his sword to prove his loyalty. And Satan was just lapping it up. A different strategy was called for.

Bad cleared his throat. "The thing is, Keeffe seems pretty turned off by our split personality."

"I'm glad you get that." McCall looked relieved. "That's why we don't think it's a good idea for you to go back. We think I should return and complete the mission on my own."

Satan was beaming at McCall the way a proud auntie beams at a clever nephew. They had planned this while Bad was off rescuing Keeffe's chisels.

"She doesn't like you," Bad said bluntly. He turned to Satan. "If you review the game films, you'll see that whenever McCall makes an appearance, the girl gets annoyed."

"That was because I didn't understand the mission. I've got it now. When I really set out to be charming, babes can't resist me."

Neither could Satan, judging by his doting expression.

"I'll get her into bed." McCall's self-confidence was as complete as it was unearned. "Once she gets McCalled, she'll give me anything I ask for."

He had no shot at seducing Keeffe, but judging by Satan's languorous eyes, if he'd been the target, McCall would have succeeded days ago.

To leave McCall here, Bad would need to convince, not just McCall but also Satan, that it was to Hell's advantage for McCall to remain Below. Deep in his pocket, Bad pressed a button on his universal remote.

The screen across from Satan's throne lit up with a giant image of Keeffe staring directly into the camera with Ernesto's Moonlight Grill in the background. She closed her eyes and lifted her face, her expression open and trusting. For a minute or two, the close-up was so tight you couldn't really see what was happening, but the audio told the story loud and clear. There was a moan and a soft sigh from Keeffe, followed by a clanging noise. The focus sharpened again as she shoved McCall away, rubbing the back of her head and looking furious.

Though not any more furious than McCall did at this moment. He opened his mouth, probably to deny the obvious facts of the video, but Bad cut him off.

"Isn't this guy incredible?" He slapped McCall on the back. "Not every inventor would be willing to share a video that shows him in an unflattering light just to prove how well his invention works."

Seth's mouth snapped closed. He looked down modestly.

Satan stroked his goatee. "We'd be able to get footage like that on all my demons?"

McCall's head popped up again. "Absolutely."

"That's why we need you down here," Bad said.

"Down here?" McCall squinted at him. "What for?"

"To implement the Gehenna Glasses rollout." Bad tapped the frame of his glasses.

Satan crossed his arms. "I haven't agreed to that."

"These things are incredible," Bad said. "In addition to recording every minute of the mission. I was able to use them to pull up research when I needed it."

Satan's arms unfolded. "Could I send orders to demons real-time?"

That was the nightmare scenario, but Bad wasn't planning to do any more missions after this one, so it wasn't his nightmare.

"Absolutely." McCall poured his smile over Satan like warm syrup over pancakes.

Satan stroked his goatee. "I can see where they could be useful." He turned to Bad. "You need to delay her start date for that residency."

"I can do that." Bad sent up a silent cheer. "Sounds like we have a plan."

McCall frowned. His face was red and sweat beaded his forehead. "But you need my body for your mission."

"I hadn't even thought of that." Bad pretended to be surprised. "You're right."

He waited for McCall to propose the logical alternative. When he didn't, Bad said, "I won't be using mine, if you want to borrow it while I finish up the mission."

McCall looked him up and down. "You're kind of short and nerdy."

"True, but my form is much better suited to the climate down here." Bad wiped his forehead and displayed his dry palm.

Satan pulled out his phone. "Let's see what Ornias has to say." He fired off a text.

Oh, great. Ornias made the centaurs look like geniuses.

A few minutes later, the double doors at the end of Ring Nine swung wide and Ornias marched in. Dressed in red-and-orange camouflage, his hair was a blond buzz-cut, showing off his perfectly formed skull and flawless features. His camo strained across a magnificent set of pectoral muscles, and his thighs looked like tree trunks. His appearance was less that of an action hero than an action figure. McCall snapped to attention.

"What's shakin', Satan?" Ornias asked as he approached the throne.

What a doofus.

Satan explained the situation. "He'll be working for you, so I thought we'd get your input. Bad thinks McCall would be better off in his body."

"Oh, he does, does he?" Ornias wrapped a beefy forearm around Bad's head and squeezed until Bad felt like his skull would crack. Then Ornias ground his knuckles into the tender spot between Bad's horns.

Bad tried not to make a sound, but when Ornias lifted him off the ground, leaving his body to dangle from his neck, he yelped.

"I can see why you'd like to jettison that body, geek boy," he said. "There's not an ounce of muscle on you. What's in it for tall, blonde, and gorgeous here?"

"Bad claims his body is more fire-resistant than mine," McCall said.

Without warning, Ornias punched McCall in the arm. McCall

stood at attention, not making a sound but, almost immediately, a purple bruise blossomed on his bicep.

"You're tough on the inside," Ornias said, "but geek boy is probably right. Human flesh isn't designed to withstand the conditions in Hell."

Instantly, McCall caved. "Well, if you think it's a good idea."

Ornias jostled him good-naturedly. "It's a great idea. And while you have his body, maybe we can bulk it up some."

McCall's eyes gleamed. "Great suggestion."

Bad didn't feel one bit good about their plans for his body, but what choice did he have? He started the process to make the switch.

When he was back in McCall's body, he climbed into the truck and drove up Ring Nine until he was out of sight. Then, he doubled back, staying behind a bank of stalagmites as he steered the truck toward a narrow, unlit passageway.

Before he left Hell, he had one more stop to make.

CHAPTER 16

*K*eeffe arrived at McCall's house early in the morning, but he wasn't there. That was probably for the best. She had a ton of work to get done and not much time to do it.

Yesterday's erotically charged massage had left her grinding her teeth and punching her pillow last night. If she was going to get this mural done in time to start at Saguaro on schedule, she didn't have time for distractions. That meant no more massages.

From a canvas duffle bag, she pulled a woodworker's pencil and a clear vinyl strip marked at one-foot intervals. Today's chore was to grid the wall to match the graph paper on which she'd sketched the planned mural. All five hundred and two square feet of it.

Might as well get to it. She plugged her iPod into the dock the way McCall had shown her the other day. Ed Sheeran's "Shape of You" poured into the room and she got to work. By ten o'clock, she'd completed a sixteen-foot section and it felt as though flames were licking up her back. She could take a break and start painting in background, but she wanted to show McCall the sketches before transferring them to the wall.

She went to find Ronnie, who was pulling a pan of buttery-smelling shortbread from the oven.

"Do you know when McCall will be back?" she asked.

Ronnie shook his head. "I don't, miss."

She ate some shortbread—it was sinfully rich—and went back to work.

By noon, when Ronnie came in to tell her lunch was ready, she'd finished nearly a quarter of the grid.

"Will McCall be joining me?" she asked, shrugging her shoulders in a vain effort to loosen muscles that had tightened into iron bars.

"I'm not certain, miss."

She wound up eating alone, grateful for the respite and the chef salad with avocado dressing. After thanking Ronnie for lunch, she grimly returned to work. The longer she worked, the stiffer her shoulders became, and the crankier she felt. Where the hell was McCall? Not that she'd accept a massage, even if he were here, but the least he could do was have the courtesy to be here so she could turn him down.

Bad made his way to the darkest, dirtiest corner of Hell, where a black gash in a wall of anthracite led to a steep trail into the bowels of the earth. He followed the downward slope for thirty or forty feet, until it grew so dark he had to take out his phone and bring up the flashlight app to see. Hade eyes were built for the dark, but McCall's weren't.

Beneath his feet, the trail grew warm, then hot. Even through McCall's volcano shoes, it was uncomfortable. Bad had never been able to get funding to install cooling panels under the streets of Hadeville. Satan insisted that Hades were adapted for scorching heat. While that might be true, McCall's body certainly wasn't. It was already awash in perspiration.

After another hundred yards, the trail made a 90-degree turn. He followed it still another 100 yards and around still another 90-degree turn before he came to an arched gateway carved into the coal. Glowing yellow lanterns on hooks flanked the opening. A sign above the entrance read *Hadeville*.

Pocketing his phone, Bad ducked through the doorway. Inside there was an expansive hallway, lined by still more arched doorways, with wooden doors and brass hardware. Gratefully, he straightened.

There were lanterns every few feet, suffusing the entire village with a soft yellow glow. The ambient temperature was probably 120 degrees. At the fourth doorway, he stooped to knock.

With a gust of cool air, the door opened to reveal a small man with ebony horns and a black tail. At the sight of McCall's hulking form, he backed up and tried to slam the door.

Bad stuck the toe of McCall's boot in the way. "It's me, Pa—Abaddon."

Pa stopped pushing on the door. "Bad?"

"Yes, it's me."

"Why are you wearing a giant's body?"

"I'm on a mission. I can't stay long."

Pa edged the door open. "Well, come on in, son."

Bad ducked through the doorway. His head rubbed against the ceiling. Pa hugged him around the waist and, clumsily, Bad patted his back. He'd never been taller than Pa before.

"Zelda," Pa called. "Bad's come to visit, but he can only stay a minute."

A woman with turquoise horns and a blue-and-green striped tail bustled out of the kitchen, wiping her hands. When she saw Bad, she stopped dead in her tracks, her eyes moving up, up, up until they reached his face.

"Bad?"

"Yeah, Ma, it's me."

Her face lit up brighter than the lanterns outside. She held her arms open and Bad walked into them, taking care not to bang into the ceiling light. The top of her head only came up to his chest, but she enveloped him in a hug nonetheless. When she released him, she pursed her lips. He bent his knees and tilted his head forward so she could kiss him where the tender spot between his horns would have been.

"Sit, sit," she said and hurried off. Bad's gaze followed her to the kitchen doorway. A young Hade with turquoise horns like Ma's and cotton-candy pink hair stood there. Even his eyebrows were pink. It took Bad a moment to recognize his brother's eldest son.

"Phoenix!" He straightened, banging his head into the ceiling. "Ow!"

Phoenix grinned. "Hey, Bad. Looking…tall."

Bad laughed. "It's a loaner. I'll have to give it back when the mission is over." He looked at his nephew curiously. "How old are you now?"

"Eighteen," Phoenix said proudly. "I graduate from high school this spring."

How had that happened? It seemed like only yesterday Phoenix had been a toddler, chewing on his tail and ramming his little horns into Bad's shins.

"What are you planning to do when you graduate?" Bad asked.

"College," Pa said.

"Not sure," said Phoenix.

"Of course you're going to go to college," Pa said. "You don't want to wind up working in the mines."

Phoenix shrugged. "Hade University is great for history and philosophy, but they don't really get technology. I'm not sure how much they have to teach me."

Bad had a sneaking feeling of sympathy for his nephew. He'd had the same feeling about college, and he'd been right. Maybe he could bring Phoenix into DemSec as an apprentice and teach the boy himself.

Phoenix checked the colorful watch on his wrist. "Oops, gotta go." He popped back into the kitchen to say goodbye to Ma, then gave Pa a quick hug. As he released Pa, the old man gave him a quick pat down and came up with a small paring knife.

The boy grinned. "You win this round." He headed out the door.

"I can't believe you're still playing that game." Bad frowned as he sank onto the sofa, the only piece of furniture large enough to accommodate him. "It's like you're teaching him to steal."

Pa hunched his shoulder defensively. "We like the challenge."

Ma returned with a tray. "It's no different than you and Pa hiding each other's flashlights."

It was, actually, but it was clear they didn't see it that way.

The tray held a cup of tea and a bowl of nectarines.

"I know how much you love these," Ma said. "We just got a shipment of fresh fruit."

That had been one of Bad's first actions in DemSec—bringing fresh fruits and vegetables to the Hades. Today's kids were taller than their parents because they ate a better diet.

"Now tell us why you're wearing a Goliath suit," Ma said.

Bad leaned forward to grab the cup of tea. McCall had become dehydrated on the trek here. Inside his jeans pocket, Ronnie's bulky skeleton key poked him in the groin. He took the key out of his pocket and set it on the end table.

"I'm on a mission," he said. "If I'm successful, Satan will put me back in DemSec, where I can do some good for the Hades again."

"We Hades are doing just fine." Ma poured him a second cup. "You don't need to consort with the likes of Satan for our sakes."

Bad didn't argue, but she was wrong. Without him to champion them, the Hades were little better than slaves, living like cave people without modern amenities.

"Why are you here, son?" Pa asked.

"There's a woman," Bad said, growing a little nervous at the sparkle that came into Ma's eyes. "She has a birthday coming up. I thought maybe I could pick a couple of pieces from the junk box so I'd have something to give her."

"What a good idea." Ma jumped up and left the room, returning with a battered bronze box. She set it on the table.

"Phaedra and Phereby—" she named his brother's younger children—"were here the other day." She wiped the box with a damp cloth. "It's all sticky."

Running water was another of Bad's upgrades to Hadeville. Hot water had been easy, but cool spring water had taken some doing.

When Ma finished wiping, Bad flipped the lid of the box open. Inside was a pile of gold and platinum jewelry—diamonds, emeralds, sapphires, rubies and dozens of other stones. The entire living room brightened as the overhead light bounced off the contents of the box.

"What's she like?" Ma asked.

"She's an artist." Bad picked through the baubles until he found a simple set of gold earrings and matching necklace.

"You can't take her that old junk," Ma said. "Your Uncle Mo made those when he was a teenager. An artist will think they're completely amateur."

"She's a human artist," Bad said. "This will be finer than anything she's ever seen."

"A human?" Ma's face fell. "Not a girlfriend?"

"Not a girlfriend," Bad said. For a wistful moment, he wished she were, even though that could never work out.

He downed a second cup of tea, put the jewelry in his backpack, and got to his feet. They walked him to the door.

"I know you hated working in the mines," Ma said, "but I wish you'd find something to do that didn't mean working for Satan. He corrupts everything he touches."

It was an argument they'd had with every visit since the day Bad went to work in DemSec.

"Life is better for every Hade down here since I started working for him." And if Bad completed this mission successfully, he'd be in a position to improve their quality of life even more.

"We don't need you to sell yourself to make us comfortable," Ma said. Tears filled her eyes.

Pa put a comforting arm around her shoulders and kissed her temple.

"Bad will be fine, Zelda," he said. "He knows right from wrong."

The trip back up the rings was eye opening. Inside McCall's body, the drive was spooky, even frightening, but an incredible sense of lightness offset that fear. Hade bodies were much denser than humans, probably due to millennia of the intense gravity at the core of the earth. The bodies of fallen angels were less dense than Hades, but still heavier than humans. McCall's form felt like his bones were made of feathers.

What didn't feel good was the guilt Bad experienced every time he thought about what he was doing to Keeffe. At some point during his quest to retrieve the chisels, he had started feeling uncomfortable about taking the statue.

Keeffe had done nothing to him, but he was exerting his considerable intelligence and skills to take from her the one thing she valued most in the world. He tried telling himself the chisels would make up to her for the loss of the statue, but it wasn't true and he knew it.

Then he thought about his parents, and all the things he could do for his people. Sometimes you had to look at the greater good.

It was nearly three o'clock before McCall showed up. For some reason, Keeffe expected him to take one look at all the work she'd done and offer praise and a back rub. Instead, he inspected her grid work with his nose almost touching the wall.

"Would you like to borrow a magnifying glass?" she asked, irritated.

He straightened. "This is how you make a mural?"

"It's how I make *your* mural." She knew she sounded disagreeable, but she couldn't seem to change her tone.

"My mural?" He wasn't wearing his glasses, but his eyes were brown. The smell of smoke overwhelmed the chocolate aroma that always accompanied his brown eyes. He must have gone camping overnight.

Even though she knew she was being completely unreasonable, it pissed her off that he'd been out playing while she was here working.

"Yes," she said. "Your mural. You know—Superman, Captain America, Green Lantern." She'd put hours into choosing characters and settings and color palettes. And the sketches were beautiful. She'd done what Ed suggested, ignoring her artistic discomfort and throwing herself into the work until the concept came alive. McCall had damned well better appreciate it.

She took the scale model from her portfolio and unfolded it. She held it out, draped across her upward-facing palms like a table runner, daring him not to like it.

Bad stared at Keeffe, trying to figure out what she was so upset about.

"I divided the room into eight panels that are each just under eight feet wide," Keeffe's shoulders were up around her ears as she gritted the words out. "Each panel will contain a different scene that revolves around one specific character. Each scene will have its own color palette. It will be set against his familiar background and feature the other characters who try to help or harm him." She glared at Bad. "Well?"

Why was she angry? He frowned at her, puzzled and more than a little concerned. She should like him more, not less, now that McCall was gone.

"That is what you wanted, right?" She spat the words at him.

It was what McCall wanted, but it wasn't what Keeffe wanted. She wanted to paint a landscape. McCall was the one who'd insisted on the superheroes. Satan didn't care what she painted, or if she painted at all, as long as Bad's plan caused her to give up the statue. He could let her paint the landscape she wanted to paint and then bring art critics here to see it. He could give her an art career. It was essentially the same trade her sister and her brothers had made—their mother's legacy in exchange for their own dreams.

"I thought you wanted to paint a landscape?" he said.

She stilled. "You said you didn't want that."

"You convinced me to change my mind."

"You never told me that."

"Yes, I did," he said. "Several times."

She looked around the room, chewing on her lower lip. He could see she desperately wanted to take him up on his offer. Then she looked at the strip of drawings in her hands.

"Before you decide," she said, "why don't you look these over?"

He reviewed them, one panel at a time. "These are great, really good, but you've sold me on recreating Sedona."

"You're kidding." She dragged her hand through her hair.

He shook his head. "Nope. I want a landscape of Sedona."

"You're serious, aren't you?" There was more than a touch of frustration in her voice.

"Dead serious."

After a long moment, excitement replaced the irritation on her face. "Sfumato." Her gaze swept around the room. Her smile blazed.

"Pardon me?" Bad said.

"Sfumato—it's a painting technique, layering these really thin glazes. Da Vinci used it a lot. It's what gives his work its amazing depth."

"Sounds intriguing," he said politely.

She nodded, but her eyes were on the walls. He could see her planning her epic landscape. The excitement she'd shown the first time she saw the room was back.

"It will take longer than painting the comics would have," she said, after a few minutes. "I figured I'd have the comic mural done in early February, but there's no way I can do justice to a landscape mural that quickly. How would you feel about me starting work on this in mid-March?"

"March?" If she started the Saguaro residency before her birthday, Lilith's fail-safe clause would mean nothing. Keeffe would have the money she needed to keep her statue before she ever started work on the mural.

It really didn't change Bad's plan, which was based on trust rather than extortion, but Satan had been very clear. If Bad didn't get to her to delay, Satan would yank Bad back Below, back to pushing a broom. He'd never see the inside of DemSec again. The improvements he planned for Hadeville would be tabled indefinitely. And in Hell, *indefinitely* could easily mean centuries.

He gestured to the nearest gridlines. "You mean, leave it looking like this for two months?"

She rumpled her hair. "I know. I'm sorry." She explained about the residency.

"This"—her wave encompassed the room— "is a great commission but working at the park will give me a lot of exposure."

"The problem is," he made his voice sympathetic, "I've already contacted *Art in America* and the *Times*—both New York and LA—about coming out when it's finished."

He hadn't, but he would.

"Just because you invited them doesn't mean they'll come."

"They'll come," he said. And they would, too. Just as soon as she agreed to sell him her statue.

Her face blazed brighter than a Sedona sunset.

"I'll call the park tomorrow and let them know I can't start there until April."

"Will they let you do that?"

Once she made that call, she would be at Satan's mercy. He would be able to exercise the fail-safe clause at his whim. But he wouldn't. For whatever reason, he wanted Keeffe to give up the statue as willingly as possible. The fail-safe method would force her to make a reluctant choice, while Bad's approach would lead to her selling the statue without being constrained in any way. It was a win-win-win. He, Satan, and Keeffe would all get what they wanted.

"I don't know," Keeffe said. "I hope so."

He hoped so, too. Satan would get her statue, one way or another. If they did it Bad's way, at least she'd get something in return.

She returned her attention to the room.

"You know what would be fun?" She turned in a slow circle, her mind clearly somewhere beyond this space. "To treat this room like you can see through the walls and paint what you would see if you could see far enough. Do you know what I mean?"

He imitated her actions, but all he saw were gridlines. "Not really. What would you see?"

She checked her watch. Her analog watch. Why was this woman so determinedly old school?

"We can't go today. It's almost five and the sun will be setting soon, but tomorrow I'll show you." She started packing up her stuff.

"What's your hurry?" He was disappointed. He'd planned to give her the chisels after dinner.

"I facilitate a group at church on the third Wednesday of the month. It starts at six-thirty."

There had been nothing in her dossier about that.

"What kind of group?" he asked.

"Grief recovery. I lost my mother when I was fourteen. It took me a really long time to get over it. In some ways, I never really have, but the grief group really helped. When the last facilitator quit two years ago, Father Xavier asked me to take over."

"Your mother must have been very young," he said. He was on safe ground. If a human died before their ninetieth birthday, their survivors felt their life had been cut short.

Keeffe nodded. "Forty-five."

He ran the calculation in his head. The average life expectancy for a U.S. female born in the 1960's was 73.1 years. Rachel had died 28 years earlier than the mean. In this case, Keeffe's sense of being short-changed was valid.

"My mother passed away last spring." That was half true—his current body's mother had died the previous April.

Keeffe frowned. "I thought you told me your parents were both still around?"

A pit yawned before his feet.

"My dad is still alive." He grasped for enough details to make himself sound credible. "And my stepmom, but my birth mother died." Internally, he winced. Ma wouldn't appreciate being killed off for the sake of one of Satan's missions.

Keeffe's face creased in sympathy. "I'm so sorry. What happened?"

Bad reviewed McCall's long-term memories. Candace McCall had crashed her car while high on cocaine.

"Car accident," he said.

"Would you like to go to the meeting with me?" Keeffe asked.

"I'm not Catholic," he said.

Keeffe put her hand on his arm. The gesture was comforting, friendly, and trusting. Exactly where he wanted to take this relationship.

"That's okay," she said. "The group is nondenominational."

The church was a cream-colored building. From the parking lot you could view the red rocks of Sedona in three different directions. Would he ever tire of sunshine and blue skies? Bad didn't think so. Keeffe led him past a statue of the Virgin Mary with an emaciated, agonized Jesus sprawled across her lap.

Other denominations might gloss over the grisly details of Christ's sacrifice, but Catholics were unflinching.

Keeffe slipped in through a side door with the comfort of long habit. She paused at the back of the sanctuary to dip her fingers in the font of holy water and cross herself.

Bad didn't attempt to mimic her. The flesh of fallen angels melted like candle wax when they touched holy water. Hade skin didn't react to it, but he didn't understand the value proposition of the ritual. Keeffe's face glowed as she performed the rite. It was clear she derived something from it. He followed her down the hall to the community room.

She started the meeting with a prayer, which Bad supposed he should have expected. Other demons complained that hearing human prayers was physically painful, but all Bad experienced was an uncomfortable compulsion to ruminate on the moral dimensions of his mission.

It was true he planned to engineer a situation to make Keeffe give up her statue, but by any objective measure, she would be better off when he left than when he arrived. By allowing her to paint a landscape and arranging for art critics to review it, he was giving her the opportunity that would make her career. At that level, this mission was morally neutral. Once you threw in the advantages for the Hade community, it was a net good.

He still felt lousy about it, though. Pa would never have treated Ma that way.

Keeffe finished her prayer and raised her head. She pulled a small book from her purse.

"Who would like to read today's devotion?" she asked.

The guy sitting on the other side of her took the book and read a passage about turning your fears and grief over to God. Keeffe put the book back in her purse and pulled out a laminated card.

"Who wants to read the ground rules?"

A fifty-something woman with reddened eyes volunteered. She read the rules in a shaking voice. The man sitting next to her squeezed her arm comfortingly.

Keeffe thanked her. "Who'd like to go first?"

Watching her with the group, it occurred to Bad that she might give up the statue willingly if she knew how much good it would do for the Hades. It was a shame he couldn't tell her. Another idea struck him. What if he convinced her he was in trouble, and the statue was the only way to save him?

She caught his eye, her face questioning, and he put the idea on the back burner for later consideration. Beside him, a middle-aged man with a balding head raised his hand.

"My daughter, Emily, died in a car crash last summer," he said, his voice husky. "The other driver was texting."

As the group made sympathetic noises, Bad shifted in his chair. Texting had been his brainchild, one he'd had no problems getting the Hellish Scientific Council to release Above. He'd thought texting would be useful for the kind of asynchronous communications he'd described to Keeffe. The Council had liked the way it dehumanized human interaction. Coupled with the distraction factor, they deemed it a no-brainer for release into the world.

The bereaved father went on to describe his wife's depression and his other children's despair. One had attempted suicide. Another was on mood stabilizers. Bad squirmed, even though these were unintended consequences.

But were they?

Well, they were on his part. It wasn't the technology, but the way the technology was used, that was the problem.

The next person to speak was a young guy with long, stringy hair. "My brother was killed in Afghanistan. Something went wrong with the controls on his plane and he flew into the side of a mountain."

Bad let out a sigh of relief. People had wanted to fly ever since the first Neanderthals set eyes on the first birds. The fact that one of the earliest applications of flight technology had been to make war was in no way his fault.

Every single person in the group seemed to have lost someone to technology gone amok. By the time the circle came around to him, Bad was itching to escape. He passed on the opportunity to share.

Keeffe went last. Tears shimmered in her eyes as she spoke.

"When I was fourteen, my mom went into the hospital for what was supposed to be a routine hysterectomy. They used one of those surgical robots. They said it would be safer and she'd heal quicker, but it nicked her iliac artery. By the time someone noticed, she'd bled out."

Bad listened with horror. DemSec had developed that technology. The Hellish Council had initially refused to release it Above because the positive aspects were so overwhelming. Feeling a little bit like Santa Claus, Bad had snuck it through as part of a wave of automation that eliminated human jobs.

Why had he thought coming here tonight was a good idea? How did humans ever enjoy life on this planet? Their existences were as prone to misery as a fire was to shooting sparks.

At the end of the meeting, Keeffe finished with another prayer. As if he weren't dejected enough, rumination swamped his brain again. As much as he preferred having his head to himself, right now he would have almost welcomed McCall's thoughts as a distraction.

What, exactly, did Satan plan to do with those statues? There was something about the four of them, in the aggregate, that wasn't true of a single statue, or even the three Satan had already collected. And it wasn't just concern that the statues might boost the power of Rachel Blackmon's crosses. Bad pictured the statues together, and a sense of doom overwhelmed him.

He tried to move on to another topic—he was even willing to go back to thinking about how badly he was treating Keeffe—but his mind stayed stubbornly fixated on the statues. Satan intended something very bad with those sculptures. He knew it. He could hack into Satan's heavily encrypted email and see if he could discover what it was, but what would he do with the information once he had it? He was relieved when Keeffe finally said "Amen."

Out in the parking lot, he walked her to her car. She put a hand on his jacket.

"It gets easier," she said.

He stared at her blankly. "What gets easier?"

"Dealing with your loss." Her mouth trembled, giving lie to her words. "Talking about it."

He felt like a louse. "I—it's okay."

"I saw you fidgeting," she said. "And how you couldn't share with the group."

"Thanks." He ran his fingers through McCall's crisp hair. "I'll—maybe I'll feel like sharing next time." There would be no next time. There was no way he'd go back into that forum and hear all the ways his inventions had destroyed people's lives.

Just when he thought it couldn't get any worse, it did. Keeffe wrapped her arms around him, like a small animal burrowing into warmth. Her hair smelled like flowers.

He put his arms around her.

She lifted her face to look at him. Would she kiss him if she knew he had a hand in the technology that killed her mother? Almost certainly not.

He thought about the plan he was hatching, the one to fool her into sacrificing her beloved statue to save him, and felt like the biggest jerk on the planet. Or under the planet.

She frowned, clearly concerned about the pain she thought he felt over the loss of his mother. His real mother would like her, he thought —a lot. She was beautiful, brilliantly creative, and deeply kind. Every month she came here and confronted memories she'd clearly prefer to forget in the service of helping others come to terms with their grief.

It was a kind of selflessness and courage he'd never seen in Hell. At least, not outside the borders of Hadeville.

But her upturned face was too much to resist. She was too beautiful, too remarkable. He lowered his mouth to hers. Her lips were soft and pliant beneath his. He stroked his hand over her midnight hair, feeling the silkiness of it against his palm. His insides seemed to light up.

How did this work? How did the simple action of pressing his lips to hers, stroking his tongue against hers, generate pin-wheeling fireworks all through his body? He'd never felt this before, not with Lamia or any of his other girlfriends over the centuries. He gathered her closer and she melted against him. Matters of conscience took a backseat to aching need, and he lost himself in the wonder of the smell and taste and feel of her.

It wasn't till the slam of a nearby car door called them back to themselves that he raised his head.

"Come home with me?" he asked.

"I would," she said, "but I need to get an early start tomorrow."

The chisels he'd rescued from Ring Seven were still in the truck. He'd been so anxious to see her he hadn't even taken his backpack into the house. If he got them out and gave them to her right now, he was 95 percent certain she would come home with him, but the idea of using her gratitude to tip the scales in his favor felt sleazy.

He gave himself an eye-roll. He had a tool that would help him achieve a desired goal, but he refused to use it. Every demon he knew would have whipped out those chisels without a qualm, especially after what he'd gone through to get them. McCall would call him a loser and Satan would point to it as proof that he was incompetent at fieldwork. But leveraging the chisels to get Keeffe to have sex with him wasn't something he was willing to do.

He kissed her again, a chaste kiss of comfort and friendship, before opening her car door.

"I'll see you in the morning," he said.

"In the morning." She gave him a misty smile and got into her car and drove away.

Bad spent the next six hours attempting to hack into Satan's email server, but someone had put up a sophisticated firewall he couldn't get past. He would crack it eventually, but it would take time. He frowned at his laptop, chewing on his lower lip.

Halfway through his marathon hacking session, Ronnie brought him a cup of coffee. He said thanks and returned his attention to his laptop but the old demon didn't leave.

When Ronnie cleared his throat, Bad looked up from his screen. "What's up?"

"Do you have my key?" Ronnie asked.

Bad patted his pockets. No key. Then he remembered. "I left it on the end table at my mom's house. Do you need it for something right away?"

Ronnie shook his head. For some reason, he looked almost pleased. "You can get it the next time you're down there."

"Thanks." Bad lifted his hands, the closest he could come to an apology. Ronnie nodded and Bad turned his attention back to his screen. Who had built this nearly impenetrable firewall? It would have taken his top two or three technology guys working together to layer on this much security. The bigger question was why they had bothered. He was the only person in Hell with technical skills that would require a firewall of this sophistication to keep him out.

What was it that Satan didn't want him to know?

CHAPTER 17

The next morning Keeffe called Annalisa at Saguaro.

"The commission I'm currently working on will take longer than I anticipated. Can I change my start date to the first of April?"

"I'm afraid not." Annalisa sounded dismayed. "The next artist-in-residence starts then. We need you here by the last week of February, at the latest, to give the staff time to prepare the cabin for him after you leave."

Keeffe calculated in her head. It would be tight, but as long as she stayed focused, she should be able to complete the mural and get herself to Tucson by then. The second task would be much easier with a reliable vehicle—the Honda needed brakes and tires.

She felt a moment of panic as she realized that her new start date was more than two weeks after her birthday. Then she told herself not to be silly. McCall had already transferred the deposit into her bank account. Even Mr. Hyde couldn't take that back now.

"February twenty-seventh will be great," she said.

When Keeffe arrived at McCall's, he was still in bed.

"Then wake him up," she said when Ronnie gave her the news. "He promised to go look at rock formations with me today."

"Bad really enjoys his sleep," Ronnie said.

Keeffe cocked her head. "Bad?"

Ronnie blinked rapidly. "It's a nickname."

"*Bad?*" she said again,

"It's meant to be ironic."

As though summoned by his nickname, McCall came into the hallway, wearing only pajama bottoms. When he saw her, he stopped yawning and stretching, but his brown eyes still looked adorably drowsy.

"Hey, Bad," she said, testing it out.

His gaze shot to Ronnie, who shrugged.

"I guess my secret is out," Bad said. He didn't seem all that upset.

"The first of many," she said. "Are we going hiking? I want to get your input on which scenes to feature."

"We are going hiking," he said, finally waking up. "Give me five minutes."

Given his narcissism, it would probably be more like an hour. Keeffe went to the mural room and started a list of additional paint colors she'd need for the new project. To her surprise, Bad reappeared about ten minutes later, fully dressed but unshaven.

She couldn't resist rubbing the palm of her hand across his jaw. His ears turned pink.

"You said you were in a hurry, so I skipped shaving."

"It's okay," she said. "I like you scruffy,"

After Ronnie fed them breakfast, Bad handed Keeffe the keys to the truck.

"You drive," he said, pulling out his phone. "You know where we're going."

His concern over what Satan was hiding on his email server had blossomed into full- fledged anxiety overnight. While he was getting dressed, he'd had a couple of ideas about how to get past the firewall. It was harder to do from a mobile device, but possible.

After a few minutes, Keeffe turned off 89A and followed Soldiers Pass Road for about a mile and a half to the Rim Shadows parking lot. Bad slid his phone into his pocket.

"Check this out." She waved beyond the windshield to her left. "If you could look due north from your house and see past all the stuff that's in the way, this is what you'd see—Coffee Pot Rock."

In the distance loomed a red rock formation in a shape reminiscent of an old-fashioned percolator.

"This is the formation you can see from Ernesto's, isn't it?" he asked.

She gave him an approving grin. "You pay attention."

"Are we hiking there?"

"Not today." She pointed to another formation, on the right. "See that one? If you look at it from the right angle, it looks like the Sphinx."

It did, but without the Sphinx's horrifying history of slave labor and death.

She led the way up Soldier Pass Trail. He followed her, typing a command into his phone as he walked. The code got him exactly nowhere.

They hiked down a dry creek bed. A trio of mule deer bounded past but he barely noticed. For a moment, he thought his next attempt would work.

Access denied.

Frustrated, he glanced up from his phone. Straight ahead, the Sphinx jutted up against the sky. Keeffe stopped walking so suddenly he almost ran into her.

"This is why I hate technology," she said.

He blinked. "What?"

"You have the most gorgeous scenery in the world all around you, but you're so focused on that stupid phone, you're not even seeing it."

His face warmed. "I'm trying to…"

"I don't care," Keeffe said.

He shoved the phone into his back pocket.

They arrived at an angular cutout in the cliff underpinning the Sphinx. A monstrous slab of red sandstone blocked the entrance.

"This is the Devil's Kitchen," Keeffe said.

Bad cracked up. It so wasn't.

She waited for him to explain, but he shook his head. "Inside joke."

Because he could tell how important this was to her, he left his phone in his pocket while they hiked to a descending series of shallow ponds connected by waterfalls.

"These are the Seven Sacred Pools," Keeffe said.

"They look more like seven puddles."

Her face fell. "They're usually deeper. It hasn't rained much lately."

"They're very cool," he said quickly. "You should include them in the mural."

She chewed on her lip. "Do you think so?"

"I do."

Her face brightened. "Okay, I will."

When they started back up the trail, his mind drifted back to the firewall conundrum. The outermost layer of security had Scrote's coding signature all over it. Scrote almost always used a hashing algorithm based on his current girlfriend's birthday. Bad hadn't talked to him since going into the maggot pit. Who was Scrote seeing these days?

He pulled up Scrote's Eternagram page. Every picture showed him with a pair of she-demons Bad didn't recognize.

Keeffe made a growling noise under her breath. "What is it with you and that phone?"

He shoved it back in his pocket.

She took him past a few other formations—Steamboat Rock, Camel Head, and Snoopy Rock.

"Are we going to hike to them?" he asked.

"You seem pretty preoccupied," she said.

"A little," he said, his mind drifting back to Scrote's possible hashing scheme.

She practically race-walked back to the truck.

When they arrived at the house, Keeffe got to work, sketching the planned mural onto the wall.

"Aren't you going to make a model?" Bad asked.

She shook her head. "With a landscape, I won't have to be so meticulous. An extra inch or two of mountain isn't like someone's eye not being in the right place."

To her surprise, instead of heading off to play video games or to his workout room, Bad settled down on a couch in the mural room with his laptop. She was still annoyed about his phone-induced distraction that morning. How many cat videos could one person watch?

She wasn't sure why it bugged her so much, but it did. Other people seemed to find so much to fascinate them on the Internet. A lot of it was stupid and a waste of time, but she felt left out nevertheless. Just before lunch, he laughed aloud at something he'd found online.

"Come check this out," he said.

It was probably something she'd have to read. "I don't have time to play around on the Internet. I have work to do,"

He looked disappointed and a little hurt, which made her feel rotten, but she wasn't about to let him see how difficult reading was for her.

When they broke for lunch, he offered her a shoulder massage, but she waved him off.

"I'm good."

He instantly stepped back, looking crestfallen.

After lunch, feeling grumpy and stupid, she drove downtown for the Senior Watercolor class. Frida was already there when she arrived. The minute Keeffe walked in the door, her sister shoved a pamphlet in her face.

"Read this," Frida said. "It will make you feel better."

On the front cover, a heavily pregnant woman smiled blissfully. Keeffe didn't have to make out the letters *I, V,* and F to know what the pamphlet was about.

"How about we get the class set up first?" Deflection had worked with Bad that morning when it came to reading. Maybe she'd get lucky and it would work with Frida, too.

"It doesn't start for another fifteen minutes." Frida dashed that hope. "No students are here yet."

Keeffe took the pamphlet. The type was small with a serif font that made the letters run together. It would take more time than she had to spend to sort everything out.

"So, what's this supposed to tell me?" She injected enough attitude into her tone to make it sound like she'd read it but wasn't impressed.

Frida grabbed the pamphlet and smacked Keeffe's arm with it. "That it's perfectly safe."

An image of Mom lying in her casket, her eyes closed, her face still and lifeless, rose before Keeffe's eyes. Mom's hysterectomy was supposed to be perfectly safe, too, but Keeffe had lived without her for the past eleven years.

As though she were reading Keeffe's mind, Frida took in a deep breath through her nostrils.

"Keeffe, seriously, you've got to let go of that. Sometimes stuff happens. We don't live in a perfectly safe world, but sometimes a fluke is just a fluke."

"True," said Keeffe, "but we can choose not to put ourselves in unnecessary danger."

"If you refuse to move with the times, you get left behind."

"That's okay. I'm perfectly happy, right where I am."

"And that's fine," Frida said, "but I'm not. I want a child. And this technology is my best option for having one."

Before Keeffe could respond, Sister Mary Grace and Father Xavier came through the door. Frida whisked the IVF pamphlet out of sight, reminding Keeffe that the Church viewed IVF as a sin. Keeffe didn't view it as immoral, just dangerous.

"What are we painting today?" Father X asked.

Like a magician, Frida produced a handful of scarves in different colors and fabrics—gold brocade, white silk, purple satin, and red velvet.

"We're going to work on color and texture."

Father Xavier reached out to stroke the purple scarf. "That looks like the stole I wore when I was an exorcist."

Keeffe gawked at him in astonishment. "You were an exorcist?"

The old priest nodded proudly. "I was the diocesan exorcist for Chicago back in the '70s."

Keeffe tried to picture him with shaggy hair and a purple stole, commanding a demon to leave someone.

"Was there a lot of demon possession back then?"

He nodded. "It was a troubled time. I drove a demon out of an anti-war protestor once. He was planning to blow up an armory." His hands trembled at the memory.

"Maybe we should set up our easels, Father." Gently, Sister Mary Grace took his arm.

"Of course." He beamed at Keeffe and Frida. "Today is our painting lesson."

They headed for the supply cupboard.

"Whew," said Frida, shaking her head.

Keeffe stared after them. "I wonder how much he's remembering, and how much he's imagining."

"It's hard to say." Frida hesitated. "Thanks for not mentioning the IVF."

"No problem." Keeffe had no problem with that part of it. She figured God could put a soul into a test tube as easily as he could a uterus.

Over the next couple of weeks, Bad mostly stayed in the mural room with her. After the first few days, he became less focused on his work and more available. When she needed to move the ladder, he jumped up to help, setting it exactly where she needed it. She tried to stay out of his way when he did that. Even the most casual brush of his arm against hers made her weak in the knees. His days of Internet distraction had given her time to remember what a creep he'd been when she first met him. She needed to keep her distance.

But it wasn't easy.

He had changed in some indefinable way since he returned from his camping trip. Well, not completely indefinable. Some of the changes were easy to define, actually. His eyes hadn't turned gray once since he'd been back. He'd stopped carrying two different cellphones. And he'd stopped spending hours in his workout room. Instead, he hung out with her, occasionally chatting as they worked on their separate projects.

Sometimes he shared a little about what he was working on, but she didn't understand much of it. He was crazy smart. What would he think if he knew she couldn't read? Okay, technically, she could read, but for all practical purposes, she might as well be illiterate. If they grew closer, at some point he would figure that out.

Another reason to stay away from him.

He closed his laptop, got up from the couch and crossed the room to where she stood on the ladder, painting Bell Rock onto the southeast curve of the room.

"What's that?" he asked.

She made a series of swooping passes with her brush. "The energy vortex at Bell Rock."

"I remember you talking about the vortices at Ernesto's," he said, but his eyes were on her jean-clad bottom.

The day she finished this mural she was going to take him up on that.

"Vortexes," she said. "Here, we call them vortexes."

"Okay." His tone was absent, his eyes still on her butt.

She swallowed. "There are four of them."

His gaze flashed to her face, sharpening. "Four?"

She nodded. "I told you about them at Ernesto's that first evening."

"Right," he said. "Remind me where they are."

"There's one in Boynton Canyon, one at Bell Rock, one out by the airport and one at Cathedral Rock."

"Can we go see one?" His eyes sparkled with excitement.

Keeffe blinked. "Sure."

"Now?"

What a strange guy he was.

She looked at the wall she'd been working on. It needed to dry before she applied another coat of glaze.

"I guess so." She climbed down from the ladder. "Bell Rock is only a few miles from here, and it's an easy hike."

He was already moving toward the door.

Bad could feel the energy pulsing as soon as he got out of the truck. A twisted juniper tree stood along the edge the trail.

"This path leads to the vortex." Keeffe pointed at a foot-worn trail leading from the parking lot. "It's about three and a half miles."

He checked the position of the sun. It was already starting its descent in the western sky. Strange, how quickly he'd grown accustomed to orienting himself to the yellow orb.

"We need to move fast, then," he said. Keeffe started up the path, setting a rapid pace and moving like she was familiar with the terrain. Every so often, she would throw a backward glance over her shoulder.

On the third iteration, he said, "No phone today." He was currently out of ideas for decrypting Ornias's firewall.

She grinned. "Good." The trail widened, and she slowed to let him draw even. His arm brushed against hers. She jerked away, muscles tense. After a moment, she relaxed. She cast a sideways glance at him.

"What?" he asked.

"Don't take this the wrong way," she said, "but why were you such a jerk when I first met you?"

A laugh burst from his mouth. "And how am I supposed to take that the right way?"

"You know what I mean."

Bad did know what she meant, but he could hardly explain his possession of McCall. "When you have things other people don't have," he said, "whether it's money or an ability, a lot of people look at you like you're this fruit tree that's ripe for plucking."

She nodded. "I hear you. There are a lot more people who want to own my artwork than want to pay for it."

He shrugged. "I learned pretty quickly to keep up my defenses if I didn't want to be taken advantage of."

She touched his forearm again, this time intentionally. The warmth spread up his arm and across his torso.

"That sucks," she said.

"Kind of."

They soon reached the base of the formation. From there, they climbed up a series of five-foot walls interspersed with plateaus. It was easy to get handholds and footholds in the porous sandstone. Like some of the formations in Hell, it sometimes gave way beneath their feet, showering pebbles on the person below.

Bad was soon perspiring, but Keeffe scrambled up the rock faces like it was effortless. The farther they went, the more strongly he felt the energy.

When they'd been climbing for a little over an hour, Keeffe came to a halt and opened her arms, like she was absorbing the energy pulsing there.

"Meditation Perch was Mom's favorite spot," she said. It was clear she was happy to be at this spot where she'd shared time with her mother.

He looked around the plateau. Next to a mesquite tree, a quail nested. Nearby stood another gnarled juniper. This one appeared to have a face twisted into its knobby bark.

"That tree was her inspiration for *Matthew*," Keeffe said. "The statue Frida used to own." She still grieved for the beauty lost to the world. He could hear it in her voice.

The first of the Evangelist statues he'd seen in Ring Nine was winged, but it didn't look much like an angel. Rachel had reproduced the gnarled face in the tree for the sculpture. It lent support to his hypothesis that there was some sort of connection between the statues and the vortexes.

Thus far, he'd only managed to read the metadata for the emails being sent from Satan's server, but that was enough to validate his suspicion that Satan had a plan that required having all four statues together. He just wished he knew what that plan was.

"Did she get the inspiration for the other statues at the other vortexes?" he asked.

"She came up with the idea for *John* at Cathedral Rock," Keeffe said. "I'm not sure about the other two."

But he was. He grabbed her hand. "When can we go see Cathedral Rock?"

She drew back. "Not today. It's too late."

"Tomorrow then?"

"Sure." She looked at the sun, which was rapidly descending, and shivered. "We'd better get going. There's a new moon tonight. A hiking trail isn't the best place to be when there's no light." She took a single step and froze.

Bad heard it before he saw it, a sound like a rattle being shaken. On the trail between them, a rattlesnake lifted her head. Her diamond-patterned scales seemed to dance in the red dust.

Bad started toward Keeffe but she murmured, barely moving her lips, "No. Stay where you are."

She moved her left foot one careful step backward, but there was a rock wall right behind her. She couldn't climb onto it without the kind of sudden movement that induced rattlesnakes to strike, and there was nowhere else for her to go. The snake raised her head another inch. Her tongue flicked out, tasting Keeffe's scent on the air. Her diamond-patterned head undulated back and forth. She seemed to find Keeffe as intoxicating as Bad did.

Keeffe slid her foot sideways, but dips in the sandstone, eroded by centuries of wind and rain, made it impossible for her to find level footing. So slowly it was as though she wasn't moving at all, she lifted her foot. The snake's head danced closer. Keeffe froze again. The single leg bearing her weight shook. Her trembling seemed to fascinate the snake.

Keeffe's eyes were so wide that white showed all the way around her irises. Moving only her eyes, she looked at the ground beside Bad, then at him, then at the ground again. There was a forked stick lying there, but the wood was too rotten to use as a weapon. The rhythm of the snake's rattles increased. It was getting ready to strike.

"Sister Snake." Bad raised his hand in greeting and hissed in sibilants the serpent could understand. "This prey's size is excessive. Go search for sustenance more suitable."

The snake whipped around to face him. Keeffe tried to scramble up onto the rock wall, but it was too high to scale in one bound.

"Brother Demon," it hissed in return. "What business is it of yours where I hunt?"

There had been bad blood between Serpentdom and Hell ever since that little affair in Eden had cost snakes their legs. Serpents believed Satan had conned them into taking the blame—and the punishment—for his actions.

They weren't wrong.

"None at all, Sister Snake." Bad bowed his head respectfully. "I simply state that you'll never be able to swallow the woman."

"She smells of flowers," the snake said. "She would taste sweet as nectar. I may not be able to eat the woman, but I can taste of her flesh."

Not without sending venom coursing through Keeffe's veins. Bad thought frantically. According to Lamia, his former girlfriend, snakes' favorite delicacies were ground-dwelling birds. Perhaps the rattler could be redirected.

He mellowed his voice into a seductive hiss.

"A quail with a nest full of eggs sleeps close by. If you move swiftly, you may surprise her."

The snake's head wove back and forth as she considered that.

"She nests just beyond that mesquite," Bad said.

After a moment, the snake inclined her head. "Thank you, Brother Demon." She slithered off through the dust.

Bad released a shaky sigh of relief. His armpits and the palms of his hands dripped with sweat, but Keeffe was safe.

"What just happened there?" Still backed against the rock wall, Keeffe watched him with wide eyes.

Bad thought quickly. "I read somewhere that if you hiss at snakes, it makes them go away." That was lame, but she would never believe the truth.

Her face didn't relax. "It looked like you were talking to each other."

Perhaps because she was an artist, Keeffe's powers of observation seemed to be much more acute than most humans'.

"Okay, you got me." Bad spread his hands, palms up. "I talked to the snake. I told her quail was more her size, and where to find one."

Keeffe raised a shaking finger to flip him off. She was still trembling from her close call.

He crossed to her. "Do I get any points for rescuing you from a snake?"

"You get all the points."

To his delight, she grabbed his head and yanked his face down to kiss him. It wasn't a gentle thank-you kiss, either—more like take-me-I'm-yours.

She could so easily have been killed. The thought horrified him. He pulled her hard against him, relieved beyond measure that she was still alive. Human exoskeletons were so fragile. It was incredible any of them survived to adulthood. He cupped his hands around her head, threading his fingers through her dark hair. He held her still, plundering her mouth, a tide of joy and relief and gratitude rolling through him like he'd never felt before in his life. He never wanted to let her go.

To his delight, she responded by grabbing his ass and grinding her pelvis against his. Blood roared into his groin. He slid his hand beneath her shirt, up her delicate rib cage, to fondle the softness of her breast inside her cotton brassiere. She arched her back and groaned against his mouth. He slipped his hand inside her bra. Her taut nipple grazed the palm of his hand. More blood forsook his brain. Gently, he tweaked her nipple. Keeffe wrapped her leg around his thigh. It was like they were back out at the lamppost.

But this time it was just the two of them.

Cupping her ass, he lifted her off the ground without removing his mouth from hers. She hooked her ankles behind his back, grinding herself against his erection. If he had any blood left anywhere else in his body, it immediately abandoned its assigned post to gravitate to where the action was.

A moment later, they were copulating on a flat rock. It wasn't slow and intoxicating, as he'd dreamed their first lovemaking might be. They couldn't get their jeans off fast enough and they didn't even bother to remove their shirts or jackets. He was on the bottom, his bare ass rubbing against the equally bare rock. As soon as he rolled on a condom, Keeffe slid her body over him, sheathing him in heat and honey and muscle. He had to grit his teeth not to lose it right then and there.

She leaned over him, grabbing his shoulders and riding him like a jockey sprinting for the finish line. Beneath him, the sandstone was cold, and it scraped his lower back mercilessly, but he hardly noticed. He had dreamed of this moment every day as he'd watched the beauty of Sedona take shape on the walls of McCall's house at the tip of her gifted paintbrush. Since the first time he'd set eyes on her, if he were truthful. He would have made love with his backside rubbing against a cheese grater if that's what it took.

After a few minutes, he knew he wouldn't be able to hold out much longer. The feeling was just too good. He wet his fingers in his mouth and reached between her legs to stroke her. A scant instant later, she screamed out her orgasm to the open sky, her muscles clutching him in a way that robbed him of self-control. He shouted his release along with her.

When the echoes died away, he gathered her against him. His hands wandered down her jacket to caress her rounded bottom. Her skin was smoother than anything he'd encountered in his entire six hundred years.

"Survivor sex," Keeffe said, stretching luxuriously. "How was it that you just happened to have a condom handy?"

Thank badness, she seemed to have forgotten her curiosity about his conversation with the snake.

Beneath him, the sandstone was like a glacier. Bad was pretty sure once his flesh warmed enough to have feeling again he'd discover friction burns on his lower back, but it was so incredible to have Keeffe straddling him he didn't care.

"I put it in my wallet the day I met you," he said.

Above him, she raised her eyebrows. "You thought I was easy?"

That surprised a shout of laughter from him. "If I did, I quickly realized my mistake. Not even your worst enemy would call you an easy woman."

She grinned. "So, what, you just hoped you'd get lucky?"

"Yes," he said. "I hoped to get luckier than I've ever been in my life." A wide smile, one he knew looked goofy and uncool, split his face. He couldn't wait to get her home and do this all over again, in a bed. "And I did."

She leaned forward to kiss him. "I think I did, too."

CHAPTER 18

That was worth waiting for, Keeffe thought as she drove back to Bad's place. She'd called it survivor sex, but the truth was she'd been lusting after her geeky sponsor since the first time she met him. Well, maybe not the first, but definitely the second.

Bad kept his hand on her knee all the way home, as though wanting to assure himself that he was really allowed to touch her. Such humility from a jillionaire hottie was flattering, and so sweet it made her eyes mist a little.

When they got to the house, he said, "I have a present for you."

"A present?" Keeffe asked, but he'd already disappeared down the hall.

He reappeared a few minutes later, bearing a gift bag that sagged at the bottom like it contained something heavy. It clanked as he handed it to her. Intrigued, she dug through tissue paper, pulling out a heavy steel chisel. It wasn't new. In fact, it looked like it had been through the fires of Hell. Despite the heat discoloration, it looked familiar. Her eyes flew to the handle. There, inscribed in the metal, were the initials "RMB." Rachel Marie Blackmon.

Keeffe's eyes brimmed with tears. She thrust her hand back into the bag, counting with her fingertips. They were all there. All dozen of them.

"Where did you get these?" she asked. "*How* did you get these?"

He grinned the goofy grin she was coming to love. It made his unnaturally handsome face look less classical and more human.

"Do you like them?" he asked.

She rubbed the chisel against her cheek. "They are the best present anyone has ever given me. How did you find them?"

"Ebay," he said. "After you told me about them, I started looking for them, and there they were." He looked embarrassed. "The case was gone. They must have gone through a fire."

"No, no, they're perfect." She offered up her mouth in a kiss, which he accepted with enthusiasm. "You're perfect."

He looked uncomfortable. "Furthest thing from."

She let that go. "How long have you had them?"

"A couple of weeks."

"Two weeks?" She was astounded. "Why are you giving them to me now?"

He blushed. "Because of the sex."

"They're a thank-you present?" That was a little weird, but the gift was so wonderful and unexpected she continued to stroke the chisel, tracing the block letters of her mother's initials with her fingertips.

He turned even redder. "No. I didn't want you to think I was trying to bribe you into sex, so I figured I'd wait until it was clear, one way or another, what was going to happen."

She stilled. "You would have given them to me either way?"

"Of course," he said, looking surprised that she would ask.

She put the chisel back in the bag and twined her arms around his neck. His mouth was gentle on hers, and warmth blossomed low in her belly.

"Again?" he asked.

"Again," she said.

"Slower this time." He took her hand and led her to his bedroom. The enormous bed had been made, the giant zebra-striped comforter placed with precision, coordinating pillows piled at the top.

"Look at that," she said. "I hope you realize what an angel Ronnie is."

His lips quirked. "I know exactly what kind of angel Ronnie is."

Bad insisted on undressing her. He unlaced her hiking boots and removed them, stopping to rub her feet with the same erotic effect as when he'd given her the massage two weeks before. By the time he stripped off her jeans, she was ready, but he really seemed to be into the foreplay.

"You have great legs." He kissed his way up the inside of her thighs. She thought he'd remove her panties, but he focused on the cuffs of her flannel shirt, unbuttoning each one with care before working his way down the front of her shirt, kissing each inch of skin as it was exposed.

His eyes seemed to glow in the dim light as he feasted them on her body. He made love with the same single-minded focus he'd displayed when they kissed. It made her feel beautiful and desirable and horny as hell.

By the time he dipped his mouth to her taut nipples, her breasts were clamoring for the touch of his tongue. He licked and sucked until she grabbed his hand and pressed it against the crotch of her panties.

"Don't be in such a hurry," he said, rubbing the pad of his thumb across the fabric between her legs. She arched toward him.

He grinned. "More?"

She clamped her hand around his wrist. "More."

"Slow down." He hooked a finger inside her panties, stroking the slick flesh there until she moaned.

"You're a little overdressed," she gasped, reaching for his fly.

"Not yet." He pushed her hand away. "Let's focus on you."

He slid her panties down over her hips, and his fingers seemed to blaze a trail of fire everywhere they touched. Once her panties were off, he spread her legs and kissed the inside of each knee.

He was going to drive her crazy.

He ran his hand up her bare thigh. "Your skin is the texture of a nectarine."

She choked on a laugh. "A nectarine?"

He nodded seriously. "It's smooth, but with an underlying firmness, like a perfect piece of fruit at the perfect stage of ripeness."

All this and poetry, too.

His lips followed his hand and she groaned with pleasure.

He slid a finger inside her, and then a second one. She closed her eyes and moaned as his fingertips stroked the front wall of her pelvis, pressing each square inch as though determined not to leave any spot untouched. When she opened her eyes again, he was watching her face, his head cocked to the side as though he were monitoring her reactions.

"What?" she said.

At that precise moment, he found her G-spot. Her eyes rolled back in her head. "Gaaah."

"That," he said with satisfaction. His fingers moved in a slow, circular motion, deft and precise. Deep inside, her climax gathered, as inexorable as the sun rising over the Black Hills each morning.

She wound her hands into the comforter on either side of her to stop herself from being swept away, but when he bent forward to lick between her thighs again, she couldn't hold on.

Her orgasm was like an explosion of brightly colored paint, covering every available surface in oranges and reds and pinks and purples, a blast of heat and pleasure and God-it's-good-to-be-alive. It rolled on and on, like a thunderstorm breaking over the mountains as his talented fingers and mouth coaxed every bit of pleasure from her body. It was only when she thought she couldn't stand it any longer, that her pelvic muscles couldn't remain clenched any longer, that he withdrew his mouth and stilled his fingers.

She lay limp on the bed, a puddle of liquid muscle and melted bone while he stroked his hands down her torso as though he still hadn't gotten enough of touching her.

Her eyelids felt like they weighed fifty pounds each, but she forced them open. "Now you."

He grinned and reached for his zipper, but the words were barely out of her mouth when her cellphone buzzed. She was going to let it roll to voicemail, but he picked it up off the nightstand and handed it to her.

"Ignore it," she said, making no move to take the phone.

He looked shocked. "What if it's something important?"

Most guys would have thought there was nothing more important than getting their turn.

Taking the phone, she tapped "answer."

"Hey, Keeffe—are you coming out tonight?" It was Camille. "Frida's running late, but Suzanne and I already have the nachos on order."

Keeffe stifled a groan. "Ugh. I forgot." Girls' Night Out was a monthly event.

"You're not coming?" Her sister-in-law's voice echoed with disappointment and a little hurt. It was one of Camille's few opportunities to be around other adult women without toddlers underfoot.

Keeffe covered the microphone with her palm and explained the situation.

"I forgot all about it." She scrunched her nose apologetically.

Bad's mouth drooped like a child denied a toy. Given that his erection looked like it was about to burst through his fly, she couldn't fault him for that. Almost instantly, though, he slapped on his game face.

"You should go," he said.

She looked pointedly at his crotch. She didn't want to abandon him in this state, especially not after all he'd done for her. On the other hand, she despised women who dumped their girlfriends as soon as a guy appeared in their lives.

"Are you sure?" she asked.

"Will you come back here tonight?"

"Of course."

He smiled. "Then I'm sure."

She kissed him, tasting herself on his lips. Today he had given her Mom's chisels, two magnificent orgasms, and quite possibly saved her life. On top of all that, he was a good sport.

"You're amazing," she said, and he blushed. Also, adorable.

"I'm on my way," she said into the phone.

Bad watched Keeffe's Honda pull away with only a mild feeling of disappointment. If there was anything Hell had trained him to do, it was to delay gratification in pursuit of a greater goal. Tonight was no exception.

Having coitus with a human woman was, without question, the most fascinating experience of his entire existence. The quickie out on the rocks had been an excellent release of tension. The real pleasure, though, was his chance to make love to Keeffe slowly and deliberately, to observe her reactions and adjust his technique to elicit the maximum response.

She had enjoyed herself. There could be no doubt about that. According to his research, the duration of an average human female orgasm was eighteen seconds. By his measure, Keeffe's orgasm had gone on for twenty-two seconds. That put it a full two standard deviations above the mean. He gave himself a mental high five. That was measurable success.

She was so different from Lamia. Where Lamia's flesh was like leather stretched over a wire frame, with no give whatsoever, Keeffe was as soft and smooth as his favorite fruit. While Lamia's coils never grew warmer than the ambient air, Keeffe's skin was hot, almost fevered. Like most nonpoisonous snakes, Lamia smelled of cucumbers. Keeffe had the pheromone-rich odor of the sweat she'd produced hiking, a smell that was surprisingly erotic. And while Lamia's genitals had practically no taste at all, Keeffe tasted like seawater—salty, but fresh and crisp.

The stimuli of Keeffe's taste and smell had slammed into him like a tidal wave. The volume of limbic activity joining with her had engendered in his brain stunned him. It had taken every ounce of his self-discipline to encourage her to spend the evening with her family instead of staying here with him. He wanted nothing so much as to bury himself inside her and bring her to orgasm again and again in shared passion. It had been worth his aching testicles, though, to see the smile on her face as she drove away.

Her joy at receiving her mother's chisels had been nearly as much fun as having sex with her. As she rubbed her cheek against the chisel, she'd looked at him as though he were an angel. It was the first time anyone had ever looked at him, a Hade, as though he were angelic. Now that he was rid of McCall, Keeffe's liking and trust of him grew every day. Soon, he would convince her that selling him the statue was the only way to keep it safe from Lilith's machinations. And once he had it in hand, he'd be back to running DemSec.

Back to the overheated, sulfurous atmosphere of Hell, never to see the blue skies or golden sun of Sedona again. Back in Hell, where every demon he met was out to get him, and there was no such thing as a lighthearted conversation. Back in Hell, where sex might be exciting, but it was never tender. Back in Hell, never to watch Keeffe paint or hear her call him a nerd or smell her flower-scented hair or taste her lips or feel an orgasm he'd triggered roll through her.

He didn't want to go back. It felt like the mammoth slab in front of the Devil's Kitchen sinkhole had just fallen on his head. The pleasure of creating new technology in DemSec paled next to the pleasure of spending time with Keeffe Blackmon, whether they were talking, hiking, making love, or he was just watching her create beauty with her paintbrush.

Somewhere along the line, the sense of achievement he'd gained from inventing things had lost its savor. The Gehenna Glasses, which were his creation even though McCall had gotten credit for them, sprang to mind. All he could think was: who would eventually be hurt by them?

Maybe he should leave Hell. Satan wouldn't like it, but Bad could still do it. The problem was, if he didn't return to DemSec, his fellow Hades would suffer. At a minimum, there would be no one to see that their lives were made easier, brighter, or cooler. Worst case, Satan would take revenge on them for his escape.

In another eight days it would be Keeffe's birthday. Two weeks after that, Keeffe would be on her way to Saguaro and McCall would return Above to collect his body. That gave Bad just over three weeks to craft an exit strategy.

To leave Hell, he would have to get Satan to release him. That was the easy part. He would also have to figure out a way to safeguard all the Hades he was leaving behind and ensure they continued to prosper. Finally, he would have to figure out a way to live Aboveworld. Humans barely tolerated other humans whose color differed from their own. His squat, hairy body, with its little pink horns and arrow-tipped tail, would be even less acceptable up here than it was Below.

Bad tried to imagine himself with Keeffe and failed. Keeffe loved beauty. If she knew what he really looked like, she wouldn't want him. What made it even more unlikely was that, despite her tough exterior, she was good to the core. If she knew the evil for which he'd been responsible, she'd be the first to order him back to Hell.

His head drooped. He was stuck. There was no way out.

On the other hand, there was a time when people believed that heavier-than-air flight, light without heat, and wireless transmission were all impossible, but he'd made them happen.

His head lifted. He just needed to be creative enough to make this happen, too.

Suzanne and Camille were already sitting in the corner booth when Keeffe arrived at Ernesto's. The aroma emanating from a plate of nachos in the center of the table made her realize how much energy she'd burned that day. She was starved.

"I love you guys." She hung her coat on a hook outside the booth, then slid in beside Suzanne and reached for a nacho. Her bones still felt like they were made of Silly Putty and she couldn't seem to control the smile on her face.

"You look happy," Suzanne said. "Is the painting going well?"

"It's going great," she said, grabbing another nacho.

The bell jangled and Frida came in, rubbing her hands against the chill.

"Jen had to work late." She slid in across from Keeffe. "She said to go ahead and order for her."

Maria came to the table and handed out menus and took their drink orders. After she left, Frida asked, "How's the mural coming along?"

"Fine," Keeffe said, thinking about Bad. He'd not only saved her life and given her the best sex she'd ever experienced, he had encouraged her to come out tonight even though his balls had to be phthalocyanine blue after all that foreplay. "I'm loving the way the sfumato technique is working out."

Maybe she should paint in two tiny figures copulating beside the Bell Rock vortex.

Frida looked up from her menu. Her eyes narrowed. "You had sex with him."

Suzanne and Camille turned to stare at her.

"No, I didn't," said Keeffe.

"You're such a liar," Frida said. "You so did."

Keeffe ducked her head, but she couldn't suppress a grin. Suzanne and Camille erupted in laughter.

"What happened to 'I don't sleep with clients'?" Frida asked.

Keeffe lifted her chin. "It's not like I'm his psychiatrist."

Frida shrugged. "True. What changed your mind?"

"Sometimes you have to celebrate being alive." She told them about the snake, minus the conversation Bad appeared to have with it.

"Are you all right?" Suzanne's face was worried.

"I'm better than all right," Keeffe assured her. "The snake didn't strike. Also—" she tried not to sound like she was squeeing—"he found Mom's chisels and bought them for me."

Frida's mouth fell open. "You're kidding."

"Nope."

"Those things have been gone for ten years. Are you sure they're really Mom's?"

Keeffe nodded. "They've got her initials inscribed on them and everything."

"Nice gift."

Keeffe beamed.

Jen came in, and Keeffe jumped up from the booth to give her sister-in-law a hug. Jen slid in beside her wife.

Frida kissed her. "How was work?"

"It was work." Jen unwrapped her silverware and put the paper napkin in her lap. "Your brothers were in."

Frida looked surprised, but Suzanne and Camille didn't. Ed must have taken Keeffe's advice and decided to try the bank instead of taking on Bad as an investor. She tried to remember why she hadn't wanted her brothers to go into business with him. The answer came back almost instantly in the form of silvery-gray eyes and an asshat attitude.

"How did it go?" Suzanne asked.

"You know how they say you can only get a loan from a bank if you can prove you don't need one?" Jen said.

Suzanne nodded.

"It's true." Jen's tone was wry.

"So, your bank said no?" Keeffe asked.

Jen shot an apologetic look at Suzanne and Camille. "They have no savings. They don't own a house. Their cars aren't paid for. In other words, they have no collateral. If this game sells, they'll be okay, but it's a crowded market. It's just not a safe investment for the bank."

Suzanne sagged with disappointment, but Camille's reaction was harder to read.

"So, they're back to letting McCall invest?" Keeffe asked.

"Do you think that's a bad idea?" Camille turned worried eyes to Keeffe.

Keeffe tried to think what to tell her. It depended on whether silver-eyed McCall was gone for good, but there was no way to explain that to them that made sense.

"You know him a little better now," Camille said. "Do you still feel as negative about him as you did?"

Frida snickered. "Guess not."

Jen paused before sticking a nacho in her mouth. "What did I miss?"

Frida recounted the snake-and-sex incident while Keeffe thought about how McCall had changed over the past couple of weeks. Bad would be an okay business partner. Maybe what he had told her on the way up Bell Rock was true—maybe he acted like a jerk when he first met people to keep them from taking advantage of him.

"I do like him better than I did." *A lot better.* She decided not to mention that. She debated whether to tell them about the split personality he had displayed when she first met him. She hadn't seen a sign of silver-eyed McCall in a while. Nor, as far as she could tell, was he on medication. "He can be kind of a jerk sometimes, but underneath he's a good guy, I think."

Maria set a jumbo margarita down in front of Frida.

Keeffe blinked. "That is one big margarita. Are you celebrating something?"

"Not yet." Frida smiled. "I'm thinking—that is, I'm hoping—this will be the last time I can have a drink at Girls' Night Out for a while."

Jen covered Frida's left hand with her right one. Keeffe looked around the table. Suzanne and Camille were beaming. It was clear everyone knew what was going on except her.

Frida said, "On Tuesday, Suzanne's going to retrieve my eggs. If that goes well, she'll fertilize them with the donor sperm and then re-implant them on Wednesday."

A rock seemed to lodge in Keeffe's throat. In the whirl of everything going on, she had forgotten Frida's quest to get pregnant.

"What time on Tuesday?" she asked through numb lips.

Frida rolled her eyes. "You don't need to come to the hospital. It's a simple outpatient procedure. Suzanne, tell her I'm not in any danger."

"She's really not," Suzanne said.

"Neither was Mom," Keeffe shot back. Beneath the table, she gripped her hands together so tight they hurt.

Frida sighed. "Nine a.m. But you really don't need to come."

"I'll be there," Keeffe said.

CHAPTER 19

On Tuesday morning at seven a.m., Bad woke to the sounds of Keeffe getting dressed. Much to his pleasure, she'd fallen into the habit of sleeping at his house. He'd never had a lover who wanted to cuddle close at night. The snuggling was almost as good as the sex.

He looked at the clock and groaned. "I thought you said her procedure wasn't till nine o'clock."

"It's not," Keeffe said, pulling on her jeans. "But I want to get there before they put her to sleep."

When he didn't move, she said, "You don't have to come."

That did it. He rolled out of bed. "Of course I'll come."

Ronnie had coffee—regular and decaf—and muffins ready to go when they got to the kitchen. Keeffe lifted up on tiptoe to kiss him on the cheek.

"You're the best," she told him.

The old demon smirked at Bad across the top of her head. Bad shrugged. One of the things he liked about Keeffe was her appreciation of the most trivial things.

When they got to the hospital, Frida was lying on a gurney in the outpatient ward with Jen by her side. Keeffe introduced them to Bad. Frida already had an IV in the back of her hand.

"You really don't need to be here," she said. "It's a half-hour process."

"Great," Keeffe said, setting her jaw. "Then I won't have to hang around long."

A few minutes later a pair of orderlies came to wheel the gurney to the operating room. Keeffe watched them go, her eyes like those of a lost child.

Bad took her hand. "You're thinking of your mom."

She turned and hid her face in his chest. "Yes."

He put his arms around her. "Frida is going to be okay. This is perfectly safe."

She stepped back and looked him in the eye. "No one has ever died from it?"

He grimaced. He'd done the research, of course.

"How many?" she demanded.

"Just one."

"What happened?"

"Would you like another muffin?" He tried to steer her toward the vending machines, but she refused to move.

"No, dammit. I want to know what happened to the woman who died during her egg retrieval."

"She bled out," he said.

Keeffe's face went so white she could have been bleeding out herself. She swayed, looking as if she might fall. Bad tightened his arms around her. His chest ached in a way he'd never experienced before.

"That was one woman, Keeffe. Out of hundreds of thousands of procedures. And she didn't have her sister-in-law looking after her."

Keeffe drew in a long, noisy breath through her nose.

"That's true. Suzanne won't let Frida to lie there for hours while her life drains away."

She didn't say it, but the rest of the sentence hung in the air, *...like my mom did.* The ache in Bad's chest grew stronger.

"How about if we talk to Jen?" he said. "She's the one whose wife is undergoing surgery."

At the other end of the waiting room, Jen sat, pretending to read a magazine. As he'd expected, thinking about someone else was the perfect distraction for Keeffe. Inside the circle of his arms, her heart still thudded in her chest, but she set aside her own feelings and crossed the big room. He followed her.

"So, what are you hoping for?" Keeffe asked when they reached Jen's side. "A boy or a girl?"

Jen smiled. "Either would be fine with us."

"Have you talked about names yet?" Keeffe asked.

"Not yet. We're just trying to get through the 'getting pregnant' part at this point."

Twenty minutes later, Suzanne came into the waiting room, her blue mask hanging around her neck, a broad smile on her face.

"We were very successful," she said. "We retrieved sixteen eggs."

"That's excellent," Bad said.

Keeffe looked at him curiously.

"Retrievals numbering between fifteen and twenty eggs are a positive indicator for live birth."

For the first time that morning, Keeffe's lips twitched into a reluctant smile. "You're such a nerd."

His ears grew warm as Jen and Suzanne laughed.

"How's Frida?" Keeffe asked Suzanne.

"She's in recovery." Suzanne turned to Jen. "In about half an hour, you can go back."

"Can I see her now?" Keeffe asked.

Suzanne's face was gentle. "She's still asleep. The nurses are watching her."

"I know, I just—can I see her now, please?"

Suzanne sighed and looked at Jen. Jen nodded.

"Sure," she said. "Go on back. She's in the third pod on the left." She pointed at the door she'd come through and Keeffe headed that way.

Bad lifted his eyebrows inquiringly.

Suzanne nodded. "You can go back with her. Maybe you can convince her Frida isn't going to die."

"Thanks," he said, and followed Keeffe.

When they got to the pod, Keeffe pulled aside the hanging curtain to reveal her sister, sleeping silently on pale pink sheets. Her color was good, and the machines monitoring her vitals all showed healthy readings. Keeffe took Frida's hand and held it to her cheek. Frida didn't stir.

"She's warm," Keeffe said.

The machine gave her temperature as 96.7.

"She's not feverish," Bad said, pointing at the readout.

Keeffe didn't even bother to look. "No, I meant she's normal body temperature."

He tried to understand what she was driving at but failed. "That's good, right?"

Tears rolled down Keeffe's face. "Mom was so cold. Her hands were like ice, but they said it was good, it meant she didn't have a fever."

"Frida isn't your mother. She's going to be fine."

"Mom was pregnant before her surgery." Keeffe's tears continued to fall.

He pulled a clean handkerchief, courtesy of Ronnie, from his pocket and handed it to her. She mopped her face.

Bad nodded. That had been in Rachel's dossier.

"She was going to name him Pablo Picasso."

In spite of himself, Bad's mouth twitched.

Keeffe smiled a watery smile.

"She was a little crazy with the name thing," she admitted. "When she was six months along, he died. She should have miscarried, but she didn't. It cut off the blood supply to her uterus. That's why they had to do the hysterectomy. And then that robot killed her."

As she said the word *robot*, her voice filled with loathing.

His robot. His invention. Keeffe's face made it clear she would carry a grudge against the medical robot till the end of time. If she knew he was the inventor, she'd never forgive him. How had he gone along for so many centuries, blissfully ignorant of the damage he was doing? No, not blissfully. Willfully.

A few minutes later, Frida's eyelids fluttered and her fingers twitched.

"She's waking up." Keeffe's whisper held the joy of someone witnessing a resurrection.

The curtains rattled and Jen came in. Frida's eyes opened and she looked around groggily. When her gaze fell on Jen, she smiled tiredly. "How did we do?"

"Sixteen." Jen squeezed Frida's hand and bent to kiss her. "Suzanne says she can implant the eggs tomorrow afternoon at her office."

Bad wasn't sure who was most relieved that they wouldn't have to go through another hospital procedure—Keeffe, Jen, or Frida.

"Call me after, okay?" Keeffe said.

Frida nodded sleepily.

Bad trailed Keeffe out the exit.

"Feel better?" he asked.

"So much better." She smiled, blinking away tears. "Thanks for hanging out."

He caught her to him. "I wouldn't be anyplace else."

That afternoon, Satan had scheduled a status update. Telling Keeffe he had an investor call, Bad left her working on the mural and locked himself in McCall's home office. He brought Ronnie along. The old demon could provide backup if necessary. Bad had one goal for this call: find out as much as possible about this mission. There were far too many unconnected dots.

"How does this work?" Ronnie eyed the computer warily.

"I'll explain while we're waiting for the boss to come online," Bad said. He brought up gotohell.com on McCall's desktop and keyed in the meeting code.

To his amazement, Satan was already waiting. The screen split into halves, and Lilith's bored, petulant face filled the second half. Satan couldn't operate a television remote. How had he managed to set up this call?

"Is that everything you need, sir?" McCall's voice asked. Behind Satan, Bad's own body appeared, at a respectful distance.

"Yes," said Satan, "but stick around in case something goes kerflooey."

"Will do." Bad's Hade face split into an ingratiating grin before disappearing off-screen. In the corner of the room, a diamond pattern undulated as something slithered away.

Was that Lamia? What was she doing there?

"All right," said Satan. "Where are we? Lilith?"

"Friday is the target's birthday," she said. "Thanks to numb-nuts there, she's within the language of the contract. I'll have no choice but to let her take the statue home."

Satan's eyes pinned Bad to his desk chair. "Well? What do you have to say about that?"

Bad tried to push up his glasses, only to realize he wasn't wearing glasses.

"Keeffe's birthday is only a deadline for Lilith. If you'll recall, the terms of our agreement were that I have another two weeks beyond that." He held up his phone, prepared to play back the audio if necessary.

Satan's face darkened. "I remember what we agreed."

"It's unfortunate that Lilith's efforts have been unsuccessful," Bad began.

"They will be completely successful once you force her to abandon that mural," Lilith interrupted, no longer looking bored. Her pupils were rectangular with fury.

Bad shook his head. "I'm not going to do that."

"I warned you," Lilith told Satan.

"Help me understand exactly how we plan to use the statue," Bad said. Two solid weeks of hacking had not given him the answer to that question.

"That's need-to-know," Satan said.

"And I need to know. I'm confident I can get the statue from the girl, but I need to understand how we plan to use it in order to identify the best method of doing so—the one that will allow the statue to retain the appropriate powers."

Satan opened his mouth, but Lilith jumped in before he could speak.

"This mission has been bottom secret for ten years," she said. "Now is not the time to get loose-lipped. That could destroy everything I've worked toward."

"Exactly what have you worked toward?" asked Bad.

Neither Satan nor Lilith responded. He sighed.

"Allow me to summarize what I've ascertained to date," he said. "Lilith's deliverables included gathering the statues, turning Daniel Blackmon into a drunk who no longer paints, preventing any of the kids from becoming artists—she failed with Keeffe—and removing as many traces of Rachel Blackmon as possible."

Satan looked impressed, but Lilith sneered. "That was all pretty obvious."

"How are you planning to eliminate her crosses?" Bad asked.

"Her journals will do that for me," Lilith said.

He wanted to ask more questions, but Satan had already begun to fidget. It was time to play his biggest card.

"Oh, and destroying the vortexes, of course," Bad said.

Both Satan and Lilith froze.

Satan scowled at Ronnie. "Did you tell him about the vortexes?"

"No, you said you wanted that kept quiet." Ronnie seemed unconcerned by Satan's scowl. There were definite benefits to having no ambition.

"Well, Lilith didn't tell him. How did he find out?"

"He's smart," Ronnie said.

This was why Bad had wanted him in the meeting.

"It's clear the four statues in the aggregate hold a value beyond the individual pieces," Bad said. "I understand the purpose of destroying the vortexes. I've felt the positive energy that emanates from them. What's less clear to me is how they fall within the parameters of this mission. They existed long before Rachel Blackmon was born."

"She grew up in Sedona. Their energy fed her, and she, them," said Satan. "And now they're feeding the girl. The longer she stays there, the more of a threat she becomes."

Bad nodded. He'd suspected something along these lines.

"Malphas is working on a ritual to invert the energy in the vortexes," Satan said. Malphas was a crow hybrid with a human torso, a hoarse voice, and a gift for destroying enemy strongholds. "He says if we place a statue at each vortex and shatter them simultaneously, their energy source will switch from the Enemy to us."

Bad listened with horror but kept his voice level. "And all the positive energy that emanates from Sedona, creating beauty and inspiration, will disappear."

"Will be replaced," Satan said, "by negative energy. I may even be able use that energy to summon up an earthquake and destroy the whole town." His burgundy face wore an expression that was as close to happiness as Bad had ever seen.

Bad was appalled. He had grown fond of the touristy little town with its beautiful scenery and continual sunshine.

"Good idea," he said. "This place is antithetical to all we stand for."

"How does this impact your plan to get the statue?" asked Satan.

Bad thought quickly. What was the best way to remove Lilith from the equation?

"Based on what you just explained, I'll need to receive it as a gift."

"A gift?"

"That will allow it to retain all of its power. In fact, because it will come to us as a voluntary sacrifice through love, it will grow more powerful."

"Love?" Satan said the word with loathing.

"She's falling in love with me," Bad said. He turned to Ronnie. "Isn't she?"

All eyes were on the old demon.

"Well," said Satan. "Is she?"

Ronnie rubbed the back of his head. "She shows all the signs."

"To the point where she'd believe whatever tale he chooses to tell her and give up the thing she loves most?" Satan asked.

"Yes," said Bad.

"Maybe," said Ronnie.

"Her feelings for me are the lever," Bad said. "I still need to figure out what will create an appropriate fulcrum."

"Understand this, Hade," Satan said. "If I don't get that statue, you will dig coal alongside your hairy brethren for the rest of eternity."

Late in the afternoon, Ronnie came into the mural room and announced that dinner would be ready in a half-hour. His thinning hair was sticking out in several places and the bags beneath his eyes were even puffier than normal.

"You work too hard," Keeffe said. "Why don't you take the evening off? Bad and I can go out for dinner." She was actually missing Ernesto's nachos.

"The master would never permit that," Ronnie said.

Keeffe blinked at him, astonished. "The master?"

"I mean Mr. McCall." Looking flustered, Ronnie backed out of the room.

After showering in McCall's white marble bathroom, Keeffe wrapped herself in the thick terry cloth robe hanging inside the bathroom door. She wandered out to the rec room, her hair still damp. There she found Bad in front of the television. To her surprise, he wasn't playing video games. He was watching TV. His face was grim.

A dinner of chicken marsala, wild rice and grilled asparagus, served with candles, cloth napkins, and crystal wineglasses, sat on the coffee table.

"You should give Ronnie a night off," she said. "He's looking pretty burnt."

Bad snorted. "There's a lot of that going around."

"Rough investor call?"

For a second he looked at her blankly, like he had no idea what she was talking about.

"Right. Yes. It was the call from Hell." His lips quirked, as though at some private joke, though not one he found particularly amusing.

She decided to let it go. Even if he explained what had happened, it wasn't like she'd understand. She sat down at the other end of the couch and picked up the remote.

"Since you're feeling so gloomy, I'll choose what we watch."

He rolled his eyes. "Not a chick-flick."

She looked at him. "Do I seem like the chick-flick type?"

"No," he admitted. He was already cheering up. She could see it on his face.

She clicked through a few channels until she found what she was looking for. On-screen, four men dressed in spandex stood beside a sled at the top of an enormous concrete luge.

"The Olympics," she said. "A positive expression of the human spirit, striving for excellence."

He crossed his arms. "With drugs, politics, corruption, and cutthroat competition."

"As a guy who has pretty much everything, you have no excuse for being such a downer."

"I have one excuse," he said.

"And what's that?"

"That I'm here and you're there."

She moved closer to him. By the time they finished eating, his expression had lightened.

Germany won the luge event. Pairs skating came on next. Keeffe sighed with pleasure.

"Really?" Bad finger-combed her damp hair away from her face.

Just the touch of his fingers made her want him. She tried to remember the last time she'd been this hot for someone. Never that she could recall.

"Admit it," he said. "This was why you turned on the Olympics. So you could watch the ice dancing."

"Pairs skating."

"What's the difference?"

"Ice dancers are judged more for the precision of their footwork. They don't do any lifts above the shoulder."

The Canadians competed first. They executed each movement with clockwork precision, but something about their performance left Keeffe cold.

"Now those are athletes." Bad's tone was admiring.

Keeffe slapped her forehead. "What am I even doing here?"

He looked at her warily. "Adding beauty and culture to my life?"

She nodded toward the TV. "We have nothing in common. You realize that, don't you?"

He looked mystified. "What did I say?"

On screen, a Latvian couple started their routine. They lacked the perfection of the Canadians, but they eyed each other adoringly throughout their dance. At the end, the boy lifted his partner above his head like a man holding up something for the gods to bless. His arms wobbled a little on the lift, but it didn't matter. The crowd went wild.

"Why are they cheering?" asked Bad. "It wasn't even a clean lift."

"You're a barbarian," said Keeffe. "Look how in love they are."

The male skater brought his partner back down with a tenderness that made it clear how precious she was to him. As the music faded away, they gazed into each other's eyes as though the crowd had disappeared.

"Aww," Keeffe said.

Bad groaned. "You've got to be kidding. This is worse than a chick-flick."

The scores came up and the Latvians edged out the Canadians by a tenth of a point. Keeffe cheered.

"You can't tell me you thought they were as good as the Canadians?" Bad was outraged.

"You are such a philistine," she said.

He pointed at the TV. "I do not get that. The Canadians were better in every way you can measure. Explain that to me."

"The Latvians were better in ways you can't objectively measure." She tried to think how to explain it in a way his numbers-driven brain would understand. "There's technical merit and then there's artistic merit. Part of any art form will always be subjective. It was the artistry and the emotion that the crowd responded to. The judges, too, apparently."

Bad snorted. "Or, the Latvians have more friends among the judges than the Canadians do."

"A philistine and a cynic." Keeffe wriggled away from him, perching on the front edge of the couch.

Bad pulled her back against him. "Maybe we should stage our own Olympics," he whispered into her ear. "See if we can earn perfect scores for artistry *and* technical merit."

Desire flooded her, stiffening her nipples and dampening the area between her legs. His breath on her ear raised goose bumps all the way down to her toes. He pushed the sleeves of her robe aside to run his hands up and down her arms.

"Are you cold?" he asked.

God, he smelled good. Felt good. The desire in his eyes made her feel like a goddess. Was this what love felt like?

She twined her arms around his neck.

"Just the opposite," she said.

CHAPTER 20

*L*ate the next afternoon, Keeffe's cellphone rang. It was Frida.

"How did it go?" Keeffe asked.

"Okay. I'm fine. A little crampy, but fine."

Fear clutched at Keeffe's gut. "Are you sure you're not hemorrhaging?

"I just left Suzanne five minutes ago. I'm pretty sure she'd have noticed. She says the cramping is normal."

"When will you know if it worked?"

"I can take a pregnancy test in nine days."

Keeffe prayed as fervently as she'd ever prayed for anything that the implantation was successful. She didn't think she could go through this again.

On Friday morning, Keeffe awoke to Bad bringing her breakfast in bed. The tray contained a glass of orange juice, a cup of what he assured her was decaf coffee, three strips of bacon, and a blueberry muffin with a lit candle in it.

"Happy birthday," he said.

She struggled to a sitting position. He set the tray across her lap and leaned in to kiss her.

She eyed him in wonder. "You got up early to make me breakfast."

He ducked his head. "Ronnie made it."

"You got up early to bring me breakfast that Ronnie made."

He laughed. "I did."

He sat down on the edge of the bed and leaned over to retrieve a quartet of boxes in graduated sizes from the floor. Each was beautifully wrapped. Keeffe's eyes went wide.

"You got me presents?"

He grinned.

She touched one foil-wrapped box with a reverent finger. "Even the wrapping is beautiful."

"Ronnie wrapped them."

She took her finger away, her lips quirking. "Of course he did. Did he pick them out, too?"

"He did not." Bad looked indignant.

Frida always bought Keeffe presents for her birthday. So did the boys, when they thought about it, but Dad just gave her cards with money in them. She couldn't remember getting this many presents since Mom died.

"Can I open them now?" she asked.

"Of course." Bad moved the tray aside and she tore into the boxes. The top one was small, the size of a jeweler's box, so it came as no surprise that it contained beautifully wrought gold earrings. The next box was long and slender. It held the matching necklace. The gifts reminded her that he was a billionaire, something she didn't think about very often. She thanked him politely.

"My uncle is a jewelry maker," he said.

She held the necklace up, looking at it more closely. "He made this?"

"He did."

"The craftsmanship is beautiful." She slipped the earrings into her earlobes.

The next box contained a set of sable paintbrushes. She threw her arms around Bad's neck and kissed him.

"Note to self," he said. "Don't waste your time getting her jewelry. Buy her paintbrushes instead."

Keeffe laughed.

The final box was the biggest. Inside was a pair of Keen hiking boots in shades of red and eggshell white, along with several pairs of thick socks.

She stared at the boots, stunned. "Those are gorgeous."

She swung her legs over the edge of the bed and pulled on socks and then the boots. Half a dozen steps assured her they fit perfectly. She grabbed Bad and kissed him thoroughly.

"This is the best birthday I've had in years."

"Good. That was the goal. Now eat your breakfast."

She took off the boots and got back into bed. He returned the tray to her lap.

"You know, a lot of women would have been most impressed with the jewelry and least impressed with the boots," he said.

"I'm not most women." She took a bite of muffin and an explosion of blueberry goodness filled her mouth.

"Truer words were never spoken." He filched a piece of bacon from her plate. "I was thinking you might take a day off painting so we can go hiking." He wiggled his eyebrows suggestively. "I thought maybe I'd bring a blanket this time."

Not a bad idea, but… "Maybe later. I have plans for this morning."

Bad's face fell, then brightened again. "Staying in bed?"

"Yeah, uh, no."

He looked so disappointed she had to laugh. "I'm going to Dad's to get my statue."

Bad's face lost all expression. Then he blinked. For some reason, it reminded her of the reptilian blink that Lilith gave when she was caught in a lie. That couldn't be true in this case—he hadn't even said anything.

"Right," he said, setting the bacon back on her plate. She couldn't tell what he was thinking. "Your contract with your dad and Lilith expires today."

"Technically, it's just with my dad, but yes." She frowned. "Is it okay with you if I leave the statue here for a while?"

Bad blinked again. "Of course. What are you planning to do with it long term?"

She sighed. "I'm not sure. I'd hoped to send it on a museum tour with the other three. Now that they're no longer available, I don't know if any museum will want it."

He smiled lightly. "Maybe you should sell it to me. I'd take good care of it and then you'd have enough money to go anywhere in the world and paint."

Acid churned in Keeffe's stomach. "Not just no, but hell no. I'm not selling the only thing I own that was my mom's."

He looked taken aback. "You have the chisels."

Her spine went rigid. She set down her fork. "Is that why you got them for me? So I'd sell you Mom's statue?"

He looked hurt. "No."

"But it's part of it."

He hung his head. "Originally, that's why I went after the chisels, but later I just wanted you to have them. I wanted to see your face when you opened them."

The burn in Keeffe's gut subsided, but only slightly. Then something in his words caught her attention. "'Went after?' I thought you bought them on eBay?"

He blinked again. "I did. Someone else wanted them. It was a fight to the finish to see who would get them."

She was sure he was lying. What she couldn't figure out was why.

After she finished breakfast, he took the tray away and she got dressed. Ronnie, angel that he was, kept her small stock of clothing clean and ironed, but she needed something different today. Back at the trailer she had a silvery-gray puffy vest. It would be good for later, when they went hiking, but it could also double as armor for her upcoming joust with Lilith. She didn't know why she was so sure Lilith would resist giving her the statue, but she was. After she pulled on her jeans, a slouchy sweater, and her wonderful new boots, she grabbed her car keys and headed for the front door.

Bad was there, waiting for her. His brown eyes looked troubled.

"Okay if I go with you?" he asked.

Keeffe frowned. She'd pictured this confrontation as a one-on-one.

"I guess so," she said without enthusiasm.

He immediately took a step back. "I don't have to."

But he looked hurt, and he'd just given her a stack of fabulous gifts, to say nothing of the best present ever: the chisels.

"No, sure, it's fine. I'm driving my car, though."

He got into the Honda's passenger seat without comment, but she could tell he wasn't impressed with the car's torn seats and faded dash. She wilted a little. If her car didn't impress, her trailer would underwhelm him. When they arrived, he followed her through the flimsy aluminum door.

"It's what I could afford." She crossed her arms.

He swiveled in a complete circle, scanning the mural in progress on her walls. "It's incredible."

She relaxed a little. "Really?"

"If you'd invited me home that first night, we wouldn't have wasted all that time on superheroes."

Her defensiveness dropped away like a scorpion's outgrown shell. "If you like this, you should see my bedroom."

His face lit up. "Okay."

She put up her arm to bar his way. "Statue first. Sex later."

He drooped comically. "Okay."

She laughed. "Maybe we'd better put off viewing the bedroom for another time." She went back into her bedroom by herself and grabbed her puffy vest from the closet. Back in the living room, she put it on like she was donning chain mail.

"Are you ready?" he asked.

"Not quite." She walked over to the footlocker and removed all the candles and books, then stripped off the fringed shawl. The manila folder holding the contract lay right out on top, from when she'd reviewed it a month before. She picked it up, revealing the worn leather journal beneath.

Bad's eyes focused on the journal like a pair of laser beams. "What's that?"

"It's the journal my mother kept while she was sculpting *John*," she said. "I kind of swiped it when I was fourteen, right after she died."

"Does anyone know you have this?" His tone was oddly urgent.

Her face warmed. "No."

He closed the lid of the trunk. "Keep it that way."

"Okay." She'd forgotten how weird he could be. She tucked the contract under her arm. "Let's go."

Bad followed Keeffe from the car to the front door of her dad's house. In her hand she held a manila envelope containing her sales receipts—all on paper, of course—and a copy of both contracts. He was really going to enjoy carting that statue out of here, right under Lilith's nose. Even though he hadn't gotten Keeffe to agree to sell it to him, if it were in his house, the advantage would be his.

He thought about what Satan planned to do with the statue—destroy the positive energy that swirled in Sedona, possibly even destroying the pretty little town itself. Unlike the bad outcomes from the inventions Bad had created over the centuries, there was no way to pretend he wasn't to blame for this one.

What would Ma and Pa say if they knew? Nothing good, that was for sure. What was it Pa had said when Bad last visited? He'd told Ma not to worry, that Bad knew the difference between right and wrong. That was true; he did. What he didn't know was how to balance what was good for Keeffe and Sedona with what was good for the Hades.

Keeffe rang the bell and a moment later Lilith answered. Her charcoal-lidded eyes swept over Bad.

"Hello, Seth."

She was reminding him of her relationship with McCall. He mumbled "hi."

"Your dad's out of town," she told Keeffe.

That rocked Keeffe back on her heels. "Where is he?"

"China," said Lilith. "Working out some details for the next round of reproductions."

Keeffe frowned. "You always go with him."

"I wasn't up for a thirteen-hour flight," Lilith said, "so he went by himself."

It was more likely she'd sent Daniel away so he wouldn't be there when Keeffe came to pick up her statue. Bad's solar plexus tightened.

Keeffe's fists clenched at her sides. "It doesn't matter. I'm here because it's my birthday."

Lilith made no effort to open the door any wider. "Happy birthday. I'm afraid you'll have to wait until Daniel comes home to get your present. Maybe he'll bring you a little something from his trip." She gave Keeffe a saccharine smile.

Keeffe flushed a dull red. "I don't care about that. I came to pick up *John*."

Lilith pressed her lips together, and Bad's abdominal muscles tightened some more. She had something up her sleeve.

She swung the door wide. "Come in."

She led the way through the house, her nosebleed stilettos clattering every step of the way. In the family room, a box and some packing materials sat on the pool table near the statue. Bad breathed a sigh of relief. Despite her behavior at the door, she must be planning to give Keeffe the statue without argument.

Keeffe moved toward the sculpture like she was being pulled by a tractor beam. She lifted it off the pedestal.

"Not so fast," said Lilith.

Shit.

Keeffe set the statue back down and turned to Lilith. "It's. My. Birthday."

"Yes, you mentioned that at the door."

Keeffe held up the manila envelope. "I have the documentation right here proving I met your terms. This is the day, legally, when I can collect my statue."

Lilith cleared her throat. "Your father and I discussed this before he left. Because Seth's commission isn't completely fulfilled yet, and your meeting the terms of our contract rely on his commission, we're not comfortable letting you take the statue just yet."

Bad glared at her. Satan hadn't told her to do this. She was just so determined not to share credit she'd decided to do it on her own.

Anger blazed in Keeffe's eyes. "What are you talking about?"

"Until you complete Seth's commission and he accepts the mural, there's a possibility things could fall apart. If that happens, you won't have fulfilled the terms of our contract and the statue will revert to us."

He should have known Lilith wouldn't give up without a fight. He wished he could point out that the deposit, which he'd already paid to Keeffe, meant she'd already met the terms of her agreement with Lilith and Daniel but he was supposed to be on Satan's side. He couldn't say anything.

Rage swept red into Keeffe's cheeks. "McCall loves what I've done so far." She turned to Bad. "Don't you?"

"Yes," Bad said. "Yes, I do."

Lilith shot him a look like acid.

The shoulders of Keeffe's down vest were up around her ears. Bad wanted to tell her to calm down, that she was reacting precisely the way Lilith wanted her to, but she was too angry to hear him.

"The only way I could fail to meet the terms of the contract would be if I abandoned the mural without finishing it," Keeffe said. "And that's not going to happen."

"The problem is—" Lilith made a pretense of sympathy, but there was no disguising her pleasure—"you're sleeping with Seth."

Keeffe had been spending her nights at his house. Had Ronnie told Lilith about that? For that matter, Keeffe had told him their relationship had been the subject of discussion on Girls' Night Out. Someone must have told Lilith.

Keeffe gasped. "What possible business is that of yours?"

Bad exhaled a tiny breath of relief. Keeffe didn't suspect her stepmother was McCall's mistress.

Lilith said, "In my experience, artists and clients who become lovers often wind up having bad breakups, breakups that sometimes cause the artist to walk off the job."

Keeffe stuck out her lower jaw. "Not gonna happen. I took the commission knowing he can be a real asshat. No offense." She threw the last comment over her shoulder at Bad.

"None taken," he said. At all.

"That was before you became involved with him," said Lilith. "Your father and I agreed that, since you lack the self-control to avoid getting involved with a client, your judgment really can't be trusted."

A vein beat in Keeffe's temple. Bad suspected Daniel would be astounded to hear that harsh judgment ascribed to him, but he couldn't be sure. Beijing was fifteen hours ahead of Sedona. If they called, he would be asleep. Even worse, what if they woke him and he agreed with Lilith? Keeffe would be devastated. She was already fighting tears.

"What are you proposing?" he asked, since Keeffe seemed incapable of speech.

"That the statue remain here, under our control, until Keeffe finishes the mural and you pay her in full." As though the movement was completely unconscious, Lilith brushed her hand across the packing materials on the pool table.

Keeffe drew in a sharp breath. "If those aren't for me to pack up *John* to take home, what are they for?"

"I'm sending that little thing to the auction." Lilith pointed to a statue of a she-demon with long black hair and tiny jeweled horns that stood nearby.

Bad recognized it. Sculpted in the sixteenth century by a lover of Lilith's who'd gone on to commit suicide, it was a full six inches taller than the eagle statue.

"That sculpture won't fit in that box," Keeffe said.

Lilith touched a fingertip to her lower lip. "I believe you're right. I'll have to find another box."

Keeffe's eyes narrowed. "That demon statue has been here as long as you have."

Lilith shrugged. "I'm bored with it."

At her sides, Keeffe's hands twitched like she wanted to strike Lilith.

"How much longer until you finish the mural?" Bad asked quickly.

She shook her head. "I don't know. With the sfumato technique..."

"You can add finishing touches later," he said. "How long till the walls are completely covered and I can sign off and pay you?"

Lilith didn't move or make a sound, but her pupils morphed into rectangles.

Keeffe took a step back. Interesting. She could see Lilith's goat-eyes and she knew exactly what they indicated. Very few humans could perceive demon eyes. Had she been born with this talent, or was it a product of spending so much time near Sedona's energy vortexes? No wonder she and Lilith got along so badly.

"I don't know—a week, maybe?" Keeffe said.

He grabbed her arm and pulled her toward the door.

"We'll be back in a week," he told Lilith.

CHAPTER 21

Keeffe handed Bad the keys as they walked back out to the car. Another time, his look of relief would have been comical, but she wasn't in a laughing mood. He didn't say anything until they turned out of Dad's subdivision onto 89A.

"Do you think your dad knows anything about this?" he asked.

"Probably. Maybe. I don't know." Keeffe stared out the window. Normally, the sight of Sedona's businesses coming to life cheered her, but today she passed the bundled-up tourists lining up for their Pink Jeep tours without a smile.

"No matter what crap Lilith pulls, he just lets her get away with it," she said. "That's why you had to buy my mother's chisels on eBay for a fortune when they should have just come to me after she died."

"I get that," he said. "But it's just another week. Can't you just be patient?"

"You saw that packing material," she said. "She's planning to send *John* to New York to be auctioned off while Dad's still in China. She sold Frida and the boys' statues to private collectors. She's determined to keep my mother's work from being seen."

"They won't take it without the appropriate provenance," he said.

"Lilith is a reputable agent. They've been doing business with her for years. She sent the other three statues there. They won't even think to question her."

"There has to be some paperwork that accompanies it."

"She can fake that."

"But she won't," he said. "To your point, she's a reputable agent. She's not going to throw her reputation away selling something that doesn't belong to her. That's theft, Keeffe. Grand larceny. You'd have the right, not just to sue her, but to pursue criminal charges."

Why he was trying so hard to convince her?

"My dad would never allow that to happen," she said.

"He couldn't stop you."

"Yes, he could. Don't you get it? I lost my mother." The world outside the car swam underwater as her eyes filled with tears. "I can't lose my dad, too."

Bad didn't respond to that, just stared through the windshield, his eyes narrowed in what she'd come to think of as his brainiac mode.

"Do you still have the contract?" he asked after a few minutes of silence.

She held up the manila envelope.

"Good. We're going to go through it with a fine-tooth comb and figure out exactly what our options are."

Keeffe's hands grew clammy. It had been a month since she'd read through the jumble of letters in the contract. Did she remember it clearly enough to fake reading it? She forced herself to relax. She didn't need to add stress on top of stress. She'd just have him do the reading.

Back at the house, he settled himself on the leather sectional. She removed the contract from the envelope and offered it to him. He waved it away.

"Read it to me." He leaned back and rested his head on the back of the sofa, staring up at the ceiling, still in brainiac mode. "I process auditory input best."

There was no way she remembered the contract clearly enough to recite it.

A rush of panic filled her chest. "What's the point?" Her voice was harsher than the circumstances warranted. "Lilith has my sculpture, and she's not giving it up."

Bad turned his head to look at her, his expression calm and logical. "The point is for us to understand the details so that we can take effective counter-measures."

"This is stupid." Keeffe clutched the folder. He wasn't going to let this go, and she was going to look like the illiterate idiot she was. "I should just take this to a lawyer. I've got the money to do that now."

"And it may come to that," he said, "but let's at least give it a look-through first. Come on, it's only a few pages. What's the big deal?"

She looked down at her feet. She was wearing her beautiful new hiking boots and the gold earrings his uncle had made. On his dresser, back in his bedroom, lay a set of sable paintbrushes, along with a gold necklace. More valuable than any of those was the set of chisels at her trailer. He'd proven he cared about her.

"I can't read." She forced the words out.

He sat up. "What?"

Heat rushed into her face. "I have dyslexia, okay? Reading is really, really hard for me." She folded her arms across her chest, willing back tears of humiliation.

He looked stunned. "How in the world did you get through four years of college?"

He thought she was stupid, just like she'd been afraid he would. She hurled the contract at him.

"Tutors," she yelled and ran from the room.

Bad spent the next half-hour reading through the contract, figuring Keeffe needed time to calm down before he tried to talk to her. He'd skimmed it before, when he was reviewing the mission dossier, but now he focused on the details.

It quickly became clear that Lilith had no legal grounds for keeping the statue. She'd sent Daniel out of town so she could bully Keeffe into letting her hang onto the sculpture until Bad either convinced Keeffe to sell it or manipulated her into abandoning the mural and walking away.

Which he'd had every intention of doing, right up until the moment Keeffe had yelled, "I can't read."

Shame filled him. Here was a woman who had made it through college on pure guts. Sure, she had loads of artistic talent, but her difficulty in deciphering the written word would have made the grind of college coursework far worse than his time as a janitor—and she'd stuck it out for four years, not a measly two weeks.

Yet here he was, determined to rip from her hands the one thing she valued in life. And for what? So that he could return to DemSec and resume churning out inventions that made life on this planet easier in some ways, but infinitely harder in others.

For the first time, he looked at DemSec's long history of innovation under his leadership—the cotton gin, TNT, the internal combustion engine, computers. All had brought progress, but with each came a large measure of misery. And then there were medical robots. If Keeffe knew of his involvement with the machine that had taken her mother's life, she'd want nothing more to do with him.

Bad had always viewed himself as morally neutral. He'd focused his attention on the upside of the inventions he'd sent to Earth, ignoring the harm he'd caused. Now he saw himself as he really was— a purveyor of evil. Shame threatened to choke him.

He thought about Satan's threat to return him to the mines. It was his worst nightmare. His kith and kin had labored there for ten thousand years. Most didn't seem to mind, but he had worked his entire life to avoid their fate. Just the idea of being stuck down a mineshaft, digging coal, made him break out in a sweat.

But what about the well-being of the Hades? It was only because of him that Hades mined using machinery and not pickaxes. He weighed further gains for his people against the purpose of this mission and realized there was no decision to be made here. He would not be party to taking Keeffe Blackmon's statue away from her, to removing Rachel Blackmon's healing influence from the Earth, to destroying the beauty of Sedona. Few of his people would want him to.

Having reached that resolve, he went in search of Keeffe. He found her in the mural room, slashing red paint onto the walls with sweeping strokes that gave form to her inner turmoil. He crossed the room to the foot of the ladder.

"Dyslexia is nothing to be ashamed of," he said. "It doesn't mean you're stupid. It just means your brain is wired differently from other people's."

She didn't respond, just painted harder.

"Do you know how few people can do this?" He gestured around the room, which was half covered with the rock formations she loved so much, and which he was coming to love, too.

"Lots of famous people are dyslexic," he said, "Steven Spielberg, Whoopi Goldberg, Steve Jobs."

She stopped slashing at the walls, standing very still on her ladder, but she still wouldn't meet his eyes.

"Not to mention Pablo Picasso," he said. "You're a genius with light and color and shapes."

Finally, she looked at him. "I can't read that contract. Not without drinking a gallon of coffee and studying it like it's a physics textbook."

"So what?" he said. "The world is full of people who can read contracts." He gestured around the room again. "There aren't many who can do this. I can't."

She stepped off the ladder. "Really?"

"Not if my soul depended on it."

He pulled her into his arms.

"The next time someone tells you you're not smart, you tell them Bad McCall thinks you're a freaking genius."

An hour later, Bad watched Keeffe's naked body stretch lazily across the black satin sheets of McCall's big bed. He'd hoped she would agree to snuggle and take a nap, but sex seemed to have given her a second wind.

"What did you figure out about the contract?" she asked.

"There's really nothing to figure out," he said. "Lilith has no legal grounds for retaining possession of the statue, but there's probably nothing you can do till your dad gets back. Any idea when that might be?"

She looked chagrined. "I didn't think to ask."

Bad shrugged. "I doubt Lilith would have told you the truth anyway."

Keeffe wriggled to a sitting position against a king-size black satin pillow. "What do we do to keep her from shipping it off to New York and selling it?"

"She's not going to do that." He loaded all the conviction he was capable of into his voice, hoping it would convince Keeffe.

It didn't.

"All the other statues have gone to anonymous buyers," she said. "Or maybe just one buyer, there's no way to know. If it sells anonymously, or to a buyer from another country, it will probably be impossible to get it back."

He wished there were a way to reassure her that wasn't going to happen, but he couldn't think of anything that would do that but the truth—Lilith wasn't really planning to send the sculpture to New York. She was planning to send it to Hell, and it was useless to Satan if Keeffe didn't part with it through her own choice.

He could tell her the truth, he supposed. Since she was able to perceive demon eyes, she might even believe him. It would probably explain a lot of things she'd observed over the years, most recently McCall's split personality. The problem was, if he did, she would stop trusting him, and he was the only one on her side.

"She won't do that," he said again.

"I'm not willing to take that chance." Keeffe slid out of bed and pulled on her jeans.

"Where are you going?" he asked.

"Where I should have gone a month ago," she said. "To see a lawyer."

Bad offered to go with Keeffe to the lawyer's, but she turned him down. "I want her to pay attention to the contract. You're too distracting."

He grinned his geeky, goofy grin, his ears turning a little pink. She couldn't get over how unaware he was of his own good looks. At least, his Dr. Jekyll side was. Mr. Hyde was all about his own hotness, but she hadn't seen him since that overnight camping trip three weeks ago, and that was fine with her.

Emma Lawson, now Emma Lawson, Esquire, had graduated from Red Rock High School a few years ahead of Keeffe. She had a one-room office in a strip mall off 89A. Her long, slightly mournful face reminded Keeffe of the horses that plodded up and down Monument Trail with tourists on their backs.

Keeffe explained about the statue and showed her the contract.

"And you want me to look it over and see if I can break it?" Emma asked.

Keeffe shook her head. "I doubt there's much you can do. My stepmom prides herself on her iron-clad contracts. There are artists she hasn't represented in ten years who still pay her a commission. What I really want is to stop her from shipping the statue to New York while my dad is out of town."

Emma scanned through the contract. Keeffe watched enviously. What would it be like to simply zip through page after page of printed material like that?

"The good news is, we can absolutely stop her," Emma said. "We can file an injunction requesting that the statue not leave Arizona until a judgment can be made about whether you're in compliance with the terms of the contract."

Keeffe released a breath she hadn't even realized she was holding. "That would be great."

"If you like," Emma said, "we can ask to have the statue placed in escrow, in the hands of a neutral party, citing bad faith on your stepmother's part."

Hope joined gratitude in Keeffe's chest. "That would be even better."

"How were you planning to pay for this?" Emma asked, but she didn't sound especially concerned. That was what happened when you wore gold jewelry and expensive hiking boots.

"Credit card," Keeffe said. It actually had open credit on it, thanks to Bad's deposit.

"I'll get to work on the injunction," Emma said.

Keeffe heaved a sigh of relief. "How long will that take?"

Maybe she'd just wait around till Emma was done and see if her former classmate wanted to go for drinks to celebrate. In high school, she'd avoided Emma as too smart for her. Now she was coming to realize Bad might be right. Maybe she was smart, too, just in a different way.

"I'll file it first thing Monday," Emma said.

Keeffe stared at her in dismay. "Lilith was getting ready to pack up the statue when I was there this morning. Monday may be too late."

It might already be too late.

Emma's face grew even longer. "It's four-thirty on Friday afternoon, Keeffe. To file it before Monday, I'd need to request an emergency injunction and make a judge come back into work on a weekend."

"Do that," Keeffe said.

Emma shook her head. "Judge Meyer is on call this weekend. He hates being called out unless it's life-and-death. This won't qualify."

Keeffe's disappointment was all the more intense for her momentary hope. She stuffed the contract back into the envelope.

"Thanks, anyway," she said. "I'll just have to think of something else."

Out in the parking lot, Keeffe called Bad to tell him what Emma had said.

"That sucks," he said, "but I'm sure it will be okay. Come on back and I'll take you out to dinner for your birthday."

His nonchalance pissed her off.

"I'm heading back to my place," she said. "I need some time to think."

"But it's your birthday." He sounded so disappointed you'd have thought he was talking about his birthday, rather than hers. "I had more celebrating planned."

"We can celebrate after I get my statue back." She hung up.

Back at her trailer, she paced the threadbare carpet of her narrow living room, trying to come up with another option. Beyond her picture window, the sun dropped behind Coffee Pot Rock in a flame of brilliant reds and pinks and golds, but the sky remained light. In the mountains, dusk lingered for a long time. She still remembered her first night at art school in Pasadena. She was shocked when the sky went dark fifteen minutes after the sun dropped below the horizon.

There had to be some way to stop Lilith from shipping *John* off to New York. After a half hour of pacing, she called Frida.

"I need to keep Lilith from selling it before Dad gets back," she said.

"Keeffe, she's not going to sell a statue she doesn't own."

"That's what Bad said. I think you're both wrong."

"If Dad's out of the country and you can't get an injunction, there's not much you can do."

"Maybe I should just steal the damned thing." Keeffe pictured herself dressed head to foot in black, sneaking into Dad's house to grab the statue. She giggled, but her giggle had a slight edge of hysteria to it.

"You know better than to try that, right?" Frida didn't see the humor. "Even if you got out of there without being arrested, where would you keep it?"

"Your house?"

"And become accessory after the fact? Think again." Frida's voice was sharp. She drew a deep breath, and her tone became gentler. "You're at the finish line. Just complete the mural and collect the statue."

"There may not be a statue to collect by the time I finish."

"The boys and I gave ours up willingly. She's not going to sell your statue out from under you. That would be crazy, not to mention illegal. Just hang in there and don't let her taunt you into doing something stupid, okay?"

It was pretty much what Bad had said.

Keeffe hung up the phone. Frida was right, of course. Breaking into Dad's house was crazy, even for Keeffe. Unfortunately, she couldn't rid herself of another mental picture, one of an auctioneer shouting "Sold!" as *John* passed into the hands of a stranger.

That couldn't happen. She couldn't allow it to happen. Removing the sculpture from Lilith's control wouldn't really be stealing. It would just be placing it in escrow, as Emma had suggested.

If she were to go after the statue, she'd have no problem getting into Dad's gated subdivision. The security in the complex focused on the front gates. All she'd have to do was hike in from Chimney Rock trailhead and cut through the neighbor's backyard to Dad's house. She'd done it dozens of times when she was in high school.

The more she thought about rescuing her statue, the more reasonable it seemed. Lilith was famous for leaving the back door unlocked. The house had a security system, but they hadn't changed the code since they moved in. Like many people who live in gated communities, they seemed to think the guard at the front gate made their home impervious to break-ins. Keeffe could slip in, scoop up *John*, and be gone before anyone was the wiser.

A bigger problem was what to do with him once she had him. She couldn't bring him back here to the trailer. Despite what she'd told Lilith the day McCall tried to buy it, she'd never store her mother's work inside her flimsy trailer. Even if Frida were willing to hide the statue, and it was clear she wouldn't be under the circumstances, her house would be Lilith's second stop.

Then Keeffe realized that didn't matter. Just as she couldn't line up law enforcement to help her wrest the statue from Lilith, Lilith would also be unable to use them to take it from her.

Keeffe was pretty sure Bad would be okay with housing the statue until she could complete her arrangements with the museums—if they were even interested in exhibiting a single statue.

She stopped dead in the middle of the room. Was she seriously considering breaking into her own father's house? Was she crazy? The image of someone boarding a plane carrying *John* in his Plexiglas case flashed across her mind. Once he was gone, she would never see him again. Was she just going to sit on her thumbs while that happened?

Not just no, but hell no.

CHAPTER 22

*B*ad hung up the phone feeling edgy. Something in Keeffe's voice set his Hade senses tingling. She was planning something crazy. He could hear it. He could feel it.

From McCall's garage full of high-end machines, he selected his own Mini Cooper as the least noticeable vehicle, only to discover that McCall's frame didn't fit inside the little car nearly as easily as his own. McCall's Lexus GX was his second choice.

He drove it to Ernesto's, pulling around to the side and parking it in the shadow of the restaurant. The driveway of Keeffe's mobile home park was clearly visible, but she wouldn't see the GX unless she looked right at it. Even if she did, she'd never seen the car before. She was unlikely to recognize who it was in the darkness.

Settling himself down to wait, he turned on the radio. Heavy metal roared from the speakers. He turned down the volume and changed the station to the alternative rock Keeffe favored.

It was tempting to pull his laptop from his backpack and continue researching how to stop Satan from destroying Sedona, but he stopped himself. If he became engrossed in the search, he might fail to notice Keeffe leaving.

At 11:30, his patience was rewarded when Keeffe's Honda nosed out onto 89A and headed west. Traffic was light, so he gave her a couple blocks' head start before following. After a few miles, she turned onto Dry Creek Road, the street leading to her dad's subdivision. Just as he'd suspected. The only question was, what exactly did she plan to do once she got there?

To his surprise, instead of driving to her dad's house, Keeffe turned into a parking lot with a wooden sign announcing the Chimney Rock trailhead. Bad cut the lights and let the GX coast to a stop off the side of the road well short of the entrance. To avoid making noise, he lowered the driver's side window and levered himself through. Then he reached back inside to grab his backpack. The tech it contained might come in handy.

By the time he got to the parking lot, Keeffe was already heading up the trail. She hiked the stony path by the half-light of the moon and a small flashlight like she'd done it a hundred times before. He grinned at an image of rebellious high schooler Keeffe sneaking out at night and putting one over on Lilith.

He gave her a good head start before following her. He didn't want to chance turning on his flashlight app, but that was okay. Hades were bred for darkness. Even though McCall's human eyes were less efficient in the dark than Bad's own, they were adequate in the moonlight. He moved silently up the rock-strewn path. Once or twice, Keeffe stopped and looked back, as though sensing someone behind her, but each time he retreated to the shadows. After forty-five minutes of up-and-down climbing, a development of upscale houses came into view.

Directly ahead lay Lilith's sprawling home, backed by an Olympic-sized swimming pool. Keeffe scaled the low wall that surrounded the pool and flitted across the patio to a full glass door. The doorknob turned beneath her hand.

The entire back of the house was made up of windows. Inside, she gravitated to a wall-mounted box with a glowing red diode in one corner. Crouching in the shadow of the wall, he eased his backpack off his shoulders.

Keeffe flipped open the plastic cover and tapped in a code. The diode continued to glow red. Her shoulders tensed. Urgently, she tapped in the code again. Still red. Her shoulders rose practically to her ears.

Inside the backpack, Bad located his universal remote. As Keeffe tried to disarm the alarm a third time, he pressed a button. The diode winked green. Keeffe's shoulders relaxed and her pent-up breath released.

She crossed the room into shadows where he could no longer see her. A moment later, she reappeared, the Plexiglas case containing the eagle statue in her hands. She was almost to the door when Lilith and Daniel rushed into the room. Daniel was weaving on his feet. Was he jet-lagged or drunk? With a sense of horror, Bad made out the outline of a gun in his hand.

Bad surged to his feet, ready to hurl himself between Keeffe and the gun, but McCall's sluggish human reflexes weren't nearly quick enough. Before he could get over the wall, Daniel's finger jerked on the trigger. The floor-to-ceiling window directly in front of Bad shattered. The bullet sped straight toward him and smashed into the wall, sending shards of concrete flying. His cheek stung as a fragment struck him in the face.

"Don't shoot," Lilith screamed. She grabbed Daniel's arm, very nearly causing him to fire again. "It's Keeffe."

What the hell? Lilith's reflexes were plenty fast enough to have stopped Daniel from firing the gun. Was she trying to kill Keeffe?

Lights in the room came on, putting Keeffe on display. She clutched her statue, her eyes wide with shock. Lilith, Bad noted, was dressed in an embroidered dressing gown and marabou slippers. Pretty stylish for someone awakened without warning.

"Keeffe?" Daniel staggered back, the color draining from his face, leaving him so pale he looked green. Under the harsh glare of the overhead lights, his nose was a network of broken blood vessels. "What are you doing here?"

He was shaking like the leaves on an aspen tree, but Bad couldn't tell if it was adrenaline from coming after the burglar, horror that he'd nearly shot his own daughter, or just a reaction to the icy air sweeping into the house through the shattered window.

Beside him, Lilith looked horrified, but the sparkle in her eyes told Bad it was a pretense.

He checked out the pool table. The packing materials that had been lying there earlier today were gone, as was the little she-demon. Lilith had deliberately lured Keeffe here. But for what purpose?

Bad crossed the tiled patio. "Keeffe? Are you okay?"

"I'm fine." Keeffe threw him a testy look. "What are you doing here?"

"What are *you* doing here?" Daniel's fear was morphing into the shamed anger of a drunk who had very nearly killed his own child.

"I came to get my statue. Today—" she checked her watch "—that is, yesterday was my birthday."

For an instant, Daniel looked remorseful, but anger quickly overwhelmed his guilt. "So you show up, unannounced, in the middle of the night and just break in?"

"I was here this morning." Keeffe's hands tightened on the Plexiglas case. "Lilith refused to let me have him."

"And you couldn't just wait and talk to me tomorrow?"

"I didn't know when you were coming home, and Lilith was packing it up to send to auction."

"Keeffe, I told you that wasn't the case." Lilith managed to look sad and disappointed and offended all at the same time. "We all know how you feel about me, but do you really think your father would allow that?"

When Keeffe didn't respond, Daniel's face reddened. "You really think I'd just let Lilith sell off the last sculpture your mother ever made?"

"You're Switzerland, remember?" Keeffe's tone was bitter. "You don't want to get involved."

Blood suffused Daniel's face, the rising tide of crimson offsetting the blue that had begun to tint his lips. "You thought—you actually thought—I'd let her take your statue and sell it out from under you?"

"Maybe Switzerland was a bad analogy," Bad said. "Maybe he meant he's like a referee, trying to keep the fight fair."

"Shut up," Keeffe and Daniel said at once. Lilith smirked.

"You haven't stopped her from any of the other things she did to this family," Keeffe said.

Daniel looked like he might burst a blood vessel. "Such as?"

"Like getting rid of Mom's stuff. Like selling off Frida's and the boys' sculptures."

"I didn't force them to sell their sculptures," Lilith said. "They made the decisions. I just handled the transactions to maximize the amount of money they received. I trust you don't have a problem with your siblings getting a fair return for giving up their sculptures?"

"And making me sign that contract." Keeffe remained focused on her dad, as though Lilith hadn't spoken.

Bad silently willed her to shut up. Raking up past grievances was a sure-fire way to lose an argument. No one wants to relive old guilt.

Lilith threw up her hands. "We were just trying to help you choose a career that wouldn't have you living on welfare for the rest of your life."

"Has it ever occurred to you I might be a good enough artist so that wouldn't happen? That I might be successful?" Keeffe watched Daniel. He didn't meet her eyes. "Well, has it?"

There was a short, painful silence.

"Despite everything I've done, every gallery in town has dropped you." Lilith's voice softened, like she regretted what she was saying, though Bad knew she was delighted. Things were going exactly as she'd hoped. "Your technique is strong, but your work just doesn't connect with people emotionally."

Keeffe flinched as if she'd been slapped. She turned to Bad. "He likes my work. Tell them."

"I love your work," Bad said. "The mural is turning out to be incredible."

"Would you like it as much if she weren't sleeping with you?" Lilith asked.

Keeffe's face flamed.

"Yes, I would," Bad said, but the damage was done. If Daniel hadn't known Keeffe was sleeping with her client before, he did now.

Lilith looked at Keeffe pityingly. "Seth gave you that commission because I begged him to. I know you think I'm trying to take your sculpture away from you, but it's not true, Keeffe. I'm just trying to make you see reality."

Keeffe turned to him, her face pleading with him to deny Lilith's statement.

"It's true Lilith asked me to give you a chance." Bad chose his words carefully. The mural had been his idea, not Lilith's, but now she was trying to turn it to her own advantage. In his mind, things were clear. He was on Keeffe's side, but until he figured out the stuff with the vortexes and how to keep her safe, it needed to look like he was playing Satan's game. Otherwise, the boss would redouble his efforts, possibly even pull Bad off the mission.

"But I do really like your work." His caution made his words sound lame and insincere.

Keeffe scorched him with a look of betrayal.

Daniel said, "All we're asking is that you wait to collect the statue until you finish the mural."

Fieldwork sucked. It was one thing to work behind the scenes, creating technology that had the potential, if used in certain ways, to make people's lives uncomfortable. It was another to be right here, face-to-face with someone you had conspired to undermine and make miserable.

Then Keeffe's head lifted. Bad drew a sigh of relief.

Resting the case on her hipbone, she said, "I'm going to put *John* in my old bedroom till you get the window fixed. It's the farthest from here, so it should be safe from the weather."

Bad wanted to cheer. Keeffe might be a little bloodied, but she was not beaten. Her inner strength made a mockery of ten years of effort on Lilith's part. She left the room.

"Do you have any plywood?" he asked Daniel. "We should patch up that hole."

While they boarded up the window, Keeffe swept up the broken glass and Lilith looked on, like a queen observing the labors of a group of peasants. When Keeffe finished, she put away the broom and dustpan and walked to the back door.

"The next time I come here, I'm taking my sculpture home with me," she said, her voice hard.

"The next time you come here, please use the front door," Lilith said.

A wave of color rushed up Keeffe's neck into her face. Her eyes went to her dad, begging him to side with her this once, but his eyes were on the floor.

"And please call first," Lilith added.

Daniel said nothing.

"A lot of help you were." Keeffe's voice was bitter as they made their way back down the trail. "Did Lilith really beg you to let me paint your mural?"

Bad was concerned about Lilith's next move. He'd planned to use the walk back to the cars to consider the possible gambits she might try and what his response should be to each one but it sounded like Keeffe needed to talk. He considered his answer carefully.

"She asked," he said. That wasn't true. The mural had been his idea, but outing Lilith's lie might open up more questions he wasn't prepared to answer. "And I agreed to consider you. I chose you because you're good, though, not because she asked me to."

She halted and turned to face him. "So why couldn't you say that back there?"

"I did."

"Only after she made it sound like a pity commission." Keeffe moved on, skirting a twisted mesquite tree. "Was it fun, watching me fail?"

Bad ran a hand through his hair. Even though he was accustomed to dealing with anger—anger was the most frequently expressed emotion among demons—hers threw him off-stride.

"You didn't fail. Why would you say that?"

"Do you see a sculpture in my hands?"

"No, but that wasn't the purpose, was it? I mean, you didn't really want to subject *John* to 30-degree temperatures and 17-percent humidity out here tonight."

She whipped around to face him. "He's made of rock. He can withstand a little cold."

Bad came from a tribe of miners. He knew rock. If the stone from which Rachel had sculpted *John* had an internal flaw, sudden exposure to the cold might very well cause it to crack. Keeffe's face begged him for reassurance. Now was not a good time to point out that if she'd been successful in removing the statue from her dad's house, it may have been at the cost of destroying it.

What would that have done to Satan's plan? It didn't matter, he supposed. Destroying the statue might stop Satan, but it would also devastate Keeffe.

He returned to his previous argument.

"Your purpose was to prevent Lilith from sending him to New York and you accomplished that goal. You also had a secondary goal—to show your dad that Lilith was behaving unscrupulously. You were successful there, too."

Keeffe shoved her hands deeper into her pocket. "That's not true. He believes all her lies."

"I disagree. I think your dad sees Lilith pretty realistically. He's just afraid of being alone, so he ignores what he doesn't want to see."

Keeffe threw up her hands in quick denial. "He wouldn't be alone. He has four kids and two grandkids. Not to mention millions of fans."

Bad spoke gently. "Four kids who have their own lives. And while he might have millions of fans, he's lost the respect of the art community. So he clings to the only person who's there for him."

In doing so, of course, Daniel was making a mistake. The last person he should lean on was Lilith, who was untrustworthy even by demonic standards, but Keeffe needed to calm down and take a more logical approach to this problem before she did something that played into Satan's hands.

Keeffe glared at him. "You don't understand how awful she is."

"I know exactly how awful she is. But you're not going to win going head-to-head with her. You've been trying that for ten years without success." Overhead, the clouds moved and an errant moonbeam struck Bad's face.

Keeffe reached out to touch his cheek. "What did you do to your cheek?"

He touched it with his fingertips. "When your dad's bullet hit the wall, a chip flew up and cut me. It's nothing."

Keeffe stopped suddenly to lean against an immense boulder along the edge of the path. "That bullet could have killed you."

"Or you," he said.

"Oh my god," She started to shake.

"Are you all right?" He put his hand out, then took it away, not sure what to do.

"No," she said. "You just made me realize I probably owe Lilith my life."

He snorted. "Think how I feel. I owe mine to your dad being a lousy shot."

That made her laugh, a laugh that indicated the release of pent-up nerves. His laughter intertwined with hers and soon they were staggering down the path, hooting and bumping into each other and gasping for air with tears running down their cheeks. Every few minutes she'd try to stop, but then he'd catch her eye, or her gaze would fall on the cut on his cheek, and she'd go off again.

They were halfway to the bottom before they got themselves under control.

"You're right," she said. "Your analysis is completely accurate. I'm okay, you're okay and there's no way Lilith can ship *John* off to New York. Everything's good. I just have one question."

"What's that?" he asked, still smiling.

"Why did you follow me?"

He picked his way down a steep spot in the trail and then held out his hand to help her down. When she released his hand, he said, "I was concerned about you."

She stared up at him, and he wished he knew what she was thinking. The moonlight leached the color out of everything, making her eyes into dark pools. She took his hands and laced them around her waist, then slipped hers around him. She laid her head against his chest.

"You get me," she said.

He gathered her close and pressed a kiss on the top of her head. She sighed and tightened her arms around him.

"I like to think I do."

They stood there, in the moonlight, just holding each other for a long time. It was one of the best moments Bad could ever remember.

After Keeffe fell asleep, Bad lay awake, thinking. Lilith was practically purring when he and Keeffe left her dad's house. She had something else planned but he didn't know what. She was determined to get the statue, and a little setback, like the fact that Keeffe's birthday had come and gone, wasn't going to stop her.

His earlier thought about the statue's fragility returned. What if, somehow, the statue were demolished before Satan could acquire it? Without a statue at each vortex, Malphas's spell would be incomplete and probably unworkable. Then he thought about Keeffe's desolation if that happened. Destroying the statue might stop Satan, but there had to be a way to do that without also devastating Keeffe.

He looked at the problem from every possible direction and found only one viable solution, given the array of demons they were up against. The best way to ensure that Keeffe's statue wound up safely in her hands and to safeguard her mother's legacy was to tell Keeffe the truth. He would have to make sure there were no electronic ears listening, so that his confession didn't make its way back to Hell. What was less clear was how he would convince Keeffe to believe him.

"Lilith is a demon" might be a statement Keeffe could easily accept. "I'm also a demon, in possession of an Internet billionaire's body, but

I'm on your side" would be a harder sell. He needed to set the stage in a way that would make her accept his story without losing her trust.

At his side, Keeffe snuggled more closely against him. Where there was a will, there was a way. He had the will to solve the problem. He just needed to figure out the way.

The next morning he pulled up a copy of Keeffe's dossier on his laptop and combed through it, line by line, looking for something to allow him to connect with her on a deeper level. Research should have continued to update her dossier since he came Above, but there was only one entry dated after his arrival, a note about her favorite painting that he'd added himself. Much more had come to light since then, but no one had bothered to add it. The work being done in DemSec under Ornias's leadership was atrocious.

With a sense of surprise, Bad realized he didn't care. He didn't care that Ornias had control of DemSec. He didn't care that they were doing lousy work. He didn't even care that he was reduced to working within the limitations of human invention.

In fact, there was nothing he'd like more than to stay right here on this wretched, technologically backward, sun-warmed, dew-sprinkled planet with Keeffe and see what he could do to make things better.

At what point had he changed sides? The change had actually begun that first afternoon, when the Sedona sun had pierced him with its beauty, allowing all the other wonderful, hopeful, luminous things about this world to seep into his consciousness.

No wonder the Almighty continued to love this screwed-up, pathetic, struggling planet, despite all of its flaws. With a sense of surprise, he realized the Almighty was no longer his adversary. They were on the same team now. Would that gain him any help if push came to shove? It was hard to say.

He needed a gesture, something romantic and original, to demonstrate his feelings for Keeffe, something that would get through to her in a way that words or gifts would not. He read through her dossier again and paused at the note saying her favorite painting was *The Sleeping Gypsy*, by Henri Rousseau.

What was it she'd told him when he'd given her the phone? She'd said she liked the painting, in part, because the setting reminded her of Sedona. He thought about all the formations they'd visited and an idea took shape in his mind. He made a list of what he needed to re-create the painting. Everything he needed but one item, a life-sized stuffed lion, should be available right here in Sedona.

He ordered the lion online. According to the website, it would arrive next Friday. He'd spend the week till then working as Keeffe's gofer, moving the ladder, rubbing her shoulders, and doing anything else that might help her finish sooner.

On Tuesday, while Keeffe was working on an area that didn't require his assistance, he drove into town to buy the remaining items he needed to re-create the painting.

His first stop was a pottery store, where he picked up a terracotta urn. An outdoor store yielded a rainbow-striped sleeping bag, a pink bath towel, and a walking stick. Then he headed for the music store. The shop had a lute in the front window, just like the picture on their website.

He went inside. "I'd like to purchase that lute."

The clerk was short, with olive skin and black hair. If he'd added a pair of horns and a tail, he could have been one of Bad's cousins.

"It's not for sale," he said. "It's just for display."

Bad pulled a wad of cash from his pocket. The clerk's dark eyes sparkled.

"I'll give you a thousand dollars for it," Bad said.

Reluctantly, the clerk shook his head. "The owner would kill me."

The clerk wasn't the owner. Bad didn't know why that bothered him, but it did.

"He'll kill you if you pass up getting a thousand bucks for a hundred-dollar instrument."

The clerk looked torn.

"I guess I could call him." He checked the clock hanging behind the counter. "He might be up by now."

The clerk made the call, but no one picked up.

"Sorry," he said.

"He'll probably reward you for your initiative." Bad added another hundred to the sheaf of bills he was holding out.

The clerk grabbed them. "I'll get it for you."

Bad's final two stops were at a florist's and a chocolatier. He walked back to his car, taking in the bustling business district. Sedona was such a beautiful little place. He thought about Satan's words—*I may even be able to destroy the whole town.* That couldn't happen. He wouldn't let it happen.

Keeffe was vaguely aware that Bad had been gone a good part of the day, but she was too busy to pay much attention. Today she was working on the Seven Sacred Pools. She was determined to get the water, and the sunlight sparkling on it, just right. She had just achieved the perfect level of luminosity when Bad strolled into the mural room holding something behind his back.

When he saw the pools, his mouth fell open. He dropped a box of chocolates and a bunch of red roses wrapped in cellophane onto a tarp-covered library table and hurried forward to inspect the painting more closely.

"How did you do that?" he asked, peering at the wall. He stretched out a curious finger, then snatched it back. "It looks so real, like I could jump in and get wet."

Keeffe beamed, pleased beyond measure at his reaction. She would never in a million years have expected the guy she met at Lilith's that first day to be enough of an art connoisseur to truly appreciate what she did, but it was clear he was awed.

"That's what sfumato gives you," she said.

He leaned in a little closer. "That's incredible." Then he straightened, wrapped his arms around her and kissed her. "You're incredible."

She stood quiet for a moment, breathing in the delicious scent of him, relishing the strength of his arms. She liked this new, more relaxed McCall a lot better than the guy she'd met that first day at Dad's. When he released her, he turned her around and began massaging her shoulders without being asked. She sagged with pleasure under his hands.

Then she caught sight of the candy and flowers. "What's up with the goodies?"

"It's Valentine's Day," he said, nuzzling her ear.

She turned to him, scrunching up her face in dismay. "Oh, crap. I forgot all about it."

She hoped he understood. The only time she'd taken off since her birthday was for a quick trip to confession on Saturday—the priest assigned her to perform an act of public service to make up for her sins, and she figured her next grief group would cover that nicely— and on Sunday to go to Mass.

"You can make it up to me," he said.

"How?" she asked.

"Friday night, whether you're done here or not, you take time off to do something with me."

"Deal," she said. Across the room, she noticed a tiny area of the seventh pool that wasn't quite right. She picked up her paintbrush.

On Friday, the lion arrived as promised. Fortunately, Keeffe was immersed in the mural, so Bad had no problem spiriting it out to the garage and stowing it in the trunk of the Lexus. There was just one more thing he needed to do before outing himself, a kind of insurance policy in case things went awry.

Grabbing a set of car keys, he made a detour past the mural room, where Keeffe was working feverishly on a depiction of Cathedral Rock. Once she completed that, all that remained was a single blank spot in the southeast corner of the room.

He walked up behind her and massaged her shoulders with the

touch he'd perfected over the past few weeks. She melted under his hands, as she always did. Would he ever get used to that?

"I have some errands to run," he said.

"More roses and chocolates?"

"Something like that."

She twisted to lift her face and he kissed her. She smelled of paint and sweat.

"I find the scent of your pheromones irresistible," he said.

She rolled her eyes. "You're such a sweet-talker."

His ears got hot, a sure sign they were turning red, and she laughed. He pulled her roughly to him and kissed her, hard, and she stopped laughing. Her lips were open and she was breathing fast. He grinned with satisfaction. She was as attracted to him as he was to her.

Her eyelids swept down. She peeped up at him from beneath her eyelashes. "So don't resist."

He dropped to his knees and unbuttoned her jeans, sliding them down to her ankles. She started to kick them off, but he trapped them with his hands. He buried his face between her legs and proceeded to nuzzle and lick and kiss her until her knees started to shake. He added a couple of skillful fingers into the mix and she started breathing faster. After a few minutes, her spine arched as she climaxed. He grabbed her ass to keep her from crumpling.

It was only when she came back to herself that he released her. He dragged her jeans back up over her hips and fastened them.

"Now you?" she asked, weaving a little.

It was tempting but he needed to get his backup plan in place. *John* wouldn't be safe until he was out of Lilith's hands.

"Maybe later. You need to get back to work."

"Did I ever tell you you're the perfect boyfriend?"

That made him smile, but he shook his head. "I'm not. In fact, I'm probably the least perfect guy you've ever met."

She squinted at him, looking adorably woozy.

"None of us lives up to the dreams God has for us. That's what forgiveness is for."

He just hoped she remembered that tonight when he told her who he really was.

Glancing around to be sure no one saw him, he pressed a button on the universal remote in his pocket and unlocked the flimsy door to Keeffe's trailer.

The candles and shawl intended to camouflage the footlocker were still piled on the couch. He opened the hasps and lifted the lid. Inside were stacks of sketchbooks and a pile of bank statements. *Perfect.* Keeffe's addiction to old-school had worked in his favor, as he'd hoped it would. The manila envelope containing the contracts Keeffe had signed with Lilith and with him were in there, too, along with her mother's brown leather journal.

He fanned the pages of the journal. Only the first dozen or so pages were filled. Rachel's handwriting was a series of artistic, looping swirls that were difficult to read until you figured out the code. Bad picked a random entry and deciphered it:

"September twentieth. Ed and Claude have decided they want to major in graphic storytelling. Not sure how their love of video games is going to support them, but Mom said the same thing about my sculptures, and I've done all right."

Keeffe's brothers would have been high school seniors then, so Lilith's claim that she redirected them away from fine arts degrees was a lie. No surprise there.

The sound of a car outside the trailer dragged Bad back to the present. He checked his phone. Ronnie would be serving lunch soon, and lunch was one of the few breaks Keeffe was taking this week as she raced to finish the mural so she could collect her statue.

Where were those drawings? He searched the footlocker until he found the scale model of the original superhero mural Keeffe had proposed, rolled up in a tight scroll and stuffed into a corner. He unfurled the scroll and looked at the beautiful detail. All the characters, even the minor ones, had individual, expressive faces. You could tell what each one was feeling just by looking at him or her—Batman was grim, Black Widow sensuously pleased with herself, Captain America determined. Keeffe would have been as good at portraiture as she was at landscape, if she'd been interested.

He rolled the scroll back up and put it in his backpack. In exchange, he extracted a bill of sale he'd printed at McCall's. It said: *Sold to Abaddon, Demon of Sloth, for $15,000, one scale drawing of superhero scenes.* He'd backdated it to the day before Keeffe's birthday. Using the number on her bank statements, he deposited the money into her account, adjusting the date on the deposit to match the bill of sale.

He closed the footlocker and got to his feet. If he wasn't able to convince her of his true identity, or if she believed him but wanted nothing more to do with him, he'd provided her with some protection.

"Can I take off this blindfold now?" Keeffe reached for the knot at the back of her head. Bad had tied it around her eyes before they left his place, and that was about twenty minutes ago. She'd tried to keep track of their turns, but she had no idea where they were.

"Not yet." A gentle swat landed on her hands. "Sit here for a minute while I get everything ready."

His car door opened. Footsteps crunched on gravel. There was a metallic pop as the trunk lid opened. From sounds alone, she couldn't identify the items Bad removed from the trunk. He walked away.

Once his footsteps faded, the car was silent, in the way that the desert was silent in the winter. The air coming in through the open door was crisp. She tried to think what lay twenty minutes from Bad's place. Lots of things. Sedona was a small town surrounded by many sightseeing spots, though most of them weren't open to the public at night.

Off in the distance, a coyote howled. She breathed in through her nose, but the fragrances that would be present in the warmer seasons were missing in February. The air smelled like nothing but clean, fresh air, with a hint of dark chocolate. After a couple of tries, she got a hint of mesquite and salt-bush, but that didn't tell her anything. Those plants were everywhere.

Bad returned to the car and collected more things from the trunk, then walked away again. A few minutes later, the smell of wood burning wafted to the car. Then more footsteps and her car door opened.

"Milady?" He took her hand.

She unbuckled her seatbelt and let him help her from the car. Once she was on her feet, he pulled her against him and lowered his mouth to hers. His kiss was deep and intimate and sexy as all Hell, but her curiosity was overwhelming.

"What's going on?" she asked. "Where are we?"

"Be patient."

She growled, and he laughed. He closed her car door and led her maybe fifty paces. Then he removed her blindfold.

In the distance, beyond a free-flowing stream, a full moon hung above the center spire of Cathedral Rock. At Keeffe's feet lay a down sleeping bag, spread invitingly. In the moonlight, the rainbow stripes of the sleeping bag were pastels. A terracotta water jug stood at one corner of the bag. Alongside it were a black lacquer lute and a stout walking stick. Best of all, on the far side of the bag, a life-sized stuffed lion stood guard.

"You made the painting." Keeffe clapped her hands in delight. "*The Sleeping Gypsy.* You made it."

His grin was almost as bright as the moonlight. "Do you like it?"

"I love it." She couldn't stop her cheesy grin.

"I thought it might be fun to make love inside your favorite painting."

"The. Perfect. Boyfriend," she said.

His smile seemed to dim a little. "Just keep thinking that."

She stripped off her clothes and slid into the down bag, shivering. In the bright moonlight, the planes and shadows of his body were riveting, though he wasn't quite as cut as he'd been when she first met him. He hadn't been in his workout room since that camping trip. She actually liked him better this way. He looked a little more human.

"I should paint you like this," Keeffe said. "Or sculpt you. I haven't tried sculpture since I was in college, but you'd make a magnificent subject."

He nudged her hip with his foot. "If you don't let me into that sleeping bag, you'll have to sculpt me without a penis because mine is going to freeze off."

Giggling, she scooted aside. He slipped in beside her.

Making love in a single-person sleeping bag was not the easiest thing they'd ever attempted. While trying to roll the condom on, she almost kneed him in the groin. His yelp, as high pitched as the bark of a prairie dog, made her collapse into laughter.

"You are not taking me seriously." He proceeded to do things with his hands and mouth that made her take him very seriously indeed.

The feel of him, steel sheathed in velvet, replaced the urge to giggle with the urge to have him inside her. She wrapped her legs around his waist, giving a strangled cry as he penetrated deep into her core. The scent of dark chocolate wrapped itself around her, and he filled her. His lips nibbled her collarbone, and his breath was warm and damp against her skin. It had never been this good. She squeezed his ass, marveling at the strong muscles beneath his skin as he stroked in and out, each stroke bringing her nearer her climax. Finally, she could hold back no longer. With a muffled cry, she let herself be swept away. As though he couldn't bear to be left behind, he followed.

What seemed like hours later, she floated back down to earth. She rubbed her hands over his sweat-slicked back. "God, that was good."

"How good?"

"A ten."

"For artistic merit? Or technical?"

She glanced around at the beautifully staged setting. Where in the world had he acquired a life-sized stuffed lion? She kissed the base of his throat, where his pulse still hammered.

"Both," she said. "You have it all. No wonder I'm in love with you."

It wasn't till his dark eyes widened in surprise that she realized what she'd said. He opened his mouth to reply, but she put her fingers over his lips.

"Don't," she said. "Don't say anything. If you say it now, it will feel like I manipulated you."

"But I—"

"Not yet," she said and kissed him to stop his mouth.

Bad looked down on Keeffe's sleeping face in the moonlight and smiled so wide it felt like McCall's lips might split. Her unexpected confession left him humbled and more determined than ever to tell her the truth. If she truly loved him, she would believe him and trust him.

He stretched out his hand to wake her, but he couldn't bring himself to disturb her rest. She'd been working on the mural day and night since her attempted burglary a week ago, and she was wise to do so. Even though Lilith didn't have a leg to stand on legally, the fact that she'd gotten Daniel to side with her tied Bad's hands. Keeffe could, with perfect legality, remove the statue from Lilith's possession but that would mean confronting Daniel, a risk Keeffe had made clear she wasn't willing to take.

Once Keeffe finished the mural, Daniel and Lilith would have no excuse to hold onto the statue. Unfortunately, knowing Lilith, she was already scheming against that eventuality. And even though the receipt he'd put in Keeffe's footlocker was a good backup plan, the one thing that would truly allow her to protect herself and her statue was his confession.

Right now, though, she needed her sleep. Tomorrow, first thing, he'd tell her the truth.

CHAPTER 23

The next morning, Frida's call woke Keeffe. Bad's side of the bed was empty. From the sounds coming from the bathroom, he was in the shower.

"It's supposed to get up to seventy degrees today," Frida said. "Dad and Lilith are hosting a barbecue this afternoon. They want you to come."

Keeffe's jaw clenched. "I told them I wasn't coming back until I could pick up *John*."

"That's why Lilith wanted me to call you. She said you'd say no to her. How close are you to being finished? Are you going to make it to your residency on time?"

Keeffe had two, maybe three hard days of work remaining. Longer if Bad commandeered an evening, as he had last night. A smile touched her lips as she thought about the scene he'd created for her.

"My residency doesn't start till the twenty-seventh," Keeffe said. "I still have a week, and I'm almost done with the mural."

"So, declare it done, get McCall to pay you, and collect *John*. Easy-peasy."

Bad had offered to do that a week ago, after her attempted burglary on her birthday, but it felt dishonest to get him to lie and say

250

the painting was done when it wasn't. She might be willing to steal a statue that was hers anyway, but her integrity as an artist was sacred. And, despite their differences, Dad had made it clear the sculpture wasn't going anywhere and she believed him.

"I can't," she said. "There's still one blank spot on the wall, where I'm planning to paint the Chapel of the Holy Cross."

"This invitation is an olive branch," said Frida. "If you toss it back in their faces, there may not be another one."

"I don't want to toss it back in their faces. I want to beat Lilith over the head with it."

"Come on, Keeffe." The plea in her sister's voice reminded Keeffe that Frida was supposed to find out if she had successfully conceived yesterday.

Maybe that was why she wanted everyone together—to announce her long-awaited pregnancy. Keeffe looked around the room, where, over the past month, Sedona's beauty had unfolded, replacing bare white walls—except for that one remaining bare spot. She was almost done, and Frida's announcement, after two years of trying, was too big an event to miss.

"We'll be there," she said.

A few minutes later, Bad joined her, still in his bathrobe, his hair wet and rumpled. His eyes were a warm brown. She rose up on tiptoes to kiss him.

"Frida just called," she said. "Lilith and Dad are hosting a family barbecue this afternoon and they want us there.

Bad grimaced. "Do we have to?"

"Kind of. This will be the first time I've seen my dad since we broke into his house."

"*You* broke into his house."

"You were an accessory."

"All the more reason to stay away."

She looked into his brown eyes and realized he wasn't joking.

"Frida wants us there. I think she's going to tell everyone she's pregnant."

His eyes darted around like a trapped animal's. After a minute, his shoulders drooped and he sighed.

"Okay, we'll go." He kissed his way down her neck, leaving a trail of fire everywhere his lips touched. "But you owe me when we get home."

She drew in a deep breath through her nose, smelling chocolate and cayenne and soap from the shower.

"That doesn't have to wait till we get home."

Bad had rehearsed what he was going to say while he was in the shower, and he was pretty sure it would go well.

"I have something to tell you," he said.

Keeffe smiled at him, her eyes languorous from the great sex they'd just shared. It got better every time. McCall's body had become as familiar as his own, and as he and Keeffe learned each other's preferences and the connection between them deepened, sex had gone from an acrobatic and pleasurable workout to a soul-shattering communion.

"What's that?" she asked.

It was clear she expected him to say he loved her, and he wanted to, but first there was his confession to get through.

"Promise me you'll hear me out," he said. "No matter how crazy it sounds."

"Were you banking points?" she asked, stretching like a cat, as if her body were knit from cartilage rather than bone.

That was exactly what he'd been doing. He licked his lips, hoping her perceptiveness would work in his favor.

"You have something to tell me," she prompted.

Before he could speak, a discreet knock sounded on the bedroom door.

"What?" he roared.

Keeffe poked him in the ribs. "Don't be mean to Ronnie."

"What is it, Ronnie?" he called, in a more moderate tone.

"Excuse me, sir"—Ronnie's voice was muffled by the heavy panel—"you have a visitor."

"A visitor?" He frowned. McCall never got visitors.

"Yes, sir. He's in the rec room waiting. He asked to talk to you privately."

Bad growled, making Keeffe chuckle.

"It's probably just as well," she said, checking the clock. "I need to get some painting done before we leave."

She kissed him and disappeared into the bathroom.

Irritated, Bad got dressed. It was probably some business acquaintance of McCall's. Bad had nothing to say to such a person. Ronnie should have gotten rid of him, and so Bad would tell him once the visitor was gone.

He got to the doorway of the rec room and stopped dead. His own body, still dark and hairy, but looking a little more buff than Bad remembered, perched on the sofa. *Shit.* McCall was back. As he watched, his body capsized like a marooned sailboat. Before he could marshal his defenses, McCall streamed up his nose.

Bad shot Ronnie a look of betrayal. "Why didn't you warn me?"

"The girl was with you," the old demon said. "I couldn't very well tell you Mr. McCall was back, wanting his body, could I?"

Bad supposed not.

"Your mission was supposed to end on Keeffe's birthday." It felt strange to hear words that he hadn't thought issuing from his lips. "That was a week ago."

"No, it wasn't," Bad said. "He gave me six weeks, two weeks beyond her birthday."

"He changed his mind."

Bad told himself not to panic. "He can't do that. I have his promise recorded on my phone."

McCall snorted. "Good luck with that. The boss wants this over with."

McCall now viewed Satan as his boss. Bad wanted to panic, but he no longer had a monopoly on McCall's adrenal glands.

"Don't worry," McCall said. "I'm not going to kick you out. He sent me up to help you finish up."

That didn't make things any better.

"It didn't work well with Keeffe when we tried coexisting before," Bad said.

Their right hand waved that away. "Not to worry. I'm down with the program now."

From across the room, Ronnie watched them cautiously.

Their head tilted down. Their eyes raked their body from shoulders to feet.

"I have a paunch." McCall sounded completely horrified. He lifted their arm and checked his triceps. "And chicken-fat arms. You let my arms turn into chicken fat."

He glared into the mirror over the fireplace. "Have you worked out one single time since I've been gone?"

"I've been busy," Bad said.

McCall bounced on the balls of their feet. "My legs don't feel too bad."

"I've been doing lots of hiking."

McCall grabbed their glutes and squeezed. "And having lots of sex, feels like."

Bad didn't want to go there, so he looked at his own abandoned body on the couch. "If you want a workout, help me put my body in storage. Keeffe will be out here any minute."

With Ronnie's help, they hoisted Bad's body off the couch and hauled it to the room where they'd put it last time. Ronnie disappeared out the door. Later, when Keeffe wasn't around, they'd have to roll it in a tarp and hide it in the garage.

McCall plucked the Gehenna Glasses off Bad's body's face and pressed a button on the nosepiece, turning them off. What was it he didn't want reported back to Hell? He looked at himself in the mirror.

"When you were in Hell," he asked, "did you know a chick named Lamia?"

"The serpent?"

"Right," McCall said.

"We went out a few times," Bad said. "Why?"

"No reason." McCall pressed the button again and resettled the glasses on their nose so that every glance, every conversation, was recorded and transmitted back to Hell.

Worse than that, Bad could already tell that McCall was stronger, more in control, than he'd been before he left. Someone had tutored him on maintaining the upper hand.

Would Bad be better off abandoning McCall's body and reentering his own? Back in his own form, he could go ahead and talk to Keeffe, tell her what was going on. How likely was she to listen to a hairy little guy with horns and a tail? Especially since he'd told her his Hade body was a robot? The more lies he had to confess before he got to the truth, the less disposed she'd be to believe him.

Did she really need him?

With the deposit he'd made to her bank account for her superhero drawings, he had assured she could keep *John*. Unless, of course, McCall declared the receipt a forgery. He needed to stay right where he was until he was sure Keeffe would keep her statue.

He also needed a game plan for keeping McCall from taking over.

When they got back to the rec room, he fished the bottle of orange pills out of the drawer in the end table and twisted off the lid. "Bet you've missed these," he said, shaking the bottle the way a dog owner shakes a box of treats at their pet.

McCall screwed the lid right back on.

"Not when we're working. Drugs are for future clients, not demons."

Bad heard him with dismay. He sounded far more focused than he'd been before.

A moment later Keeffe appeared in the doorway. She paused, eying him warily. "You're wearing your glasses again."

Bad waited for McCall to jump in with an explanation, but he didn't speak.

Say something, McCall hissed inside his head.

"I've been experiencing some eyestrain lately." Bad smiled weakly. "Too much screen time, I guess."

She stepped closer and inspected his eyes carefully. Evidently, she was satisfied with what she saw because she said, "Are you ready to go?"

Bad tried to think of anything he was less ready to do and failed. "Sure," he said.

When Keeffe and Bad arrived at Dad's, Bad handed her the keys to the Lexus.

"Put those in your purse, please."

She looked at the keys, then at him. "Why?"

"I may have a few beers."

"Are you that nervous?" she asked.

His lips twisted wryly. "The last time I was here, your dad almost shot me."

"In that case," she said. "I should be the one doing the drinking. He was aiming at me."

Their laughter brought back the memory of staggering down Chimney Rock trail, laughing like children. She put the keys in her purse. It was a small thing, but it made her feel like they were a couple.

On the patio, Dad was grilling burgers. Ed and Claude stood nearby. Camille crouched near the pool, trying to explain to Andy and Noah that, yes, it was warm enough to be outside without a jacket, but no, it wasn't warm enough to swim. Frida and Jen had kicked back in a couple of chaise longues, soaking in the February sunshine. Keeffe didn't see Suzanne, which probably meant she was delivering a baby.

Lilith stepped out of the house, wearing red short shorts and stiletto sandals that should have looked ridiculous on a woman her age but instead looked fabulous. A tiny smile curled the corners of her lips, for no reason that Keeffe could see.

Keeffe wore a denim skirt and a pair of high-heeled sandals that showed off her own long legs. Legs that were twenty years younger than Lilith's. Slipping her arm through Bad's, she smirked right back at her stepmother.

The plywood that Dad and Bad had put up to cover the broken window was gone, replaced by glass. On the far side of the room, *John* lifted his head and aimed himself toward heaven. Keeffe set her jaw. She should be taking him home. She told herself to let it go. It wasn't worth making a scene. In a few more days, it would all be over.

She lifted her face and drank in the sunlight. Other than the outing with Bad the night before, she had barely left the mural room since her burglary attempt. It felt good not to be working for a change.

Bad wandered over to the grill and Claude handed him a beer. Keeffe headed for the chaise longues.

"How are you doing?" Frida asked, her eyes on Bad.

"Good," Keeffe said. "I'll finish the mural on Monday, probably. Then I can take *John* home, and we'll be done with this crap once and for all."

Frida grinned at her slyly. "Whose home would that be?"

Keeffe's ears grew warm. "We're not living together. It's just more convenient for me to sleep there while I'm working such long hours. I've got the residency coming up, remember?"

"That's only for a month," Frida said. "I'm guessing a certain someone may decide he needs to spend time in the southern part of the state soon."

Keeffe looked over at Bad. As though he could feel her eyes on him, he turned and smiled at her. Behind his glasses, his brown eyes looked anxious. She wanted to tell him he had nothing to worry about. The way she felt about him wasn't going to change.

He mouthed *I love you* and Keeffe thought she might melt into a puddle right there on the deck. It was the first time he'd ever said it. She'd been sure he was going to after they made love this morning, but then Ronnie interrupted.

It occurred to her that she hadn't asked who his visitor was, or why he'd left so quickly.

"Oh, my god," said Frida. "I feel like I'm trapped inside a valentine. I don't think I've ever seen you so smitten."

Keeffe told her about Bad's re-creation of *The Sleeping Gypsy* the night before.

"It was so beautiful," she said, knowing she sounded completely sappy and not caring a bit.

"Did he get a photograph of it?" asked Jen.

Keeffe shook her head. "No. He said he knows how I feel about technology, so last night was about being technology-free."

Frida looked over at Bad and shook her head. "All that and romance, too. That guy is almost too good to be true."

"It feels too good to be true." Keeffe fought the urge to cross herself. To change the subject, she asked. "What did Suzanne say yesterday? Are you pregnant?"

Frida's face lit up like a tiki torch.

"I'll take that as a yes," Keeffe said.

"We're planning to announce it later," Frida said. "So don't tell anybody, but I am."

Keeffe squeezed her hands. "That's wonderful. Congratulations!"

Frida and Jen's faces were radiant.

Keeffe looked over at Bad to share the news, but his eyes were on Lilith's butt. Keeffe frowned, confused. This was the first time she'd seen him and Lilith together since the day her stepmother had introduced them. Had her initial impression been correct, after all? Overhead, a tiny cloud scudded across the sun, obscuring the bright sunlight for an instant.

But wait, that wasn't true. He'd been with her on her birthday, both in the morning and later that night, and he'd shown no signs of being fascinated with Lilith either time. Keeffe's confusion deepened.

Lilith walked into the house then, her hips swinging back and forth like a metronome, drawing attention to her perfectly shaped ass. No wonder he was staring.

"Do you think she's had work done?" asked Frida.

"Yes," Keeffe said. "No woman in her mid-forties could possibly have an ass like that naturally."

Especially since Keeffe had never known her to exercise.

Bad was all too aware of Keeffe's distress, but McCall refused to drag his eyes away from Lilith's derrière.

Come on, dude. Keeffe is going to kill us.

Give me a break, McCall replied. *I haven't had a chance to look at that ass in a month.*

Was that true, or had Lilith visited McCall while he was Below? Probably not, at least not for sex. There was no way Lilith would have had intercourse with a Hade body.

Grimly, Bad bullied McCall out of their frontal lobe, but by the time he'd managed to regain control of their eyes, the door had closed behind Lilith. He tried to throw Keeffe an apologetic glance, but she refused to look at him. Great, just great.

Keeffe decided she'd been mistaken about McCall—no, Bad—ogling Lilith's butt. His eyes were still a deep, warm brown. Mr. Hyde hadn't reappeared. Bad was probably just shocked that a woman of Lilith's age would dress that way at a family barbecue.

Other than that minor incident, Bad behaved like the perfect boyfriend. As soon as the burgers were done, he brought her one cooked medium rare, just the way she liked it. When Frida and Jen announced their news, he congratulated them with as much enthusiasm as anyone.

"I have an announcement, too," Lilith said. "I received the advance reader copies of *The Artist's Soul* this week, if anyone wants to see it."

Frida and the boys quickly assured her they'd like to have a copy.

"What about you, Keeffe?" Lilith asked, smirking.

Keeffe thought about the app on the phone Bad had given her. She could scan the pages and have it read the book aloud to her.

"Sure," she said. "I'd love to read it." She glanced at Bad. He grinned, as though he knew exactly what she was thinking. Down by his side, unnoticed by anyone but her, he gave her a thumbs-up. Her heart could barely fit in her chest.

The book cover had a picture of Mom's face superimposed over the cross she had created for a church in Catalonia. Keeffe didn't love the picture of Mom. In it, she looked cold and calculating. What was Dad thinking?

He was thinking how best to stay in Lilith's good graces.

Bad spent most of the afternoon chatting with Ed and Claude about video-game creation. He participated in the discussion with an earnest nerdiness that made her smile.

Around three o'clock, Suzanne showed up and the women's talk turned to co-sleeping. Camille was a proponent, citing the improved mother-child bond, but Suzanne was concerned about the danger of rolling over on the infant. They asked Frida what she planned to do.

"I don't know," she said. "Oh my gosh, I need to figure that out, don't I?" Happy tears filled her eyes.

Did life get any better than this?

Bad mingled with Keeffe's family, thinking how lucky they were to live all together in this beautiful place, and relieved that McCall remained silently in the background. Other than the incident when McCall refused to stop staring at Lilith's butt, he had allowed Bad to run the show without interference. Bad was talking video games and eating a burger that was substantially less spicy than the normal burger in Hell when Lilith went into the house, pausing on the doorstep to glance over her shoulder at McCall.

A few minutes later, McCall told Bad he needed to empty their bladder. That was verifiably true, so Bad didn't resist going inside. After they urinated in a bathroom off the main hall, McCall exited through a second door that led to the master bedroom. There, on the king-size bed, lay Lilith, naked as the day she was formed.

Bad lunged for McCall's thalamus, hoping to incapacitate him before he could act, but McCall had apparently planned for this. He had about a million neurons posted around his pain center. The next thing Bad knew, they were copulating with Lilith, skipping over any foreplay to get right to the action.

If Bad had been struggling with McCall over one of the higher functions, like problem-solving or decision-making, he might have stood a chance. But sex required very little from the pre-frontal cortex. It took almost no brain to rut. Even sea sponges could copulate. All that Bad could do was close his eyes and hope they would finish quickly.

From across the patio, Ed called, "Where's McCall? We need his opinion on something."

Keeffe looked around but didn't see him. "He must have gone into the house."

She returned her attention to the co-sleeping debate, which was growing more intense as her sisters-in-law each tried to draw Frida to their way of thinking.

A few minutes later, Dad couldn't find the hot sauce.

"Where did Lilith go off to?" he asked. "She knows where everything is."

"A uterus isn't a tracking device, Dad," Frida said.

"There is nothing wrong with a little division of labor."

"There is if all the homemaking chores fall to the woman."

They wrangled amicably about Dad's not-so-latent sexism, but Keeffe was uneasy. Bad had been gone for quite a while.

She hoped he was okay. Dad's seasonings were sometimes too much for people who hadn't been raised in the Southwest. Excusing herself, she went into the house. Neither Bad nor Lilith was in the kitchen, nor in the little bathroom off the main hall. Could he have gone out to the car for some reason?

As she stood at the entrance to the hallway that led to the bedrooms, trying to decide whether to check the car or just return to the patio and wait for him to reappear, she heard a rhythmic squeaking coming from the master suite. *Eee-eee. Eee-eee.* It was a cartoonish noise, but it didn't make her smile. It almost sounded like... Something clutched inside her chest.

Don't be ridiculous, she told herself. Last night, he had shown her more clearly than words that he loved her. A muffled laugh, low and throaty, floated down the hall.

The air in the room seemed to grow heavy, like the atmosphere on Courthouse Bluff before a thunderstorm. The coward inside Keeffe begged her to walk back out to the deck and pretend she hadn't heard anything.

Frida's words came back to her: *that guy is almost too good to be true.*

Mom had always said if something seemed too good to be true, it probably was.

With leaden feet, Keeffe walked down the hall. Her fingertips felt numb, as though she could drag them along the rough stucco walls till they bled and not feel a thing.

Outside the six-panel mahogany door to Dad and Lilith's bedroom, she paused. On the other side of the door, the pace of the rocking increased. Feral grunts and the slap of flesh on flesh came through the door.

She stared at the square panels, feeling nauseated. It couldn't be true. Bad would never... Even Lilith wouldn't... Quietly, she opened the door.

On the California king-sized bed, a nude Lilith was on all fours. Bad, still wearing his T-shirt, knelt behind her. His big hands were on her hips and he slammed into her like a jackhammer. He was so absorbed he didn't hear the door open, but Lilith did. Her head swiveled to the door in alarm, but when she saw it was Keeffe, a small, satisfied smile flitted across her face. Deliberately, she reached behind her to rake her fingernails down Bad's thigh, leaving four red stripes on his perfect skin.

"Oh, you want to play rough, do you?" Releasing her hips, Bad grabbed her breasts hard enough to leave bruises.

Lilith arched her spine in perverse pleasure.

Keeffe had seen all she needed to see. She slammed the door and stumbled down the hall, her eyes so filled with tears she couldn't see where she was going. She didn't stop until her hipbone crashed into the granite kitchen counter. Pain radiated through her pelvis, but it was nothing compared to the pain in her heart. She crumpled across the counter.

How long had this been going on? How many clues had she failed to pick up on? Her first impression when he tried to buy *John*, that he was an opportunistic womanizer, was correct. She should have trusted her instincts. She felt like an idiot—a blind, foolish, love-struck idiot. Her shoulders heaved and tears beaded on the black granite. She would never be able to erase that image from her brain.

At the end of the hall, the door opened. "Keeffe?"

No. She did not want to talk to Bad. She fled across the kitchen and out the back door. Where was her purse with the car keys?

"Keeffe?" Camille's lovely face looked concerned.

If she stopped to explain, Bad would catch up with her. And she couldn't explain, anyway. She couldn't tell Dad that she'd just seen his wife having sex with a man thirty years his junior. She clattered across the tile flagstones, cursing her high-heeled sandals. She'd worn them to compete with Lilith, she realized now. Even before she discovered what was going on, she knew her stepmother was competition.

Keeffe ran around the house to the driveway where Bad's Lexus sat. Footsteps sounded behind her.

"Keeffe!" Bad's voice sounded lost and broken.

She sprinted the rest of the way to the car, yanking open the door and jumping into the driver's seat. Before he could catch up, she drove off like the hounds of Hell were after her.

CHAPTER 24

Bad chased Keeffe out to the car, but she had too much of a head start. She was halfway down the street by the time he reached the driveway. He returned to the patio, where her whole family stared at him suspiciously.

"She's upset," he said, striving to keep his tone light. "Guess I need a ride."

Frida and Jen took him home, a journey filled with awkward silences and sidelong looks in the rearview mirror.

"What was wrong with Keeffe?" Frida asked when they were about halfway to his house.

"Just a misunderstanding," he said.

"Uh-huh." She pulled out her phone and fired off a text. It was clear she was Team Keeffe all the way, and he was glad. If he couldn't turn this thing around, Keeffe was going to need people in her court.

A few minutes later, Frida's phone dinged. A bittersweet sense of satisfaction filled him. If Keeffe got nothing else from this relationship, at least she could now participate in the digital world.

"She says it's okay to drop him off," Frida told Jen.

What would they have done if Keeffe had told them not to let him go home? Dumped him beside the road?

When they got to McCall's place, he was relieved to see Keeffe's Honda sitting in the oval driveway,

Frida pinned him with a glare. "Whatever you did—fix it."

"I'm going to try," he said, and meant it.

He walked into the house, cursing himself for putting off telling Keeffe the truth. If he'd confessed last night, he wouldn't be in this jam.

He started for the mural room, but against his will, McCall rerouted them to the bedroom where Bad's body lay. McCall had been silent since they left Lilith's bedroom, but now he spoke up.

"It's time for you to go." He pointed at Bad's demon body. "Hop in there and go home."

"Not gonna happen," Bad said. He might not be able to prevent McCall from grabbing control once in a while, but McCall couldn't dispossess him either. That required that either the demon agree to leave, or some outside agency, like a priest.

"The boss wants you back," McCall said. "He has a few things to discuss with you."

That was exactly why Bad had no intention of returning to Hell. He didn't want to go back, even to run DemSec, and after what he'd done Above, DemSec was no longer on the table. If he returned, he'd spend the rest of his days digging coal in penance for his disloyalty. That meant contributing nothing to improve the lives of Hades, so he wasn't going back. He was going to stay right where he was and live out his life beside Keeffe.

McCall couldn't hear his thoughts, but he must have read Bad's intentions from his silence.

"Get out!" he roared.

Bad shrugged. "Make me,"

"Okay," McCall said. "Just remember, you brought this on yourself."

He slammed out of the bedroom and headed for the mural room. Worried about what McCall might say to Keeffe, Bad tried to redirect him, but he no longer had any control. He gathered some electrons to shoot into McCall's thalamus, but his access to that brain region was gone. He was now confined to a small area near the hippocampus. Somehow, he had gone from commanding McCall to being caged inside his brain.

There was no way McCall had figured out how to do this. Some demon with vast amounts of field experience must have taught him.

Ornias.

Ornias wanted to stay in charge of DemSec, and his best chance at doing that was to prove Bad couldn't handle fieldwork. Well, the joke was on him. He could run DemSec till the Apocalypse made everything moot. Bad wanted nothing more to do with it.

In the mural room, they found Keeffe painting like a madwoman. The sable paintbrushes Bad had bought her for her birthday lay on the floor like a child's abandoned toys. Bad's heart, an organ he'd never known he possessed until these past few weeks, twisted in his chest.

"I will be finished and out of here by Tuesday at the latest," Keeffe said without turning around. She was trying to sound cold and unemotional, but her voice vibrated with pain and anger. Bad scrabbled at the corners of his prison, looking for a weak spot, but there were none. His cage was indestructible.

McCall leaned against the doorway. "So, here's the thing—I'm not loving this mural."

Keeffe's paintbrush froze mid-stroke. "Really? When did you decide that?"

"I asked for superheroes."

"And you changed your mind." She whirled to face him. "I sketched superheroes, but you told me to paint a landscape."

McCall shrugged. "I wanted in your pants. I would have said anything."

He was trying to bait her into walking out. *Don't do it,* Bad pleaded silently.

Color surged into Keeffe's face. "I hope it was worth thirty thousand dollars."

"Not even close," McCall said.

She looked so furious that for a moment Bad thought she might attack them with her paintbrush, but then her eyes narrowed.

"Gray," she said.

"Huh?"

"Your eyes are gray."

"So?"

"You're always a jerk when your eyes are gray. What happened to brown-eyed McCall?"

Bad wanted to cheer for her powers of observation.

"He's back at your dad's," McCall said, "screwing Lilith."

She flinched like he'd slapped her, but she just said, "Whatever."

"Look, there's no point in finishing," he said. "I'm just going to have someone paint over it as soon as you're done."

For an instant, her shoulders hunched forward, like she'd taken a knife to the heart, but then she straightened.

"You do whatever you have to do," she said, and resumed painting.

CHAPTER 25

*K*eeffe painted until midnight, then went home and cried herself to sleep.

She'd gotten exactly what she deserved. She'd known better than to get involved with Mr. Hyde. She just wished she could forget Dr. Jekyll.

She had half a dozen texts from Frida. She pushed the buttons McCall had shown her and listened to them but couldn't summon the energy to respond. After the sixth text, she typed in "I'm ok," and hit send. The texts stopped, but at some point she would have to tell her sister the Valentine-perfect love she'd witnessed at the barbecue had turned out to be false.

McCall stayed up until three a.m., playing *Call of Duty* online. There were few things more boring than watching someone else play a video game, but Bad didn't dare fall asleep for fear of what McCall might do to ensure Satan got what he wanted. When the other players finally called it a night, McCall loaded up *Tetris,* of all things. Bad fought to

268

stay awake, but the hypnotic quality of the game finally overwhelmed him. He dozed off.

He awoke a few minutes or a few hours later, to see Ronnie disappearing out the rec room door, wearing a windbreaker.

"Where is he going?" Bad asked.

"None of your business," McCall said, and called it a night.

Once McCall was finally asleep, Bad tried again to break free of his neuron prison, but the bars were impenetrable.

The next morning Keeffe returned to McCall's at seven a.m. If she hit this hard enough, she could finish the mural tomorrow and be done with him forever.

She couldn't bring herself to think of the gray-eyed monster who lived here as "Bad" anymore—Bad was the brown-eyed good guy who'd made the painting and convinced her that having dyslexia didn't make her stupid.

To her surprise, the door was locked when she arrived. Ronnie was an early bird, so she leaned on the bell until he came to the door. He was yawning and still in his bathrobe.

"Sorry," she said. "I didn't realize you were still asleep."

"Would you like some breakfast?" he asked. He looked exhausted and impossibly old, and he smelled like a campfire. Had McCall made him go camping?

"No, thanks." She held up a McDonald's bag. "Why don't you go back to bed?"

"I believe I will," he said.

Bad was already awake when Keeffe arrived, but he couldn't rouse McCall and he could no longer move their body without McCall's participation. Whatever techniques Ornias had shown him, they were rock solid. Bad was tempted to exit McCall's body and return to his own, but that was exactly what McCall wanted him to do.

McCall finally awoke around eleven and stumbled into the shower. Bad had tried to convince him to shower the night before. The idea of going to bed still sticky from Lilith squicked him out.

"If you don't like it, get out," McCall had said.

The hot water felt good, but it was weird to have someone else's hands soaping his chest, washing his balls. He had developed a proprietary sense toward McCall's body that was probably inappropriate, but it was the body he'd always dreamed of.

After they toweled off, McCall wiped down the mirrors.

"Man," he said, "you let my body go to Hell while I was gone. I'm gonna have to spend a lot of make-up time in the workout room."

That was okay, as long as he stayed away from Keeffe—at least till Bad figured out how to regain control.

On the vanity were a contact lens case, a glass spray bottle, and an unlabeled spray can that hadn't been there the day before. McCall lifted his left arm and trained the nozzle of the can on his armpit and sprayed. It smelled like chocolate. After spraying his right underarm, he spritzed himself with the contents of the bottle. Still more chocolate. What was he doing?

Inside his walk-in closet, McCall pulled two identical navy T-shirts from a drawer. Bad couldn't remember ever seeing them before, either. McCall put on one of the shirts. Then he inserted the contact lenses into his eyes. When he looked in the mirror, the eyes looking back at him were a dark, chocolaty brown.

McCall was impersonating him. Why? For what reason? Bad hurled himself against the bars of his cage without results.

"That should do it," McCall said, looking satisfied. "Let's go talk to Keeffe."

Bad slammed himself against his cage all the way to the mural room, but McCall remained in complete control.

In the mural room, Keeffe had completed the first layer on what had been the remaining bare spot on the wall. The bottom third was a reddish brown, like the rest of the mural, and the top third was sky blue. In the center third, she'd blocked out a white trapezoid rising up from the rocks.

"What's that?" McCall asked.

"The Chapel of the Holy Cross," Keeffe said, without turning around.

A shudder of aversion ran through McCall but aloud he said, "It's really beautiful."

She stilled for an instant. Bad watched as she took in a deep breath through her nose. With the lavish amounts of cologne McCall had sprayed on, she had to smell chocolate. *Don't believe it.* Frantically, he beamed his thoughts at her, knowing they wouldn't get through. She turned to inspect his eyes. When she realized they were brown, a joyous smile lit her face.

"You're back," she said.

"I'm back," McCall agreed.

I'm not back, Bad screamed. He tried to force his head between the bars of his prison, but it wouldn't fit.

"Why did you do it?" she asked. It was a plea for any story that would allow her to forgive him.

McCall groaned. "I should have told you the truth when I had the chance."

She stilled. "What truth?"

He bowed his head like he was making a shameful confession. "There are two different guys inside me."

What was he doing?

"You have bi-polar disorder?" She nodded as if she'd already thought of that, but her mouth drooped. The thought didn't seem to give her much comfort.

"No, not one mentally ill man," said McCall. "Two different men."

Her eyebrows drew together in confusion.

"Think about it." McCall's voice was low, urgent. "You've commented yourself on how sometimes my eyes are gray and sometimes they're brown. You may have noticed I even smell different sometimes."

Uncertainty flickered in Keeffe's eyes.

McCall was telling the truth, but there was no way his intentions toward Keeffe were good.

Leave her alone! Bad shouted till the echo nearly deafened him, but McCall ignored the voice in his head. Bad tried to pry apart the bars of his prison, but they didn't move.

"I'm listening," Keeffe said. Her arms were still folded across her chest, but her forearm muscles weren't as rigid as they'd been before. McCall was making headway, damn him.

"How do you explain sleeping with my stepmom?" she asked.

"Demon possession," he said.

Keeffe drew back like she'd been slapped. Tears sprang to her eyes.

"You asshole." She drew a shuddering breath. "You total asshole."

But the depth of her anger was a measure of how deeply she longed for a valid explanation. McCall just might pull this off—but what was his purpose?

"Think about it." McCall grabbed her elbow, but loosely. He was calibrating his performance just right. "The first day you met me, you thought I was a jerk. The gray-eyed demon had control then. But that night when you had nachos with me, I seemed like a different guy. Different eye color, different smell, different guy. That was me, the real me."

He was turning everything around—but why?

Keeffe's hands balled into fists. She blinked away more tears. "How stupid do you think I am?"

"I don't think you're stupid at all. I think you're one of the smartest women I've ever met. You know how you've always said you have the stepmother from Hell?" McCall asked.

She nodded.

"You really do. Lilith is a demon. That thing her eyes do? That's an indicator."

Keeffe sucked in a breath. "I thought I was the only one who could see that."

"You're the only human who can see it," McCall said. His tone was admiring, calculated to make Keeffe feel like she was exceptional.

She thrust her jaw out. "If you're possessed by a demon, why don't your eyes do that when he's in control?"

Bad wanted to cheer.

"Because I'm not a demon. I'm just a human being possessed by a demon."

Bad wilted as Keeffe nodded like she found that explanation logical.

"Father Xavier said Lilith was a demon," she said grudgingly.

He was winning, damn it.

"He's right," McCall said. "And we need his help."

All at once, the picture became crystal clear. He tried to squeeze through the bars again, nearly crushing his rib cage in the attempt, but he couldn't get through.

"To be the man you want me to be, the man you fell in love with, we have to get rid of the gray-eyed demon," McCall said.

"How do we do that?" Keeffe asked. She still sounded wary, but she was falling for it.

"Exorcism," McCall said. "You need to get a priest to exorcise me."

No wonder he had been unconcerned when Bad refused to leave. He had a backup plan, one masterminded by Ornias, no doubt. If a Catholic priest performed the rite of exorcism correctly, Bad would have no choice but to vacate McCall's body. That was the agreement Hell had made with the Adversary, and the terms of that agreement were immutable. The Adversary tolerated Hell, but only to a point.

But Keeffe was a tough cookie.

"That's the biggest bunch of bull I've ever heard," she said.

Inside his prison, Bad cheered, but McCall was furious. His adrenal cortex went wild, sending anger hormones coursing through his system as he flung himself out of the room.

Instead of stomping to the weight room to work off his rage as Bad expected, McCall headed for the master bathroom again, where he popped out his contact lenses. Then he took off his shirt and dropped it on the floor. He wiped down his arms and torso and sprayed on more cologne—his signature sandalwood and leather scent this time. Finally, he replaced his shirt with the second navy T-shirt.

Then he returned to the mural room. Grabbing Keeffe by the wrist, he dragged her into the hall. She resisted, pulling away from him, dragging her feet, even latching onto the door frame, but he hauled her to the room where Bad's body was stored. Bad watched, helpless to intervene.

"What about this guy?" McCall shouted, pointing at the bed. "How do you explain him?"

Keeffe shrank away, trying to peel McCall's fingers from her wrist. With his other hand, he grabbed the back of her head in a hard grip, forcing her to look at the creature on the bed. Her eyes widened and her face turned ashen. Bad wanted to shrivel up and die.

"You told me that was a robot," Keeffe said.

"I lied," McCall said, flinging her wrist free. "I am the demon Abaddon. That's my body, but I can't get back into it without help."

Keeffe stepped closer to the bed. Bad closed his eyes. He couldn't bear to see the look of revulsion that was sure to come over her face.

"You have two choices," McCall said. "You can deal with me in your life, living in your boyfriend's body, or you can set me free."

CHAPTER 26

That night brought Keeffe no rest. She twisted and turned and punched her pillow, but sleep eluded her. Whenever she lowered her guard, the image of McCall and Lilith's joined bodies, and Lilith's feline smile of triumph, invaded her mind.

Was he really a demon? Or did Keeffe just want to believe that so she didn't have to admit that her boyfriend was having an affair with her stepmother? Was she just trying to evade the truth—that she'd fallen in love with a lying, cheating, manipulative jerk?

The next morning, clouds hung heavy in the sky as she left the trailer. El Niño winds were bringing the spring rains.

She stopped at the drug store and bought a two-ounce bottle, the kind used to carry fluids onto airplanes. Then she drove south to Chapel Road beneath the lowering sky. The gloom suited her mood. She couldn't believe she was actually doing this. On the other hand, she was still having trouble believing McCall had had sex with Lilith—and she'd seen that with her own eyes.

The Chapel of the Holy Cross came into sight above her, a rectangle of white limestone against a backdrop of gray sky. The front wall consisted of a soaring sheet of glass, split into quadrants by a white limestone cross. The cross extended below the foundation of the church, cleaving the red rocks on which the building stood.

Keeffe followed the twisting road the rest of the way up the hill to the parking lot and got out of the car. She hated feeling like a victim. Anything was better than doing nothing.

The only people in the tiny chapel were two old ladies kneeling near the front of the church and a young Latina woman lighting a votive candle at the back. Beyond the floor-to-ceiling front windows, clouds scudded ominously.

Keeffe dipped her fingers in the holy water of the font and made the sign of the cross. The water was cool against her forehead. She retrieved the bottle from her bag and unscrewed the cap, holding it under the water till the air bubbled out, replaced with blessed water.

Was she really going to do this?

Once she'd filled the bottle, she slipped over to the nearest pew and pulled out the kneeler. From her messenger bag, she retrieved her rosary. Kneeling, she traced the sign of the cross on the crucifix and recited the Apostle's Creed—"I believe in God, the Father Almighty, Creator of Heaven and Earth…"

The familiar words reminded her of coming here when she was a little girl and kneeling next to Mom. On the large bead of the strand, the one next to the crucifix, she prayed the Our Father, followed by three Hail Mary's on the next three, smaller beads. Despite the turmoil of the past two days, a feeling of peace descended over her as she worked her way around the rosary. When she was done, she put it back in her bag and got to her feet.

She would do what she needed to do.

McCall was lounging on the couch in the rec room, playing a video game, when Keeffe walked in. He tossed the controller aside.

Time for Act Two, he told Bad.

Bad struggled with the bars, knowing his efforts would be fruitless. He'd tried everything he could think of to escape, but his prison must have been reinforced with some kind of curse because nothing worked.

From her purse, Keeffe extracted a small bottle and unscrewed the cap. She crossed to the couch. "Can we talk?"

"Did you contact a priest?" McCall asked.

She dumped the contents of the bottle on his arm.

"Ow!" McCall howled, cradling his arm. Drawing on skills Ornias must have taught him, he raised blisters beneath his tattooed flesh. "What is that stuff?"

Keeffe watched the blisters erupt in wide-eyed horror. "Holy water. I wanted to see if you really were possessed by a demon."

McCall blew on the blisters and waved his arm in the air as though trying to cool a burn.

"I guess you believe me now?"

"I don't know." Keeffe gnawed on her lower lip. "This is just so crazy." She dug in her bag again and pulled out her rosary. "I believe in God, the Father Almighty, Creator of Heaven and Earth..."

As she spoke, all around the room, small objects quivered. A bong rattled its way to the edge of the mantelpiece and crashed to the tile floor. The logs in the fireplace burst into flame. McCall had spent his time well with Ornias.

"*Omnes Ave satanas,*" he chanted in a guttural voice straight out of the old *Exorcist* movie. "*Satanas est autem stellam matutinam.*"

Keeffe shuddered. "I didn't know you knew Latin."

"McCall doesn't know Latin," the guttural voice said, "but I do."

Keeffe's lips twisted skeptically. "Why would a demon know Latin?"

Bad wanted to cheer.

"You're a thief," McCall screamed so suddenly Keeffe jumped back.

"You stole Frida's lipstick on her prom night."

Keeffe turned pale, but quickly rallied. "Lilith could have told you that."

"Lilith," he said. "All I have to do is tell Lilith you abandoned the mural, and she'll sell your statue to the highest bidder."

"That's not true," Keeffe said. "I haven't abandoned the mural."

"Well, you didn't exactly come here today to paint, did you?" he said.

"I'll tell my dad—"

"You'll tell your dad what?" McCall demanded. "That I'm boffing Lilith?"

Keeffe winced. "No, that I didn't abandon the mural. That I plan to finish it."

Bad could sense McCall's rising levels of frustration at Keeffe's resistance.

"If you're not going to help me return to my real body," he roared, "then you can join me in Hell." He advanced on her.

Keeffe backed toward the door, but he followed her. By the time she reached the hallway, she was barely out of reach of his long arms. Eyes huge, she threw her rosary at him. He screamed as the beads struck his bare skin. She ran helter-skelter for the front door.

McCall pounded down the hallway after her. She wrenched the front door open and raced for her car with McCall on her heels. She dove into the driver's seat and slammed the door. McCall grabbed onto the door handle, but before he could yank open the door, she put the car in gear. McCall refused to release the handle. Bad thought the tendons in their wrist and fingers would tear as she drove off.

McCall lifted the door handle and shook it in triumph.

Back inside the house, McCall laughed till their sides hurt.

"Did you see her face? I totally freaked her out."

"You're an asshole," Bad said. McCall was letting him use their voice, but it didn't matter. After this, there was no way Keeffe would come back to finish the mural.

"This is the first time I've had any fun since you showed up. I told you I'd make a better demon than you."

"Yeah, well you're not going to be a demon. You're going to be client, damned to suffer in Hell for all eternity."

"Satan promised me," McCall said, his voice smug. "If I deliver the statue, I can become a demon."

"Satan promises a lot of people a lot of things," Bad said. "He lies a lot."

McCall shrugged their shoulders, unconvinced. "Even if that's true, it beats playing a harp."

"Bless me, Father, for I have sinned." Keeffe's voice was hushed inside the tiny wooden confessional. "It has been nine days since my last confession." That one had been a doozie—she'd had to confess to burglarizing her dad's house as well as a dozen acts of fornication with brown-eyed McCall. At least she hoped he was brown-eyed then. At the thought of having sex with the gray-eyed demon, she shuddered.

The presence on the other side of the screen spoke. "If any man sins, we have an Advocate with the Father, Jesus Christ the righteous."

She relaxed a little on the padded kneeler as the familiar invitation to confess came through the screen. She led with her big-ticket item. "I fornicated five times with a man I'm not married to. I wished my stepmother would fall off her high heels and break her neck. I took the Lord's name in vain."

When she'd gone through every sin she could remember from the past nine days, she expressed her contrition.

The voice on the other side of the screen said, "This man you fornicated with—do you plan to continue to have carnal relations with him?"

Keeffe hesitated. This was the tricky part.

"Actually, Father, that's what brought me here. I mean, I'm sorry for my sins, truly sorry, but here's the thing. This guy I'm seeing is possessed by a demon."

There was a rattle on the other side of the screen, as though the priest had dropped his rosary.

"What?"

"My boyfriend is possessed by a demon."

"What makes you think that?" The priest's voice sounded calmer now.

"He had sex with my dad's wife at a family barbecue."

"My daughter, a lot of young men behave badly." The priest was sympathetic but firm. "That's not an indication of demon possession. This may just be an excuse for his bad behavior. At worst, if he's telling the truth, it's a better indicator of mental illness than demon possession."

Inside the stuffy wooden cubicle, Keeffe clenched her fists in frustration. "There are other signs, physical signs. His eyes change color when the demon is in control. He even smells different. He says Satan is his boss."

"He sounds like a very troubled young man," the priest said.

"I sprinkled holy water on his arm. It made his skin blister." Keeffe produced this proof with a feeling of triumph.

But the priest just sighed. "As hard as it may be to understand, people are capable of raising blisters on their own skin through psychosomatic reaction."

"He didn't know it was holy water."

The silence on the other side of the screen said she hadn't convinced him. She played her last card. "When I prayed the rosary in front of him, a wind sprang up in a closed room. Objects hurled themselves off the mantelpiece. The logs in the fireplace burst into flame without anyone touching them."

The presence on the other side of the screen went very still.

After a long moment, the priest said, "I'm sure the incident with your boyfriend and your stepmother was very distressing." His voice was soothing.

Keeffe was so aggravated she wanted to scream. As things stood, she couldn't safely return to McCall's house to finish the mural, which meant Lilith would soon declare victory and confiscate *John*. Keeffe believed what he'd said about her stepmother with no reservations. Being a she-demon explained so much about Lilith.

Should she tell the priest about the demon body that lay in

McCall's guest room? Perhaps hearing of a living, breathing figure with horns and a tail would convince him. After a moment, she decided against it. She barely believed in that body herself.

She forced herself to remain calm. "When I drove away, he ripped the door handle off my car."

"How old is your car?"

Fifteen years.

"Not that old," she said. "Let me repeat that: he tore a metal handle off my car door."

Finally, reluctantly, the priest said, "This does sound as though there could be a demon at work."

Keeffe breathed a sigh of relief. "Can you exorcise him?"

"In real life, exorcism doesn't work like it does in the movies," the priest said. "First, an authority from the Church would need to observe these phenomena firsthand. Then, we'd need to rule out mental illness and chicanery. Then, if demon possession is actually verified, the Catholic Church requires an order from the bishop of the diocese where the exorcism is to take place."

"So, what do we need to do to get him to do that?"

"A good first step would be to take your boyfriend to see a doctor, a mental-health expert, to screen him for a physical or mental illness that might be at the root of the problem."

"Father, I saw six *Star Wars* action figures jump off a mantel when no one was near them. That wasn't caused by schizophrenia. Unless you think I'm the one who's ill."

The silence from the other side of the wall told her the priest viewed that as a genuine possibility. She was glad she'd decided against telling him about the demon body.

After a long moment, he said, "I empathize with what you're saying, but the exorcism process is very clearly defined. Your best approach is to get your boyfriend in to see a doctor. If he comes back with a clean bill of health and he continues to manifest symptoms, we can talk about next steps."

"All right," Keeffe said, because there wasn't much else she could say. It wasn't like arguing would change his mind.

"Please recite the Act of Contrition," he said. She could almost hear the relief in his voice at being back on familiar ground.

Obediently, she recited the prayer, but her mind was elsewhere. All these steps would take time—time she didn't have. A week from today, she had to be in Tucson and she didn't want to abandon McCall to fight the demon alone.

The priest went on to assign a penance, but Keeffe had stopped listening.

Aside from the state of McCall's soul, if she didn't return to complete the work, the demon living inside McCall would claim she had abandoned the mural and demand his deposit back. Then Lilith would tell Dad that Keeffe had failed to meet the terms of their contract and sell off *John* to the highest bidder.

Would Lilith do that? For the first time, it occurred to Keeffe that perhaps her stepmother wasn't planning to sell *John*. If McCall harbored a demon and Lilith was a demon, what made more sense was that they wanted the statue for some mutual, evil purpose. She thought about *Matthew, Mark* and *Luke*, her siblings' statues. They had disappeared without a trace. She'd assumed that they'd gone into private collections, but if demons were real—and she was now convinced they were—maybe they'd been sucked down to Hell. She would willingly give up *John* to save Bad, but without knowing what Lilith planned to do with the statue, it was too dangerous.

If the official church wasn't prepared to help her, she would just have to take a shortcut.

CHAPTER 27

The next morning, Keeffe signed in at the front desk of the St. Ignatius Home for Retired Religious. Clear plastic slipcovers shrouded the sofas in the lobby area and the place smelled overwhelmingly of pine cleaner. She asked for Father Xavier's room number.

The receptionist directed Keeffe down a long hallway to Father X's room. When she got there, the old priest was napping. The sound of the door closing behind her woke him.

He struggled to a sitting position and smiled happily at the sight of her. "Did you come to look at my painting?"

Keeffe's heart sank. There was no hint of the fiery priest in the old man's childlike eyes.

"Actually, I came to talk to you about demons."

"Demons?" A glint came into his eyes. "You mean that stepmother of yours?"

"No, this is something different. I think my boyfriend has been possessed by a demon."

Keeffe told him what had happened. With every word, his spine grew a little straighter. When she got to the end and described McCall ripping the door handle off the car, he clutched the crucifix hanging around his neck.

"This is the work of the Evil One," he said.

"That's what I thought," she said. "Can you exorcise him?"

He frowned. "The bishop would have to approve it."

That put her back at square one—getting McCall in to see a doctor. Even if he were willing, it could take days, if not weeks, to get a diagnosis when she already knew the real problem wasn't his mental health.

Crossing her fingers behind her back, Keeffe said, "I talked to the bishop. He said it was fine if you were willing."

"Oh." Father X's face cleared. "All right."

Keeffe headed to the closet for his jacket, but he didn't move.

"I'll need to go to confession first," he said.

If he confessed to another priest, that priest would put a stop to the exorcism. Sister Mary Grace seemed to manage Father X primarily by distraction. Keeffe gave it a shot.

"Father, if we don't get rid of the demon today, my mother's statue of John the Evangelist will be sucked down to Hell and lost forever."

He looked troubled. "I suppose I could settle for an Act of Contrition."

"Great." Keeffe pulled his jacket from the closet and held it out to him. "Can you say it on the way to his house?"

Father X got to his feet, but instead of putting on his jacket, he wandered over to a small wooden bureau and opened the bottom drawer.

"I have a surplice," he said, "but I'll need a purple stole."

"Where can we get that?"

"I can request one from the bishop."

"Can't you just do the exorcism in your surplice?"

He shook his head. "I must be appropriately garbed and in a state of grace, or the exorcism may not be successful."

On the other hand, every day that went by with the demon in possession of Bad's body put his immortal soul at risk.

"It could even be dangerous," Father X said. "The demon you describe sounds powerful."

Keeffe thought quickly. "What about Frida's stole—the one you painted at art class? Would that work?"

His happy, childlike smile returned. "That was a beautiful stole, wasn't it?"

"It was," she said.

"I'll need holy water, too."

"We'll stop on the way." She folded his surplice and shoved it into a plastic bag.

At the front door, Sister Mary Grace was standing beside the reception desk.

"Why, Keeffe—" she looked curiously from Keeffe to Father X— "I didn't know you were here."

"Father X and I are going to—" Keeffe cast frantically for an excuse —"paint. *En plein air.*"

The nun looked disappointed. "I wish I'd known. I would have gone with you."

"Next time," Keeffe promised and herded Father X out the door.

At Frida's, she parked in the driveway and told Father X to wait in the car. She had texted a few more times since the barbecue and spoken to Frida once, but this was the first time she'd seen her sister.

Inside, Frida was sitting on the couch, reading *The Artist's Soul.* She was scowling.

"Have you read this?" she asked, holding up the book.

"Not yet," Keeffe said. "Can I borrow that purple scarf we painted in class the other day?"

"What for?"

Keeffe tried to imagine explaining everything that was going on to Frida. Even if her sister believed her, she couldn't leave Father X sitting in the car that long. "I'm trying to match that shade for something in my mural."

"Okay." Frida went to get it.

"Let me know what you think of the book," she said, handing Keeffe the scarf.

"Will do," Keeffe said, and hurried out the door.

Their next stop was the Chapel of the Holy Cross. She wanted Father X to wait in the car again, but he insisted on going inside and kneeling and reciting the Act of Contrition. On the way to McCall's, he instructed her in her role in the exorcism. Her job would be to repeat whatever he said, mostly verbatim.

By the time they reached McCall's house, it was after two. Keeffe retrieved the bag containing the surplice and stole from the back seat. When Father X put them on, he seemed to gain in stature and gravity.

Keeffe rang the doorbell, but no one answered. Inside one of the sidelight windows, movement flickered.

"That's odd," she said. "He has a butler who always—" She stopped. Something was off about Ronnie, but she couldn't put her finger on exactly what it was. He'd always been super nice to her, and he didn't seem like someone who would be in cahoots with evil McCall, but she no longer trusted her own judgment. She rang the bell again with no response. "I don't think he wants to let us in."

Father X smiled fiercely. "Of course he doesn't."

Since no one answered the door, Keeffe opened it and yelled hello into the foyer. No one responded, but she could hear the sound of the video game from the rec room.

Together, they walked down the broad hallway and found McCall on the couch with a controller. He looked up when Keeffe appeared in the doorway.

"Are you back again?" he said, looking annoyed. His eyes were gray today.

She wasn't sure whether to be upset or relieved.

Keeffe moved aside to allow Father X to enter the room. At the sight of the priest, McCall grinned. He set down the controller and got to his feet.

"That was quick." He rubbed his hands together.

Something felt off, but Keeffe couldn't figure out what it was.

"Lord, have mercy," Father X's voice, sonorous and authoritative, seemed to ring from the rafters. He traced the sign of the cross over McCall, then over himself, then over Keeffe.

"Lord, have mercy," Keeffe repeated.

McCall stuck his thumbs in his pockets. His fingers framed his genitals. That was the demon all the way, but Keeffe still felt uneasy.

"Christ, have mercy," Father X said. He sprinkled each person in the room, including himself, from a vial of holy water.

"Okay, little demon," McCall said, grinning. "Time to go."

Why was the demon talking to himself as though he were someone else? Keeffe's unease increased.

"Christ, have mercy," Father X repeated, a little louder.

"Christ, have mercy," Keeffe parroted.

"Adios, amigo," McCall said.

"Lord, have mercy," said Father X.

"Lord, have mercy," said Keeffe.

McCall shuddered and his eyes turned brown. He looked beseechingly at Keeffe.

"Please don't do this, Keeffe. I love you."

"Christ, hear us," said Father X.

McCall sounded so sincere Keeffe hesitated. Why had his eyes turned brown? The demon was still inside him.

"Don't listen to the demon," said Father X. "God, the Father in heaven."

Keeffe steeled herself. "Have mercy on us."

"God, the Son, Redeemer of the world," said Father X.

"Keeffe, please. I love you. Don't send me away." McCall's face moved like he was being torn apart.

Tears filled Keeffe's eyes. "Have mercy on us."

Father X began to recite the names of the saints. McCall grabbed onto the armrest of the sofa, like he was trying to keep himself from being dragged away. With each name, a tremor ran through him.

"I adjure you, ancient serpent, by the judge of the living and the dead, by your Creator, by the Creator of the whole universe, by Him who has the power to consign you to Hell, to depart forthwith in fear, along with your savage minions, from this servant of God, who seeks refuge in the fold of the Church."

That didn't exactly describe either McCall. Keeffe's sense that something was off grew stronger. She put out her hand to stop Father X.

"He killed your mom," McCall said suddenly.

Keeffe stared at him, horrified. "He did what?"

"He killed your mom."

"Don't engage with the demon," Father Xavier warned her.

She couldn't believe anything the demon told her. He was a liar.

"He invented surgery robots," McCall said. "And then he sent them up here to kill people."

Keeffe gazed at him, feeling a little sick. Father X continued to chant. She repeated his words with emphasis. After a few more moments, gray smoke drifted from McCall's nose. It formed into a small gray tornado and moved toward Keeffe.

"No," she cried.

Father X moved to block it, and she hid behind him. At that, the tornado seemed to wilt. One solitary drop of water, like a tear, formed midway up the funnel and ran down the side, dripping from the bottom. Keeffe's sense that something was amiss exploded but it was too late. The tornado gathered itself and streamed out of the room.

A door opened and closed down the hall.

"Should we go after him?" asked Keeffe, shivering.

"Let's kill it," yelled McCall, picking up a pool cue.

Before Father X could respond, the hairy little guy with the horns and tail appeared in the doorway. He stood there for a moment, looking at her with the saddest brown eyes she'd ever seen. She watched him with a feeling of unreality. What were Bad's eyes doing in that body?

"Goodbye." He sounded like the word was choking him.

Involuntarily, Keeffe took a half step toward him, but he held out his palm as though to ward her off and shook his head. He disappeared from the doorway. A horrible thought seized her. She turned back to McCall, who was brandishing the pool cue. His eyes were gray as flint. Down the hall, the back door opened and closed. Something was wrong, very wrong.

Beside her, Father X crumpled to the floor.

"Father Xavier." She dropped to the floor, putting her arms around his shoulders. "Father Xavier! Are you all right?"

He looked up at her. There was no light of recognition in his eyes, only confusion. She squeezed his shoulders. He had warned that the exorcism could be dangerous if he wasn't in a state of grace and wearing the proper vestments. Intent on ridding McCall of his demon, she had insisted on proceeding anyway. What had she done?

"Oh, Father," she wept, "I'm so sorry." There weren't enough Hail Marys in the world to absolve her of this sin.

He blinked, and his eyes seemed to come into focus.

"Is it dinnertime?" he asked, and she felt an overwhelming sense of relief. He didn't seem to be any worse off than he'd been before.

"Almost," she said, helping him to his feet. "Let me take you home."

Even though Father X had rid him of his unwelcome visitor, McCall didn't offer to help her get the old man to the car. McCall sat on the couch, his arms stretched along the back watching as she hoisted Father X to his feet. He was the same arrogant asshat she'd met that first day at Dad's.

"Are you coming back later?" McCall asked, giving her what he clearly considered to be a come-hither look.

What a jerk.

"No," she said.

He followed them toward the front door, and for a moment she thought he might assist with getting the priest into the car, but when they got to the weight room, he stopped.

"Time to get back into shape," he said, and headed for his weight bench.

Keeffe drove back to the nursing home, keeping a watchful eye on Father Xavier. His face was pale and his head kept drooping. She prayed he hadn't sustained any permanent damage from his unauthorized exorcism.

She walked him back to his room and waited until his evening meal was served before leaving.

It was only when she was back in her car that she allowed herself to think about what McCall's rudeness and narcissism and, most of all, his gray eyes meant. Common sense said the little demon who'd trudged out the door, his tail dragging behind him, had to be the bad guy, but his brown eyes begged her not to believe it.

She was exhausted when she got home. She considered going across the street to Ernesto's, but without Bad to razz her about her hopeless addiction to nachos, the thought held no appeal.

She wasn't much for books, but she was rarely wrong about people, especially people she'd spent any amount of time with. It defied common sense, but the more she thought about it, the more certain she was that, somehow, she'd gotten rid of the wrong guy.

CHAPTER 28

*B*ad was barely out of the car before a pair of demons, the same ones that had escorted him to the maggot pit ten years ago, grabbed him by the arms and dragged him to Satan's throne room.

They hurled him to the floor, obviously hoping to leave bruises, but Hades had tough hides. Bad picked himself up and brushed the lava ash off his arms. Today was the day his six-week mission was due to end. With luck, he could convince Satan that he was a failure rather than a traitor.

"You were right," he said. "Fieldwork is harder than it looks."

"Don't try to bullshit me." Satan held up his cellphone. "McCall texted me what you were up to."

Bad supposed he should have seen that coming.

"You're never going back to DemSec," Satan said. "Not for the rest of eternity."

Bad shrugged. He had no desire to return to DemSec.

"Where shall I put you?" Satan mused. "Shall I toss you in the Lake of Fire and obliterate all trace of you?"

Bad didn't respond. With his heart aching at the thought of never seeing Keeffe again, oblivion didn't seem like such a bad option.

"No, you're right," Satan said. "That's overkill. Hades may have tougher hides than angel stock, but they're not immortal."

Just very long-lived.

"No, I think justice would be served best by returning you to where you came from. In the mines, you won't have access to technology. That will punish you and it will keep you from interfering in other missions."

It also meant he would never again invent anything that harmed anyone Above. It felt like a gift.

When Bad didn't respond, Satan's eyes blazed. He crossed to where Bad stood and held out his hand imperiously. "Give me your backpack."

Inwardly, Bad groaned. All the tech he needed to track what was happening Above was in that backpack. With any luck, he'd at least keep the cellphone and the universal remote in his pocket.

"Empty his pockets," Satan instructed the guards.

The guards went through his clothes, removing his cellphone, his universal remote, and his keys. They found Keeffe's scale model of the mural room and for a moment he thought they'd toss it on the nearest brazier. Bad watched them apathetically. It might be easier if they took away that last touchstone. Satan must have read his expression.

"Leave him that," he ordered. "He can look at it and think of all he's lost."

By the time they were done, they'd completely stripped him of all technology.

"Give that stuff to Ornias," Satan ordered.

"Will do," said the guard on his left.

"What do you want us to do with the prisoner?" asked the guard on his right.

Satan's eyes blazed with triumph. "Dump him in Hadeville."

Keeffe didn't sleep much that night. Every time she closed her eyes, she saw the brown-eyed demon turning to look at her over his shoulder as he left McCall's house. The little body with horns and a tail she'd seen in the guest room wasn't a robot, as he'd told her initially. It was a demon.

She punched her pillow. If Father X had expelled that demon from McCall but the asshat version of him was still there, what did that mean? Maybe the demon had left behind traces of evil that would take a while to wear off?

Except the brown-eyed demon that had walked away hadn't seemed evil. He'd seemed like a very sad version of Bad. She thought about that last pitiful look he'd given her and her ribcage seemed to squeeze her heart.

If she were smart, she would finish up the mural and put all this behind her like a bad dream. She'd move on to her residency in Tucson and forget all about him. Despite what Bad had said, she must not be very smart because she had no desire to forget him. She wanted to remember the hiking and the lovemaking and the laughter. She wanted to hang on to the memory of the night he'd made the painting —was that just four days ago?—and she'd told him she loved him. He'd started to say it back, but she'd cut him off.

Now she wished she hadn't.

Except that wouldn't have changed anything. Some version of McCall would still have humped Lilith the next day and Keeffe would still have broken up with him.

In the morning, she would return to McCall's house. Once she confirmed that the brown-eyed version of him was truly gone, she would finish up the mural, get her final paycheck, and say adios.

Keeffe arrived at McCall's the next morning to find a white panel van parked outside his front door. The logo on the side read *Jimenez Brothers Painting*. She stared at it in shock. Despite what McCall had said Saturday, she hadn't believed he would have her beautiful mural painted over. She'd thought that must be the demon talking.

Inside the house, a trail of tarps led her to the mural room where a pair of Latino men in white coveralls were spreading still more tarpaulins over the hardwood floor. In the middle of the room sat a small machine with a blue power cord and a thick, corrugated hose with a nozzle at the end. The younger of the two men knelt beside it.

"What are you doing?" she demanded.

The man on the floor looked up. "The owner wants the walls in this room repainted."

"That can't be right," Keeffe said. "I just finished painting this mural."

"I told you the paint looked fresh," the older one said. He finished laying out the final tarp and walked over to the machine. He picked it up by its handle, carrying the hose in his other hand. When he reached her depiction of the Honanki ruins, he flipped a switch on the machine. A dull roar filled the air.

"Stop!" She shot across the room and yanked the sprayer from his hand. He turned off the machine and the roar silenced.

"You can't do this," Keeffe said. "I just spent nearly six weeks of my life painting this."

He shrugged. "I'm sorry, lady." He flipped the switch again, but Keeffe wasn't about to let this desecration happen. Flinging her arms wide, she used her body to block his access to the wall.

"You have to wait," she said. "Let me talk to the owner and find out what's going on." McCall was an asshat. They'd established that beyond all doubt yesterday. But even an asshat had to have some appreciation of art.

After maybe thirty seconds of staring contest, the man sighed. "We'll take a break. Ten minutes, no more. When we get back, unless he tells us to stop, we will have to go ahead."

"Thank you," Keeffe said gratefully.

The younger man nodded toward the nearest wall. His dark eyes were sympathetic. "It is a very beautiful painting."

"Thanks," Keeffe said again. She hoped they weren't the only human beings other than McCall who would ever see it.

She found McCall in the rec room playing a video game. When he didn't put the controller down, she stepped between him and the console. He leaned to the left, trying to play around her, but she'd learned enough over the past six weeks to know exactly where she needed to stand to block the game.

He tossed the controller onto the leather couch and slumped back against the cushions. "What do you want?"

"I came over to seal the mural and pick up my check."

He picked up two sheets of paper off the coffee table. With a sense of foreboding she recognized the contract she'd signed to do the painting by the ribbon of brown at the edge of the paper and the smudged thumbprint below his signature.

"You abandoned the mural," he said.

"What?" Keeffe stared at him. "No, I didn't."

"Yes, you did, and I want my deposit back."

She felt completely numb, as though someone could slap her across the face and she'd feel nothing. Maybe they already had. "I did not abandon the mural."

"Sure you did. Yesterday, before you left, I asked 'are you coming back?' And you said, no."

"I meant not yesterday."

"That wasn't how I interpreted it," he said.

"I'll get a lawyer."

"Go for it," he said. "By the time you get back, those walls will be white again. There will be nothing to show you ever painted anything."

With a sick feeling, she realized he was right. Those men could completely cover up weeks of effort and energy and creativity in an hour or two. She charged back down the hall and pulled out the cellphone McCall had given her. Except it wasn't McCall. It was Bad, the little brown-eyed demon who had inhabited him.

They must have been in cahoots. She should have gotten that stun gun she'd thought about buying. She should have used it on him that first day when he'd offered her a massage. What kind of guy offers a massage to a female employee? The sleazy kind.

Except the massage had been amazing and completely respectful, so what did that say?

It said she was never going to figure out what had happened here.

Heart aching, she took a photograph of each scene—the Honanki ruins, Coffee Pot Rock, Snoopy Rock, the Sphinx. When she got to Cathedral Rock, the spot where they had made love inside a replica of her favorite painting, her eyes filled with tears, but she dashed them away. There would be time to mourn her losses later.

When she had documented each scene, she set the camera for panorama and slowly turned, taking a 360-degree picture of the mural in its entirety. She would get Frida to build her that website she was always talking about and post the photos there.

McCall came into the room. When he saw what she was doing, he said, "If you blow me, I'll let the mural stay for a few days so you can show it to people." He put his hand on her shoulder.

Keeffe knocked it off so hard he yelped.

"Not just no, but hell no." She held up her phone. "I'm taking these to my lawyer."

His eyes turned mean. "You're wasting your time. That contract was written by Satan's lawyers."

"Why is Satan part of this discussion? Father Xavier exorcised your demon yesterday. We're done with all that."

McCall laughed. "More like, he exorcised *your* demon yesterday."

"What do you mean?"

He opened his mouth, then closed it again, blinking rapidly. He walked over to the doorway and looked up and down the hall, as if spies might have infiltrated the house while they were talking.

"I just spent three weeks down there." McCall's voice was just above a whisper. It was clear he was dying to brag about his exploits. It was equally clear he didn't want to be overheard. "I worked in their technology division while Abaddon used my body for the mission. Satan is totally impressed with me."

A piece of the puzzle slid into place. That was why she hadn't seen gray-eyed McCall for so long. He'd spent several weeks in Hell, leaving the brown-eyed guy in charge of his body.

"Abaddon?" she asked.

"Short, dark, and hairy," McCall said.

"That's his name? Abaddon?"

McCall nodded. "They call him Bad."

So that was where his childhood nickname had come from.

McCall shot another glance toward the doorway. Was it the painters he was afraid of? No, she could hear them outside, speaking in Spanish. If not the painters, then who? The only other person around was Ronnie.

"His mission—did it have anything to do with my statue?" Keeffe asked.

He scowled. "That little freak spilled his guts to you, didn't he?"

"He may have said something," she lied.

"Satan should never have sent him. Hades aren't real demons. They can't be trusted to do the Master's work."

"Hades?"

McCall's chest expanded. "Real demons are fallen angels. Hades are just the grubs who lived in Hell before Satan showed up."

So Bad wasn't a true demon. The thought gave her some comfort, but only for a moment.

"If he's not really a demon, how did he possess your body?"

"He found some old book that told him how to do it."

"Why did he sign me to that contract?"

"He thinks he's so smart, but he's a moron." McCall sounded disgusted. "He was supposed to come up here and either help Lilith get the statue or talk you into selling it to him. But somewhere along the line he changed his mind. He was going to pay you for the mural and let you keep the statue."

Why had he changed his mind? Keeffe set that aside to process later. She wanted to get as much information as she could while McCall was in a mood to talk. "Where is he now? Back in Hell?"

McCall snorted. "In his own private hell. He broke the cardinal rule."

"What's the cardinal rule?"

"Satan's minions aren't allowed to fall in love."

A tide of warmth swept through her. Her instincts hadn't lied. Bad, the demon-who-wasn't-a-demon, really had loved her.

"Didn't he know that would get him in trouble?" she asked.

"He thought he had it all figured out. He knew there was no way I could get rid of him on my own. He figured he'd just keep my body and stay up here."

"But you talked me into having him exorcised." The picture came together. McCall and Satan had used her as a tool to their own ends. Bad had apparently started out doing Satan's bidding, but somewhere along the way he'd changed sides. Because he'd fallen in love with her.

McCall tapped his nose. "You got it."

"Why does Satan want my statue?"

There was a noise out in the hallway. McCall stiffened, but it was just the painters, returning from their coffee break. She was running out of time.

"That's need to know," McCall said, "and you don't need to know."

"In other words," she said, "you don't know. You're just a grunt they don't tell anything."

He looked affronted. "I know everything."

If she could take him far enough down this road, he'd tell her what was going on.

"You're just a puny human," she scoffed. "Why would they tell you anything?"

His head came up and his shoulders went back, like he was some kind of weird cadet reciting a pledge. "Our mission is to destroy your mother's legacy."

Then he smirked, ruining the effect.

"Lilith will demolish her reputation. Every church that owns one of her crosses will chop it up for kindling." He smiled spitefully. "And your dad will drink until his liver gives out, which shouldn't take much longer."

Keeffe's insides seemed to freeze. She'd long suspected Lilith was on a mission to destroy her mother's legacy; she just hadn't realized it was a mission assigned by Satan. Or that it affected Dad, too. But McCall wasn't done yet.

"I'm stripping all the intellectual property from your brothers' company. In six months, I'll call in the balloon payment on their loan and bankrupt them. Not bad for a grunt, huh? The boss is thrilled with me. He says destroying their business is the cherry on top of his ruin-the-Blackmon-family sundae."

Keeffe eyed him with loathing.

"Guess you wish you'd never introduced them to me, huh?" he said.

But she hadn't. She'd introduced them to Bad, the guy she'd fallen in love with and who, according to McCall, had loved her enough to risk Satan's wrath for her.

One of the workmen appeared in the doorway. "Are you ready for us to paint?"

"Go ahead," McCall said. He gestured at the walls containing the mural she'd slaved over. "I want this mess gone by nightfall."

Bad's demon guards took him to the black gash in the wall of anthracite and tossed him through. He tumbled down the sharp slope before slamming into a thick timber supporting the ceiling of the cavern. A sprinkle of pebbles and black dust rained down on him.

When the rockfall stopped, he picked himself up and, with his well-adapted Hade eyes, followed the twists and turns to the arched entry to Hadeville. Back in his own body, there was no need to duck, and the heat was only a minor discomfort. At his parents' door, he knocked before letting himself in. The living room was empty, so he went on through to the kitchen, where Ma was chopping root vegetables and Pa was reading the paper.

"Bad," Ma cried when she saw him. She put down the knife and hurried over to give him a hug. Then she looked more closely at his face. "Are you all right? How did your mission go?"

"I've messed everything up," he said, hanging his head.

"I'll put on some tea," Pa said.

"It can't be that bad." Ma kissed the tender spot between his horns.

"It's worse," Bad said. "My entire life has been a disaster. I've brought people nothing but misery."

She took him by the upper arms and held him away from her.

"You brought electricity and fresh water to the Hades. Air-conditioning and Wi-Fi. I don't know what went wrong Aboveworld, but we Hades are better off for your efforts."

Bad's shoulders sagged. The town leaders had a laundry list of improvements they still hoped to see and now he wouldn't be able to help them. He was glad Keeffe would keep her statue and Sedona was safe but he wished those things hadn't come at the cost of all future improvements for the Hade way of life.

"That progress will stop now," he told Ma. "Satan will never let me back into DemSec again."

"He'll get over it," Ma said. "He always does."

"Not this time," Bad said. "I won't be able to do anything to improve the lot of the Hades from now on."

"I wouldn't worry about that too much," Pa said. "Phoenix and some of his friends have a plan to take over where you left off."

Bad frowned. "DemSec is not a good place for him."

"He's not joining DemSec," Pa said. "He plans to set up a lab here in Hadeville."

In spite of his misery, Bad smiled. "He's really something, isn't he?"

Pa nodded. "He's a lot like you were at his age."

"Why are you so sure Satan won't let you back into DemSec?" Ma asked.

Bad's chin dropped to his chest. "I broke the cardinal rule."

Ma's pixie face split into a wide grin.

"You fell in love?" She squeezed him in another hug.

In spite of himself, he felt a little better. It was hard to stay down in the presence of Ma's effervescent optimism.

She clutched his arms and her eyes turned wary. "You're not in love with that snake, are you?"

"Lamia? No, Ma."

"Good." Ma sniffed. "That girl was cold to her core."

"You remember that girl I talked about, the artist?"

"The one you gave Mo's junk jewelry?" Ma's jaw dropped.

"Her name is Keeffe."

Pa dropped the teakettle into the sink with a metallic clang. "An Aboveworlder?"

Bad's face grew warm. "Yes."

"Did she love you back?" asked Ma.

He lifted his chin. "Yes, she did."

"How did that happen?" Ma looked astounded.

"Gee, thanks, Ma."

She shook her head. "I don't mean that. Any woman who got to know you was bound to fall in love with you. But Aboveworlders see only the outside of people. They always fall for those nasty angels."

"Not this one," Bad said proudly. Then his shoulders drooped. "At least, not completely."

"Maybe you'd better tell us what happened," Ma said.

Keeffe left McCall's numb with shock. It wasn't enough that painters were whitewashing over her beautiful mural like so much graffiti, or that, after years of uphill struggle, she was losing *John* anyway. No, it was far worse than that. Those setbacks were part of a larger plan to erase her mother's legacy, kill her father, and demolish her brothers' dreams.

She did feel bad about introducing the boys to McCall, but with a plan this elaborate and far-reaching, Satan would have gotten to them some way. Her heart ached at the thought of their devastation when they learned they were about to lose everything they'd worked for. But why had her family been targeted?

Except it wasn't her entire family. Frida was missing from the mix. Why would that be? Because she'd left the Church? Frida had stopped attending Mass after she came out. She said the Catholic Church had no place for lesbians.

Still, something felt off. When Keeffe turned out of McCall's subdivision, she headed south, toward Oak Creek. When she got to Frida and Jen's, Frida was lying on the sofa, her face so pale it looked almost green. Keeffe's hands went clammy.

"What's wrong?"

"I'm spotting." A tear rolled down Frida's cheek. She cupped her belly with her hands, as though to keep her precious cargo safe.

"You mean…?"

Frida nodded. "Suzanne says I may lose the baby."

Frida hadn't been exempted from the family curse after all. The thought made Keeffe feel physically ill. She went to her sister's side, feeling helpless. "Is there anything I can get you?"

"No, Jen made sure I had everything I needed before she left." The coffee table was stacked with books and magazines and snacks. Another tear rolled down Frida's face. She scrubbed at it with her fist.

Keeffe had planned to tell Frida about the demon, but she couldn't risk upsetting her sister any further.

"Did you read the book?" Frida asked.

Ugh, the book. She'd forgotten all about it. Now that she knew about Hell's plan to destroy her mother's legacy, the book took on a whole new significance. She swallowed. "Not yet."

An issue she'd have to fix as soon as she got home.

"That damn Lilith," Frida burst out.

Keeffe froze. Did Frida somehow know about McCall and Lilith? Warily, she checked her sister's face. Frida was glaring at the book on the coffee table, not looking at Keeffe with pity in her eyes. She didn't know. Keeffe expelled a tiny sigh of relief. "What did she do?"

Frida pointed to the book lying on the coffee table. "It says Mom died trying to have Pablo aborted."

Keeffe gasped. "That's a lie."

Frida's face was grim. "But it's a believable lie. Mom's journal entries talk about how unhappy she was when she found out Pablo had Down syndrome."

"That much is true." Frida had been away at college, but Keeffe was still at home when Mom got pregnant with Pablo. When his test results came back, Mom had struggled to accept his condition. "She was pretty upset."

"And how she considered aborting him," Frida said.

A shock ran through Keeffe. That she hadn't known.

"She came to terms with it, though," Keeffe said. "Before she died, she reached a point where she was looking forward to his birth. She said all children are a challenge, and he'd just be a different kind of challenge."

"That's not what the book says." Frida's lips trembled, and her eyes swam with tears. "At the end of her last journal, she was thinking about aborting him. Then she went into the hospital and died. The book makes it sound like she died trying to get rid of him."

"That's not true." Keeffe was horrified. This must be the scheme McCall talked about, the one aiming to tarnish Mom's reputation so that churches would destroy her crosses. As a plan, it was fiendishly clever. Abortion was such a hot-button issue. Churches would be bound to come out strongly against a woman who appeared to have killed her unborn child because of a genetic handicap. Then what Frida had said sank in.

"That's not where her last journal ends," Keeffe said.

"But Lilith said—"

"Lilith doesn't have her last journal. I do."

Frida stared at her blankly. "You what?"

"I have her last journal. I took it off Mom's bookshelf after she died, before Lilith moved in. Mom wrote the last one while she was working on *John*, so I wanted to see it. Then when Lilith started getting rid of everything Mom had ever touched, I decided to hang onto it."

"What does it say?" Frida asked.

"I don't know," Keeffe said. At Frida's look of surprise, she added, "Her handwriting is really hard to read."

"You've had eleven years." Frida pointed out.

Heat washed up Keeffe's neck and into her face. She started to make the same kind of lame excuse she'd always made. Then she remembered Bad telling her she was just wired differently from most people. Even though he was gone, even though he'd turned out to be some kind of demon, the recollection made her more confident.

"I don't read very well," she said. She steeled herself against Frida's judgment.

"You never really outgrew your dyslexia, did you?" Frida sounded sympathetic, but like it was no big deal.

"No." It was all Keeffe could do to say that aloud.

"That damn Lilith," Frida said again. "She told us you'd worked through it but not to bring it up because it embarrassed you that you'd had so many problems learning to read."

"And she told me not to tell anyone because they'd think I was stupid."

"That damn Lilith," they said together. They laughed, but their laughter was tinged with grief. On the plus side, Frida's color was a lot better than when Keeffe had arrived, and she'd stopped cradling her belly.

"I'll go get the journal," Keeffe said. Maybe Frida could decipher Mom's handwriting. Mom had accepted Pablo's condition and was looking forward to his birth. Keeffe was certain of that. The only question was, had Mom committed those feelings to paper?

"I just need to figure out how to get back up there," Bad said as he concluded his story.

Ma and Pa exchanged a glance.

"Will she want to see you again, now that she knows who you really are?" Ma asked.

What she meant was, would Keeffe want to see him now that she knew he'd created the surgical robot that had killed her mother. It was a good question.

"Or," Pa said, "you could stay down here and help Phoenix set up that lab."

Bad stared at Pa without enthusiasm. He didn't want to stay Below.

Pa rubbed his hands together. "You could focus on technologies by Hades and for Hades. You could create jobs for our community, jobs that don't involve mining or metalworking. You've always said we need to diversify our economy."

"That's a great idea, Pa," Bad said, though the idea of spending the rest of his life below ground, away from the sunlight and blue skies of Sedona, made him feel like the walls were closing in. "But I can't really focus on that until I know Keeffe is okay."

He excused himself. In the bathroom, he pulled the roll of superhero sketches from his pants leg and returned to the kitchen to display the black-and-white drawings.

Ma looked impressed. "She's very talented."

"Very nice, son," Pa said.

"This isn't even her best stuff," Bad said. "You should see the mural she painted." He described Keeffe's colorful rendering of the Honanki ruins, the Sphinx and the Seven Sacred Pools.

"It sounds lovely," Ma said. Pa nodded but their faces told him the words meant nothing to people who had never seen sunlight.

"If you were to set up that lab," Pa said, "you could decorate it with these cartoons."

"Wouldn't that be nice?" Ma gave him the same cheery smile she'd given him when he was a kid when they would visit her mother, a cantankerous old woman who smoked a pipe. Granny would rap him between the horns with her pipe whenever she thought he was "sassing her," which included any disagreement with her unscientific views. She steadfastly refused to believe in gravity until the day she died, no matter what proof he presented.

"That's not really the point," Bad said. "I messed up Keeffe's life. I need to make sure she's all right."

And Keeffe would only be all right with him at her side. When he pictured them together, though, it was McCall's body he saw standing next to her. He shoved that image away.

"I left her a bill of sale for these sketches, to ensure she had enough earnings to evade Lilith's contract." He bit his lip. It was driving him crazy, not knowing what was going on up there. "If she doesn't look in her footlocker, she may not know about the bank deposit in time."

Ma gasped. "What were you thinking, getting in the middle of one of Lilith's doings? You know what a she-devil she is. You'll be lucky if she doesn't convince Satan to send you back to the mines."

Telling Ma that Satan had already threatened to do just that would only worry her for no reason. Even though Bad had once been a rising star in Hell, Satan had probably forgotten his existence by now.

According to what Bad had learned in school, when Satan first arrived in Hell, he had carved out enough terrain to set up his nine rings and demanded the Hades pay him tribute. It had created quite a furor at the time. There had been talk of making war on the angel community but it quickly died away in the face of reality. Angels were immortal. There were more Hades than there were angels, but Hades could be killed. There was no way Hades could win such a war. Although the more warlike among the Hades had prophesied that giving in to Satan would be the first step down an oily incline, the Hade leaders had ceded him the territory he wanted and begun paying annual tribute in the form of precious metals and jewels.

Fortunately, Satan seemed content with the area he started with, only occasionally expanding one ring or another in response to trends in human population and transgressions. And though the Hades complained when they paid their taxes, they mostly turned in junk jewelry created by metalworking students. These days, Satan paid no attention to the Hades as long as they paid their tithe and didn't threaten his supremacy. By now, Satan had forgotten all about Bad, especially since he'd stripped him of his devices.

"You know—" Pa eyed him obliquely, "—if you were to set up that lab, you'd be able to use the tech to tap into cameras Above and check on her."

"That's true," Bad agreed, but every fiber of his being rebelled at the idea. He didn't want to spy on Keeffe. He wanted to talk to her and laugh with her and feel her joyful orgasms, the orgasms he gave her with his hands and his mouth and his—. Except that those hands and that mouth and that penis didn't actually belong to him. They belonged to Seth McCall. Seth McCall, who might very well be using those attributes to elicit those same responses from Keeffe even as they spoke.

That wouldn't happen. It couldn't happen. Keeffe was too

observant, too perceptive, too smart, to fall for McCall's dubious charms.

"The man she fell in love with was a human." Ma seemed to read his mind. "And not just any human, but one who looked like an angel. Do you really think she could love a Hade?"

Even Bad's power of imagination didn't extend to seeing Keeffe in love with his Hade self. "I'd need to get back up there as a human."

Ma's thick eyebrows drew together. "How would you do that?"

Bad had been thinking about that. "I could possess Seth McCall again."

"Would he let you do that?"

"Not voluntarily." Drugged, though, he wouldn't be able to resist, and Bad would make sure McCall stayed drugged this time.

Ma looked shocked. "You mean, take someone else's body without their permission?"

"Don't think of it like that," Bad said.

Ma put her hands on her hips. "I did not raise you to act like an angel."

"I know that," Bad said. "I just…"

"You're just going to have to forget her, son," said Pa.

Ma's face was sympathetic but firm. "Pa is right, Bad. You're never going to see her again. You have to move on."

Back at the trailer, Keeffe opened the lid of the footlocker and frowned. It looked like things had been moved around. When she didn't immediately see the journal, her heart missed a beat. She found the journal beneath the envelope containing her copy of the contracts she'd signed with McCall and Lilith.

Was it with McCall? Or the demon Bad? McCall had gray eyes the day Lilith introduced them, but both had been around that night at Ernesto's. It was the brown-eyed guy who'd talked in her into that first kiss by the lamppost, but after he banged her head against the post so hard her ears rang, his eyes were gray. Gray eyes hadn't disappeared until that camping trip, which, it turned out, was actually a trip to Hell. It felt like she was living inside a Salvador Dali painting. She tried to imagine sharing everything that had happened with Frida and failed.

She pulled the journal from the footlocker and a piece of paper fluttered from between the pages. In large, clear letters, it read, *Sold to Abaddon, Demon of Sloth, for $15,000, one scale drawing of superhero scenes.* It was dated February 10th, the day before her birthday.

She stared at it blankly. What? She went back and re-read it, tracing the letters with her fingertip. Yes, that was what it said, all right. She riffled through the contents of the trunk. The rolled-up scroll she'd made of the sketches appeared to be missing, too.

She removed everything from the footlocker, including the bag of chisels. She hefted the bag in her hand, feeling their weight. He hadn't bought them on eBay, she realized. He'd rescued them from Hell.

When the footlocker was empty, the scroll of sketches she'd done for the superhero mural still hadn't turned up. It was gone. Did that mean the fifteen thousand dollars was real?

Putting everything but the journal and the receipt back in the trunk, she raced out to her car and drove straight to the bank. At the counter, she requested her balance. The number on the slip the teller handed her almost made her eyes bug out. She had nearly twenty-nine thousand dollars in her account, and the date of the deposit was February tenth. Even if she had to refund McCall's money, she had enough to save *John*.

Whether Bad was a demon or a Hade, whatever that was, he had been looking out for her.

CHAPTER 29

Ma and Pa meant well, but Bad couldn't simply abandon Keeffe to take her chances against the demon world. His first order of business was to determine what was going on Above. Had Keeffe figured out that she'd exorcised the wrong guy? Had she found the receipt? Had she managed to stop Lilith and McCall's evil plans?

One of the worst parts of returning Below had been losing his tech gear—his phone, his laptop, and his universal remote. It was as if all his skills had been stripped from him along with his devices. But that wasn't true. He still had a brain. He just needed to use it.

To get a window on what was going on Above, he would need to reacquire his tech. Satan had told the guards to turn his equipment over to Ornias, so it was probably in DemSec. Bad just hoped Ornias hadn't destroyed the devices trying to figure out how they worked.

Where in DemSec would they be? He could picture three possibilities: Ornias's office, the secured room where DemSec kept technology still under development, or in the cage where small items that had a tendency to walk away were stored. Unfortunately, all three of those areas were kept locked and only a handful of demons had keys.

From under the bed in his old room, he pulled a set of lock-picking tools he'd acquired when he was a teenager. If Ma knew that he'd gotten them to sneak into Hell's power station to see how it worked she would have had his hide. He put them into a backpack and pulled it onto his shoulders.

The best way to get to DemSec without passing through any public spaces was via the tunnels that had been in place before Satan arrived. Bad had built the tech hub at the conjunction of several of these tunnels. Even then, he'd known he might someday need to enter or exit DemSec unseen. He checked his watch. If he left now, he should arrive after everyone was gone for the day.

"I'm going for a walk," he called to Ma and hurried to the door before she could ask questions. Outside, he ran into an obstacle in the form of Phoenix, who was just lifting his hand to knock when Bad opened the door.

The boy eyed him curiously. "Where are you going?"

"Nowhere," Bad whispered.

"Why are you whispering?"

Bad pulled the door closed behind him. "Shh."

Phoenix's eyes sharpened. "Are you sneaking up to the Rings?"

Sneaking up to the Rings was a favorite pastime of Hade youth. "Of course not."

Phoenix raised his pink eyebrows skeptically.

Bad drew him away from the door, "I'm going to DemSec to retrieve something."

"Something Satan wants you to have?"

Bad gave that the eye-roll it deserved.

"I'll go with you," Phoenix said.

"You can't. Go visit Ma and Pa and keep them occupied."

Phoenix smirked. "Like, by telling them where you went?"

Bad glared at him. "If I get caught, it will be bad. And Satan won't go easy on you just because you're a kid."

Phoenix drew himself up. "I'm not a kid."

"I mean, Lake-of-Fire bad."

Phoenix blinked, but immediately stiffened his spine. "I'm not scared."

"You should be," Bad said.

Phoenix just shrugged.

It might be Lake-of-Fire bad for Bad, but it was probably only maggot-pit bad for a youngster. Bad glared at him. "Okay, you can come, but keep quiet."

He set out in the direction of the nearest tunnel that led to DemSec. Phoenix fell into step beside him. Briefly, Bad explained what they were looking for. Phoenix's eyes lit with excitement. "Drastic."

Bad looked at him blankly. "What?"

Phoenix gave him a pitying look. "It means…cool, I guess would be your word for it."

Bad hoped it didn't turn out to be anything drastic. Kids today were so sheltered. He expected to have to reiterate his order to be quiet, but Phoenix popped in his earbuds and lost himself in music.

It took a couple hours of rapid uphill walking to reach DemSec. By the time they got there, Bad was grateful to McCall for getting his body into better shape. It would have been humiliating to have to stop to rest with young Phoenix loping along beside him like a mule deer.

As they neared the spot where the tunnel intersected DemSec, he touched Phoenix's arm and raised his finger to his lips. Phoenix pulled his earbuds out and nodded silently. Ahead lay a brightly lit hallway. They crept along the tunnel until they reached the corridor.

Motioning Phoenix to stay behind him, Bad poked his head out into the hallway. It was deserted. He checked his watch. The workers should be gone by now.

The cage would be easiest to break into, so Bad decided to try it first. He slipped through the hallways like a phantom, Phoenix on his heels, till they came to the warehouse area that housed the cage.

He inspected the door. He hadn't been here in ten years. What if they'd wired it since then? Despite the need for speed, he made himself take time to check carefully. No sign of wires.

"If an alarm goes off," he murmured to Phoenix, "you take off and get yourself back to Hadeville. Okay?"

Phoenix nodded silently, his brown eyes wide beneath his pink eyebrows.

Bad set to work with his lock-picking tools. In a matter of moments, the lock clicked. Squeezing his eyes shut, Bad turned the handle and swung the door open. He breathed a sigh of relief when no alarm sounded.

"You take that side—" he pointed to the left, "—and I'll take this side."

A rapid but methodical search of the cage turned up no sign of his confiscated tech.

"What now?" Phoenix asked.

"The secure room," Bad said and led the way.

After another quick stop by the trailer, Keeffe drove to her father's house and rang the bell beside his sulfur-colored door. The cloth sack containing Mom's chisels was inside her backpack. A moment later, the *rat-a-tat-tat* of high heels on the parquet floor sounded. The door opened a crack.

It was the first time Keeffe had seen her stepmother since the barbecue. Back then, she hadn't believed Father Xavier's assertion that Lilith was a she-demon. Now she knew it to be true.

"What do you want?" Lilith said. She was dressed, as usual, in red and black.

"*John,*" Keeffe said.

Lilith smiled, the same taunting smile she'd worn the afternoon of the barbecue.

"According to Seth, you walked out on him and abandoned the mural. Your dad's already booked a flight to take it to New York for auction." She tried to close the door, but Keeffe shoved the toe of her hiking boot in the way.

"I didn't abandon the mural but it doesn't matter." Keeffe held up the bill of sale, along with the balance slip the clerk at the bank had given her. "Even without it, I'm good."

Lilith scanned the documents. Her face darkened till it was as red as her miniskirt. "That little turd."

"My statue, please," Keeffe said, opening and closing her hand in Lilith's face. "Or do I need to come back with my lawyer?"

Lilith threw the door open so hard it slammed into the foil-covered wall. The doorknob gouged a hole in the drywall. She stalked off down the hall. Keeffe followed her.

In the family room, Lilith pointed to *John* with a shaking finger.

Keeffe lifted him off his pedestal. "You are going to see so many great museums."

"Take him and get out." Lilith snarled. Her pupils were rectangular. Keeffe felt the same burst of satisfaction she'd gotten as a teenager when that happened.

She set *John* down on the pool table and rummaged in her backpack. "Not so fast. I have a deal to offer you."

Lilith went very still. "A deal?"

Keeffe set the cloth sack on the pool table and removed the chisels, one by one, laying them out on the green felt.

"Where did you get those?" Lilith's face turned red.

Keeffe looked her dead in the eye. "They were a present from my boyfriend. I think you know him as Abaddon."

Lilith digested that. "So you know?"

"That you're a demon from Hell? Yes."

Lilith picked up one of the chisels. "That little shit must have rescued them from the incinerator in Ring Seven."

Keeffe almost got the sense she admired Bad. "Is that a big deal?"

"River of boiling blood, armed centaurs, harpy-filled woods—you could say that." Lilith shook her head. "When Satan finds out, geek boy will be in even more trouble than he already is."

Keeffe's heart missed a beat. "What kind of trouble?"

"You're in love with him." Lilith looked stunned.

"I just want to know he's okay," Keeffe said. He would be fine, she assured herself. Someone as smart as Bad could figure his way out of a jam.

Lilith eyed her. "Let me give you a piece of advice. Forget about Bad."

She never would. She wasn't sure she even wanted to try.

"Since you went to all the trouble of stealing them," Keeffe said, "I thought maybe you'd be willing to make a trade to get them back."

"What kind of trade?"

"I'll give you the chisels," Keeffe said, "if you convince McCall not to destroy Ed and Claude's company."

As soon as the words were out, she knew she'd made a mistake. Lilith's rectangular pupils smoothed back into ordinary circles, and she stopped looking like she wanted to murder someone. Keeffe's ribs seemed to tighten around her lungs.

Lilith smiled. "Let me offer you an alternative arrangement. You give me the statue and I call off Seth."

Keeffe hated to see the boys lose their business, but she hated the thought of *John* disappearing into Hell even more.

"No deal," she said, expecting a return of Lilith's fury.

"No?" Lilith seemed unconcerned. "I don't blame you. That's not really an even trade, is it? Let me sweeten the deal. Give me the statue and I'll not only have Seth completely forgive the boys' loan, I'll let Frida keep that wretched fetus she's so intent on giving birth to."

Keeffe felt the blood drain from her face. "You can't do that." Surely Lilith didn't have that kind of power.

"What?" asked Lilith. "Make her miscarry? Of course I can. Who do you think kept her barren all these years so she'd sell her statue?"

Keeffe stared at her, feeling sick. Suzanne had always said there was no medical reason that Frida wasn't getting pregnant. Suddenly, it all made sense.

"Well?" said Lilith. "Are you going to keep a worthless hunk of rock and destroy not only your brothers' business, but your sister's happiness—not to mention your little nephew or niece? If I work it just right, I can set up an infection that makes it impossible for Frida to ever have a child. With the proper inattention during treatment, it might even kill her."

Now it felt as though the blood had drained from Keeffe's entire body. "You wouldn't do that," she whispered through numb lips.

"Sweetie, I'd not only do it, I'd enjoy it. Over the last ten years, I've had a bellyful of the Blackmon family. The idea of there being one less of you tickles me to death."

Keeffe looked at her stepmother's face. She meant every word. Blinking back tears, Keeffe picked up *John* and set him back on his pedestal. When she turned back around, Lilith was holding out a slip of paper, along with a scarlet quill pen.

"You don't mind using my pen, do you?" Lilith asked. A tiny, almost invisible barb protruded from the shaft.

The paper looked similar to the bill of sale Keeffe had brought with her, except that the amount was a quarter of a million dollars. Lilith wasn't even trying to screw her out of the actual value of the statue. She must want it very badly.

Why would that be? A shiver went down Keeffe's spine at the thought, but when she considered the possibilities against Frida losing her baby, there was no question what she would do.

She crossed her arms. "How do I know you'll keep your word?"

Lilith's eyes darted from the statue to the bill of sale. She licked her lips. "I can draft an addendum, if you like, specifying my end of the bargain." Her charcoal eyelids swept down to cover her eyes. "What do you want it to say?"

Keeffe thought for a minute. She wanted to ensure that Dad, Frida and her brothers were all unchained from the demonic influence that had infected their lives for the last ten years.

"In return for the eagle statue sculpted by Rachel Blackmon," she said, "I, Lilith Blackmon, commit that Frida Blackmon's baby will be born unharmed by demon influence. I further commit to freeing Daniel Blackmon to return to painting. Finally, I commit that Seth McCall will release his interest in Blackmon Gaming in exchange for $250,000."

Lilith's eyes widened. "You're giving the money to Seth?"

"Did you really think I wanted your blood money?"

Lilith walked over to the bar and typed briefly into a laptop sitting there. "Let me just print that out and then we can both sign it."

Keeffe retrieved the cellphone Bad had given her from her messenger bag. "Do that. There's a text-to-voice app on this phone. It will let me verify that nothing got missed or misstated when you were typing it up."

Lilith's jaw tightened. She turned back to the laptop and typed again, for longer this time. She pressed another key and then disappeared, presumably into her office to retrieve the printout.

Uneasily, Keeffe wondered if she should have included something about *The Artist's Soul* in the agreement but if McCall had told the truth, and the purpose of Lilith's mission was to destroy Mom's legacy, she wasn't likely to give away the very thing that would let her achieve her goal.

When Lilith returned, Keeffe snapped a picture of the document with her phone and pressed a few keys. A robotic voice read out the text. It was word perfect.

"Satisfied?" Lilith asked. This time she didn't offer Keeffe her pen.

"Almost," Keeffe dug into her pocket and pulled out her Swiss Army knife. She stabbed the tip of her finger and, with the welling blood, signed the bill of sale. Then she held out the knife to Lilith.

Her eyes blazing with dislike, Lilith did the same.

It wasn't great, but it was the best Keeffe could do.

Bad and Phoenix flitted through the halls of DemSec like a pair of bats. Bad wished he could stop and point out some of the more interesting areas where exciting work was underway—at least, it had been underway when he went into the maggot pit ten years earlier— but it wasn't safe here for the boy. They needed to retrieve Bad's tech and get out.

After ten minutes of covert movement, they arrived at the secure room. Bad stared at the door with misgiving. In his day, it had not only been kept locked, but it was also wired with an alarm and the room inside was surveilled by closed-circuit cameras. On the other hand, without his tech he'd never know how Keeffe was doing. The only good news was, there was a tunnel nearby, hidden behind a stack of skids and camouflaged by a Hade charm. He showed Phoenix how to access it.

"If you hear or see anything," he told Phoenix, "I mean *anything*, you head for that tunnel and get out of here. Understood?"

Eyes huge, Phoenix nodded.

Bad unzipped his backpack and took out his lock-picking kit again. Why had he never thought to hide a duplicate of his universal remote somewhere outside of DemSec? Because he'd never thought he'd need it. He'd given no thought to the damage he was doing from his ivory bunker, so he'd had no reason to think he'd need to subvert his own efforts.

There was no point in trying his shims—he'd designed the doorframe to prevent easy entry. He prodded the cylinder with a wafer reader but, again, he'd intentionally designed the lock on this room to resist unauthorized access. He was just about to pull out his scope and plug it into an old tablet he'd given Dad for his birthday years ago when he heard footsteps.

Turning to Phoenix, he jerked his head. "Go."

To his intense frustration, Phoenix didn't move. "I'm not leaving you here."

Whoever was coming toward them was still out of sight, down one of the many hallways that crisscrossed DemSec, but he or she was drawing closer.

"Go," he said, even more urgently.

Phoenix folded his arms across his skinny chest and shook his head. Bad grabbed him by the shoulders and pushed him in the direction of the tunnel. "Go!"

But it was too late.

"Yo! You there! What are you doing?"

Phoenix stared beyond Bad, his eyes enormous. Bad whirled to face the oncoming threat. A gangly demon with earlobes pulled long by the weight of oversized grommets jogged toward them. His Converse gym shoes slapped the tile floor like the echoes of doom.

"Scrote?" said Bad.

"The very same," Scrote said, offering Bad his hand. They exchanged a complicated handshake that went on for several seconds. Finally, he wrapped his pinky around Bad's little finger and they bumped the tips of their thumbs together. "How you doing, man?"

"Good." Bad couldn't help grinning. "I'm good. You?"

"Can't complain." But Scrote immediately undercut that by shaking his head gloomily. "You need to come back to DemSec, man. Ornias is a total dick to work for."

Bad could have predicted that.

"He keeps giving me noogies." Scrote tilted his head forward to display a bare patch between his horns.

"I'm sorry about that," Bad said.

Scrote's eyebrows nearly climbed off his forehead. "You can apologize?"

Bad blushed. "A little." It had been a source of constant lamentation for Scrote that, once he started working for his old schoolmate Bad, he'd lost the ability to say he was sorry.

"Congrats." Scrote held up his palm and Bad slapped it.

Bad cleared his throat. "I don't suppose you could let us into this room?"

Scrote seemed to notice Phoenix for the first time. "Is that your kid, man?"

"No, he's my nephew."

Scrote nodded sagely. "Giving him the tour of the old workplace?"

It was tempting to lie, but the consequences for Scrote if Ornias learned that he'd let Bad into the Development room were too serious.

"I'm trying to grab back some tech Satan took from me."

"Wow." Scrote thought that over. Then he reached into his pocket and pulled out a key and unlocked the door. "I'll erase this from the tapes after you leave."

Bad heaved a sigh of relief. "Thanks, Scrote."

CHAPTER 30

Keeffe wanted nothing more than to return to her trailer and howl out her grief and frustration at losing *John*, but if the public believed Mom had died trying to kill her unborn baby, her crosses—her beautiful, inspirational crosses—would become poison to the Church. Before Keeffe could process her grief, she needed to know if there was anything in that final journal that could stop Lilith from destroying Mom's legacy. Keeffe turned the car once again toward Oak Creek.

When she got to Frida's house, her sister looked much better than she had that morning.

"Are you still spotting?" Keeffe asked.

"No." Color had come back into Frida's cheeks and she was no longer cupping her abdomen with her hands. "It stopped about a half hour ago, and my cramps are gone."

Keeffe drew a deep breath. It was what she'd expected, but she was still relieved.

"Did you bring the journal?" Frida asked.

"Are you sure you want to read it?"

"Of course." Frida looked puzzled. "Why wouldn't I?"

"What if I'm wrong? What if Mom never came to terms with having a handicapped child? What if she was planning to abort him?"

Frida shrugged. "Then we forgive her and move on."

Keeffe handed over the journal.

"Sheesh," Frida said, scanning the first page. "You weren't kidding about her handwriting."

In spite of her misery over losing *John*, Keeffe felt vindicated. It wasn't that she was illiterate. Mom's scrawl really was difficult to decipher. After about ten minutes, Frida said, "I think I've figured out the pattern." She pointed to a letter in the journal. "That letter that looks like a curlicue?"

Keeffe nodded.

"It's an uppercase *I*."

"Okay."

"And this one that looks like a pennant?"

Keeffe nodded.

"It's a *P*."

"Sure. I can see that."

Frida translated a few more characters and pronounced herself ready to read. Keeffe's mouth was dry, but she nodded at Frida to begin.

"*September first.* John *is coming along marvelously. I think he will be the best of the bunch. The alabaster I selected for him has fewer occlusions than the stone I used for* Matthew, Mark *and* Luke. *At first I thought he would be huddled inside his wings, cowering from the Apocalypse, but as I chipped away I found a different version, soaring for the sky. He reminds me to keep my eyes on God.*"

"*September eighth. Pablo is active today. I think he's practicing his high dive, using my bladder for a springboard. When I try to picture him, I see a tiny face that's a bit like Keeffe's. I'm not sure which she's more excited about having: a baby brother or her very own sculpture.* John *is coming along well. I should finish him in the next few weeks.*"

Despite the seriousness of the situation, Keeffe smiled. The passages from the journal made it feel like Mom was back in the room with them.

"September tenth. Frida came by today with her friend, Jen. I wish she would come out and admit they're lovers. This closet thing drives me crazy. Daniel says be patient, she'll tell us when she thinks we're ready. I'm ready, for heaven's sake."

Frida blinked back tears. "I'm glad I came out before she died."

"It was a good decision," Keeffe said. "She adored Jen."

"September twelfth. Daniel showed me his newest painting today, a cottage in a dark forest. It's so welcoming I wanted to go inside, sit down, and have coffee with the owners. He swears this will be the last of his night scenes, but he enjoys painting them and his fans love them."

"I never thought I'd say this," Frida said, "but I wish he'd paint another night scene."

"I think he will soon," Keeffe said.

Frida raised her eyebrows. "Really? Why is that?"

"No reason," Keeffe said. "It's just this feeling I have."

Frida returned to the journal.

"September fifteenth. Went to Keeffe's open house tonight. Most of her teachers were suspiciously polite. Lord knows she's not an easy child. Her art teacher loves her, though. He should. She's brilliant. She will grow up to be an amazing artist."

Keeffe flushed with pleasure. "I wasn't that bad."

"You were a nightmare," said Frida, but she said it with an affectionate smile.

"September seventeenth. Heartburn kept me awake half the night. Sister Mary Grace says that means Pablo will have lots of hair. How did a nun come to know that old wives' tale?"

"September twentieth. It's hard to believe Ed and Claude are high school seniors this year. They are looking for a college that offers a major in graphic storytelling. Not sure how their love of video games is going to support them, but Mom said the same thing about my sculptures, and I've done all right."

Frida turned the page again. Mom's scrawl filled the left side, but the right had only a couple of lines. Frida riffled the remaining pages. They were blank.

She bit her lip. "This is it."

Keeffe wrapped her fist around the tiny crucifix hanging from her neck and took a deep breath. "Go ahead." The final entries had to provide them with the evidence they needed to put a stop to Lilith's destructive plan. They just had to.

"*September twenty-sixth. Went to confession this morning. Told Fr. X about Pablo, and about looking into abortion. Assured him I'm past that now. I really want this baby. I think Daniel and I are the ideal parents for this child.*"

Frida's shoulders slumped with relief. Keeffe let out the breath she was holding. "Oh, thank God."

"*Fr. X was very troubled that I'd ever considered getting rid of the baby. I'll be saying Hail Marys for months. But the God who sees all, forgives all. This child will be a blessing to our family.*"

On the next page came the final entry:

"*October tenth. Pablo hasn't moved in nearly a week. Seeing the doctor this afternoon.*"

That doctor visit had resulted in the surgery, which, in turn had killed Mom. Keeffe grappled with that for a moment. Frida reached over and squeezed her hands.

"That's pretty indisputable," Keeffe said. Her voice was husky.

Frida nodded, blinking back tears. "It is. I'll take it to Lilith and let her know *The Artist's Soul* paints a misleading picture. I'll tell her that if she doesn't suspend publication and correct that, we'll release the journal and sue for defamation of character."

Keeffe's heartbeat quickened. A trap loomed before them. "You can't do that."

"Why not?"

"Once Lilith knows this journal exists, she'll do anything to destroy it."

Frida's expression said she thought Keeffe was exaggerating. "I'll make a copy first."

A dozen copies wouldn't be enough to safeguard the journal. Keeffe had tried to make her agreement for the statue as airtight as possible, but she was playing on Lilith's home court. There was no way to know how binding their contract was. If Lilith found out about the journal, Dad's future, Blackmon Gaming, and Frida's baby could all be at risk.

Keeffe picked up the journal and tucked it into her bag. "Don't mention this to anyone—not even the boys. I'll bring it back once I'm sure I've got it secured."

For that, she needed more help than she could find in Sedona.

Bad gazed around the Development lab in frustration. He and Phoenix and Scrote had looked in every drawer and cubbyhole, but there was no sign of Bad's missing tech.

"The only other place I can think of that it might be is Ornias's office," he said.

Together, the three of them made their way through the maze of hallways to what had once been Bad's office. It was not only locked, but the lockset that had been there in Bad's day was now an electronic lock with a retinal scanner. Bad's shoulders drooped.

"I don't suppose you have access to this room?" Bad asked.

Scrote shook his head regretfully.

But Phoenix pulled something from his pocket. "Try this." He held up the skeleton key that Ronnie had loaned Bad when he'd come to Hell for Keeffe's chisels.

"What are you doing with that?" Bad asked.

Phoenix stepped back. "I was returning it."

Right. The game. "How did you get it past Pa in the first place?"

"I stuck it down my underwear."

Bad fought the urge to wipe the key on his jeans. Instead, he held it up to the retinal scanner. The eye on the bow glowed and seemed to come alive. A second later, the lock clicked.

This time they didn't have to search for very long. Bad's confiscated tech was in Ornias's lap drawer. Bad put the universal remote in his backpack and shoved his phone into his back pocket. It felt like he had his arms and legs back.

Out in the hallway, he and Scrote exchanged their complicated handshake again.

"Seriously," Bad said. "I don't know how to thank you."

"Come back to work," Scrote said. His long face grew even longer. "Ornias makes us do calisthenics."

Bad gazed at him in horror. "You're kidding." He didn't have the heart to tell Scrote that he'd never be returning to DemSec.

"You should come work for me," said Phoenix.

Scrote scratched his scraggly goatee. "You have a tech lab?"

Phoenix blushed. "Not yet, but I will soon, and I'll be looking for techies."

Scrote smiled amiably. "Drastic, dude. Keep me in mind."

Bad had just said goodbye to Phoenix at the edge of Hadeville when "Shape of You" issued from his phone. He stared at the phone, not believing his ears. He'd set that as Keeffe's ringtone the first time he heard her play it while she painted.

Fingers shaking, he pressed the Accept icon.

"Keeffe?" He half expected a howl of demon laughter as the call turned out to be someone's practical joke.

"Bad?" The voice on the other end was tremulous.

It was Keeffe. For a moment, the joy of hearing her voice erased all rational thought from his brain. "Hi," he said, and immediately felt like an idiot.

"Are you in Hell?" she asked.

"I—yes." He waited for her to hang up on him.

"You sound different," she said.

His face warmed. "I, uh, the other voice was produced by McCall's larynx."

He waited again for dead air to telegraph her rejection of his Hade self, but all she said was, "Duh. Of course."

"Are you okay?" He hoped against hope that she'd say yes.

"No."

He wasn't surprised. Hell was gonna do what Hell was gonna do. "What's wrong?"

She told him about McCall painting over her mural. The thought of so much beauty carelessly wiped out made him feel physically ill.

"I'm really sorry." He hung his head. This was his fault. "If I hadn't signed you to that contract, this never would have happened."

"I forgive you," Keeffe said.

It couldn't possibly be that easy. "I was trying to get you to sell me *John.*"

"I know."

"But I wasn't trying to trick you out of him. Lilith added that part."

"I figured."

Her words were like balm. He sent a prayer of thanksgiving northward. "So now McCall says you abandoned the mural, which means Lilith... Did you find the bill of sale for the superhero sketches?"

"I did," she said. He heaved a sigh of relief, but his relief was cut short when she added, "I gave it to Lilith to save my brothers' company. I made her sign the agreement in blood. Is that legally binding? By demon standards?"

"It's brilliant," he said. "Contracts signed in blood are the only kind that are enforceable in Hell."

"Lilith made me get blood on the first one and then you gave me a paper cut on the second one, so that's what I figured."

"Smart girl," he said. She was so observant. "It sounds like you've got everything under control."

"Not really." A choked sob came through the phone. It felt like she had reached into his chest and squeezed his heart. "It sucks here without you."

He'd never meant to hurt her. As soon as the thought crossed his mind, he called himself out for a liar. He had meant to hurt her. He'd meant to take from her what she valued most in the world. He was done with making excuses for himself. "You should try being down here without you."

She gave a watery chuckle. "That's probably worse. Come back."

They were the words he'd longed to hear, but it wasn't what was best for her.

"You've seen what I really look like," he said. "There's no place for a guy like me up there."

"I don't care about that," she said. "I want the guy who made the painting to come back."

"The guy who made the painting also made surgical robots." He clenched his teeth, waiting for her to run out of forgiveness and finally hang up on him.

"McCall told me," she said. To his amazement, there was no censure in her tone. "My mom died but a lot of people lived because of those things. You have to take the bad with the good."

Bad drank in her words. They felt like absolution. In the end, though, they didn't change anything.

"I can't be the guy who made the painting anymore," he said, "but I can be your lifeline at the other end of the phone. I can be the best friend you ever had."

Someday she would call to tell him she'd met someone. The time Satan had stabbed him in the belly with a burning pitchfork hadn't hurt half as much as that would, but he'd take that pain, and worse, if it would ease her life even a tiny bit. In the meantime, he would drink in the sound of her voice like a life-giving elixir. "What else is going on?"

She told him about Lilith and *The Artist's Soul* and about the final journal. "That's really why I called. How can I keep it safe?"

"Scan it into your phone and text me a copy." That, at least, was something he could do for her. "I can safeguard it."

"Thank you," she said. "I wasn't sure if I should call."

"Of course you should call," he said. "Anytime. Night or day. I'm here for you." They sat in silence for a moment. He'd stay on the phone all night, just to listen to her breathe. "That was really smart, getting Lilith to sign that contract in blood. I'm sorry about the mural, but at least you saved *John*."

"No, I didn't," she said. "Didn't I tell you? That's what Lilith demanded in return for letting Frida keep her baby."

"What?" A world of horror opened up in front of him. "Lilith has *John?*"

"I didn't have any choice. She was going to make Frida miscarry."

Sweat broke out on his forehead, something that had never happened to his Hade body before. "You need to leave Sedona. Get your family out, too. And anyone else you can convince to leave."

"What?" She sounded astonished. "Why?"

"Because Satan is planning to destroy the town."

Keeffe spent the next hour arguing with Bad about her next move. Bad wanted her to abandon Sedona and save herself, but she had never been a fan of half steps. Using Mom's final journal as leverage, she could save Sedona. If she worked it right, she could free Bad from Hell, too.

"Don't come down here," Bad said. "It's too dangerous for you."

"I'll see you in a couple of hours," she said, and hung up. Her plan required letting Satan destroy Mom's legacy. The idea broke her heart, but Mom would have considered it a worthwhile trade-off.

It was well after midnight when she arrived at McCall's mansion. She put her thumb on the doorbell and left it there, listening to the *Star Wars* theme chime over and over again. After a few minutes, McCall came to the door.

He jutted his pelvis toward her. "Looking for some hot stuff?"

She barged in past him. "Actually, yes. Where's Ronnie?"

"In bed."

"Where does he sleep?"

"What is your deal?" He glared at her. "You weren't kidding with all that flirting you were doing with him, were you?"

"You're an idiot," she said. "I want him to take me to Hell."

"You don't need him for that," McCall said. "I can take you there."

"Not bad-date Hell," she said. "Real Hell."

"I can do that," McCall insisted. "Bad showed me how."

He grabbed her arm. He must be talking about when they went on that camping trip that wasn't a camping trip. She let him drag her to the back hallway, where he plucked a set of keys from a little cabinet just inside the door. He led her to the smaller of his two garages and walked over to a pickup truck.

"We'll take this one," he said. "I just had the headlights modified so that they're bright enough for Hell."

"Why are you doing this?" she asked.

"I've been wanting to get back there anyway." He put the truck in reverse and backed out of the garage. Keeffe squinted. He was right about the headlights. "There's a chick down there that's hot for me."

What a doofus.

He pulled out of his subdivision and turned south on 179. After passing through Oak Creek, he shoved his foot down on the accelerator.

"Yee-haw!" he yelled as the vehicle's speed climbed.

Keeffe grabbed the safety strap over the door. "What are you doing?"

"Taking you to Hell, baby. Keep an eye out for the portal to open."

"What portal?" Keeffe asked.

"It will be off over to the side," he said. "Like a black doorway."

"It's dark," she said. "Everything looks like a black doorway."

The truck's speed continued to climb. They were at ninety miles per hour when Keeffe heard a *whoop-whoop* from behind them. Blue lights flashed.

McCall looked in his rearview mirror and then scanned the terrain outside the passenger side window. The moron was considering driving off the road and hoping for the best. She could see it in his face.

"Slow down," she yelled, punching him in the thigh with one knuckle jutting out for maximum effect, the way her brothers had taught her.

"Ow!" He yanked his foot off the accelerator and rubbed his thigh. "That hurt."

"Good," Keeffe said. "You were going to get us killed."

The police car drew nearer. Reluctantly, McCall braked, pulling over at a wide spot in the berm.

He assured the officer he hadn't been drinking, but the cop made him take a sobriety test anyway. He passed, but then the officer noticed the headlights.

"Those exceed allowable limits," he said. "You can either drive this straight home and replace them, or I'll impound this vehicle."

By the time they made a U-turn and headed back toward his house, McCall was the possessor of a three-hundred-dollar traffic ticket and a court date. When they reached his house, he jumped out of the truck.

"Now can I talk to Ronnie?" Keeffe asked, following him to the door.

"Go home," he yelled, and slammed it in her face.

If Satan really planned to destroy Sedona, she couldn't do that. She circled the house, peeking in windows until she found the room Ronnie slept in. She banged her fist on the glass, wincing. Her knuckle was still sore from punching McCall's thigh.

After a few moments of her pounding, Ronnie sat up. He wore striped, old-man pajamas. When he saw her, he slid his feet into a pair of house slippers and padded over to the window and opened it.

"Miss Keeffe," he said. "What are you doing here?"

"I need you to take me to Hell," she said.

He didn't even blink. "The master doesn't like tourists."

"He let McCall in," she said.

"McCall is more of a future resident, if you get my drift."

She so did.

"Here's the thing," she said. "I have a journal proving that my mother did not, in fact, abort my younger brother, and that the book Lilith is about to publish is intentionally misleading and can be debunked. I think Satan would want to know that's not going to work."

"Ah," Ronnie said, smoothing the few strands of hair he had left over his crown.

"If you will take me to Hell," she said, "I am sure your boss will be pleased at the deal I have to offer him."

He thought about that. "Meet me at the garage."

When she got to the garage, McCall was with him.

She groaned. "What's he doing here?"

"If anyone is going to Hell, I am," said McCall, sticking out his chest.

Keeffe exchanged a glance with Ronnie. Ronnie shrugged.

"Whatever," Keeffe said. "Let's go."

Instead of turning right on 179, as McCall had, Ronnie made a left, and then followed the roundabout onto 89A. It wasn't until they turned into her dad's subdivision that Keeffe realized where he was going. He parked in front of the house and walked up to the front door. Producing a key from his pocket, he unlocked the door and opened it.

"If you stand in this doorway," he said, "and tap your heels together three times and say 'There's no place like Hell,' it will transport you to Ring Nine."

Keeffe stared at the doorway with narrowed eyes. "You're joking."

But McCall stepped onto the doorsill, his face shining with eagerness. He tapped his heels together three times in rapid succession, chanting, "There's no place like Hell. There's no place like Hell. There's no place like Hell." As soon as the last "Hell" was out of his mouth, he vanished.

Keeffe blinked.

"Portals usually only require that the person being transported cross them at a specified pace—say, a jog—to operate," Ronnie said, "but Bad recoded this one. He set it up so it wouldn't be triggered accidentally by your nephews."

Another example of why Bad didn't belong in Hell, but Keeffe didn't tell Ronnie that. He appeared to be on board with giving Satan what he wanted. She suspected he'd be less supportive if he knew she was planning to spring Bad from Hell.

Keeffe stepped onto the doorsill, but before she could launch into the magic phrase, Lilith appeared in the entryway. She wore the same embroidered dressing gown and marabou slippers she'd worn the night Keeffe tried to steal *John*. When her gaze landed on Keeffe, she looked surprised and annoyed. When they fell on Ronnie, understanding swept over her face, followed by anger.

"What are you doing?" she demanded.

"Ferrying her to Hell," Ronnie said. He jerked his chin at Keeffe. "Go ahead."

"Why does she want to go to Hell?" asked Lilith.

"She says she has something that will please the boss."

Lilith's gaze zeroed in on Keeffe like a laser. "What does she have?"

Keeffe didn't like being spoken across like she wasn't even there. She opened the flap of her messenger bag just enough to give Lilith a peek at the journal.

Lilith's eyes flashed instant understanding. "Your mother wrote another journal?"

Keeffe nodded. "While she worked on *John*. It was her last one."

Lilith advanced on Keeffe, her red-lacquered nails like claws.

Keeffe wrapped her arms around the messenger bag and clicked her heels. Before Lilith could reach her, she blurted out, "There's no place like Hell. There's no place like Hell. There's no place like Hell."

CHAPTER 31

Keeffe knew she was in Hell before she even opened her eyes. The ambient temperature felt like Sedona in July and the air reeked of sulfur. Warily, she peeled her eyes open. She stood in the middle of a gigantic cavern that looked like it had been painted by an artist whose palette was limited to red and black. Giant spikes of limestone hung from the ceiling and jutted up from the floor.

She looked around, orienting herself. Nearby, three pedestals held *Matthew, Mark,* and *Luke.* A fourth pedestal was empty. Where was *John?* Lilith must not have delivered him yet.

The cavern held the most diverse array of creatures she'd ever seen assembled in one place. Some looked like exceptionally beautiful humans. Others looked like animals, sometimes a single creature, like a stork, but more often a horrifying hybrid of two or more different animals, like a bull, a raven and a man, or a lion and a bear. Some appeared in columns of flame or smoke.

McCall had already crossed the cavern to an immense ebony throne, where a skinny little maroon guy lolled. He had horns and a tail. Except for his skin color and his unpleasant expression, he looked a lot like Bad.

McCall bowed deeply from the waist. "Your highness, I've brought you the girl."

Satan's skinny eyebrows drew together. "The girl? What would I want the girl for? DemSec's probability calculator computes the chances of her becoming a client at point zero one percent."

That was good to know. Her fourth-grade teacher had calculated her chances much higher.

McCall's mouth opened and closed. He hadn't bothered to ask her why she wanted to come to Hell.

Satan leaned over and whispered something to one of his guards. The guard, a hulking cross of man and bull, disappeared down a corridor.

Keeffe was trying to think how best to open negotiations when Ronnie materialized beside her.

"The young lady has a journal she believes you'll be interested in acquiring." He took her arm and led her toward Satan's throne. His grasp on her elbow wasn't exactly a tight grip, but it didn't leave much room for resistance, either.

Satan leaned forward. "A journal? What kind of journal?"

Keeffe removed the book from her messenger bag and held it up. "My mother's last journal, showing that she did not, in fact, die having my little brother aborted. Which I can use to stop the publishing company from releasing *The Artist's Soul.*"

Smoke issued from Satan's horns.

"Why did no one tell me of this journal?" His tone was a threat.

"You'll have to ask Lilith that question," Ronnie said.

All the other demons, both the beautiful ones and the animal hybrids, shivered. Why were they so afraid of this scrawny little clown?

"Oh, I will. Believe me, I will." Satan turned to Keeffe. "What do you want in exchange for Mommy's diary?"

The very fact that he tried to minimize the value of the journal told her how much it was worth to him.

"I want you to leave Sedona alone."

Satan's face darkened a shade. "How does she know about the Sedona plan?"

No one answered.

Keeffe said, "And I want the demon Abaddon to return Aboveworld with me."

"Ah." Satan put two and two together. "Do you know what he really looks like?"

"A lot like you," she said, "except for his coloring." She cocked her head. "If I were painting you, I'd have to buy extra magenta."

Somewhere at the back of the crowd, someone tittered. Satan's skin darkened to the shade of a ripe beet. "Silence!"

He turned back to Keeffe. "Bad's here for the duration. You don't realize it, but I'm doing you a favor. He's the source of a lot of misery in your world."

Keeffe crossed her arms. "And a lot of good."

A puff of smoke issued from Satan's left horn. "I'm just starting to realize how much."

Beside the throne, McCall gazed out over the crowd, like he was looking for someone. His face was pink and a rivulet of sweat ran down his temple.

"I don't release demons," Satan said harshly. "Ever."

Keeffe thrust her chin out. There was no way she was going back to the surface without Bad.

"No deal."

Satan eyed her calculatingly. "But I am willing to offer you a deal on Sedona." Before she could respond, he said, "Where are my manners? Can I offer you some refreshments?"

He was stalling. Why?

"No, thanks." Keeffe hadn't forgotten the myth of Persephone and the pomegranate seeds. She'd skip the refreshments.

The guard Satan had sent away returned. A small, horned figure was with him. Keeffe caught her breath.

He was even shorter than she'd remembered, and the hair on his arms was thick as fur. For an instant, her heart quailed. Then she saw his eyes, dark brown and warm with love for her. All her misgivings melted away. It was a different body, but he was still her Bad.

"What are you doing here?" he asked, his hands clenching into fists.

"I came to get you," she said with more confidence than she actually felt. "And to make a deal to save Sedona."

"Go back," he said.

"Not without you."

He held out his hands. "Please, Keeffe, for the love of God, go back where you belong."

Shrieks echoed through the cavern. The beautiful demons, who must be fallen angels, bent double. All the ones who had arms wrapped their arms around themselves, as though trying to ward off pain.

"How dare you mention the Enemy's name!" Satan roared.

Bad tried to pull free from his guard, but the minotaur's hamlike hands held him securely. In the middle of this uproar, Lilith appeared. She had exchanged her dressing gown and slippers for her usual miniskirt and stilettos.

A single puff of oily black smoke emitted from Satan's left horn at the sight of her.

"Where's my statue?"

"All in good time," Lilith said. "It passed from the girl to her father. I need a little more time to convince him to give it to me."

"Malphas needs to have all four statues stationed at the vortexes by moonrise tomorrow night." Satan gestured at a small delivery van parked beyond some stalagmites. "The others are ready to go. We're just waiting on the last one."

Keeffe caught her breath. When she'd talked to Bad, he hadn't known the timeline for Sedona's destruction.

Lilith smiled at Satan. Her white teeth reminded Keeffe of a shark. "You'll have it."

He seemed to accept that at face value, and he was right. Dad never stood up to Lilith about anything.

Then Satan's face darkened again. "Would you like to explain how you missed Rachel Blackmon's last journal?"

"Certainly." Lilith minced across the uneven lava floor of the cavern on her nosebleed heels, taking her time. Keeffe couldn't stand Lilith, but she had to admire the woman's—no, make that demon's—moxie. When Lilith reached the throne, she leaned over and whispered something in Satan's ear. As she spoke, Satan's expression changed from enraged to gleeful. Keeffe's mouth went dry.

"You're sure this will work?" he asked Lilith.

Her gaze swept over Keeffe. Her lip curled. "Absolutely."

"Very well." Satan turned to Keeffe. "I have an offer for you, Ms. Blackmon. I would like you to read your mother's journal, aloud, to my minions. I think they will find it instructive."

Keeffe blanched. She had not read anything aloud since seventh grade, when her stumbling performance in English class had made her the butt of jeers and laughter. The next year, she'd taken three weeks of detention rather than endure that humiliation again.

"If you're successful," Satan said, "I will allow Sedona to survive and return all the statues."

All four of Mom's statues, back in the family's possession? The desire to say yes and damn the consequences was overwhelming.

A smile played around Satan's lips. It was clear he could see how tempting his offer was.

"I will also allow you to keep the journal," he said, "and I'll return you Aboveworld. No harm, no foul."

She looked at Bad, expecting him to be shaking his head frantically. Instead, he was in brainiac mode, head cocked to the side and lips pursed, as though he was working through the implications of Satan's offer.

"Will Bad go with me?" Sweat matted her hair to her head and her knees knocked together, but she refused to give him up.

"Let me see if I can put this in terms you can understand." The smoke coming from Satan's left horn grew darker, oilier. "You have a better chance of building a ski resort down here than you have of taking the Hade home with you."

She didn't have to know Satan well to realize he was reaching the end of his patience.

"Let it go, Keeffe," Bad said. "Take me out of the equation. He's offering you everything you could hope for."

He wasn't offering her Bad. She looked at her lover. The truth was, humans weren't very kind to anyone who looked different. With his horns and tail and short, hairy body, his life on Earth might be even harder than what he dealt with down here. Maybe he didn't want to come back to Sedona.

"Don't you love me?" she asked. Satan shuddered. All around the room, demons covered their ears and screamed.

"More than life itself," Bad said. "But he's never going to agree to let me go, no matter what you offer him. I want you out of here, and safe."

She swallowed. Was that really the reason, or was he unwilling to face the miseries that would go with a life lived above the surface? If it was, she couldn't blame him. She turned back to Satan. "What if I fail?"

Satan smirked. "Then I destroy Sedona and your mother's reputation."

Except for leaving Bad behind—and having to deal with the humiliation of looking like an illiterate moron in front of a vast crowd —it was a better deal than she'd hoped for. She eyed Satan warily. "That doesn't sound like I have anything to lose."

"Oh." He did a theatrical double take. "Did I forget to mention your soul?"

Her lips seemed to go numb. "My soul?"

Satan shrugged. "Take it or leave it."

"What do I have to do to win?"

Satan conferred with Lilith again. "You have to read the entire journal aloud."

"She'll never make it through," Lilith sneered.

In her heart of hearts, Keeffe knew she was right.

From the other side of the cavern, Bad called, "You can do it, Keeffe."

Keeffe looked at him blankly. "What?" She got why he might not want to return with her to the surface. Was he trying to keep her below with him?

Bad's body was small and hairy, but his eyes were the same deep, dark brown they'd been when he rescued her from the snake, when he'd told her she wasn't stupid, when he'd made the painting.

"You've got this," he said. "You can save Sedona and your mother's legacy and take the statues home. I believe in you."

Satan beamed at him. "I knew you were really a demon at heart. Maybe I will let you return to DemSec."

Bad didn't even seem to hear. His gaze remained intently on her.

Keeffe gripped her hands together. "I can't do that," she said. "You know I can't."

"Of course you can." Bad smiled at her. His eyes were so warm and confident she completely forgot what his body looked like. "You've gotten much better at reading since you started working on the mural."

"From reading all your stupid texts," Keeffe said. With the electronic voice validating her understanding and reinforcing her confidence with every text.

"Exactly," he said. "You can do this."

"But if I fail..."

"You won't fail." He spread his hands. "I have faith in you."

The question was: did she have faith in him? He'd admitted that he came to Earth to take her statue away. Could she really believe a demon had fallen so deeply in love with her that he was willing to give up his entire future for her? Did she truly trust that he was staying below out of love for her? She looked into his deep, brown eyes. She did. He loved her, and he believed every word he said. Suddenly, she did, too.

She opened the first page. The curlicues were capital *I*'s, Frida had informed her, and the pennants capital *P*'s. Her mouth was so dry she could barely speak.

"September first," she read, stumbling over the word *first*.

Throughout the cavern, demons howled in derision. Her underarms instantly went damp.

"*John…is… combing, no, coming*, along marvelously."

"You read like a first-grader," taunted one demon.

"Like a kindergartner," said another.

Tears of humiliation sprang to Keeffe's eyes. She started to close the book. She couldn't read this. Why had Bad thought she could?

"You can do this," he said. At a sign from Satan, his guard stuffed a dirty sock in his mouth. Even gagged, he beamed encouragement at her.

She couldn't back out now, she realized. Not just Mom's legacy and Sedona were on the line. Her soul was, too. She had to believe in herself as much as he did. She swallowed and tried again.

As she read, a strange thing happened. The demons in the cavern continued to jeer and hoot, but it stopped bothering her. She had always believed that having people realize how badly she read was the worst thing that could happen to her. Now she knew it wasn't. Not by a long shot.

Bad thought she could do this.

She remembered some of the entries from hearing Frida read them aloud. Some of them she sounded out, consonant by consonant, syllable by syllable, making mistakes and going back and correcting herself. Satan hadn't specified any standard of perfection for the reading, just that she needed to get through it.

When she was halfway through the book, she glanced up. Bad's eyes were shining with pride. Satan's gaze was calculating. As she watched, he made a subtle gesture with his hand and the noise level increased dramatically. Jeers became shrieks. Cackles became howls.

Then McCall, who sat on the steps to the throne, drenched in sweat, yelled, "Give it up, Duckling."

Her mouth went dry as dust. In an instant, she was a child again, flooded with shame at her inability to read. The other demons quickly realized McCall's taunt had struck home and took up the chant, growing louder with each round. "*Duckling. Duckling. Duckling.*"

Her entire body burned with humiliation. Tears flooded her eyes, making it impossible to even see the pages in front of her.

Why had she thought she could do this? Why had Bad encouraged her to risk her soul when she was sure to fail? She threw him a furious, mortified glare but when her eyes met his, he didn't look away. Instead, he gave her an encouraging nod. *You can do this*, his brown eyes seemed to say.

She returned to the nearly illegible scrawl in front of her, painstakingly sounding out the words. When she got to the last page, she looked up again. Bad held up both thumbs, grinning.

"...the God who sees all, forgives all." She read the words directly at Bad, saw him flinch and then slowly straighten. The screams in the cavern became screams of pain.

"This child will be a blessing to our family," she read.

Then she came to the final entry. She took a deep breath.

"October tenth. Pablo hasn't moved in nearly a week. Seeing the doctor this afternoon."

The pain implicit in the entry made her blink back tears. She closed the book and took a deep breath. "I'll take my statues, please."

Smoke rolled from Satan's horns like the thunderheads that formed over the Black Hills in the rainy season. Furiously, he turned on Lilith. "You said she couldn't do it."

Lilith put up her hands as though to fend him off. "I thought...."

"You thought wrong," he screamed.

He snapped his fingers and a pair of minotaurs rushed up to the throne. They grabbed Lilith by the shoulders. Keeffe watched in horror as they dragged her stepmother away. Satan pointed to McCall.

"Take the girl and get out of here," He pointed at the delivery van.

McCall sat up from where he'd been lolling on the steps. He looked more alert, like he was starting to revive. Now that Keeffe had made it through her trial by fire, it didn't feel nearly so warm down here.

She crossed her arms. "Not without Bad."

"I told you. I don't release demons. Get out." Satan's face was the color of dried blood. Smoke streamed from his horns. "Unless you'd like to stay permanently."

She looked over at Bad. His hands were in his pockets and he was no longer making any effort to pull free from his minotaur guard. If he had indicated he wanted to come with her, she would have held her ground, but he hadn't. She crossed the cavern and picked up *Matthew* and hauled him to the van. Inside the cargo door was a wooden crate lined with excelsior. She lifted out a handful of the excelsior. What remained conformed precisely to *Matthew's* silhouette. This must be how Satan had planned to transport the statues to Sedona. She set *Matthew* down in the padded compartment and replaced the wad in her hand.

"I could use a little help here," she called to McCall, but he was talking earnestly to Satan in low tones she couldn't make out.

She checked the three remaining crates, identifying which one was for *Mark,* which for *Luke* and which for *John,* before crossing the cavern again. She was getting used to Hell—it no longer felt hot to her. In fact, the air blowing from the vent felt downright cool.

She loaded up *Mark* next, taking care to ensure he was fully padded before returning for *Luke.* Inside her thin jacket, she shivered a little. As she placed *Luke* in the van, something cold landed on her cheek. She touched it and her finger came away wet. She gazed around Hell in amazement. All around her, fat white snowflakes fell.

Somewhere along the line, the air temperature had gone from Sedona in July to Juneau in January. Cracks and pops sounded overhead. A colossal stalactite fell from the ceiling, crashing to the floor. Demons screamed and ran in all directions. The snow started coming down in earnest.

Satan turned to Bad, his face purple with rage. "This is your doing."

Bad pulled the sock from his mouth. "It is." He sounded pretty cheerful about it.

"Well, it's not going to work."

There was another loud pop and the stalactite directly over Satan's throne snapped loose. He dived from his chair an instant before it stabbed through his seat like a giant dagger. He jumped to his feet and took two steps to his right, his feet slipping in the snow. Another stalactite fell, once again nearly impaling him.

A demon who looked like an action figure from a combat game hurried up. "Sir, the Lake of Fire is freezing over. Tectonic plates are shifting. Hell is becoming unstable."

Satan screamed, "Enough!" He turned to Keeffe. "If you want him so much, take him."

Keeffe ran to Bad and threw her arms around him. "You're brilliant."

"Are you sure you're up for this?" he asked, touching his horns.

"I'm up for anything," she said, "as long as it's with you."

He turned to Satan. "You're really prepared to release me? And we don't have to worry about you coming after us?"

Through chattering teeth, Satan said, "Yes, anything to have you out of here!"

Bad reached into his pocket. The snow stopped and the air started to warm.

Keeffe turned to McCall. "Are you coming with us?"

Behind Satan's throne, a snake with diamond-patterned scales slithered across the floor.

McCall knelt in front of Satan. "I petition you to stay, sire."

Keeffe's mouth fell open. "You're not really going to do this?"

McCall wouldn't meet her eyes. "Maybe. If Satan allows it."

"Why?" Keeffe asked. McCall was an idiot, but he had excellent self-preservation skills.

He turned to Bad. "What's my probability of coming here when I die?"

Bad typed something into his phone. "Ninety-eight point two percent."

"Exactly." McCall turned to Satan. "Can I stay?"

Satan looked at him wearily. "Why not?"

McCall turned to Bad. "Switch bodies with me."

Bad blinked. "What?"

"Switch bodies with me. This one can't handle the heat down here. Besides," he looked lovingly at Satan, "that one looks like the boss."

Keeffe watched in disbelief as they exited their bodies in the form of smoke and streamed up each other's nostrils.

Bad, now clad in McCall's body again, grabbed her hand. "Let's go."

As they hurried toward the van, a pair of small, horned figures, one male, one female, appeared in the entryway to one of the side tunnels. They looked a lot like Bad, only older.

"Bad?" said the woman, her mouth trembling.

"Son?" said the man, looking at Bad sadly.

Bad's newly acquired shoulders sagged. Stooping a little, he put his brawny arms around them. Keeffe stared at them in fascination, taking in Bad's mom's turquoise horns, his dad's scarlet tail. These must be her future in-laws. Or out-laws. She had no idea where Bad planned to take this relationship.

"Will we ever see you again?" His mother's eyes filled with tears. Keeffe's welled up in sympathy.

No mother should have to see her son disappear off to some distant, unknown place, knowing she might never see him again. Keeffe stepped forward, sticking her hand out. She introduced herself. Bad's mother shook her hand, looking lost.

"Of course you will." Keeffe smiled warmly. "You're welcome to visit anytime."

"Aboveworld?" asked Pa, his eyes wide.

"It's great," Bad said. "The sun shines all the time."

"Hade eyes aren't meant for the sun."

"I'll make super-dark sunglasses for you."

Pa touched his horns. "I don't know…"

"Sedona's a pretty open-minded place," said Keeffe. "And my family will love you."

"Our house is huge," said Bad. "You'd never have to leave the property if you didn't want to."

"Maybe sometime," Ma's hand fell away from Keeffe's. It was clear she was just being polite.

Bad looked so heartbroken Keeffe cleared her throat. "I was wondering…"

Ma looked up at her, tilting her head to the side inquiringly.

"I don't have a mom." Keeffe put her hand on the older woman's arm. "I could use help planning the wedding."

"I always wanted a daughter." Ma squared her shoulders. "As soon as you set a date, you just let us know and we'll be up."

Bad kissed their cheeks and squeezed their hands.

"I'll call you next week. And Pa—could you tell Ronnie thank you?"

CHAPTER 32

*B*ad couldn't take a chance on hitting a pothole or running over a spike and damaging their precious cargo, so the drive back up the rings was painfully slow. That gave Keeffe far too much time to look out the windows.

They'd only been on the road for an hour when she caught sight of the fortune-tellers with their backward-facing heads in Ring Eight. The one-time seers wept copious tears, saltwater running down between their shoulder blades to the cleft of their buttocks.

"Why are the like that?" Her eyes were wide with horror.

Bad winced. "They falsely claimed they could tell the future. Now they're doomed to only look back."

He thought about all the other things she was likely to see as they made their way up the rings. If he didn't distract her, by the time they arrived at the surface she'd be completely traumatized.

"I can't believe you proposed to me." He fanned his face like a beauty pageant winner fanning back tears. "I mean, it was so sudden."

Keeffe's gaze swung back to him. "Don't be a jerk. I couldn't leave your mom thinking she'd never see you again."

"Oh," he said. "So that's why. Nothing to do with me suddenly inheriting this very buff body?"

Her lower jaw thrust out. "I was prepared to take you with horns and a tail."

He reached across the gearshift to catch her hand and lift it to his lips. "I know you were. That's just one of the million reasons why I love you."

Her face softened. "I wondered if you'd ever get around to saying it."

Then her gaze wandered back to the window. Outside, the hounds of Ring Seven pursued the squanderers. She moaned and covered her eyes. It came as no surprise that her reaction was nothing like McCall's had been.

"The center of this ring is where I found your chisels," Bad said. By the time he'd finished recounting the story of rescuing the chisels, they'd left Ring Seven and were entering Six. He handed Keeffe a blanket from behind his seat.

"I need you to put this over your head," he said.

"Why?"

"Because the Gorgon lives here. If you accidentally lock eyes with her, you'll turn to stone."

"Since you put it that way." She drew the blanket over her head. A moment later, her disembodied voice asked, "Why does Satan look like a Hade rather than an angel?"

"Good question," Bad said. "I don't know for sure. Legend says he was the most beautiful angel in the universe when he was in Heaven—God's morning star. But after the Great Rebellion, after he chose to abandon God and arrived Below, he began to wizen. After a few centuries, his horns popped up. He tried getting them removed, but it was very painful and they just grew right back. A century or two after that, he grew a tail."

"Did looking more like a Hade make him friendlier to the Hades?" Keeffe asked.

"Not that you'd notice."

"Then why did you go to work for him?"

It was a question he'd known would come up at some point.

"I thought I could make life better for my people."

At her look of confusion, he explained about the Hades—how they'd lived in Hell long before Satan arrived with his squadron of fallen angels and how the Hade's lives had changed after the invasion.

"And did you make things better?" she asked.

"Yes. That was why it was so hard to give up targeting you. Because failure meant I wouldn't be able to help the Hades anymore."

A few minutes passed before she spoke again.

"I feel bad about taking you away from your people," she said in a small voice.

He hastened to reassure her. "The Hades will be fine. My nephew, Phoenix, is going to take over where I left off. He's smarter, though, so he won't work for Satan. He's going to work directly to benefit the Hades."

"Why did you ask your dad to thank Ronnie?" she asked.

He told her about the skeleton key Ronnie had loaned him.

"Why would he do that?"

He shrugged. "I don't know. I have a hypothesis, but that's all it is."

She giggled. She was definitely better off with the blanket preventing her from seeing the nightmares occurring outside the van. "What's your hypothesis?"

"I think it was because he liked you so much."

"Aww. Really?"

"I think so." He launched into a long and intentionally dull story about the history of the Hades and the angels. After a few minutes, a soft snore issued from beneath the blanket. She slept the rest of the way to the surface.

It was dawn when they arrived back in Sedona. The light must have woken Keeffe because she pulled the blanket off her head.

"Ahhh," she said. "Sunlight."

He knew exactly how she felt.

"Where to, milady?" he asked as he drove through the portal and onto 179.

"Home," she said. "I've been in these clothes for forty-eight hours. I need a change."

He parked the van on the apron outside her trailer. They had agreed they'd keep the three statues at McCall's—no, now it was his, no, *their*—house.

"I'll just be a minute," she promised and scampered up the steps.

The aluminum door had barely closed behind her when Bad heard her shriek. His blood ran cold. Satan must have lied and pursued them after all.

In a flash, he was out of the car and into the trailer. Inside, he found Keeffe weeping and shaking. He scanned the living room but saw no sign of Hellish devastation.

He put protective arms around her. "What's wrong?"

She pointed at the kitchen table. On it sat *John*, wings extended, his gaze fixed on heaven.

Bad crossed to the table and picked up a small, sealed envelope lying there. He handed it to her.

Inside the envelope was a card with picture of a devil on it. The front read, "What the devil? I missed your birthday!" Inside, it said, "Hoping this little gift makes up for it. Love, Dad."

THANKS TO READERS

Dear Reader,

Thank you for reading *The Demon's in the Details*.

I know that your spare time is limited, and I'm honored that you chose to spend it with Keeffe and Bad.

If you enjoyed the book, please consider leaving me a review on Amazon, Goodreads, Bookbub, or your blog or website. Word of mouth is also good—please tell your family, friends and fellow readers.

Book 3 of my *Touched by a Demon* series will be coming out in 2020. In *The Demon Wore Stilettos*, Lilith finally gets her own mission—and her own chance at love. (Or what passes for love in Hell.)

To be notified of upcoming releases, author interviews, appearances, blog tours, and giveaways and to receive special content that's for newsletter subscribers only, please sign up for my monthly newsletter at www.jeanneestridge.com. The newsletter signup form is at the bottom of the page,

To follow me on Facebook: www.facebook.com/JeanneEstridgeFanPage

To read my weekly blog posts: www.EightLadiesWriting.com

To follow me on Twitter: www.twitter.com/JeanneEstridge

To see what I'm posting on Instagram www.instagram.com/jeanneestridge

Again, thanks so much for reading!

Jeanne Oates Estridge

EXCERPT FROM THE DEMON WORE STILETTOS

Chapter 1

"Hell must be empty," Megan Swensen murmured into her wineglass as she gazed around the Manhattan bookstore her publishing house used for their launches, "because all the demons are at this party."

Luminaries from the publishing world along with a host of B-list celebrities with books to push thronged the aisles of Acheron Books. Megan knew most of them, at least by sight, but interspersed in the crowd was a handful of people she didn't recognize. The strangers had two things in common—supernatural beauty and an unpleasant "I've seen it all" smirk. She surveyed them grimly. Even though she'd never met any of them, she had a pretty good idea what they were.

"Get thee behind me," she muttered.

"I beg your pardon?" A silver-haired man rummaging through the bargain bin next to her paused in his search.

Megan gave him an apologetic smile. "Nothing."

On the other side of the store, Conrad Ovid, tonight's star and a former classmate of Megan's from grad school, autographed copies of his debut volume of poetry. The crowd surrounding him hung on his every word. It should have been the best night of his life, but his plump face was sweaty, and so pale he looked faintly green. He hooked his finger inside his collar and dragged his polka dot bowtie away from his throat.

Catching his eye, Megan threw him an encouraging smile. The smile he sent back wobbled but it was a smile, and some color came back into his cheeks. She drew in a breath of satisfaction. It was probably false comfort, but at least she'd made him feel a little better.

But not for long. A raven-haired woman with ruby lips, red snakeskin Jimmy Choo's and a little black dress that screamed "Paris," minced up to Conrad and began fussing with his tie. The crowd around him scattered like sparrows at the approach of a cat.

Good decision, little sparrows. The woman was Lilith Rojas, Megan's literary agent. Conrad's, too, for that matter. That was Megan's fault. Conrad had met Lilith at one of her book signings.

Beneath Lilith's dagger-like fingernails, Conrad twitched like a fish on a line and the color drained out of his face again. She gave his tie one last tug, so violent he had to step forward to keep his balance. As she drew her hands away, one of her crimson nails grazed his throat. A bead of blood appeared.

"Tsk, tsk." Lilith retrieved a hankie from a tiny feathered purse that looked like it had been constructed from the corpse of a songbird. Knowing Lilith, it probably was. She pressed the hankie against Conrad's neck for a moment. When she pulled it away, he stared at the blood-specked tissue with a kind of horrified fascination.

"There." Lilith's teeth, white and gleaming, always made Megan think of a shark. "All better." She patted Conrad's cheek and sauntered away on her stilettos to disappear through a door marked Restrooms.

Megan picked up several copies of Conrad's book from a nearby table and headed in his direction.

She wasn't really Conrad's audience—his themes were a little too gloomy for her tastes—but they shared a deeper bond. As well as having the same agent, they'd both signed contracts with Tophet Publishing, which meant they both—she shut the thought down before it could finish forming.

She handed Conrad the pile of books. "How are you holding up?"

He signed the top book. His hand trembled so badly the inscription was barely legible.

"This is it," he said. "I know it is."

"Don't be silly." Megan cast a swift glance around to be sure no one was listening. "This is your first sale, your first reading. They won't take you that quickly."

He looked at her, his face a mask of tragedy. "That's all I asked for."

Megan caught her breath. "What?"

"You signed when you were twenty-two." He clutched the little poetry book to his chest like a shield. "You still thought you could succeed on your own, so you drove a hard bargain. I was thirty-five."

Had she driven a hard bargain? With help from James, her law student boyfriend at the time, she had squeezed seven years of fame from her deal with the devil. Now, with repayment looming on the horizon, it felt more like seven minutes.

"Thirty-five isn't old," she said. For her it was still six years away.

"I was desperate," Conrad said. "My parents were insisting I move home to Dubuque and teach English. Can you imagine me teaching high school English in Iowa?"

Plump, balding, and given to wearing pastels, Conrad was a bully magnet. Working in a public high school would have been torture, but what was coming up for him was even worse, and it wouldn't end with a nice retirement after thirty years.

"Why didn't you ask for more?" Megan asked, feeling sick. "Why didn't you tell them you wanted to be Poet Laureate? There's probably a waiting list for that."

He smiled sadly. "I was a little drunk. It was your release party for *Lilies of Winter*. There was free wine. Lilith and this gorgeous guy stopped to talk to me. He seemed so interested in my career. I was flattered. I told him I would be satisfied if just once I could give a public reading of my poetry in a Manhattan bookstore to raucous applause. The next thing I know, he pulls a contract out of thin air, promising me just that."

"I should have warned you." Megan hung her head. Her pale hair fell forward past the frames of her oversized glasses, blocking her peripheral vision. Despite her feelings of guilt she quickly she lifted her head. This wasn't a safe place to lose sight of what was going on around her.

Conrad shook his head. "By the time I knew enough to believe you, it would have been too late."

"If you were drunk, the contract shouldn't be binding."

His mouth twisted in a wry smile. "I don't think Hell follows the same rules we do up here."

Probably not.

Megan caught her lower lip between her teeth, her gaze darting around the room. "I can ask people not to clap."

"No one will listen to you," he said. "You'll just come off looking jealous and petty."

That was probably true. And even if everyone she knew agreed not to clap, she was pretty sure the gorgeous people she'd noticed earlier were demons, seeded into the crowd to ensure the audience response met the terms of the contract.

A bead of sweat ran down Conrad's right temple and past his chin to the scratch on his throat. It sizzled when it reached the tiny cut.

"It burns," he whispered.

She pulled a tissue from her purse and dabbed away the sweat, but the pain had rattled him. His teeth chattered uncontrollably.

She clutched his arm. "Don't read. Tell them you're sick."

"I can't," Conrad said. "Failure to deliver on my end of the contract constitutes grounds for immediate collection of my soul."

Megan's mouth went dry. Her contract had a similar clause. She'd had to deliver seven novels on a yearly schedule or face instant deportation to Hell. Luckily, she responded well to pressure.

The high-pitched whine of feedback squealed from speakers at the back of the store. Everyone in the store—at least, everyone that was human—cringed. A staggeringly handsome man Megan recognized as Raim, the store owner, tapped a microphone attached to an oak podium. Exaggerated thumps, like the gates of Hell slamming closed, replaced the squeal. Conrad turned paler, if that was even possible.

Raim had tried to seduce Megan at her first launch party, but it was soon after her breakup with James and she wasn't interested. By the time her second launch party rolled around, she'd known from Raim's inhuman beauty that he was part of the Hellish hierarchy and kept her distance.

Lilith reappeared. Conrad swallowed, the muscles in his throat working convulsively. What if he couldn't read? What if his throat locked up? Surely they wouldn't enforce the collection clause in that case.

Megan's shoulders drooped. Of course they would.

Lilith's gaze swept up and down Megan's body, taking in her sapphire wool sheath and matching Christian Louboutin boots. "Nice ensemble. I taught you well, grasshopper."

Heat crawled up Megan's neck and face. She pressed her lips together to hold back the rude words that wanted to burst out. When she first met Lilith, she'd had no idea how to dress or talk or carry herself as a celebrity. Lilith had taught her everything she needed to know about being a famous author—except how to enjoy it. That wasn't part of the deal.

"Did you come to see Conrad's triumph?" Lilith's eyes were as black as licorice. Weirdly, she always smelled like licorice, too. A hateful smiled played around the corners of her mouth.

Megan locked eyes with her. "I came to support a friend."

"That's so sweet. Maybe someone will do the same for you when it's your turn in—" Lilith checked the date on her phone—"thirty days now, isn't it?"

Megan's hands went clammy. Her seventh book was scheduled to release in a month. As soon as it hit the *New York Times* bestseller list, it would fulfill Satan's end of their bargain and she'd be bound for Hell. She licked her lips.

Lilith threw back her head and laughed. The she took Conrad's elbow. "Come on, Connie-poo. It's time for your big moment."

She led him to the podium like a lamb to the slaughter. He shook so hard he could barely walk. Megan clenched her teeth. She wished desperately she could rescue him, but after nearly seven years of trying, she hadn't come up with a way to rescue herself.

Raim introduced Conrad as an up-and-coming poet with much to tell the world. Everyone clapped politely except for the beautiful strangers in the crowd, who stomped and whistled, confirming Megan's suspicions.

Conrad read his first poem, his voice thin and strained. The poem was a description of children playing on the Alice in Wonderland statues in Central Park. It received only mild applause. Megan felt a stirring of hope. Maybe she'd misread the crowd. Maybe Conrad wouldn't receive the ovation that would allow Hell to claim his soul.

Then he read a second one, about a homeless man camped out in front of Tiffany's in a refrigerator box. Filled with misery and despair, it garnered a warmer response. Conrad began to sweat.

Pick another happy one, she silently willed him. Angst might appeal to people who had plenty, but anyone who had grown up in real misery didn't need to go looking for it.

His third poem was a piece of blank verse that likened the subway station on Elmhurst Avenue to a gas chamber. It brought the house down.

At the podium, Conrad's shoulders rose till he looked like a turtle trying to pull its head into its shell. The clapping slowly died away. He looked around warily. Nothing happened.

In by inch, his shoulders lowered. He read another poem. Still nothing happened. A smile like the sun coming up broke across his face. Megan smiled, too, almost boneless with relief. He read a few more poems, each to more and louder applause. After about thirty minutes he took questions from the audience, his smile growing broader and his gestures more animated with each answer.

When there were no more questions, Raim shook Conrad's hand.

"Thank you for being with us tonight." He asked for, and got, another round of applause.

Conrad beamed. "You're very welcome."

Megan breathed a long sigh of relief. Conrad was okay. Maybe, just maybe, she'd be okay, too.

Conrad took a step away from the podium and his face went

blank. For a moment, he teetered. Then he crashed to the ground like a tree falling.

Megan's hand flew to her throat. Raim dropped to his knees beside Conrad. Rolling him over on his back, Raim started CPR. Lilith pulled out her phone, punched three numbers and spoke urgently.

"An ambulance is on its way," she announced, pocketing her phone. It all felt like playacting.

Megan fought her way to Conrad's side. When Raim's rhythmic chest presses yielded no results, she grabbed Conrad's hand.

"Come back." She squeezed his lifeless fingers. "Come back, Conrad. We need you here. We love you."

Conrad's limp body didn't respond. Across from her, Raim smirked, that same unpleasant expression she'd seen on the other demons earlier. She wanted to slap it off his face but instead she gripped Conrad's hand tighter and called him even more urgently as her tears dripped onto his fingers. She got no response.

Two minutes later, a pair of EMT's, one blonde, one dark, came in through the back of the store, rolling a stretcher. Megan clutched Conrad's hand, which was already growing cooler to the touch. She hadn't heard sirens. How had the ambulance gotten here so quickly in Manhattan traffic? The EMT's shooed Raim and Megan out of the say and started their own attempt at CPR.

She got to her feet, scrubbing at her eyes with the back of her hand. It came away smeared with mascara.

The EMT's worked on Conrad with the appearance of skill and professionalism but their expressions said they didn't expect to succeed. They were two of the most gorgeous men she had ever seen. Her jaw tightened. She'd bet the royalties from her last book they didn't work for the city.

After twenty minutes of CPR, they loaded Conrad onto a stretcher and trundled it through a metal fire door leading to the stockroom. There were almost no alleys in Manhattan—real estate here was too expensive to waste on alleys. In retrospect, that alone should have warned her that something was off about Acheron Books.

She slipped through the door after them, sheltering behind a stack of boxes. Instead of heading out the back to the alley, they threaded their way through cartons of books to what looked like an old freight elevator.

The blonde EMT pushed the elevator button. A moment later, a mechanical groan issued from the battered wooden door. The arrow on the brass dial above the elevator slowly began to move.

Something felt wrong about the dial. They were on the ground floor of a twenty-two story building, but the number "1" was dead center on the dial. The numbers to the right ranged from two to twenty-two. The ones on the left started with "V" and descended backwards to nine.

A vestibule and nine rings. Megan's blood seemed to freeze in her veins.

When the pointer on the dial came to rest on the number "1," the blonde EMT opened the wooden door and shoved a brass folding gate to the side. The dark-haired EMT reached beneath the stretcher and pulled out what looked like a butterfly net. The netting material was made from some kind of silvery thread that looked almost liquid. Dread swamped Megan's lungs, making it hard to breathe. The blonde EMT bent over Conrad. Applying his lips to Conrad's mouth, he sucked in a huge breath. As his chest expanded, his eyes glowed like red coals. Megan's own breath stopped.

He pulled his mouth away with an audible pop. A wispy gray shadow, like a misty version of Conrad, issued from Conrad's mouth. Its eyes were black holes and its mouth was open, as though in a scream. It tried to stream away, but the dark EMT snagged it in his butterfly net. The net jumped around as Conrad's spirit frantically tried to escape, but the EMT twitched the handle with the skill of long practice.

Conrad remained trapped, his black eyeholes peering through the net, terrified, as the dark EMT stepped onto the elevator and closed the metal gate. The blonde EMT slammed the wooden door and the motor whined to life. On the brass dial, the arrow fell steadily to the left, finally stopping at seven.

The outer circle of Ring Seven, if Megan remembered her Dante correctly, was reserved for blasphemers. That must be where they stuck poets. Novelists, too probably. Her heartbeat, which had been thudding so loud she could hear it in her hears, seemed to halt.

The blonde EMT rolled the stretcher, with Conrad's corporeal body still strapped to it, out the back door and loaded it into the waiting ambulance.

Megan stumbled back into the bookstore, shaking with horror. Her lips and fingers felt numb. While she was in the back, the crowd that had come for the reading had disappeared, leaving behind stacks of Conrad's books. Hell hadn't promised him sales, she realized. Just applause.

Nearby, Lilith surveyed the abandoned books, tapping her crimson lips with one crimson fingernail. "We have got to come up with a more cost-effective way to do this."

Raim shrugged. "Tell Legal to write tighter contracts."

Lilith laughed. "I'll pass that word along."

Megan shivered. If Lilith was in a position to give feedback to Hell's legal department, she must be very high in the demon hierarchy.

Lilith's glance fell on her. Lilith nudged Raim. He followed her gaze and his face lit with laughter. "What were you doing in the back? Checking out the transport to your final destination?"

"Or perhaps you've decided you might as well go now," Lilith said, "and save us the trouble of dialing 666 when the time comes."

The pair of them were so startlingly beautiful and so utterly without pity her marrow seemed to freeze inside her bones. But as they stood there, smiling their nasty smiles, a resolve to beat them at their own game rose in her. Her spine stiffened and she lifted her chin.

"My book release is still a month away," she said. "Until then, my soul is my own."

And she was going to keep it that way.

ACKNOWLEDGMENTS

It takes a village to write a book—at least, it does to write one of my books. The following people contributed in so many ways:

My gym buddy, Cynthia Adayemi, who, when I talked about Keeffe visiting her lawyer about the statue, said, "She should just break into her dad's house and steal that statue." The book became about 1000% more active thanks to her.

The plotting group at Central Ohio Fiction Writers—Linda Rice, Julia Blaine, Linda Munn, Andrea McCardle, Sandra Rice and especially Saralee Etter, who suggested that the most logical reason the Catholic Church might decry Rachel Blackmon would be abortion.

Amanda Hope Cook, painter extraordinaire and Pauline Persing, water color genius, for their guidance on the art portions of this book.

Jerry Morris, the brilliant software developer who answered questions about video game production.

My long-time writing group, Teri Piatt, Joe Downing and Mark Thaman, who read an early draft and helped identify many, many issues.

My sisters, Carla Voisard and Lelane Oates, who provided much input and guidance along the way.

The Eight Ladies (www.eightladieswriting.com), who provide inspiration and support in so many ways.

The Persisters, RWA® Golden Heart® class of 2018, who cheer each other along each step of the way.

And finally, my wonderful neighbor, beta reader, and practicing Catholic, Gina Slaughter, who walked this Protestant through how confession works and how you pray the rosary.

Despite all the assistance I got from these people, I suspect there are still many mistakes. Any errors are not on them, but a result of my failing to ask the right questions or correctly understand their answers.